"Bogey man, bog[...]
The crea[...]
I will catch with skill."

This was definitely wrong. Just as it occurred to Bob to speak to the officials about postponing play, a little, little man with a long beard and red, pointed cap bounded up onto the tee. Bob almost dropped his club.

"Whaaa?"

"You've got to play," the little man told him. "It's sudden death."

"Jim, it looks like a garden gnome," the commentator said.

"Play?" Bob asked.

"If you don't continue, well, the consequences . . ."

"Consequences? What consequences?"

"Why, sudden death!"

An official strode up to the green with determined strides. "This is not acceptable," he said.

"It appears the official is conferring with MacDuff and the garden gnome, Jim," the commentator said.

The gnome whirled and pointed at the commentator. "I am not a *garden* gnome. My name is Robertson and I'm a *golf* gnome."

"I don't care what kind of gnome you are," the official told him. "You are interfering—"

Robertson waved his hand at the official. The man vanished, his empty clothing—smart yellow blazer, plaid slacks, golf hat, and all—collapsing to the ground. Within moments, a toad hopped out from beneath the hat.

"Interference!" it croaked.

—from *"Chafing the Bogey Man"* by Kristen Britain

Misspelled

edited by
Julie E. Czerneda

DAW BOOKS, INC.
DONALD A. WOLLHEIM, FOUNDER
375 Hudson Street, New York, NY 10014

ELIZABETH R. WOLLHEIM
SHEILA E. GILBERT
PUBLISHERS
http://www.dawbooks.com

First Printing, April 2008
1 2 3 4 5 6 7 8 9

Acknowledgments

Introduction © 2008 by Julie E. Czerneda
Trippingly Off the Tongue © 2008 by Lesley D. Livingston
8 rms, full bsmt © 2008 by Kristine Smith
Eye of the Beholder © 2008 by Kevin G. Maclean
Cybermancer © 2008 by Janet Elizabeth Chase
Eye of Newt © 2008 by Marc Mackay
Chafing the Bogey Man © 2008 by Kristen Britain
A Perfect Circle © 2008 by Kent Pollard
Reading, Writing, Plagues © 2008 by Kell Brown
Totally Devoted 2 U © 2008 by John Zakour
The Mysterious Case of Spell Zero © 2008 by Rob St. Martin
Crosscut © 2008 by S. W. Mayse
Bitch Bewitched © 2008 by Doranna Durgin
The Witch of Westmoreland Avenue © 2008 by Morgan S. Brilliant
A Spell of Quality © 2008 by Kate Paulk
Demon in the Cupboard © 2008 by Nathan Azinger
Untrained Melody © 2008 by Jim C. Hines
Yours for Only $19.99 © 2008 by Shannan Palma

Table of Contents

Introduction

What's the difference between a good cook and a great one? Between a capable chemist and a famous inventor? I think it's a willingness to experiment with ingredients and procedures. The best make intelligent, reasonable substitutions and observe what happens. If something unexpected occurs, they recognize when they've struck gold. Key Lime Pie and Post-it Notes™ come to mind.

The worst? Because others are willing to experiment too. The results can be memorable. Poor cooks and sloppy chemists. You know who I mean. People in a rush, who never finish (or start) reading the directions or bother to understand why this and not that is listed in a recipe. They leave out steps, toss in whatever's handy, omit what they don't have, and hope for the best. Occasionally, this works. Just as often, family and friends go home feeling ill—or there's a crater where the lab used to be.

That's real life. In fantasy, much relies on the uncanny skill of wizards, the long memories of witches, and the years of learning required to properly cast spells.

Come on. Not everyone is going to learn it all before they try some magic. Not everyone will read the manual first or be careful. It's simply not in our nature. Which means someone will goof a spell—at least once. When magic's involved, what might be the consequences?

Welcome to *Misspelled*.

Julie E. Czerneda

Trippingly Off the Tongue

Lesley D. Livingston

Narrator: *The final exam. The ultimate test. That moment in time when success or failure is measured by what you accomplish under pressure. Or, in the case of Michaela duLey, what she can accomplish with the help of her lab partner and a single, dangerous spell. There's only one problem . . . Michaela hasn't been quite herself lately. She'd better be very careful indeed.*

"Careful with that!" Michaela duLey froze, her eyes panic-wide in the dusky air.

Vinx, her lab partner, stiffened at the squawk of admonition and cocked his head, eyeing the beaker of bilious green liquid he held—rather carelessly—in one hand. "You don't trust me," he mused, raising a tangled eyebrow at Mickey and gently sloshing the beaker's contents about.

"I really don't!" Mickey was agog at the notion.

The stuff was becoming vaporous the more Vinx agitated it. Mickey knew how much he enjoyed goading her to elevated flights of nervous tension, but she was in no mood for shenanigans. Besides, they had work to do. She turned the scorch-factor way up on her glower and Vinx relented, stifling whatever nefarious impulses he might have. Contenting himself with a smug chuckle, he deposited the catastrophically explosive substance near the back of the workbench and out of harm's reach with a delicate flourish.

Mickey watched as faint vaporous swirls of mist settled in the glass, and she wiped a sleeve across her sweating brow. Then she shrugged the tension from her shoulders and turned back to the work at hand, a heavy sigh escaping her lips. They'd been toiling over various final exam projects for the past week and a half, and tonight's was the last. Mickey was tense to the point of snapping. "What I wouldn't give for a nice cold bier just now," the sorceress-in-training pined.

Vinx cocked an ear in her direction, feigning innocence. "Oh, I don't think it's as bad as all that, Mick!" He tut-tutted. "You're not quite *dead* yet . . ."

"Pardon?" She raised an eyebrow at the apparent non sequitur.

"Nothing . . . nothing . . ."

It's wayyy late for this, Mickey groaned inwardly, not prepared to deal with Vinx's bizarre sense of humor. Not that she wasn't well acquainted with it—they'd been paired up as study buddies for two semesters in a row—and usually she could handle him just fine. But tonight he was getting on her nerves. She glanced at her watch, but it was a useless gesture. The hands just spun in a slow backward circle, as they always did when she was in the middle of a spell-casting. Something to do with arcane energies or magnetic field generation or dimensional flux yadda yadda. Mickey didn't quite grasp the specifics, but that didn't stop her from finding the phenomenon truly irksome. Struggling to keep her cool, she turned back to her lab partner and asked politely, "Vinx, what's the thyme?"

"It's that greenish-gray aromatic stuff over there—very nice on pork roast."

Mickey snarled in frustration and turned back to the work muttering, "Demented demon spawn . . ."

"Why, thank you." Vinx bowed very slightly from the waist, an amused grin stretching the scaly, eggplant-hued skin across the craggy landscape of his features. In the flaring light of a dozen torches, the red glint of his eyes sparkled with an alien mirth and he picked up the beaker of liquid again, swirling it in the glass. "You were saying about this?"

Mickey glared violently. "Just bee careful. That's awl."

"I'm always careful around bees—allergies, you know. And awls for that matter—got a nasty poke in the thumb once." Rumbles of barely contained demon-giggles bubbled up from deep within his barrel chest, and the membranous wings sprouting from his massive shoulders ruffled slightly with amusement.

Mickey gritted her teeth as the lightbulb finally went on above her head and Vinx's cryptic banter suddenly made sense after a fashion. She must be doing it again. "Eye'm doing it again," she sighed, "aren't eye?"

"Yup." *Rumble rumble. Ruffle.*

"Dammit!" The young apprentice threw a delicate pair of sterling silver calipers down on the workbench, seething with frustration. "This is yore fault."

"Umm . . ." Vinx held up a single, yellowed talon. "*You* were the one doing the incantation, Mick . . ."

"That's only because *somebody* was so apocalyptically hungover after yet another pan-dimensional village pillage that *he* was incapable!" Mickey threw her hands in the air. "Even though ewe gnu perfectly well that eye wood knot bee able too handle that stupid Karnalaquiann dialect myself!"

"Well, granted, it *is* somewhat impossible if you only have a single tongue . . ."

"Rite!" Mickey barked. "Besides—how was eye two no that *unduuruu* and *unndurru* were pronounced *that* differently, anyway?"

"They're not." Vinx shrugged a massive, leathery shoulder. "They're pronounced exactly the same."

"Ewe sea my difficulty."

"Clearly . . ." *Giggle giggle rumble.* The demon's amusement sounded like the beginnings of a rockslide. "Although I'm not sure sheep are all that fond of the water!" Vinx turned away before he lost it completely.

"Bloody mystical homonyms . . ." Mickey fumed.

"Homo*phones*, actually." Unable to contain his glee any longer, Vinx collapsed in a large, quivering mess of burbling, boiling guffaws.

"Vinx, it's bean a weak . . ."

In Mickey's defense it had, indeed, "bean a weak." Off and on, at least. But she was truly sick of the weird looks she kept getting at the bank and in coffee shops whenever the awkward side effects of her botched Karnalaq soothe-spell took hold. Every now and then she would just erupt into bouts of saying one thing and—utterly unintentionally—meaning something else entirely to whomever she was speaking. And, of course, *she* couldn't tell when she was doing it. Not, at least, by the sounds she was making. Only by way of blank or puzzled stares. "Seven daze! When's it gonna stop?"

After a long moment of squeezing every ounce of enjoyment out of Mickey's sound-alike plight had passed, Vinx relented. The demon wiped a tear from his rumpled cheek and reached into the pouch hanging from his belt. "Here. I've been working on this. A pinch of powder up the left nostril ought to do," he said as he poured from a thin, blown-glass vial into the palm of Mickey's hand.

Mickey sighed and, pinching her right nostril shut, snorted the sparkly purple crystals, trying hard not to sneeze as she felt the tingly snap of synapses rearranging themselves ever so slightly deep within the vault of her skull. "Huzzah," she cheered blandly, eyeing the demon with mixed scepticism and gratitude. "I'm cured."

"Oops."

" 'Oops'?" Mickey asked warily. "*What* 'oops'?"

Vinx looked like he was trying *really* hard not to bust out laughing again. "When you said 'cured,' just now, you meant 'like bacon.' "

"I did not."

"Did. And that *is,* in fact, a homonym." He popped the cork on the vial again. "Did I say left nostril or right?"

"You said 'left.' "

"As in 'I *left* a package at the door.' " The demon pointed at the novice spell-slinger with moderate triumph. "See? You're speaking in homonyms. I should have said 'right.' "

Mickey ground her teeth and snorted purple crystals again. "As in—I'm gonna tear your head *right* off if this doesn't work?"

"Ah—see!" Vinx slapped his massive palms together, beaming benevolently at his fellow student. "All better!"

"Lucky for you."

"Now. Where were we?"

"Still stuck in a cave . . ." Mick grumbled, now thoroughly mired in ill-humor. "Why does anything to do with dark magick always have to be performed in a cave?"

"Something to do with the dark?" Vinx asked dryly as he reached for a small clay pot.

"That is so lame." Mickey rolled an eye at him. "It's such a stereotype. Like—evil has to be ugly."

"I'm not exactly *evil* . . ." the demon sounded hurt.

"Not you, Vinx. Well, actually, yes—you." Mickey plucked the jar from his taloned grasp. "Also the entire cheerleading squad at my old high school. All very pretty girls and—here's the thing—PURE EVIL."

Vinx nodded appreciatively.

"Yah. You would've like them." Mickey peered at the pot, looking for a label of some kind. That would, of course, be *way* too easy. "Seriously, man. Uh— demon. I was under the impression that warding- amulet spells were pretty straightforward. Why was the Conclave being all dire and cryptic with this assignment?"

"Perhaps they're just encouraging us to stretch a bit. This is your final project, after all. And, contrary to *your* middle-of-the-road approach, *I* happen to think that even the simplest spells can be interesting if you use a little imagination, Mick."

"Like last week's transmogrification?" She pegged him with a sharp gaze.

"What was wrong with that?" Vinx shrugged innocently.

"*Dragon* was not on the approved list of morph targets, you maniac."

"Oh, fine. Go ahead," he huffed. "Be boring. Turn yourself into a hedgehog again, my little kitchen witch. And then I'll barbeque you with my mighty dragon's breath!"

"You are such a drama queen." Mickey turned the pot around and around.

"It *would* be one less student in the class for me to go up against on a bell curve . . ."

"You wouldn't." She knew that not every student would advance to the next level of training. There would be cuts. Elimination. A figure of speech, hopefully. But, on the other hand, Vinx might be taking this competition thing a little too much to heart. Wherever his was. *What*ever his was . . . Mickey shifted uncomfortably under the demonic gaze. "Vinx?"

"Oh, I'm joking!"

Of course he was. Mickey reined in her apprehension and told herself she was just being silly. After all, Vinx could hardly gaze at her in a way that was *un*demonic . . .

"Cheer up, Mick." Vinx's expression shifted mercurially, and he grinned a lopsided grin. "This project is, after all, the kind of casting you're fond of—a protective spell to ward *against* the blackest of sorceries."

"Sure it is," Mickey sighed, surveying the staggering array of toxic and otherwise injurious articles arranged on the table. "Only that it just happens to employ deadly poisons and other noxious substances in the process. Really, I'm tickled." She already decided against all of the assorted weaponry—it wasn't her style. Too much collateral mess. Toxins were just that much tidier, she thought as she unstoppered the clay pot and wrinkled up her nose, sniffing with great caution at the contents. The odor was pungent—sharp and bitter. "Wormwood. Isn't that the stuff in absinthe?"

"Makes the heart grow fonder . . ." Vinx fluttered his wiry eyelashes.

"That was terrible," Mickey groaned and resealed the pot.

"And the mind go wander . . ."

"Stop it."

"Sorry." He stifled another rumble.

Mickey put the wormwood aside. Mild hallucinogenic properties notwithstanding, that darling of the Victorian artiste wouldn't do. It might be the bitterest herb known, but it was hardly lethal. Next.

Vinx nodded silent approval as she rejected the

"greene faerie" and handed her the next item on the table—a small bunch of leaves, stems dotted with white berries, tied neatly with a silver wire.

"Mistletoe," Mickey correctly identified the bit of shrubbery.

"For the kissing thereunder." Demon lips twisting, Vinx puckered up into a grotesque parody of kissyface and dangled the foliage over his head.

Mickey shuddered. "I *will* exact a terrible revenge, you know."

"Sorry." Vinx appeared instantly contrite. "Truly."

Mickey wasn't fooled for a second. She also wasn't buying those wares. She waved off the mistletoe. To be sure, there were rare cases where the ingestion of mistletoe had caused cardiac collapse, but usually only with preexisting conditions, and you had to have eaten an awful lot of the stuff. Mostly though, ingesting mistletoe usually just resulted in some unfortunate intestinal discomfort. It was not, in and of itself, lethal. And lethal was what Mickey needed. She must choose her spell-cipher carefully.

The whole idea behind this particular spell-casting was to create something protective out of something destructive—to render something lethal harmless by releasing its killing spirit and capturing that essence in the amulet. Harnessing deadly power to protect against deadly power. Or something like that . . .

Mickey ran her fingertip along a line of spidery calligraphy on the weathered page of the ancient spell book. Her eyes were stinging and there was an itchiness in her sinuses that was either an oncoming cold or—and this was probably a good deal more likely—she was allergic to one or more of the ingredients in Vinx's purple whammy-dust. Great. Just what she needed—another distraction. She pushed aside the sense of discomfort and furrowed her brow with renewed concentration. She really hoped she could nail this amulet spell, mostly because if she *didn't*, there was no way she could pull her sagging grades out of the fire. The Conclave would fail her. And *that* was not a prospect that rewarded protracted mulling. Mickey scrunched up her nose, snuffled fiercely, increased brow-furrow depth by 10 percent, and calmly asked her demon helpmate to hand her the next candidate ingredient.

Vinx removed the glass cover from a small platter and passed the dish over with a flourish. It contained, at first glance, a small bundled sheaf of innocent un-winnowed barley heads. Except that, upon closer inspection, the bearded grain appeared to be covered with a faintly iridescent, grayish slime that resembled snail trails. Even Mickey could recognize *that*.

"Ergot!" she exclaimed. "Jeezus, Vinx!"

"Yessss . . ." Vinx had earned an A++ last semester in poisons—they were a passion of his—and he positively beamed at the stuff in the dish. Like the proud owner of a darling new puppy. "In the proper proportions—"

"In the proper proportions," Mick interrupted with a squeal, "it can cause convulsions, hallucinations, ex-·treme fiery pain in the extremities and—if you're *really* lucky prior to it killing you horribly—gangrene!" She stared in horrid fascination at the harmless looking stuff.

"Oh, yesss," the demon hissed gleefully. "Marvel-ous, isn't it?"

Okay. Granted, she needed something lethal. Not necessarily lethal and violently, devastatingly painful! Ergot was out. Not in the least because if this spell were performed incorrectly, instead of providing a charm to ward off death, the enchantment would often turn and *inflict* death upon the hapless practitioner by whatever means naturally employed by the cipher element. Mickey had, on more than one occasion, overheard the more advanced students telling horror stories about such cases. And, frankly, gangrene?

No. Ergot was *definitely* out.

The young sorceress shook herself out of a gruesome reverie and looked over at her lab partner. Vinx was staring at her from under the shadowy escarpment of his browridge, his expression unreadable.

"You're learning, Mick. Quickly and well."

She ignored the uncharacteristic praise and turned back to the table, picking up a carved wooden box with a brass identifying tag. "So tell me, Vinx, just what are the proper proportions for—" she translated from the Latin automatically "—*Destroying Angel?* Sounds delightful. What *is* that, exactly?"

"What does it look like?"

She lifted the lid and peered inside. A fecund, peaty smell assaulted her nostrils. The box was half full of soil from which sprouted a solitary occupant.

"A mushroom, Vinx?" Mickey said, raising an eyebrow. "An armed and dangerous side dish? I'm terrified. Truly."

"Would you care to test that theory?" Vinx leaned closer, fetid demon breath undisguised by the handful of catmint he'd filched from the stores of herbs and had been munching on idly.

Mickey blinked, eyes and nasal passages burning. "Uhh . . . I don't like mushrooms."

"Then you have nothing to fear. It isn't a mushroom. Not really." Vinx plucked it out of the dark soil and held it up to the light of a torch.

"It looks like one."

"That is its power."

Terrific, Mickey thought. *Fungi power. Shazam!*

"It masquerades as one thing when it is, in reality, something quite different," Vinx continued on casually. Conversationally.

And yet there was something in the tone of his voice that made the pit of Mickey's stomach all squirmy. She tilted her chin up so that she could look him square in his glowy red eyes. "You don't say."

He grinned and, shrugging, plunked the thing back into the soil of its box. "The only visible disparity between this—you might call it a toadstool—and what you might call a mushroom is a slight variation in the color of its gills. And it is *very* slight."

"So?"

"So the one goes very nicely with a steak, sautéed in a little butter. Maybe a touch of garlic."

"And?"

"And the other causes hypertoxemia in the kidneys and liver. Extreme abdominal pain. Death within forty-eight hours of consumption." Demon eyes glittered coldly.

"Right." Mickey slammed shut the lid on the box and put it up on a shelf. A high shelf. Hypertoxemia? Higher than the ergot shelf. She turned back to the table. "This is the last one," she said, poking at another bunch of twigs, this time labeled with a small, white tag with the words *Taxus baccata* written on it in careful, somewhat childish block letters.

"Ah, a branch of the wondrous yew." Vinx scooped up the shrubby, dark green bough festooned with bright red berries. He looked as though he was about to wax positively rhapsodic, so Mickey figured this stuff must be particularly dangerous. *More* particularly dangerous. If that was possible . . .

"*That's* lethal?" she asked, sceptical. "It looks like a Christmas decoration."

"Bite your tongue!" Vinx actually shuddered at the word 'Christmas.' "*This* is yew! It is a symbol of immortality. It is sacred to the Druids. It is highly toxic in leaf, bark, *and* stem!" His expression actually got a little misty at that point. "Nary an inch of this little tree that won't kill you! It's one of my personal favorites. If you couldn't dispatch a man with the poison of the yew seeds or tea made from yew bark, you could always dip an arrow in yew sap and shoot him with a yew bow. So versatile in its lethality!"

"Ohhh, yah. I remember now." Mickey frowned, recalling details from her spell tome cram session of the previous night. "And death from yew poisoning is almost always asymptomatic: sudden and without warning."

"Such elegant efficiency, Mick!" Vinx cooed. "Use this one. For me? Please?"

"Gah!" Mickey shuddered. "All right, all right. Yew it is. Just quit with the kitten face, will ya?"

"Oh, goody!" The demon clapped his meaty mitts together like a little girl at a birthday party who'd just gotten a pony.

Mickey plucked up the branch and placed it a shallow bronze dish. "Is the circle ready?"

"Drawn from the finest sea salt and bonemeal."

"Why do you always have to make it sound like you're baking cookies when you spell-cast?" Mickey sniffed, her head feeling stuffy.

"Would you rather have me intone gravely and with menace?"

"Uh . . . no. Actually. Cookies are good." She put the dish down in the center of the circle. The pressure in her sinuses was actually becoming painful. *Concentrate, dammit!* Mickey admonished herself sternly. She took up the beaker of green liquid, the medium used for all student spells; it was a brew of mystic and highly secret substances, ladled out in carefully controlled portions by the Conclave *Grande Sorciere* at the beginning of term. The stuff smoked and hissed a little as she poured enough into the dish to cover the shrubbery. For all the dire warnings that accompanied the use of the beaker's contents, Mickey had always had a sneaking suspicion that it was probably nothing more than the magical equivalent of Pop Rocks and Mountain Dew, meant to scare the apprentices into cautious behavior when spell-casting (it was a theory she kept to herself).

Over in the corner of the cavern, Vinx lounged casually against the wall, watching.

Mickey drew the amulet receptacle from an inside pocket of her robe and held it over the dish of yew. It was beautiful—a rainbow-colored empty glass bulb about the size of a Victorian locket, hung from a delicate, box-link silver chain. She carefully filled it with more of the chartreuse liquid and, leaving it unstoppered, placed the amulet around her neck.

Then she stood and prepared to speak the enchantment.

The thing about casting, Mickey always thought, was that to the untrained eye it looked so damned easy. A few ingredients, a couple of muttered phrases, and whammo!—instant spell. Except that everything important that took place in a casting *really* went on behind the scenes—in the spell-caster's mind and heart. Even in her or his soul for some spells. *That* was the hard part. The words? They were more of a focus for the power. A lens used to capture the picture. Which was why spell chants could come off as a little . . . dull. And that was the reason so many sorcerers spoke their spells in Latin. Or ancient Greek or Gaelic. Mickey even knew one hotshot who did all his casting in Toltec—and he was from Winnipeg! Contrarian that she was, Mickey did all of hers in plain ol' English. With really simple rhymes. Because— hey—just 'cause they were the easy part, it didn't meant you couldn't seriously screw 'em up.

She took a deep breath.

From the corner of her eye, she saw Vinx lean forward.

"Fire burn bright!" she began.

"Flame burn true!" She wished her nose would stop itching.

"Keep me from harm"—*Oh, God! Not now*—the sound of her sneeze echoed off the cavern roof, and a cloud of sparkly purple danced before her eyes. There was a tingling in her skull, but she pushed on, desperate to finish the chant—"Ashes of *you!*"

And Vinx burst instantly into flame.

Mickey was still standing there, stunned, when the air shimmered, and the Conclave Elders appeared to grade her on her project results.

The letters appeared before her eyes in a silvery burst of light.

A++ across the board.

What? she thought. *I just flambéed my lab partner! How is that a good thing?*

"A clever ruse, Michaela," Chya, her primary instructor was saying, his voice pitched so that the other sorcerers could plainly hear. "Using a Karnalaq curse to alter the meaning of your chant."

"Wha—?" Mickey murmured numbly.

"The other Elders were not sure that you would recognize your fellow student as the most deadly cipher in the room—and therefore the most useful for your warding amulet." Chya bent low and scooped up the branch in the dish, from which the red berries were beginning to drop. "Nor were they certain that you would deduce that the demon had substituted a harmless, costumed evergreen for the *Taxus baccata*, meaning to destroy you utterly after you had spellcast a useless warding amulet. Which, of course, would have earned *him* the A++."

"He wha—?"

"*I*, of course, never doubted you for a second." Chya's black eyes glittered in the torchlight. Mickey could have sworn that he winked at her. "Congratulations, First Apprentice duLey. Enjoy your summer break!"

And then they were gone.

Mickey stumbled out of the circle and over to the pile of smoking, aubergine ash that had been her study buddy. "Demented demon spawn," she said, shaking her head half in anger, half in sadness. *Of all the dirty, rotten . . .*

But then, out of the corner of her eye, off to one side of the worktable, she spotted the leather pouch that Vinx had always worn on his belt. She picked it up and opened it. Inside was the vial of purple crystals and a tiny scroll of parchment. She unrolled it and read the block-lettered script:

Mick ~ Congratulations!
I hope they gave you an A++.
Here is the rest of the ex-Karnalaq.
Use it sparingly . . . who "nose" when you might need
   it again!
Cheers,
Vinx'ythnial Warburton-Smythe III

With a tear in her eye (just one, mind you—were the situation reversed, he *would* have killed her horribly, after all), Mickey knelt and carefully scooped up a bit of what was left of her lab partner and added it to the glass amulet hanging around her neck, stoppering it tightly. Then she poured a pinch of Vinx's purple powder into the palm of her hand and, as she felt the familiar tingling snap in her head, Mickey could almost swear that the amulet on her breast bubbled with the faint echoes of a deep, rumbling laughter . . .

Narrator: *Competition can be a healthy thing— for the winner. Fortunately for Michaela duLey, a misspell was exactly what she needed.*

LESLEY D. LIVINGSTON is a writer and actor living in Toronto, Canada. She has a master's degree in English from the University of Toronto, where she specialized in Arthurian literature and Shakespeare. For over fifteen years she has appeared in lead roles on Toronto stages, chiefly as a principal member of Tempest Theatre Group. Fans of Canada's nationally broadcast SPACE Channel may remember her as the SpaceBar's Waitron-9000, a holographic barmaid with an encyclopaedic knowledge of obscure B-movie trivia. Lesley's short fiction has appeared in *On Spec* magazine, and her debut novel *Wondrous Strange*, a young adult fantasy, is soon to be published. She is thrilled to be a part of the *Misspelled* crew.

8 rms, full bsmt

Kristine Smith

Narrator: *Selling a house involves attention to those little details, the ones that make such a difference to prospective buyers. Fresh paint, tidy cupboards, enhanced curb appeal. And, of course, don't forget to call the house cleaners.*

"That makes five so far." I ducked down behind the storage bin just as a gout of flame jetted through the space my head had occupied. It struck the wall behind me with a sound like a thousand metal zippers opening at once, a brilliant orange fireball that blazed, then vanished in a puff of wet, black smoke.

I stared at the chrysanthemum-shaped char that blistered the paint to the base cement. Started breathing again, and coughed as the burned hair stench of the smoke drifted around.

"He's gone." Jamie dove in beside me from his hiding place behind the washing machine. "I saw him scoot back down the hole."

"Probably went back to his nest for reinforcements." I scrolled through scuttle demon characteristics in my head. It kept me from thinking of other things, like how we were going to get out of this base-

ment alive. "How do you know it's a 'he'? You can
only sex a scuttle surgically."

"Alliterative today, aren't we?" Jamie chuckled and
rocked his head back and forth. "Sex, scuttle, surgically—
that's good." Soot coated a wide-eyed, pale face
framed by spiky red-brown hair, a shirt that had once
been orange, and khakis that would never be khaki
again.

Bambi, I thought, *caught in the path of a blowtorch.*
I'd met a few Bambis over the years, but they had all
been women. It always seemed to slip everyone's mind
that the Bambi of the movies was a guy. *Try naming
a boy "Bambi" these days and see what happens. The
poor kid would*—I stopped the panicked giggle in my
throat. Breathed deep. Coughed.

"There are subtle differences. Shading around the
gills and thickness of the webbing between the fingers." Jamie's voice sounded light and easy, an "all
the spells are working and we'll be out of here by
lunchtime" lilt. "I'll go over them with you after we
get out of here."

"*If* we get out of here."

"Caro, my girl. Have I ever led you astray?"

"Yes." I fielded his surprised look and tossed it
back. "That day you tracked me through the university library and told me that I absolutely needed to
take you on as a partner."

"Luckiest day of your life."

"Even more than the day I broke my leg, lost my
car keys, and found out that refrigeration won't prevent demon eggs from hatching."

Jamie grinned brightly—the expression wavered as
he looked me over. "Do I look as bad as you do?"

"How do I look?"

"Like an exploding cigar with legs."

I felt for my eyebrows, assured myself of their presence, then pushed my hands through my hair—the last

couple of fireballs that the scuttle and his friends had tossed at us had whizzed a little too close. *Hair's still there*. No shorter than it had been when we arrived at dawn and likely blacker than ever given all the soot floating around. *It pays to wear black on this job*. I gave the front of my T-shirt a self-congratulatory pat and raised a small cloud. "I'd say we look equally riveting."

"Hottest housecleaners in town, in more ways than one." Jamie took hold of my hand and squeezed. "So, that makes five, you said. One scuttle, two storms, a wattle, and a stench." He glanced at his watch. "Ten ante meridiem, and we're still in the Minors. Pokey little First Housers. Twelve demon Houses to go."

"That agent didn't expect to show this place today, did she?" I looked up at the ceiling and the floor joists visible through the gaping holes in the tiles. "I didn't see a sign out front."

"Kincaid Associates doesn't do signs. They show by appointment only. You go to one of their offices, and look through their catalog—" Jamie mimed leafing through pages "—while they look through your bank account."

"Doesn't seem to be anything special about this place. Eight small rooms. Only one bathroom." Besides the flame-scorched washer and dryer, I could see the smashed remnants of some storage cabinets. In one corner, a set of golf clubs. Assorted empty boxes. "Full basement's nice, but still. Nothing special at all." Beyond the fact that it came equipped with a passageway to the underworld and was infested with demons to a degree I had never before seen. "We should be able to pay it off eventually."

Jamie frowned. "What are you talking about?"

"Well, we broke it, didn't we? You break it, you buy it."

"We won't have to buy it."

"I always wanted a nice little ranch in the 'burbs."

"Will you shut up?" Jamie worked into a sprinter's crouch. "On the count of three, let's go."

"Go where?"

"To seal up the hole. Things keep emerging. We need to stop them. That's our job."

"I've already tried every sealing spell I know!"

"So, try one you don't." Jamie peeked over the top of the bin. "I have the utmost faith in your powers of improvisation."

"I can't—" I lifted my head as high as I dared, ready to dive back down at the first sign of further demonic hiccupping. "I can't do it by myself. You don't help, and I can't—"

"One."

"Damn it, Jamie Sheridan, if we live through this—"

"Two."

"—I'll bloody kill you myself!"

"Three!" Jamie plunged forward into the dark.

"Did you hear me?" I scrambled to my feet and bolted after him, dodging around melted mangles and through a do-it-yourself passageway that had once been part of a wall.

"You can kill me later." Jamie slid to a stop behind the smoking husk of a television cabinet. "Having you kill me would be infinitely preferable to anything else that could happen, believe me."

I ducked in beside him and peered around the side of the cabinet. We stood in the finished half of the basement, which contained a fireplace, wet bar, and pool table. The remains of a pool table. Distant pool table memories.

Now, in its place, there was a hole. It had opened up unbidden soon after we'd arrived, swallowing the table, a throw rug decorated with an ace of hearts, and a small figure of a donkey holding a daisy in its mouth. It seemed to curve upward above the level of the floor, like a shallow bowl. It also . . . pulsed. Which didn't make sense as there shouldn't have been anything there to pulse, seeing as "nothing" was sort of the definition of "hole," except— *It's like a vast black heart.* If I concentrated, I could hear the sound it made, like the *thrum* you get when you crank up the volume on a set of cheap speakers. "It's as though it's alive."

"It is." The lightness had left Jamie's voice. He seemed transfixed by the hole, like the proverbial deer in the headlights.

"Does it lead down to Hell, you think?"

"Eventually. But it makes a few stops along the way."

I shivered, even though the area close to the hole had grown warm enough to make me sweat. "I might have something." I had to repeat myself three times before Jamie finally looked at me. "It's not an officially recognized spell. I read it in one of my mother's grammars. It might not work."

"All the ones you tried that should've worked didn't. What've we got to lose?" Jamie tried to smile, but this time he couldn't quite pull it off. "Don't answer that."

I backed away from him, then stood still for a time, hands clenched. Fear had me by my soul's throat, and my mind was a scatter. I needed to focus, to clear my head so I could concentrate. Normally, I'd fix on something innocuous, a plant or a picture frame or the sound of my own breathing. But everything down here had been either burned or broken, and my breathing stuttered in counterpoint to my heartbeat. I had nothing solid. I needed rock to stand on and could manage only sand.

Then came the throbbing hum, worming past my thoughts, offering itself to me. I trusted it like a salesman's smile, but it was all I had. The only sliver of light in my darkness.

I stepped out from behind the cabinet. Shook off Jamie's restraining hand and positioned myself before the maw. I had no trappings, no accoutrements. Candles, feathers, charms—all had been shattered or incinerated over the course of the morning. **All I've left is me.** Well, that's what it always came down to in the end, didn't it?

I closed my eyes, felt the vibration come up through the floor. Did you ever listen to a band at a club, and find yourself at just the right place in the room? That place where the sound hits your ears perfectly and the bass rattles your bones, settles in your sternum and takes over for your heart? Pumps your blood? Drives your brain?

I let the pulsing dark take me. Let it go to that special place in my brain. Let it open the door and release the words.

Let the beast trap itself.

"Clean for the—" I staggered as the floor quaked. Scrabbled for the cabinet, missed, and fell backward. Felt arms close around me from behind and jammed my elbow back. Felt it connect with—

"It's me, you idiot!" Jamie held me, steadied me. "That got a reaction." He pushed me upright but stayed close, hands resting on my hips. "Try the rest of it."

I stepped closer to the hole. Felt its heat through my T-shirt. It looked different now, the empty throbbing gone gray instead of black. The beat of the vibration had quickened. "Clean for the new. Cleansed of the—"

The hole flared dirty white. The floor buckled upward and snapped like a whip end.

Three guesses who stood at the end of this particular whip. First two don't count.

"—*ooold!*" I flipped and spun through the air like a human daisy cutter. Luckily for my bones, I landed on an old overstuffed sofa. Unfortunately, the impact smashed it into the wall behind, sending loose chunks of wallboard and sheets of paper-thin paneling raining down. Shaken, but not stirred—lucky, lucky me.

I closed my eyes to keep the plaster dust out. Jamie must have thought I'd passed out because next thing I knew, he had crouched beside me and started patting my cheeks. "I'm fine." I opened my eyes wide, then batted his hands away.

Jamie stared at me as if he didn't believe me. His eyes looked strange in the half-light, the brown darker, the whites brighter. Crayon eyes. "Caro?" His voice sounded strange as well, throaty and rough, as though he had a cold.

"I don't think anything's broken." I moved my legs, and flexed my knees.

"You're fine." Jamie's voice sounded more normal as he worked to free me from the splintered pile. "Do you remember the title of that grammar?"

"*Assorted Spells and Cookery.*"

"Spells *and* Cookery. You're sure this is a *spell* you're remembering?" He grabbed my hand and pulled me to my feet. "I can see the headlines now. 'Giant Beef Wellington Avenges Ancestors and Devours Town.'"

"*You want to do this?*" I yanked away my hand and brushed off a layer of plaster dust that had already mixed with the soot to form a milky gray layer. "Because I have reached the limit of my expertise." I scratched my arm—the stuff irritated like itching powder. "I need help."

Jamie shook his head. "You're the spellworker. I handle research and accounting."

"No reason why you couldn't try. You have some ability. I keep telling you this, and you keep blowing me off." I took a step toward him—he took a step back. "We could double the power."

Jamie eyed the stairs the way a lost hiker would eye a cell phone. "I can go to the house and pick up your grammars."

"I can't handle this one alone. It isn't a simple haunting or visitation. This is something else."

"I can go to the house—"

"I don't need more words. I need power, and I don't have it. All you'd have to do is stand there and clear your mind. I'd hold your hands—"

"No."

"Why?"

"*No*, all right. Don't ask me again." A darkness fell across Jamie's face that had nothing to do with the surrounding dimness, a dying light in his eye that put an end to any argument. "I can't help you."

"What happened?" Behind me, I heard the noise from the hole elevate in pitch, paining my ears like a change in air pressure. "Someone died because of a spell you worked?" Jamie only looked at me, and I jammed my hands into my pockets to keep from grabbing and shaking him. *No time—not for this.* I needed him with me, and I knew that for the first time in the three years we'd worked together, he might not be there. Knew that the things in the hole would sense his inner turmoil and use it against both of us. Knew that we needed to talk, now, at this, the worst possible time. "You hurt someone . . . ?"

"Some people . . ." Jamie folded his arms, hunched against the fractured wall. "Some people shouldn't do magic." He looked at me, shrugged. "You've known a few. Something happens to them. They forget that others can break. That others can bleed, and weep. I'm one of those forgetful ones. I become . . . not myself."

I felt a rumble come up through the floor and rattle

my knees. "Could 'not myself' close that hole? Because if it's tears and blood you'll be needing as payment, you could wind up with more than you'll ever spend." I looked back toward the hole. It had grown more active, the air around it shimmering dully, like tarnished silver. "I don't know if it's going to stay this small. I don't know if the things we've seen come out of it are as bad as it gets or the point demons for something we really don't want to see." I took a deep breath, and uttered the words I dreaded. "We need to call in a specialist."

"An exorcist?" Jamie shook his head. "Exorcists mean permits, and permits mean publicity. People call us because they want to avoid publicity."

"People also call us when they want to get by on the cheap." I positioned myself so I could watch Jamie and keep my eye on the hole at the same time. "I'm a housecleaner. An unlicensed technician. Simple spells for simple demons. Cleaning out the odd bodkin that gets caught in the corners." The ceiling above the hole reflected movement in waves and flutters, shadowy hints of convection currents and steam and whatever else drew near the surface. "This isn't something that got lost and wants help finding its way home. This wants to stay, and I can't clean things that don't want to leave." I sniffed the air, and swallowed hard. That smell that hits you when you open a shed on a hot summer day and you know something crawled in there and didn't get out in time . . . that smell. "Our client—"

Jamie watched the hole now, too. "Rina Kincaid."

"Rina Kincaid." I had only caught a glimpse when she visited the office. Patrician blonde. A navy blue suit so severe you could slice a finger on the seams. "She underestimated her problem. She needs to call—" My heart skipped as something struck my arm, then started beating again when I realized it was Jamie tapping me with his hand to get my attention. "What's wrong?"

He pointed toward the shattered television cabinet. "We have company."

I looked toward the cabinet. Saw nothing. Squinted to try to sharpen the gloom and saw only diffuse shadow.

Then the shadow darkened and began to flow toward us. Stopped. Then started to flow again, more slowly this time, as though it knew we'd seen it but thought it could fake us out all the same. *See—I'm moving so slow that you don't see me . . .*

"What is it?" I looked at Jamie, who watched it draw near with what I had come to call his "science stare," curious but detached.

"Could be a shadow or a stench." He sniffed and winced. "Stenches usually have a more solid form, though."

"If it's a stench, we can't make any sudden moves—"

"—or it could go off like a skunk. I'm glad you remember that from the last time." Jamie smiled sadly. "Not much imagination to these names, is there? Scuttle. Stench. They are what they appear to us to be and nothing more. Not much of a life."

"You always say things like that. It's as if you feel sorry for them." I struggled with the urge to step out of the way as the demon drew near and the smell grew stronger. "Is it dangerous?"

"It could nauseate you." Jamie edged his foot toward the stench. It wrinkled to a halt, then straightened and curved around his shoe like a ghost of a reptile. "Ruin your clothes."

"Like that's an issue at this point." I tried to sidestep the demon, but as soon as I moved, it sped up, snaking out a tendril that wrapped around my ankle while the rest of it formed into a ball and stilled in front of me.

Then, slowly, it stretched out until the front half rested atop my shoe.

"I've never seen anything like this." Jamie's voice emerged soft with wonder. "I think it's laying its head on your foot like a dog."

I looked down at the shadowy mass and imagined it staring up at me with rheumy, bloodshot eyes. "It's making some sort of noise." I strained to hear it through the hole hum. "Kind of like wheezing."

Jamie bent close to the stench, and listened. "Snoring." He looked up at me with watering eyes. "I think he fell asleep."

"How can you possibly tell that it's a 'he'?" My head started to pound as another sound cut to the front of the line, past the humming and the demonic snoring. The worst sound of them all. "Did the front door alarm just beep?"

Jamie looked down at his watch. "Oh, *hell!*"

I fought to stay upright as the floor rippled and the stench slid off my foot and darted into a corner. "I don't think you should say that word."

"Hello?" A woman's voice, from the head of the basement stairs. "Jamie?"

Jamie closed his eyes. "We're—we're down here, Ms. Kincaid!"

"Kincaid?" Just when you thought things couldn't get worse, fate went and slammed your fingers in the door. "What is she doing here?"

"I told her we'd be finished by eleven." Jamie's face flared. "Don't give me that look—this has never happened before. This is Elysian Fields subdivision, not the House on Haunted Hill."

"You never saw *Poltergeist,* did you?"

"Yes—you forced me to watch it three times. Need I remind you that it was a *movie.*"

"In my house, it was a training film. This is what happens when you get in over your head. This is when a smart housecleaner bails and calls a pro." I looked around the blasted basement and swore under my breath while the stairs squeaked, announcing our client's descent.

Rina Kincaid wore taupe and pearls and held a thin brown briefcase in one manicured hand. "I'm sorry I took so long—" She stopped in her expensively shod tracks, eyes widening as the condition of her surroundings sank in. "What—?"

"Ms. Kincaid." I nodded to her but kept my distance. Every time I moved, I shed plaster dust and soot, and I didn't want a bill for a designer suit on top of my impending mortgage payment. "You have a portal problem, which is beyond the expertise of any housecleaner. We can't help you, but I can refer you to one of several discreet licensed practitioners."

Kincaid's well-glossed lips moved, but the only sound that emerged was a stricken "Jamie?"

Jamie tried to approach her, but he stopped as she took a good look at his filthy appearance and backed away. "Rina—"

"You said she was good. You said she could help."

"She is. She can. She—"

An ear-splitting shriek blasted out of the hole. I clapped my hands over my ears, then looked at Jamie and Kincaid to find them arguing as through they hadn't heard.

"What happened to my pool table?"

"Rina, please calm down—"

"It was *my* pool table, and I *liked* it."

"What do you mean, *your* pool table?" I shot a look at Jamie, who turned his back to me. "This is *your* house?"

"It was . . ." Kincaid hesitated. "My first house." She looked toward the hole and shivered. "I thought I lost him, but he's found me." She rummaged through her briefcase and pulled out a cigarette case and a gold lighter. *"It's not fair."*

Jamie held out a hand to her. "Look, I know—"

"Well, it's *not.*" Kincaid stuck a cigarette in her mouth, then lit it with a shaky hand. "Everything I've worked for all these years." She took a deep drag, then pulled the cigarette from her mouth and paced back and forth, like Bette Davis in a thirties melodrama. "Everything I've built—" Another drag. "If he thinks for one damned second I'll let him take me away—" Another drag. "—he's got another thing coming."

My mouth went dry as I watched Kincaid stalk back and forth and smoke while the air around her remained as clean as . . . really clean air. Even the smoke that emanated from the cigarette found its way to her nose and . . . vanished. *She isn't exhaling.* She didn't have to. Hers was a breathing-optional sort of life. "You're a demon."

Kincaid wheeled to stare at me. Yup, it was Davis, down to the pencil-thin eyebrows and the go-to-hell look in her eye. "Oh, you're fast, aren't you, Miss Worthless Housecleaner? Nothing gets past you, does it?"

"Well, it's not as though you'd *want* her to figure it out just by looking at you, is it?" Jamie's voice sounded as it had when he thought I had passed out, roughened by temper and guttering fast.

In all the time I've known him, I've never seen him angry. Come to think of it, he hadn't seen me torqued, either. "You knew she was a demon?" When he tried to turn his back again, I grabbed his arm and spun him to face me. *"You knew?"*

"Caro, please."

"If he thinks he's taking me back, he's in for a bumpy night!"

The second shriek silenced us all.

Then came the flies. They swarmed out of the hole in a thick ribbon and lit on the walls, the ceiling, and floor, coating them like paint, their buzzing drowning out the pervasive hum.

Then came—

I felt the presence before I saw it. It entered my brain as the hole itself had, but there the similarity ended. The hole had been gentle, in its way. It sought to conquer through persuasion. The presence didn't care. It drilled like an ice pick, driving me to my knees.

I hunched into a ball. Closed my eyes so tight and saw only the pulsing white. Felt the cold steel spike.

Screamed.

"Caro."

Felt arms around me, opened my eyes, and found Jamie kneeling beside me. Jamie, who hadn't told me the truth. Who had known our client was a demon and didn't tell me.

"I wanted to tell you, but I didn't know how."

Jamie, who knew everything about demons and pitied them. Who couldn't risk aiding a spell because he had learned that he couldn't trust himself with the power.

"Caro? I'm sorry."

I looked in his eyes and saw them go strange again. Heard how his voice had deepened and realized I was the only human in the room.

I pushed him away and sprang to my feet. Circled the hole and watched a head emerge, then shoulders, in a sick mockery of birth. "What House are you?" I looked at Kincaid, who had backed into the shadows and was visible only as a dot of cigarette light in the dark.

"House?" The dot whipped around. "What do you know about our Houses?"

"Answer the damned question!"

"Damned quesstion," a voice intoned from behind. "Sso amussing."

I turned to find the demon had emerged from the hole. Almost. Pretty much.

"She iss Sseventh Housse." Even though he still stood in the hole up to his knees, the top of his head grazed the ceiling. Bottle blue as the flies that attended him, with wings that beat so quickly they seemed a blur. Compound eyes set in a humanlike face. Naked. And definitely a "he." No question at all. Surgical examination not necessary, nope.

"Seventh House," I said, just to say something. "She's an emotion of some sort."

"Sshe iz exzaperation, and zelfishness."

I can see that. I shut up so I could breathe through my mouth—the thrumming wings kicked up the remains of the stench's stench and mixed it with the effluence that flowed from the hole. Rotted flowers. Sweat. Shit and spoiled food. "What are you?"

He looked down at me. "You have to asssk?" Disgust colored his voice. He drew himself up so that his head bumped the ceiling, sending tile crumbling down about him like snow. "I am Lord of the Fliesss."

"I should have guessed."

"Thiss iss not your conzern, cleaner." He looked toward Kincaid, who still stood in the shadows. "Rina?" At least, it sounded like "Rina," as uttered by a mouth that wasn't quite human. "You never write. You never call." The glitter in his eyes dimmed. "You are missed."

Kincaid stepped into the light. She held a fresh cigarette, which she jabbed in her mouth between short, clipped sentences. "I'm not going back." Pull. "You can't make me." Pull. "I'm staying here."

"It izzn't your choize to make." The Lord of the Flies lifted one leg out of the hole, then bent forward and leaned, elbows on knee, like a farmer at a fence. "To live amid the ssoundss and the ssmellss iz not for one ssuch az you. He wantz you back." The buzzing voice lowered. "We all want you back." He stilled, then slowly turned toward the far wall. "You are not alone here."

I searched the shadows along the wall and caught sight of Jamie trying to make himself very small in a junk-strewn corner.

"You." The Lord of the Flies pointed to Jamie. "You sought to vanquish us! To keep us from her! We, who love—" The arm fell. The jaw snapped shut. Compound gaze darted about the room.

Even demons commit sharing violations. I looked at Rina, who stood chin held high.

"I told you it was over." She paused to light another cigarette, the lighter flame flaring blue in the aromatic atmosphere. "It wasn't working. I'm a Seven, and you're . . . with headquarters. No room to maneuver. No sense of adventure. Just work, work, work all the live-long millennium."

"It iz never over, when you are forever." The Lord of the Flies straightened. More ceiling tile flaked down. "You will return az well, hider in cornerz, zo we may dizcusss your rule breaking." He eyed Jamie sidelong, and smiled. "We will enjoy that."

I circled around, positioning myself between the Lord of the Flies and Jamie. "So, Buzzy, you want her back?"

The Lord of the Flies looked down at me, eventually. Faceted eyes narrowed. "Yess."

"She came here, to a place you despise, to live among the humans you disdain, and you still—"

"Yess." He pounded his fist into the flat of his hand. "And yess, again."

"She had all that any demon possesses. Eternal life. The power of her House. Knowledge." I made a show of looking around the basement. "And yet she chose to live among us, in a place like this. She has to hide her true nature, hide her powers. She weighed all you could offer, and made that choice. She proved herself stupid beyond belief—"

"Hey!"

"—and you still want her back?"

The Lord of the Flies shot a look at Rina. Then he bent low and plucked something from beneath a broken chair. It was a cue ball, a survivor of the hole's creation. He pondered it for a time, then pressed it between his palms. The humming of the flies didn't quite drown out the crunching. "There musst be dizzipline," he said as he wiped the plastic dust from his hands.

"Or all the demons would bail? What the hell kind of Hell are you running that even the staff want out?" I held up a finger. "I would like to confer with my partner for a few minutes, if it's all right with you."

The Lord of the Flies laughed, a wet, treacley sound. "I can hear all you ssay. You cannot keep ssecrets from the dark, human—" He fell silent as a black stream shot up from one corner and fluttered along the walls and through the flies, driving them from their perch and luring them to follow.

It's the stench. I almost laughed out loud as it led the flies back to their master in a solid mass that wrapped around the demon's head and neck, blocking his vision. Distracting him for just along enough.

"Down!" The Lord of the Flies bellowed, with as much success as any owner of an overexcited dog. "Down! Sstay! Ssstill!" His hands were tied, figuratively if not literally. He couldn't strike at the stench without harming his pets.

Which meant I had a little time.

"Jamie?"

He was beside me like a shot. "Caro, I—"

"We don't have time." I turned to him and tried not to flinch. The nearness of his master had altered him—he seemed blurred around the edges, his features drawn rather than formed. "How long have you lived as a human?"

"About eight years."

"What about her?"

"Five." Kincaid wedged between us. "What can you do?"

I saw the fear in her eyes. It may have been a selfish, exasperating, demonoid fear, but it was all I had. "I'm going to try one more spell. It's my last shot." *And yours, too.* "You have to want to stay."

Kincaid rolled her eyes and nodded once. "Would I be going through all this if I didn't want to stay?"

"I do, too." A bit of the old Jamie shone in his eyes and smile, then vanished too quickly. "You know I do."

"Hold that thought." I turned and walked back to the hole. "Clean for the new."

"What?" The Lord of the Flies held the stench in one hand like a dirty rag, and used the other to herd his pets back to their perches.

I took a deep breath, gagged, then finally found my voice. "Cleansed of the old."

The demon stilled in midsweep. "You call that a spell? I have known the greatest warlocks—"

"All you be waiting, return to the fold."

"—blood sacrifice was made to us! The virtue of maidens—"

"Your father is calling. Best not make him wait."

That got his attention. He tilted his head. Listened. "He calls to me. How did you—?" He clenched his fists, then started as flies fell crushed to the floor. "I will be back."

"For what? You feel the pull of the spell." I pointed to Jamie and Kincaid. Definition had returned to Jamie's face, telling me that the connection between him and the Lord of the Flies had weakened, that I had made the right choice. "They don't feel that pull. They may not be completely human, but they're just human enough. What you'd take back with you wouldn't be the same thing that left, and how would your father feel about that?" I smiled. "Oh, the trouble they could cause."

Even the demon's wings stilled. A hush settled over the room. "If we let them."

"It won't get that far." I held out my hands to Kincaid and Jamie. Jamie grabbed and squeezed, while Kincaid took my fingers between hers in a cold fish clasp. "You believe the spells can drive you away. They believe the spells can keep you away. It's a subtle difference. But it means the world."

The Lord of the Flies looked into my eyes. "We harbor a few down there who think in the way you do. You would feel at home."

"Now's not my time. It's not theirs, either." I took another deep breath and didn't gag at all. "Clean for the new. Cleansed of the old. All you be waiting. Return to the fold."

"I will be back."

"Your father is calling. Best not make him wait. Your time here is passing. Your hour is late."

"Bah!" The Lord of the Flies looked down at the stench, which flipped and twisted in his grasp like a fish. He shook it loose, then slapped it in midair, sending it flying toward me.

"Go!" I turned aside just before the stench hit me in the face. It struck my shoulder and clung, scrambling across my upper back, draping itself like a particularly pungent scarf. *"Go! Go!"*

The flies peeled away from their perches and funneled down toward the hole, drowning the yells of their master as he lowered after them.

"You have not won!" The hole closed like an eye as his head vanished beneath the surface, then shrunk to a point and winked out.

Kincaid yanked away her hand as soon as the last light extinguished. "I've never heard that spell before." She rubbed at a soot smear and glared at me. "Sounded like a nursery rhyme."

"Whatever it was, it did what it had to." Jamie edged close, and tried to catch my eye. He looked as he always had, his features returned to normal, the connection with his old home broken. "He knew where he belonged. I guess we know where we belong, too."

Kincaid cocked her head, a touch of wonder softening her sharp features. "We've become human?"

"Human enough." Jamie reached out to touch her arm, then stopped and wiped his grimy hand on the front of his shirt. "Are you sorry?"

"No. It's what I wanted." At some point, Kincaid had stashed her briefcase under the stairs. She reclaimed it now, and dug a checkbook out of the depths.

I watched her fill out the spaces as the strain of the last hours began to ebb and the anger moved in to replace it. "I'm guessing he'll return at some point." Damn me, but part of me relished the lick of fear that flashed across Kincaid's high-boned face. *Bad Caro.* "I suggest you contract the services of a really good warlock. You're going to need them." I unwound the stench from around my neck and handed it to Jamie. "Don't bother to thank me." I took the stairs two at a time. I had never been so happy to walk out a door in my life.

I walked down the street to the place where we'd left the car, shedding flakes of soot and plaster with every stride. Birds sang. Children's voices sounded in the distance.

"Caro!"

I quickened my step.

"I knew you could do it." Jamie caught me up, then fell in beside me. "Believe what you want. I'm sorry I didn't tell you, but how do you tell someone that you . . ." He stuffed his hands in his pockets. "I mean, do I take you out, buy you a few drinks, wait until you've relaxed a bit and then say, oh by the way, I'm a demon?"

"Which House?" Why did I ask that—it wasn't as though I cared.

"Fifth," Jamie blurted, eager to keep the conversation going. "I'm a susurrus. Was a susurrus. The voice you think you hear when you're alone. The murmur on the dead phone line."

"Doesn't seem like there's much room for advancement. Not a lot of variety."

"It is limiting." He smiled. "There are more of us about than you think. Mikey, the meat manager at Scholl's. He was a tender of the flies."

I slid to a stop beside our car. "He works with *meat*? That people *eat*?"

"He can tell if it's fresh or not. He doesn't do anything to it." Jamie stood, hands on hips. "You know, that's the sort of thing we'd run into, if humans knew." His eyes dulled. "If we were lucky, that's what we'd run into." He shifted his feet, stared at his shoes. "The new mechanic at the auto place was a speed demon."

I popped open the trunk and pulled out bath sheets and a plastic bag of predampened washcloths. "That doesn't surprise me." I opened the car doors. Jamie helped me spread the sheets across the front seat to protect the upholstery, as we'd done so many times before.

"We don't fit in downstairs." He straightened his side of the sheet, then took the washcloth I handed him and wiped his face. "We prefer it here, even through we don't quite fit in, either. We like the quiet, and the soft colors, and the light." He concentrated on massaging the soot from his fingernails. "We like humans, too."

I tried to wipe the plaster dust and soot from my arms. Gave it up as a job for the shower and made do with brushing the worst of the grime from my clothes. "We've been working together for three years, and I never would have guessed." My eyes filled, and I blamed the soot. "Now I feel like I never knew you at all." I tried to open the plastic bag so I could stuff the dirty cloths inside, and as usual I couldn't pull apart the blasted interlocks. Sensed a presence beside me and did my best to ignore it.

"You know me." Jamie took the bag and, as usual, worked a thumbnail into the seam and opened it quick-as-you-please. "You know Rina. You know us all." He stuffed our grimed cloths inside, sealed the bag, and walked to the back of the car. "We're dust devils. The rustle of leaves. The shadow in a darkened room. The voice that you can't quite hear. We're part of you. You might as well be expected to notice the air." He tossed the bag into the trunk and shut it, then remained still. "You outwitted the Lord of the Flies." The look in his eyes held admiration and something else that made my heart skip. "You could be something, you know?"

I shook my head. "I come from a long line of cleaners."

"I come from a long line of sounds." He walked around to the passenger side door, steady gaze never leaving my face. "You never know until you try."

We stared at one another over the roof of the car. Smiled, eventually.

Then we sniffed the air and looked back down the road just in time to see a shadow dart behind a tree.

"I thought he'd stay at the house." Jamie looked

everywhere but at me. "The simple ones don't like to stray from their point of origination."

"Unless, say, they have another ex-demon to follow."

"I don't know what you're talking about."

"Oh, my mistake." I got into the car and put the key in the ignition, moving slowly so as to flake as little as possible. "He can sleep in your room."

"Be that way." Jamie got in beside me. Laid his head against the seatback. Yawned. "This could be the start of . . ." He smiled. ". . . something special."

I pulled away from the curb. Checked the rearview mirror in time to see a shadow flit into the street and give chase. "I thought you were going to say something else."

"I know." Jamie closed his eyes. "I'm full of surprises."

"Tell me." I turned on the radio and settled in for the drive back to our office.

Narrator: *A happy homeowner is a joy indeed. As for our housecleaner? Caro may have misspelled the situation at first, but she did come away with an ex-demon assistant and demonic pet. Nothing like a full household.*

KRISTINE SMITH was born in Buffalo, New York, has lived in Florida and Ohio, and now resides in northern Illinois. Scientist by day and writer by night and weekend, she is the author of four science fiction novels featuring Jani Kilian, a documents examiner who deals with crime and political intrigue in far-future Chicago. In 2001, she was awarded the John W. Campbell Award for Best New Writer. The fifth book in the Jani Kilian series, *Endgame*, was released in 2007.

Eye of the Beholder

Kevin G. Maclean

Narrator: *Behold a queen with a problem. A queen with a problem she expects to be fixed, no matter who, or what, must get the job done. By royal command, you see, there will be magic.*

"I want you to understand, gentlemen, the precarious position in which you find yourselves," Prince Consort Bertrand said.

The three priests wisely stayed silent, though the leader nodded slightly to indicate understanding.

"The queen is furious."

This time all three nodded.

"Seven years ago, she came to the Temple of the God with Two Faces with a simple request—that her unborn child should be 'as white as the snow and as red as the rose.' *Most* people would have understood this as a request that the child be beautiful . . ."

"It is a sign of most extreme divine favor, Majesty," said the priest on the left. The other two stared at him in horror.

"What? To be an albino with a strawberry birthmark covering the whole of the right-hand side of her face? Do you have any idea what your typical seven-

42

year-old makes of that? She is my daughter. And she is the heir to the throne. In ten years, gentlemen, she is going to be thinking of marriage."

"The mark was quite hard to see for the year Princess Dual was black, Majesty," put in the priest on the right.

"*What* did you just call her? It better have been Jewel, not what I thought I just heard, because if you give me any good reason to suspect that you have not been acting entirely faithfully to the commission Her Majesty gave you, or contrary to my daughter's best interests—well, let us just say that so far I have protected you from the queen's wrath and that I love my daughter."

The prince sat for a moment, his face unreadable, though his left hand gently and automatically checked his sword was loose in its scabbard. Then he sighed, and the priests could breathe again. "No, gentlemen, I want my daughter to look at least halfway normal. And the queen still wants her to be beautiful. In fact, she paid you a great deal of money once, and more since, to ensure Jewel would be beautiful, and, to put it bluntly, she isn't beautiful, she's scary. And when she isn't scary, she's ugly. Every time you try to fix the problem, she's different, but a new problem appears."

The High Priest began, "We have a new—" but stopped under the prince's withering gaze.

"Are you prepared to bet your life, and that of every member of your order, that this new spell will work to the queen's satisfaction? Because that is precisely what you would be doing."

The High Priest didn't have to think about it long. "Err . . . no."

"Well, take it from me, the most pleasant part of what she has planned for you if you aggravate her again will be the ravens tugging on your entrails. Stay out of her way."

The priests stood in white-faced silence.

The prince continued, "She has lost faith in your ability to set things right. To quote her very words, 'Those two-faced priests of that two-faced god are worse than useless. Find someone who can and will do the job.' And so, gentlemen, I shall."

"Not the witches?" gasped the priest on the left.

"No. Her Royal Majesty has no wish to be beholden to the worshipers of the Triple Goddess, even if she thought they could do the job."

"Dealing with Hell always has too high a cost, Majesty," the High Priest cautioned.

"Just how stupid do you think we are?" the prince snapped. He held up his hand. "Wait! As you value your lives, do not answer that." His aide took the opportunity to slip a document where the hand had rested. "Gentlemen, Her Royal Majesty has been both patient and generous for seven years and has seen no progress. Consequently, it would be an act of prudence to offer to pay for someone else to do the job. Have I made myself perfectly clear? Ask now, because any misunderstanding could be fatal for you."

"Yes, Highness. Perfectly clear. But where will you find such a powerful mage?"

"Faery, gentlemen," the prince said. "I am sending an emissary to Faery." He waved them away. "I have taken the liberty of arranging a guided tour of the torture chamber for you. Pay close attention. If you manage things right, you may never see such a thing again. Go on, shoo! The guards will escort you."

Beth was sure she had made a mistake. No, that wasn't right. She'd made lots of them. First, she should have let Josie get her own clothes down out of the trees. Second, she should never have told her mother what she was about. Third, she should have told every-

one concerned to keep their mouths shut—no, that
would never have worked . . .

She was startled out of her reverie of self-
recrimination by the arrival of yet another interroga-
tor. This one bore himself with the unmistakable air
of a military man, and one of high rank. He was accompanied by a finely dressed man who poured a glass
of wine for him before retiring to a side table with
the rest of the wine and the remaining glasses. Beth
noted with amusement that this flunky wasted no time
pouring wine for himself and getting comfortable.

The officer cleared his throat. "I am General Robert
Longley. You are Beth Hawkins, from the village of
Grimley-on-Tyde."

Beth, of course, had heard of him, but since the last
half dozen interrogations had all been conducted by
men who held the power of life and death over her,
she was no more frightened by this one. She nodded
in acknowledgment.

"This will hopefully be the last interview for you.
Lying or attempting to mislead us at this stage will be
construed as treason. Any changes in your story will
not be held against you. We just want the truth."

"I understand, sir. But to tell the truth, I've been
questioned so long and so hard that I'm no longer
sure what some parts of the truth *are*." This brought
a scowl from the general and an understanding smile
from the flunky.

"How about you just tell us your story, and tell us
which bits you're sure of, and which bits you aren't?"

"Well, sir, me and a bunch of the village girls went
down to the swimming hole, and after we undressed,
Josie insisted on putting a religious medallion on top
of her clothes. I forget which god's it was, but she
insisted it would protect her clothes."

"And you argued over this?"

"Yes, sir, and eventually I told her that if she upset the Fae, whatever they did would be her own damned fault, beggin'-your-pardon-sir, and let her do it."

"What made you think it would upset the Fae?"

"Well, my gran's ma used to say that openly displaying any religious symbol in the woods was a bit like carrying the Pretender's flag into a royal castle. They just could *not* let it pass."

"And this grandmother's mother, she was something of an authority on the Fae?"

"Oh, aye, sir. Friends with some of them, she claimed, as much as mortal can be friend with Fae. Strange, she said they were, and uncanny."

"And she taught you about them?"

"No, sir. She died just before I was born. But Ma talked about her a lot. And I've worked out a fair bit for myself."

"Why was none of this in the reports?" The general's voice was low and terse, straining not to shout in angry frustration at his absent subordinates.

"No one asked, sir," Beth said. "They kept telling me just to answer the questions, but they wouldn't ask the right ones. They seemed much more interested in hearing about the Puck catching us naked in the swimming hole, and what Josie did when she found her knickers flying like a flag from the top of a pine tree."

The general closed his eyes in despair. "I see. And the milk and whiskey?"

"An apology, sir, and a bribe to get the Puck to bring her clothes back. He may be terrible mischievous, but there's no real harm in him."

"You've had frequent dealings with the Fae, then?"

"Oh, not that frequent, sir. Maybe twice a year, someone's cow will get lost, and I'll talk to the Fae and give them a gift, and next day the cow will show

up. That sort of thing. It's dangerous to have too much
to do with them."

"But you do know how to contact them?"

"Oh, that's easy enough, though they can be tricksy
and wild. Just a matter of etiquette. It's not like
they're scarce, y'know."

There was an awkward silence.

Finally, the silence got too much for Beth, and she
said slowly, "You didn't know?" Then it came to her.
"Of course you wouldn't. You've never been out of a
town without your weapons and armor and a great
host of men scaring away even the boldest of beasties.
No wonder they never let you see them."

There was a rustle of silk as the flunky stood. He
strolled across and perched himself on the edge of the
table and quietly poured her a glass of wine. "I think,
general, that we may have found our emissary." He
smiled at her.

"I think, Highness, that you may well be right."

To her credit, Beth did not faint.

She could have said no to the general, with his duty
and honor. She could have said no to the prince, with
his offers of honors and wealth. She could even have
said no to the queen, with her tears and her threats.
But she hadn't been able to say no to a sad-eyed little
girl, so she cursed herself for a fool.

And there she sat in the woods, under a great,
spreading oak, with a small untouched cup of good
whiskey in front of her and another set out for an
unknown guest who hadn't arrived yet. A small donkey grazed nearby, hitched to a traveling pack and its
saddlebags. She had been able to talk the queen out
of sending a full entourage but not out of equipping
her and providing a donkey laden half with traveling
supplies and half with the Prince Consort's best whis-

key. She'd tried to explain it was too much—that the Fae weren't drunks—but to no avail.

The crack of a twig announced the arrival of a guest. Politely, she turned her head toward the distraction, then looked back. The cup opposite was untouched, but a quarter of hers was gone.

"Oh, it's you, Puck," she said.

A peeved-looking Puck showed himself and picked up the cup again. He tasted it again carefully, and pulled a face. "Arr, your great-grandmother's was better. And how did you know it was me, anyways?"

"Anyone else would have taken this one," she said, and leaned over to pick up the untouched cup.

"It's the curse of all Pucks," he said, woebegone. "Too much cleverness and the compulsion to show it."

"Well then," she said and raised her cup to him. "To all Pucks everywhere—may their cleverness never fail them."

"I'll drink to that," cried the Puck, leaping to his feet with cup still in hand, and never spilling a drop.

"Of course you will," she said. "You'll drink to any bloody thing."

He clutched at his heart melodramatically. "You wound me, mistress. I may be overly fond of strong drink, but I am not such a tosspot as that."

She smiled fondly. "No, you're not, but you have to admit it was funny." She leaned over and topped up his cup.

"Could it be, mistress, that you are trying to out-clever a Puck?" The Puck appeared unsure whether or not to be offended.

Beth carefully hid her smile. "Nay, never, for that were foolhardy indeed, and doomed to certain failure."

Honor satisfied, the Puck perched himself on a great gnarly root and attended to the whiskey.

After about three cups, Beth broached the real reason for her visit.

"You want to *what?*"

"I want," she repeated slowly and patiently, "to talk to a Faery mage powerful enough to sort out what those priests have done to Princess Jewel." She topped up his cup again. "Do they exist?"

"Oh, they exist all right!" The Puck was too disturbed to even think about the whiskey. "And tell me, lassie, how long have you been hankering after death or something worse?"

"Worse?"

"They are a strange and uncanny lot, yon mages. And they all have a whimsical sense of humor and no regard for others. There's no telling what they might do to you. I saw one poor mortal turned into a fish." He shuddered.

"And what was so terrible about that?"

"He left him like that for thirty years, *and wouldn't let him die, or get near water.*" He closed his eyes in horror. "The mage was just amusing himself. Nothing personal about it at all." The Puck looked at her slyly. "Still want to talk to one?"

"I don't really have a choice."

"Then on your own head be it!" He made a single pass across her field of view with his right hand. "Sleep now!"

She slept.

Beth came awake with a start. The Puck was still sitting facing her. "How long was I asleep?"

"Who can say? An instant? A moment? Forever?" He gave an enigmatic smile. "Ask me not when, but where, for you, my lass, are now in Faery."

"It doesn't look any different."

"Can ye no see it? Look closer."

And she *could* see. There was a *difference*, something subtle in the way the light danced perhaps, a life in the wind, an awareness that even the trees might be sentient, or the rocks . . . *Or maybe it was just her that was different . . .*

The Puck stood. "Night comes," he said. "We had best be getting you somewhere out of reach of the nightwalkers."

"Nightwalkers?"

"You know what a nightmare is?" He waited for her nod. "Here, they're *real*."

Suddenly it seemed like a very good idea to be moving. She packed quickly and followed the Puck.

It was evening when they reached the palace: an alabaster edifice, elegant and rather smaller than Beth had expected.

"Who lives here?"

"The Duke of the Western Marches. He's an elven sorcerer, your best bet for getting your princess fixed."

"Is he powerful enough to do the job?"

"He's one of the great lords of Faery. The question is not *can he help* but *will he*. Catching his interest could be tricky. He has about as much care for the concerns of mortals as you do for the cares of ants."

"Oh," Beth said, chastened. She fastened the donkey's lead rope to a small tree outside of the garden perimeter. "Will he be safe here?"

"For the meantime. I'll see to moving him later."

"Thank you." She strode through a gap in the boundary hedge. "Even the garden is perfect."

"No horse shit in the courtyard neither," said the Puck. "Me, I like things a little more natural."

The guards paid them no attention, but the same could not be said of the courtiers inside, as all eyes followed them as they approached the duke. They stopped at a respectful distance and waited.

Eventually, the duke finished his other business and turned his attention to them. "Well, Puck, what have you brought me this time?"

"An emissary, Your Grace, from a queen in the mortal realms."

The duke snorted. "And what do they want this time? A sword to carve them an empire? The Key to All Knowledge? Or mayhap just a charm to smite their enemies with the Itching Pox?" The wide gray eyes fixed on her and she trembled like a rabbit transfixed by a polecat. "Well? Speak up, girl!"

"If it please Your Grace, Her Majesty is in need of a working of magic. One small to one of your obvious puissance but beyond the reach of her own powers."

"Get on with it, girl."

"Well, Your Grace, a spell was cast upon her then-unborn daughter, and, oh, Your Grace, they made such a mess of it. Instead of making the girl beautiful, she has a face straight out of a bad dream. They have tried all they know, but nothing has helped."

"There would be a price . . ."

"Her Majesty has told me she is prepared to be generous."

"Indeed? I will think on it. Steward, show our guest to suitable quarters and see she is provided for. I will send for her once I have reached a decision."

The room Beth found herself in was small but immaculately appointed. She sat down on the edge of the bed and removed her boots. She had a moment of fright when she heard the key turn in the lock behind her and realized that there was no other way out of the room, but they did not seem to intend her harm. She lay back and let herself drowse.

Beth came awake suddenly and would have cried out but for the small hand across her mouth. It was full night, and moonlight streamed through the window slits.

"It's me, the Puck," a voice whispered in her ear.

"Be as quiet as you can. Put these elf boots on. We're leaving."

Beth struggled to put the strange boots on. Eventually, the Puck gave up and put them on her.

"Now," he whispered. "Follow my lead. Be quiet. Do *what* I tell you *when* I tell you, and we'll get you out of here."

They stepped out between two sleeping guards. The Puck relocked the door and hung the key back on one guard's belt. Then they slipped into the shadows and away out of the court.

After several miles, she stopped to catch her breath.

"Come on. Come on." The Puck jigged up and down in anxiety. "We must be well away before daybreak."

"I'm not going a step further until you tell me what's going on."

"I heard them talkin'," said the Puck nervously. "They was going to put you to sleep."

"So?"

"They was arguing whether forty years would be better or fifty."

A sudden chill ran up her spine. "Oh. Thanks are definitely in order, then. And we'd best cover our tracks."

"No need while you're wearing those," he said. "Best elf boots, them. No noise, no tracks, never slip. The scout I stole them from will be livid. Now come on."

"What about the duke's hounds?"

"Well, when they wake up, in about a week, the trail will be too cold. Now come on."

And so she did.

"You can speak normally now," said the Puck. "We're safe here."

"Where are we?"

"Oh, this is just a hidey hole I made for when I

need to keep out of sight. Being a Puck means that sometimes you have to avoid certain people until they cool down. First, the water rushing past the end of that corridor is a waterfall. We get water, light, and air that way. Second, that way comes up under a rather large, unruly, and extremely thorny blackberry bush. Third, that way comes up between the roots of a tree, though you'd have to cut your way through some spiderwebbing."

"Isn't anyone who finds one of those going to investigate it?"

"Not unless they're a Puck, or one of the wee folk. Yon elves would just think it was a mouse hole. They don't have size-mastery."

"Oh. So I'd be what—half an inch tall?" Beth thought about this a moment, and decided not to think about it more, because it made her dizzy. She sat down.

"There's a bed over there," said the Puck. "It's yours as long as we're here."

"Thank you." She moved in the direction indicated, and located the bed by touch. "Is it always this dark?"

"At night, yes." The Puck was amused. "I'll shut the water door, and then we can light a candle." He did so.

Beth sat on the bed and began to remove the boots. "I still don't understand why you'd risk the wrath of one of the great lords of Faery over me," she said.

The Puck nibbled on a fingernail. "Well," he offered, "it's not like I'm unfamiliar with the wrath of great lords. But mostly, it's for your namesake, Old Beth, your great-grandmother."

"Gran's ma? But she's long dead."

"Oh, I wouldn't count on that—her being such a fearsome strong woman an' all. Half the Fae looking after her house think she's coming back. You know some people called her a witch?"

"Never to her face, I'll bet."

"No, never that. Not twice, anyway. But I owe her. And it's one of those unpayable debts."

"Why? What'd she do?"

"She faced down a King of Faery for me."

Beth looked at him and raised one eyebrow.

"He's hunting me seriously—hounds and all. They've just about caught me when I see Beth's door standing open, so I duck inside. Beth takes one look at me and grabs her staff and heads out the door I'd just come in. I hear a few yelps and sneak a look out the window. There's twenty-odd Fae hounds prowling up and down this white line she's drawn across her garden. Any of them is at least as big as her. Presently, His Majesty comes trotting up on his gray horse and looks at the line. She tells him it's a courtesy line, which is to say a line that he can cross if he really wants to but that he can't cross without crossing her, as it were. Then he demands me, and she tells him no, that I am under her protection, and that he may not hunt me, or anyone else for that matter, on her land without her permission. And at that time, the Fae reckoned her territory as stretching at least ten leagues in every direction from her house. She lets him bluster and threaten a bit as his retainers come trotting up, and then she looks at them and tells him, yes, his hunting pack is a pretty fair imitation of the Wild Hunt, but if he doesn't get those horses and hounds out of her vegetable patch quick smart, he'll get a much closer look at the real thing than he really wants. His Majesty tries to stare her down, but she just lifts one eyebrow and smiles slightly in that dangerous way she had. He jerks his horse's head around and heads off with all his retainers and other hounds behind him. And you know what? She never even asks me what I've done."

"And what had you done?"

"Well, the king has been romancing this sweet thing

for months, and finally she gives in, and the two sneak off to the royal bedroom, only to discover that some evil person has short-sheeted the royal bed."

"Oh. And the king didn't think that was funny?"

"*I* thought it was hilarious."

"*You* would. And, of course, you got blamed."

"As is only right, seein' as I'm the one what done it. A Puck's got his pride."

Beth laughed. "You're mad, I vow. Completely off your rocker."

The Puck leaped to his feet and gave her an extravagant bow. "Why thank you, Mistress. 'Tis the nicest thing anyone's said about me these many years." When Beth's giggles had subsided, he added quietly, "You know, you're not going to be able to go back."

"What?" Beth said, momentarily stunned by the rapid change. "What do you mean?"

"I mean that if you go back to Grimley-on-Tyde, you'll find all your old friends aren't your friends any more. You'll be the strange one, the one who left the village, and talked back to the queen, and went to Faery. And they'll never quite believe any of it, but they'll make those signs they think ward off evil when you walk past."

Beth's eyes filled with tears. "I know," she whispered.

"And when that happens," the Puck went on, "you'll have two choices. You can run away before they stone you, or . . ." and he posed dramatically for a moment ". . . you can move into your great-grandmother's cottage."

"I don't understand. How would that help?"

"Ah, now listen to the Puck, for he is mad. Completely off his rocker. Fear and respect are but two sides of the same coin. The one will get you stoned; the other gets you a place in the world. Your great-grandmother was a Wise Woman, and a wise woman as well. It is a place in the human world that will let you be strange, nay, even requires it in some measure. Moving into that house would be a declaration that you are to be treated with respect."

"Does it still stand?"

"Oh, aye, did I not tell ye there were Fae looking after the house? And half of them expecting *her* back? And you were named for her, because you were born shortly after she died. And half those Fae suspect there is more of Old Beth in you than would be accounted for by bloodline."

"And what do you think?"

"I think that it doesn't matter. Even if you were Old Beth come again in her entirety, you're still yourself, and that's as it should be. And you'll be a great Wise Woman."

"How can you be so sure?"

"Because I'll make sure. And, of course, because I'm mad. Completely off my rocker. Didn't a Wise Woman just tell me so?"

She heaved a chunk of moss at him and rolled over, knowing she'd've missed. "Good night."

She did not hear him leave, but then, he was, after all, a Puck.

Beth awoke to a strange crunching sound. She carefully rolled over to locate the source. The donkey rolled one eye at her but left his muzzle in the bucket of oats.

"How did you get here?" she asked.

"I stole him, of course," said the Puck, sauntering into the cavern and perching himself on a rock. "And seeing as there was no pursuit yet, I brought him here. And as to your next question, don't ask, because I ain't tellin'. Just take it from me that following the tracks he left is a waste of time."

"So what now?"

"Now, we wait until the hunt dies down. Should be only a few days. Make yourself comfortable."

"Then what?"

"Then we go looking for a mage again. Only it can't be an elf, because the duke will have alerted them all."

"Doesn't he have any enemies?"

"Oh, plenty, but they're just as nasty as he is, or worse. And it won't be so easy to escape a second time. They weren't really expecting you to up and go, because it never occurred to them that I might help you. They know better now."

"So who do we try next?"

"Well, it's no use asking a unicorn. They don't like traveling out of Faery. And they can't do magic, only undo it, so if the girl is naturally ugly, that's how she'd end up." He scratched his head thoughtfully. "I think your best bet is a dragon. They're powerful, very magical, and don't care what elves think. Yes, a dragon would be best."

"Ah, don't they *eat* people?"

"Yes, but they're intelligent. No self-respecting dragon would eat a person who could deliver them half a dozen oxen, and I imagine your queen would gladly give every ox in the country for this little job. And they're quite protective of their own offspring, so they can understand a parent's concern, which gives us a slight advantage. And don't forget they're vain. You can use that."

"I see."

"Just don't irritate the dragon, and you should be able to rely on its greed to see you through. But cheat one, insult it, steal from it, or try to harm it or its offspring in any way, and that dragon won't be happy until you've met a gruesome death."

"Such as being a dragon's breakfast."

"Exactly!"

*   *   *

A fortnight saw them in the foothills of the mountains, approaching the lair of the dragon Fwooshka.

"I'd better change back to my old boots soon. Wouldn't want him thinking we were sneaking up."

"Good thinking."

Her steps still sounded disturbingly loud to Beth by the time they crested the final rise, and there, basking in the sunlight near the opening of a cavern, was a large dragon, which Beth correctly took to be Fwooshka.

The Puck pointed toward a rock entirely too close to the dragon. "We'll just sit down there until he wakes up."

The donkey sensibly declined to follow, so they led him back over the ridge before making their way down to their chosen seating.

No sooner had the Puck sat down than an eye snapped open. The dragon sat up and stared at the Puck. "Why are you here? Could it be that you have brought me a sssssnack?" He eyed Beth hungrily.

"Oh, no, Great Fwooshka! I have come to you with a rich proposition befitting your magnificent self," Beth said quickly. "There will be many oxen in it for you, and gold."

"Oxsssen? Gold? Magnifissscent!" Fwooshka polished a claw against one massive shoulder. "I approve of your mannersss, human, and sssssince you do not offend as much as mossst of your unattractive speciesss, you may continue. Go on."

So she did, and they haggled, and finally agreed that, for a fee of eight oxen, the dragon Fwooshka would fly to the mortal lands on the night of the next full moon, and there he would inspect the princess and then negotiate directly with the queen for the correction of the spell.

*   *   *

The queen was mightily pleased with herself. For a few dozen oxen and a mere hundredweight of gold, the dragon had agreed to remove all the existing enchantments from the princess and then to make her beautiful. The only hard bit would be getting the gold out of those priests, but she could take it from the royal coffers and deal with them later.

The peasant girl had been granted the patch of abandoned land she had requested and sent on her way laden with gifts.

The oxen had already been set free in the wilds for the dragon to collect at his leisure. All she had to do now was get the gold to the agreed clearing in the forest on the night of the new moon and leave Jewel there alone with the dragon while he worked his magic. And the next morning, her little Jewel would be *beautiful*. She could make *plans* . . .

The queen and her ladies-in-waiting approached the clearing. The ladies wanted to be done and return to civilization, but the queen was more anxious to see her now beautiful heir. She needed to know the exact appearance of the princess, so she could choose which of the neighboring kings to offer her to. Red hair would be good—that would attract the lust of King Randolph, and his kingdom was large and rich and adjoined her own.

Anxiously, the women entered the clearing. The gold was, of course, gone. They looked around and spotted something.

"Aww . . . what a cute little dragon," said one of the ladies.

"Such exquisite patterning!" enthused a second.

"She's beautiful. Just look at the way the light plays on those iridescent scales," said a third.

"But where is the princess?" demanded the Queen. It was some minutes before the awful truth occurred to her.

Narrator: *The queen and Beth received exactly what they asked for, so was this technically a misspell? Alas, only the lovely princess could say for sure . . . and she's declined to be interviewed. Something about oxen and gold.*

KEVIN MACLEAN lives in Auckland, New Zealand. He gives his profession as freelance computer geek. His short fiction has been featured in *Andromeda Spaceways Inflight Magazine*, *Millennium Nights*, *Summoned to Destiny,* and a number of *Pipers Ash* collections. He is currently working on a novel that he describes as "very strange," which, considering he considers H. P. Lovecraft's work "normal," is somewhat worrying.

Cybermancer

Janet Elizabeth Chase

Narrator: *Sisters, sisters. There were never such devoted sisters. Old song. Enduring sentiment. Or is it? Witness the plight of Epiphany Jones, cybermancer extraordinaire, when her flesh and blood comes to call.*

The Aether was singing its song to me again. With my headphones on I didn't hear the knocking. The pounding I heard. When I opened the door, I nearly slammed it shut again. It was my sister. My younger sister, and she had a suitcase.

"So what'd you do this time?" I held the door open only to my shoulder. Slamming was still an option.

"Got caught at a rave," she said plainly. "Things are a little tense at home right now."

"No kidding. What else?"

"Nothing." She sounded defensive. "Mom and Dad didn't appreciate me calling them from the police station."

"I can see how that might make them upset." She knew a call to me would have meant a night spent in a holding cell at juvenile hall.

"Well?" Exasperation.

"Well what?" I wasn't going to make it that easy.

"Can I come in?"

"Want to give me one reason why?"

"We're sisters."

"That's never mattered before." And it hadn't. Bernie, Bernadette on her birth certificate, and I had never been close. My parents thought it was our difference in age. We're seven years apart. My sister and I knew it was because we quite simply didn't like each other.

I stared at her for a minute before turning around and walking back into my apartment. I left the door open.

"I'm surprised Mom didn't just give you the key," I growled. My mother had a key to my apartment for "emergencies." "Put your stuff in the spare room." I headed for the fridge and a beer. "And close the door, Bernie."

Bernie was barely seventeen. Of the two of us, I've been the least problematic, even with my chosen profession. My name is Eppie Jones, Epiphany on my birth certificate. I am a practicing Cybermancer. I deal in cyber-divination and demon summoning. I work in the Aether, known as Hel to its inhabitants. What you'd call the Internet. My sister, on the other hand, has no notable skills other the aforementioned stress-inducing ability toward parents.

I live in Santa Cruz, on the west side, far enough from downtown where the tourists usually congregated. I like the weather; fog suits me, and the city has a constant population of hippies. I get a few Silicon Valley geeks too. I've no shortage of clients. Most of them want the usual, astrological readings and divinations. They use people like me instead of the classic methods: tarot and astrology. For the locals it's modern chic while still being agreeable with their more pagan side. The high-tech geeks like the technology aspect of it. The Internet is perfect for that sort of divination, the whole random numbers thing and all.

"Mom doesn't know I'm here. Hey, this room's crammed," Bernie called from down the hall.

"Take it or leave it," I called back from the kitchen. I took a long drink of the cold beer, hoping for the latter. The spare room was where I threw everything I didn't have a place for, including my little sister. "And call Mom."

After a few minutes she came and sat at the bar, sans suitcase.

"Can I have one?" She gestured to the beer in my hand. I shrugged and motioned to the fridge. She could get it herself.

"Did you call Mom?" I headed back to the computer. I had a new client, which meant a new spell to be written.

"Yeah." She flipped the bottle cap onto the counter. "She'll be by tomorrow after work."

"Great." I put my headphones back on and began working. After a moment there was a tap on my shoulder.

"What?" I growled and pulled the headphones down around my neck. I lived alone for a reason.

"What's on for tonight?"

"Nothing. I'm working." I pulled the headphones back up and continued working on the new spell disk. After a few minutes I could hear the TV.

It was Sunday, and the portents were good that night; the spell was coming along nicely. When I finished it around 1 AM, Bernie was still watching TV. I locked up my disks as usual. These weren't the kinds of things you wanted loose on the world. I was halfway down the hall when she called out.

"Can I go online?"

"No." I headed back for the family room. "Don't touch my computer."

Unlike my parents, Bernie knew what I did for a living. I'm not sure she understood what I did, but anything crossing magic with technology was apparently cool. My parents thought I designed Web pages. They thought everyone working "in computers" designed Web pages. It was best to leave them with that impression.

"I mean it, Bernie."

"Yeah, yeah." She waved me off and went back to watching TV.

Monday came quietly. Bernie had eventually made it to bed since the couch was unoccupied. With a cup of coffee in hand, I sat at the computer for some quick clean up work on the new spell.

"What's this?" I stood up again. Bernie had left her mp3 player in my chair. I tossed it across the room, mildly aiming for the couch. I sat back down and started to check the spell. I planned on testing it that day since the portents were once again favorable, so when I finished the cleaning up, I burned the disk. The sooner I had the spell working the sooner I got paid.

"So what are you doing?" Bernie appeared, leaning over my shoulder.

"Nothing that would interest you."

"I want to see."

"No."

She sat on the desk. "Come on. I'm bored."

"By your choice not mine. Go sit down." I pushed her off the desk and pointed behind me to the couch. I lit the candles surrounding my desk. These were critical. Whatever power you were able to glean from the Aether would soon dissipate without the protective circle. This was a textbook example of where magic and technology came together, if there were textbooks for such things.

Having completed the circle, I put in Tim's spell

disk. Tim's my imp. I always call him out when I run spells. You just can't put a price on experience.

Next to me sits a sphere. The ignorant might call it a crystal ball. It isn't. It's a special computer monitor. I use it to draw power from the Aether, to run the spells I write. Without the Aether it'd be just another program disk.

Once I had the spell running I waited for the flash of light that brought Tim into my office.

"Hello," I said when I saw it, without looking up. "Ready to work?"

"Of course," he replied calmly. Tim was about six inches tall with oil slick colored skin. He also had a four inch pointed tail. His ears droop and his nose is nonexistent. He used to smell until I realized I could tell him to stop.

"Wow! You've got a—a—what are those things called?" Bernie stood up from the couch.

"Imp," Tim replied. He turned his attention back to me.

"Sweet!" She came closer.

"New spell's ready, Tim." I motioned to the sphere.

My sister leaned on my chair. "Tim? You named your imp Tim?"

"Drop it, Bernie." I tried to sound threatening.

"But wasn't Tim that guy you liked your senior year in high school?"

"Drop it." I'd regretted using that name. The high school infatuation didn't last long. Imps, on the other hand, do. The upside to naming an imp is that once you do, you have some measure of control over it. The downside of naming an imp is that once you do, you can't change it. Once the authoring protocol has been set, it's nearly impossible for it to be rewritten, not without major magic.

I loaded up the new disk and entered the parameter codes.

"What's that?" Bernie was looking over my shoulder.

"Sit down and stay out of the circle."

"Can't you even tell me what it does?" She came around to the side of my chair.

"I'm testing a new spell." I finished with the parameters and checked the candles again. "Tim, get ready."

Tim jumped to my shoulder and closed his eyes.

"So what's this supposed to do?" Bernie called from the couch.

"Locate a particular djinn."

"Why? Wait—a what?"

"Demon." I didn't elaborate, client confidentiality. One last check of the circle, and I sent the go code. I watched the spell's processes on my monitor while Tim watched the sphere.

"I see the Aether." He whispered. He always whispered when the Aether was opened. To me it looked like code on the monitor; to Tim it looked like home.

"Keep it there, Tim." I didn't need to watch him to know he was making the signs that would help control the opening. Like I said, you can't beat experience. As I watched my screen, I felt a rush of cold air. "We're losing it!"

"Working on it," he whispered.

The cold air became a push. Something was entering the circle. "Bernie! Sit!" Whether she didn't listen or I was too late, I don't know. The telltale flash of the spell happened.

I spun around in my chair and stood up, effectively flinging Tim off my shoulder. "Where the hell is she?"

"Well, by your tone I'd say you are referring to the rhetorical 'Hell.' " Tim got up from the floor, straightening his tail. "When there's a good probability that your sister is in the actual 'Hel.' "

Tim was referring to his place of origin. If the Aether is the universe, then Hel is one of the planets. Cybermancers and Zero Point Energy enthusiasts use the term Aether to describe the source of power. Everyone else unwittingly knows it as the Internet.

"How did that happen?" I growled as I dropped back down into my seat. I began a tracer on the spell. It got lost a few jumps in. I said as much.

"It did if she went over." Tim climbed up on my shoulder. "Your data tracers don't work over there. And I suspect some sort of corruption of the spell disk. How many loci are on the spell?" my imp asked.

"The default to here and the Aether." By their very nature, loci can't be corrupted. They either work or they don't.

"Well, since she's not here—" he looked around the room "—I'd say she's crossed over into Hel." He jumped on the desk. "I suggest a scan. To find out the cause at least."

I started a full system scan and several small files were flagged, files that weren't mine. They were mostly music files.

"What the hell are these?" I held up my hand, effectively stopping Tim from starting the "one *l* or two" argument again. "She downloaded music." The mp3 player on my seat made sense now.

Tim leaned over my shoulder to read the screen.

"Bernie must have gone online and downloaded a bunch of crap last night. Damn it. I knew I should have put in the lock code." I had never needed to lock my computer—as I said, I live alone. As the scan finished up, I saw she had indeed downloaded crap. She'd let in a worm and it had gone straight for the disk-burning program. Tim was right. If my sister downloaded the virus last night, the disk I burned this morning had to be corrupted.

I massaged my temples. "Shit!"

"Well, we can't find her with this thing. We need a clean computer." Easier said than done. Cybermancers aren't a close-knit group; that's the nature of programmers. We tend to be loners until we're forced to be team players.

There was only one person I felt confident would help me. "Pack up the disks. We're going to see Iraina."

"Of course we are. Sri Lanka is lovely this time of year."

Tim's sarcasm was usually wasted on me but August was a nice time. No monsoons. The sphere went into a soft-sided bag. I gathered up the disks I'd need and put them into a smaller pouch along with a new box of Rick's Razzmatazz Tea. It's always nice to bring a gift when asking a favor of a witch. Rick's was Iraina's favorite.

Now one might wonder how a twenty-four-year-old computer professional and her otherworldly imp might get to Sri Lanka from a seaside town in California on absolutely no notice. Well, I get there the way I get most places a cab can't take me: the telephone booth at the south end of Bay Street.

The streetlight over the booth was out. Neither it nor the phone booth had ever worked as far as I knew. Someone, long ago, had placed a handwritten "out of order" sign on the glass booth. I can only assume they also placed a warding spell on the booth since it was obvious that no one ever came to check on it.

With Tim on my shoulder, hidden by my waist-length hair, I stepped into the booth and traced the spell glyph that had been graffitied onto the glass. Some types of magic are easy to use even if you have no idea how they work. Tim and I stepped out onto a dark street in downtown Galle. It was sometime in the early morning hours if I remembered the time change. There was no one on the narrow lane and no streetlights to announce our arrival even if there had been. As I stepped away from the box, I felt the steady cooling sea breeze.

Iraina's apartment was the fifth house down the

street. I jogged the short distance to her place. If anyone could help it was her. And would. Iraina was overly friendly by cybermancer standards. Being a dualist had its advantages. There weren't many witches who also practiced cybermancy.

It isn't hard to find Iraina's apartment. Usually there is a distinctive odor. Classic magic always seems to smell.

"Epiphany! Darling!" Iraina opened the door before I'd knocked. She's the only one who calls me by my given name. Even my parents don't call me Epiphany. What she was doing up at this hour I didn't ask. She always seemed to be awake, no matter what time of day I appeared.

"Iraina." I handed her the box of tea as she stepped aside to let me in. She looked the same as she did when I first met her about ten years ago, fortyish. I had a feeling that she dabbled in life extension, but I never had the nerve to ask her. It's a touchy subject among witches.

"Oh, you've brought Tim!" She reached out to pat his cheek. Tim smiled. "And a box of Rick's. You need help with something, my dear." She waggled a finger at me and smiled. I tried to smile back.

As I walked into what passed for her living room I noticed the smell. It wasn't one of the usual ones.

"What is that?" I said between sniffs.

"Ah, yes!" She slipped the tea into her apron pocket and went over to the large cauldron sitting in the middle of the hardwood floor. It took up the entire middle of the small room. "Divination, dear." She stirred the cauldron.

"What sort of divination?" I asked, peering carefully into the depths of the giant pot.

"Tiromancy, Epiphany, darling." She stirred it again then looked at me, noticing my utter lack of understanding. "Cheese curds."

I just stared at her.

"New client." She smiled.

"Does it actually work?" Tim asked from my shoulder.

"I don't see why not," she answered with a shrug.

Iraina was interesting. Along with cybermancy, she was also what you'd call a classic witch; potions, spells, cauldrons, cupboards filled with all manner of dried and powdered creatures and now, apparently, cheese. Now me, I have trouble with instant rice, and I prefer to do my magic online. I like the logic of the Aether. It also keeps strange dried things out of my cupboards.

"Iraina, I need your help." I wasn't sure she was listening.

"With what?" She reached in with her hand, grabbed a handful of curd and squeezed.

"I've lost Bernie."

"Bernadette? Where, dear?" She let the liquid run through her fingers.

"Into the Aether. I think." I kept my eyes on the curds.

Iraina stopped midsqueeze and looked at me. "What did you say?"

"In the, uh, Aether." I glanced up to meet her gaze briefly.

"How in Astaroth's name did that happen?" She dropped the curd back into the cauldron and wiped her hands on her apron. The demon Astaroth is said to teach the mathematical sciences to his followers. Because of this, cybermancy is usually connected to him.

"Corrupted disk. I have to find her." I took a deep breath and let it out.

"I should say so, dear. She is your sister."

"Yeah, there's that, too." I groaned. In truth, my mother was my more immediate concern.

"You say the spell disk was corrupted?" Iraina wiped her hands on her apron.

"Yes. Bernie let in a worm. It got to the disk burning program."

"Oh, dear. That's like a witch letting her newt tongues go bad. It just isn't done, dear." Iraina's lecturing tone did little for my temper. "I would think you'd have an intrusion detector installed, dear."

"I did. The worm must have spell coding in it."

"Any time a spell is altered incorrectly strange things can happen, dear."

"I know, I know," I growled as I dropped into an overstuffed chair.

"If I may make a suggestion, Epiphany. Retrieving your sister should be done as soon as possible. As you know, viruses spread, corruptions spread. It's like when you add too much salamander lard—things just spin out of control."

"Salamander what?"

"It doesn't matter dear. What does matter is that you go get Bernadette. Now." She walked over to a scarf-covered table. She pulled off the scarves, revealing her computer.

"How do I do that? Can I send Tim?" I fought my way out of the chair.

"No, I'm afraid not. Your authoring protocol becomes null once he returns to Hel. You'd have no control over him. You'll have to go over with him. Your proximity will keep him under the control of the summoning, and his spell disk will be able to bring you all back."

"You want me to go over to the Aether?"

"Hel, actually. There's nothing really in the Aether, dear."

I knew that. Iraina was a stickler for accuracy sometimes. She motioned for me to come sit at the desk.

I did. I unpacked my disks. Iraina had nearly the same setup as I did, though her sphere was a newer model. I made a mental note to upgrade after this was all over.

"When I asked you once, I thought you said I couldn't go over." This I directed at Tim.

"I said you *shouldn't* go over. But since your sister did, the point is moot." He smiled. Somehow I got the feeling he was enjoying this.

"While you reprogram the parameters for three entities, I'll go find you some candles for the circle."

It became obvious I wasn't going to be offered another option. My sister would pay dearly for this. I didn't know how yet. I left that detail for later. I did as Iraina said and reprogrammed Tim's spell disk. The idea was simple enough; you just needed multiple placeholders. A little coding took care of that. The return locus was automatic. The address of the computer of origin was the locus by default for the reintegration point. Nice comforting logic. I knew it wouldn't last.

Iraina returned with a basket of mismatched candles. "Would you like black or white, dear?"

"Black." It fit my mood.

She dumped them onto the floor and Tim began setting them up around the desk.

"Here you go." She pulled a small wreath from her apron pocket and set it on Tim's head. She pulled a slightly larger one out next and placed it on my head.

"And this is?" I felt the wreath.

"Blue spruce, dear. Protection against enemies."

I nodded politely and wondered how much stuff she could fit in those oversized pockets. Returning to the immediate issue, I adjusted my sphere, moving several suspicious wax-topped bottles out of the way. When I glanced back, Iraina was lighting the candles. I completed a system scan on the computer, declaring it clean. I loaded my general spells subprograms disk and waited. Once the download was complete, in went the corrupted spell disk. I ran the primary program to gain access to the Aether.

Iraina set a bottle of orange liquid on the desk. Next to it she set a mortar with pink petals in it.

"See you use that before running the spell," she said as she stepped back.

"What for?" I eyed the bottle and mortar.

"It's Lammas," Iraina said as if she couldn't believe I'd forgotten.

"Great. Another ritual for prosperity." There simply wasn't any logic in classical magic.

"You really should keep better track of these things, Epiphany. You may use that," she pointed at the computer, "but it's still magic, dear. And I would suspect you could use a little prosperity about now."

It's magic all right. If it weren't, then a simple thing like a corrupted disk wouldn't send people to Hel. I removed my PDA from my bag. I would have to contact Iraina via e-mail so she would know when to run Tim's return spell. Since the Aether was the basis for the Internet, there shouldn't be a problem with the e-mails.

I typed in the same parameters for the corrupted disk as when Bernie disappeared. Adding to my list of worries was whether or not the disk had been corrupted further. I needed the same result as last time. Tim sat next to the sphere and concentrated on the Aether. I showed Iraina how to run the spell disk when my e-mail arrived, then had her leave the circle. I mixed the orange liquid in with the petals and almost gagged. Roses and sandalwood oil. The odor was almost overpowering. Classical magic. I shook my head.

I stood next to the sphere with Tim on my shoulder and pushed the go code. "Okay," I said and closed my eyes.

I didn't see the flash if it happened. My eyes stayed

closed until Tim tapped my shoulder. When I looked around, I saw a flat, orange plane. Scattered through it were rocky outcroppings. Orange.

"Not as bad as I thought it'd be," I said quietly. "Except for the color scheme." I absently scratched my head under the wreath of spruce.

"You were summoning a demon from here?" Tim sounded worried.

"Hey, cash client. I didn't ask too many questions."

"You should ask more questions." His grip on my shirt tightened. "This is not a good place."

I was going to ask him what he meant when we heard the scream. With Tim on my shoulder, I followed the sound to the far side of one of the rocky outcroppings. There we saw Bernie, and she wasn't alone. She was scrambling up one of the boulders, trying to keep her feet off the ground. When I looked lower I saw why.

"What is that?" I kept my distance. My concern for my sister was still in the mild stage and didn't outweigh my self-preservation. Not yet.

"Uh, I'm not sure," Tim whispered.

"Why are you whispering?" I whispered back.

"Don't you see it?" He pointed toward the thing but held tight with his other hand. "The Aether."

So that's what it looked like. It was fascinating and repulsive at the same time, like code made flesh. It was hard to look away. The thing started to climb the boulder holding my sister. She screamed again. I didn't think she knew we were there.

"Bernie! Climb!" I shouted.

"No!" Tim yelled.

"What are you doing?" I hissed at him. Before he could answer, Bernie screamed again. She either hadn't heard him or didn't listen because she had turned and started climbing. She only got as far as the next higher boulder. Sitting above her was an exact copy of Tim except for the fact that it was six feet tall, not six inches. I swear it hadn't been there a moment ago.

The djinn.

"Tell her not to move," Tim said. He began making hand gestures, not unlike those he used when helping me, and speaking a language I'd not heard him use before.

"Bernie! Stop, don't move."

The monstrous djinn spit something toward Tim and me. It landed a few feet in front of us. The stench was amazing. Sandalwood didn't seem so bad now. I began to back up. Tim yanked my hair.

"Stop," he hissed in my ear. "Don't move."

The djinn turned its attention back to my sister. Bernie hadn't moved, either from fear or listening to me. A glow began to appear between Tim's hands. When it was as large as a baseball he threw it at the djinn. The creature raised its hands to block the ball of light. It didn't help. With a flash, the monstrous djinn faded away, but not before it let out an ear-piercing shriek.

"That's why you should ask questions." Tim was as irate as I'd ever heard him be.

"Okay, you win. Now what about the other problem?"

"I think it's the worm from your computer. The presence of the Aether is somewhat odd, though. I suppose it's the nature of the worm. That might be why your computer didn't pick it up when your sister was online. It's got magic in it. I think it would be best if it didn't reach your sister."

Bernie hadn't moved. The worm, on the other hand, had. It reached the boulder where she stood and, in one smooth movement, wrapped itself around Bernie's leg. She collapsed before she could scream again. I made a start for the boulder when Tim yanked my hair again.

"Don't."

"What do we do?"

"Uh, well." Tim scratched his hairless head in thought. "Do you have a stick?"

"I'm serious!"

"Just kidding. My spell disk. You have an antivirus programmed in, don't you?"

"Yes!" I'd built an automatic virus scan into Tim's spell. When I had originally written the spell I hadn't known what was capable of coming over the Aether. The scan had never picked anything up before. I'd forgotten it was even there.

I got my PDA out and sent the retrieval e-mail to Iraina. Moments later I received her reply. "Starting spell now." I stepped as close as I dared to my sister and waited. It didn't take long. I saw the flash this time. I had a momentary feeling of floating that I didn't have the first time, then fell onto Iraina's floor. The candles scattered, leaving trails of quickly cooling wax.

"Are you all right, dear?" Iraina helped me up.

"Yeah. Where's Bernie?"

"Right here, dear." She pointed to the floor behind me. Tim had fallen from my shoulder and was in the process of climbing back up.

"Is she okay?" I asked Tim. There was no sign of the worm.

"I suppose." He cocked his head to one side and regarded Bernie lying on the ground. "She looks okay."

"She looks out of it." I waved my hand in front of her face. All she did was blink.

"Did something happen? The spell disk ran the antivirus program just before you returned." Iraina helped me up.

"Bernie found the worm that caused all this mess in the first place." I looked accusingly at my sister.

"Cosmic justice. Not always pretty I'm afraid." I-raina shoved her hands into her apron pockets.

"Understatement. I think I'd better get her home. Our mother is coming over." I froze. "What time is it? I mean at home." I looked at my PDA; it had switched to local time.

"Uh, sometime in the afternoon, dear. Monday," she added.

"Shit! We've got to go. Now."

"Are you sure that's wise?" She came over to look at Bernie.

"Irrelevant. I need her walking."

Iraina took a small silver box out her pocket. She opened it and pinched a bit of the powder that was inside. She put it into Bernie's mouth.

"Oh, my." Iraina touched Bernie's cheek.

"What? What?" I looked closely at my sister then back at Iraina. "What?"

"Oh, probably nothing, Epiphany. Bernadette just looks a little pale." She smiled at me. I was not reassured, but I was running out of time. A few moments later, my sister was functioning enough to walk. I threw my stuff back into my bag. With Tim on one shoulder and Bernie leaning on the other I headed for the door.

"Thanks, Iraina. I'm sorry about just taking off."

"Don't worry dear. I read your curds while you were gone. You'll be back soon." She smiled as she held the door open. "Oh, wait. You'd better take this, dear." She reached into her apron deeper than I would have thought possible and pulled out a leather pouch. It was tied with something's hair. She held it out.

"What's that for?" I reached out slowly for it.

"Just something you might need." She shrugged. "I

mean, after all, it isn't every day you send your sister to the Aether, go to retrieve her, do battle with a demon, fight a worm, and return home now, is it?" She smiled. It wasn't a simple smile. It was an "I know something" smile.

I hate those smiles.

"Uh, okay. Thanks." If I'd had time, I would have asked her more about it. As it was, I was just hopeful I could make it back to my apartment in time. I shoved the pouch into my pocket. It squished. Was there a law against witches using plastic bags?

Once back in Santa Cruz I made record time back to my apartment, considering I was dragging my sister. Once inside the apartment, the first thing I did was to drop Bernie on the couch. The second thing I did was to pack her suitcase. It was amazing how much stuff she'd needed for one lousy night. I made sure to throw her mp3 player in extra hard. I brought the suitcase out from the spare room and saw Bernie trying to stand.

"What happened?" She wobbled as she stood.

"You don't remember?" I heard the microwave beep as I went into the kitchen.

"Not really. I had the weirdest dream though."

"You were in—" Tim started. I glared at him.

"Yeah, okay." I shoved a cup of instant coffee into her hands. "Drink this. I packed your stuff already." I wanted nothing more than to get my sister out of my apartment. I wanted to clean up my computer. I wanted things the way they were. As I stood watching her, the doorbell rang.

Salvation! Our mother was here.

"Get your stuff." I went to the door and glanced back to make sure Bernie had heard me. I froze. The thing now leaning over the suitcase was shaped like my sister all right, but it had the appearance of the worm. My sister was code made flesh. My sister had been corrupted.

"Crap." I grabbed a blanket off the couch and threw it over Bernie. Grabbing the corners of the blanket I pulled her into the spare room and shut the door. "Stay in here." I didn't know if she could hear me or even understand me. I whirled around, looking for Tim. "We've got a problem." I found him sitting next to the sphere.

"I'd say so, yes." He looked up thoughtfully from the computer desk.

"Less analysis. More help," I snarled. The doorbell rang again. "Shit."

"I think your mother is here."

"That's not the kind of help I meant."

"Just can't seem to please you, can I? Well, then. Check your pocket." He pointed to the small bulge in my jeans. I reached in to find the pouch Iraina had given me. I pulled it out. Not only was it still squishy but it also stank now.

"It smells like mosquito repellent." I held the bag away from me.

"Citronella. Cleansing and warding." He sniffed the air. "And cedar wood. Healing. Also for unhexing, I believe."

"Unhexing? Unhexing what?" I stared at him.

He looked towards the spare room. "Iraina made up a medicine bag." He pointed at the pouch. "Just in case, I guess."

"And what do I do with it?"

"No idea." Tim smiled. "Not a clue."

"You're just a fount of useless information aren't you?" I didn't expect an answer, and I didn't get one. Tim simply faded out of view. Probably pouting. I grabbed my PDA and sent an e-mail off to Iraina. I marked it urgent. The doorbell rang a third time. If I didn't find out what to do with the stupid pouch soon, my mother was going remember she had the key to the apartment. I couldn't remember why I'd thought giving her the key was a good idea.

My PDA pinged at me. Iraina had replied. "It's an infusion of oils. Rub it on her, dear, of course." Of course. I didn't know if it would work. I only knew that Iraina had a keen sense for the unusual, and I'd have to trust that. I really couldn't do better than a technologically savvy witch.

As I ran back to the spare room, I yelled towards the front door. "Be there in a minute, Mom!"

I opened the door to the spare room slowly. Bernie was standing where I'd left her. The blanket was still thrown over her. I pulled the blanket off. The sight of her made me shiver. I opened the pouch and pulled out a wad of cloth. It was saturated with the oils. Keeping my hand well covered with the cloth, I began to rub my sister's face and head. I worked my way down her arms, across her chest and down her back. I heard the front door open. I kicked the room door shut and stood back and waited. The room stank of the aromatic oils. My sister no doubt stank as well.

To my relief and surprise, the coding began to fade. My sister's face was returning. She looked at me in utter confusion. As I let out the breath I'd been holding, the door to the room opened.

I turned around and smiled.

"Hi, Mom."

I shoved Bernie and her bag into my mother's arms. Then I shoved both of them through the front door, ignoring every word.

First chance I had, I planned to look up a locksmith.

With the apartment finally quiet, I felt the pull. The Aether was calling to me. Putting on my headphones, I answered its call.

Narrator: *Peace and quiet descends around Epiphany Jones once more. There's nothing quite like a family visit to make you appreciate your privacy, especially when a misspell is involved.*

JANET ELIZABETH CHASE is originally from Northern California and has her BA from the University of California at San Diego. Her past professions include working in live news, owning her own video post-production company, and the occasional stint as a corner sound person for boxing in Las Vegas. She is currently a full-time mom with a part-time writing habit. Her favorite color is green, her favorite number is seven, and her favorite food is sauerbraten with kartoffelpuffers. Janet spends her spare time playing air violin to the music of the Trans-Siberian Orchestra. She lives with her husband, two children, and an assortment of interesting pets in Pleasant Valley, Nevada.

Eye of Newt

Marc Mackay

Narrator: *The Griffith School of Magic. A hallowed place of tradition and learning. A place where students learn from renowned teachers and those teachers encourage an atmosphere of true scholarship. Which is all very well and good until there's to be a dance.*

"Eye of newt?"

Nina Whiting looked over at Mildred, who had the large grimoire open in front of her.

"Tell me you did not just say 'eye of newt,' " she said.

Mildred Gilly bit her upper lip and looked around the empty classroom as if afraid someone in the hall might have heard. Nina knew her friend didn't like this sneaking around stuff.

Mildred flipped through the pages of the book.

"That's what's written," she replied. "It's the first ingredient in the list. As a matter of fact, all the potions in here have eye of newt as one of the components."

Nina sighed. "That's typical."

"Of what?" asked Mildred.

"Mistress Truax," replied Nina. "She's very old school. I mean she still wears a pointed hat for crying out loud."

When Nina had entered the Griffith School of Magic, she and her fellow students couldn't help but notice Mistress Truax. She'd stood there with the other teachers and the headmaster, wearing a flowing black gown and a large coned hat with stars adorning it.

At first Nina had thought that Mistress Truax was playing a prank on the new students. She was later told that it was no joke. Sibley Garrath had revealed how the Mistress believed a true witch should embrace the old. Worse, she wanted Headmaster Griffith to impose a dress code. Lucky for them, he believed students should be allowed to express themselves.

"What does her being old fashioned have to do with eye of newt as an ingredient?" asked Mildred.

"Come on, Mildred, think," said Nina, exasperated. She watched her try to reason it out.

Nina and Mildred had been friends all their lives. Together they'd found out that they had the power to handle magic.

When they'd heard the news that they were both accepted into the Griffith School of Magic, the most prestigious of all the schools, they'd been delighted.

But Nina sometimes thought Mildred was a little slow on the uptake.

Like right now.

"I still don't see what you're getting at," Mildred finally said, shaking her head in frustration.

Nina sighed.

"What's the first thing that usually comes to someone's mind when they think about witches brewing potions?" she asked her friend.

"Eye of newt?" ventured Mildred.

"Exactly," said Nina. "Every time, it's 'eye of newt'

this and 'eye of newt' that." She rolled her eyes. "You must've gotten at least one newt comment when you told your friends and family you were a witch?"

Mildred nodded.

"A couple," she said. "But I still don't see what Mistress Truax being old fashioned has to do with this."

"Because she buys into all this stuff," answered Nina. "You don't have to wear the pointed hat and dark clothes to be a witch, do you?"

"No," said Mildred.

"So, she probably has eye of newt in all her potions because it's what you're supposed to use if you want to be a proper witch," said Nina. "And anyway, you know very well that Mistress Truax keeps the eye of newt jar, along with a few of the rarer components, in her quarters, and I'm not going to try and get them. We'll just have to do without."

"Maybe we shouldn't do this now," Mildred protested.

"Don't you want to show up that snotty Cwen Dana?"

Mildred nodded.

"She keeps going on about the beautiful jewelry her dad has sent her for the dance. And we really can't afford anything good for ourselves. This is a good idea," Nina said confidently.

"But all this spell does is coat anything with gold," argued Mildred. "And not even real gold at that. It doesn't make our jewelry worth any more than it already is."

"But Cwen won't know that," said Nina, with a mischievous smile. "If we do this right, ours will look better then the ones she'll be wearing. That'll stick in her craw for a while. I can't wait to see her face."

"But we aren't allowed to make any potions," in-

sisted Mildred. "We're still just learning the different
ingredients and what they do. If Mistress Truax finds
out we did this, we'll be in detention for the rest of
the year."

Nina smiled. "Think about what Caman will think
when he sees you at the dance all prettied up with
our jewelry adorning your neck and ears."

A determined look entered Mildred's eyes.

"Okay," she said. "Let's do this."

"All right then, what do we need?" asked Nina.

Mildred read the ingredients and instructions while
Nina did the work. Soon they had a small cauldron
boiling on the Bunsen burner. They'd done everything
for the spell. Now it was time to try it out.

Nina reached into her pocket and pulled out the
earrings her family had given her when she'd left for
school. They were nice, but anyone could see that they
weren't the best quality, just the best they could afford. Cwen always made Nina feel like they were
nothing but tin. Now she was going to feel the way
Nina had.

She held out her hand.

Mildred slowly pulled out a small necklace and a
pair of earrings from her pocket. They looked even
worse than Nina's.

Mildred stood there staring at the jewelry in her
hands.

"What's wrong?" asked Nina.

"I'm still not sure."

"Trust me," said Nina. "We're going to be a hit."

Reluctantly, Mildred placed the jewelry into Nina's
open palm.

"Thank you," said Nina.

Mildred started to fidget. She bit her lip and nervously flipped through the book as Nina held her earrings over the small cauldron.

All she needed to do now was drop them into the liquid, and they would come out looking like the best gold jewelry money could buy.

She let go, watching with anticipation as they fell toward the cauldron.

Mildred suddenly shrieked, "No! Don't—"

The earrings hit the liquid.

There was a tremendous flash of bright light. Nina shut her eyes, but the glow penetrated her lids. She felt hot wind flow over her, as if she'd been scalded by hot water. A rushing sound, so loud Nina was sure she would become deaf, filled her ears. Just as Nina felt she couldn't take anymore, everything stopped, and the room was quiet again.

She opened her eyes and tried to move.

She couldn't.

For a brief moment panic took over, but Nina fought it, controlling her breathing and telling herself to calm down.

When she was calmer, Nina looked around and couldn't believe her eyes.

Everything in the classroom—every piece of equipment, the chairs, the tables—was now gold. As she lowered her eyes she could see that her hand, still poised over the cauldron, was also coated with the metal.

She looked for Mildred. As she'd feared, her friend now stood covered from head to toe in gold. Her mouth was open in midsentence, and her hand was stretched out toward Nina in an aborted attempt to stop her. Frantically searching her friend's face for signs of life, Nina suddenly saw Mildred's eyes move.

Thank the gods, she thought to herself. *But what went wrong?*

She looked down at the cauldron, now empty of any liquid. The earrings were sitting at the bottom completely unchanged.

Regaining her composure, Nina heard noises coming from outside of the classroom. Normally the halls were fairly quiet during the day, what with Headmaster Griffith being a stickler for proper behavior. But now Nina could hear screaming coming from the halls. Students were all talking at once, and some of the teachers could be heard trying to calm them down. Feet could be heard running everywhere.

She strained to make out what was being said.

"What happened to Cwen?" cried a voice near the classroom door.

Nina recognized the voice as Cwen's friend Mae. Wherever Mae was, Cwen was not far behind. The two were nearly inseparable.

How far has this spell gone? Nina wondered.

"She was just standing here," continued Mae. "Suddenly there was this light and now she's like this. What's happening? Why—"

Another voice cut her off.

"Miss Mae Ogden! Please be quiet! I'm trying to get this door open. I don't want to hear another word out of you."

That was Mistress Truax's voice. Nina felt herself panicking and saw that Mildred was as well.

"But—" began Mae.

"Not one more," threatened Truax.

Nina could've sworn she heard Mae swallow. She heard the rattling of the doorknob and the creaking of the door as Mistress Truax continued to try to open it.

A loud cracking sound came from beyond Nina's vision.

"Finally!" exclaimed Mistress Truax. The potions teacher walked past Nina, looking around the room.

"Oh my, what an awful mess," she said, seemingly not talking to anyone in particular.

Her long black hair, normally tied in one long braid, was free and flowing down her back. She must have been off duty before being called out here by Cwen or Mae, thought Nina. Everyone knew that Mistress Truax hated being disturbed. Her punishments were always more severe when she had been bothered during her time off. The deep blue eyes now staring into Nina's brown ones told her she was right to worry.

Mae's voice came from the doorway. "Nina!" she said, almost spitting the name. "I should've known you were behind this."

Mistress Truax held up her hand.

"That'll be enough, young lady," she said to the girl. "Go and stay with Miss Dana."

"You're in for it now," said Mae, from her voice almost laughing, before she left.

Mistress Truax stood between the two girls. Nina could see that part of her dress was covered in gold. The teacher followed Nina's glance down to the patch.

"Ah, yes," said Truax. "When your little spell went off, I was just out of its reach, but part of my clothing wasn't. Unfortunately, the same can't be said for poor Miss Dana, who was eavesdropping outside the door."

She walked up to Nina and looked into the girl's eyes.

"She'd sent Miss Ogden to fetch me, saying someone was in here after hours. I arrived in time to see the fireworks. Now exactly what were you working on in here when you shouldn't have been?"

She looked down at the empty cauldron and reached in to pick up the earnings. Holding them in her open palm, she examined them for a bit and then closed her eyes reciting something under her breath. Then she stopped and opened her eyes.

"Oh, I see," Mistress Truax said. "You were trying to liven up your rather unimpressive jewelry collection. I assumed as much when I saw Miss Dana's condition, but it's always safer to confirm a spell before trying to reverse it."

"Darlene?" said a soft voice from the doorway. "What's going on in here?"

Mistress Sigismund stepped into Nina's view. She was the headmaster's secretary. She was also Mistress Truax's best, if not only, friend. Together they lived in a suite of rooms on the school grounds. Nina couldn't believe that anyone could be friends with Truax, but the two women could nearly always be found together.

Mistress Sigismund's eyes darted around the room, while she nervously ran her hand through her forever unruly mop of red hair. The students always said that she looked as if she had just been shocked with a thousand volts.

"Kendra?" said Mistress Truax. "Observe Miss Whiting and Miss Gilly being their mischievous selves again."

"Oh, Darlene," said Mistress Sigismund. "Don't be mean. They're just young girls. Are they all right?"

"They're all fine for now, but I must start a reversal spell."

"Are they in immediate danger?" Mistress Sigismund looked worried.

"No," said Mistress Truax. "But if it isn't reversed soon, the change will be permanent and they will die from thirst and starvation."

"What?" Nina felt the same way.

"Only their outsides are covered by the gold," explained Truax. "They still need food and water but can't take in nourishment."

"Then you must do something," Mistress Sigismund pleaded. "Quickly!"

"I will." Nina watched as Truax went to Mildred and looked over her shoulder at the grimoire. "When I feel they have learned their lesson."

Mistress Sigismund looked even more worried.

Mistress Truax let out a small laugh.

"What is it?" asked her friend.

"It seems Miss Gilly came across a little footnote in the book and she tried to stop Miss Whiting, which would explain her expression. Unfortunately, it was too late." Nina saw Mildred roll her eyes.

"What footnote?"

Mistress Truax took on the tone she used when teaching.

"Although the reasons for it are still unknown, eye of newt has the distinct property of being able to contain the spell to only a specific area, depending on the amount used. Without it, spells will go wild and can cause damage and havoc."

Mistress Truax turned to Nina.

"With the size of your potion, you could have coated everyone in the entire school as well as several acres of the forest outside. Who knows how long it would have been before anyone noticed and sent help. By then, some—or maybe all—of us would be dead."

"Why didn't it?" puzzled Mistress Sigismund.

"I keep a containment field around the classroom for incidents such as this," answered Mistress Truax. "The spell bubbled out around the door and poor Miss Dana was caught inside it. Fortunately the overall field held, or it would have been worse."

She lifted her robe to show her friend the gold patch.

Mistress Sigismund gasped. "Are you all right?"

"I'm fine, only whatever was in my pocket was . . ." Her eyes widened in realization, and she reached into the gold-covered pocket, pulling out what looked like a gold-plated flower.

"Oh, bother," she said.

"What's that?" asked Mistress Sigismund.

Mistress Truax sighed. "It was a rose. I was going to give it to you tonight at supper."

"It's not my birthday." Mistress Sigismund looked a little confused.

"I know," said her friend softly.

A big smile crossed Mistress Sigismund's face, and Nina thought she was going to jump up and down for joy. She also thought it was about time Truax focused on fixing her and Mildred's predicament instead of roses.

"May I have it?" Mistress Sigismund asked.

"Now?" said Mistress Truax in surprise. "But I have to fix it."

Mistress Sigismund shook her head. "I think it's pretty like that and besides it'll last longer than a real one. And it'll always remind us of this day. That makes it even more special."

Mistress Truax smiled the first genuine smile Nina had ever seen from her, but she hurriedly hid it away.

She held out the rose to Mistress Sigismund, who snatched it quickly from her hands as if afraid that her friend would suddenly change her mind. She clutched it to her chest.

"Thank you, Darlene," she said.

"You are welcome."

I swear, it's like they're the only two in the room, thought Nina, a little annoyed. *Can we please get on with getting us back to normal?*

Suddenly a booming voice echoed down the hall.

"What's going on here?" bellowed Headmaster Griffith. "Why's everyone just milling about? And why's there a golden statue of Miss Dana in the middle of the hall? I know she's rather fond of herself, but this is just not okay. I can't have my students making effigies of themselves."

"You go and take care of the headmaster," said Mistress Truax, shooing her friend away. "Explain what's happened while I start the reversal spell. It'll take some time, so I may be late for supper."

"I'll keep it warm," said Mistress Sigismund as she quickly left the room.

"Mistress Sigismund," said Griffith. "What's going on?"

"A moment, Headmaster," she said.

Mistress Truax turned to the two students. "While I work on fixing this mistake of yours, why don't the two of you start working on a one-thousand-word essay about the importance of eye of newt in spells."

Nina groaned inwardly.

"And you can read them to the entire class when you're done," she finished with a little smile. "That seems a sufficient start to your punishment. I'll decide what else you have to do to make up for this blunder later."

She turned and removed her pointed hat. From it she produced a small cauldron as well as other jars and equipment. She set up the equipment on the nearest table.

Mistress Truax opened one of the jars.

Extracting an eye of newt, she held it out for the girls to see.

With a grin, she dropped it into the cauldron.

Narrator: *It's said, "All that is gold does not glitter." In the case of the golden students of Griffith School of Magic, it could be said, "All that is gold should have read the entire spell first." Still, the girls have learned a valuable lesson. Or will.*

MARC MACKAY is forty-two years old and has been writing seriously for the last four, thanks to friends who encouraged this habit. "Eye of Newt" is his first sale, which is one of the best moments in his life. Marc is a technical writer for a company that makes graphics cards for computers, creating user manuals shipped with product. Previously, he was a software tester for the same company. He's had several odd jobs, including seven years as a cook with the Hard Rock Café in Montreal as well as working in a garage. When not at his regular job, he plays keyboards in a punk rock band. Unlike many other writers, Marc does not own any cats and is not currently working on any novels, only short stories. But that could change.

Chafing the Bogey Man

Kristen Britain

Narrator: *Meet Bob MacDuff. Has-been golf pro. Has-been husband. The image of failure on the road to despair. He'd do anything to turn his career around. Even read a little family history. But reading can be such a dangerous thing . . .*

Bob MacDuff rested his head on the cool surface of his desk. The house was dark and silent; much too dark and silent since Susan and the kids had left him. Well, that is the kids he had hoped to have—a boy and girl—the perfect family portrait. That seemed unlikely now.

Trophies, looking tarnished in the shadows of his den, and framed covers of sports magazines hanging on the wall illustrated the successes of his life, from a state championship for his high school golf team to wins on the amateur circuit and the rising star of his professional golf career.

Trophies, purses won, a beautiful wife, sponsors galore, this big house . . . Where had it all gone wrong?

Bob gazed at the framed photo on his desk; he was eight years old, holding his first golf club, his father kneeling beside him.

"Lost another one, Dad," he told the picture. "Didn't even make the cut to the second round."

Lately his sponsors were dropping like flies, leaving only one—a small chain of hardware stores on the verge of bankruptcy. Instead of wearing a fashionable logo like the Big Names, Bob was stuck with a shirt emblazoned with a wrench and the name "Lucky's Nuts & Bolts," the irony not lost on him or on the sports columnists who got lots of laughs at his expense. "Lucky?" they said. "More like unlucky!"

Now his wife had left, he'd received a notice from the IRS that he was going to be audited, and, worst of all, his agent wasn't answering his calls.

"I don't know what's happened to my game," he told the picture of his dad. Inside, however, he knew the late nights, the jet-setting lifestyle, the dark side of fame had distracted him from what mattered, precipitating his decline. His ancestors must be twisting in their graves.

Bob came from a long line of golfers; his forebears had helped develop the game in Scotland. A portrait of a kilted ancestor bearing a golf club in one hand and a claymore in the other actually hung in the historical museum in Troon. When his family emigrated to America, they brought their love of golf with them.

They also brought their love of single malt scotch. Bob opened a drawer and withdrew a bottle and glass. He poured the amber liquid, thinking his love of the scotch far exceeded his love of golf these days.

Some hours later, Bob still sat slumped in his chair with only his desk lamp aglow. The bottle of scotch was more empty than full. As empty as Bob felt with his career tanking and everything that mattered in shambles.

"What am I going to do; Dad?" he asked, his voice dull.

His father didn't answer, but Bob knew what he'd say anyway: *Keep trying, son.*

Bob shook his head. "I don't think I can." A swan dive off those sea cliffs at Pebble Beach held a certain appeal.

A poetic end, he thought.

In the darkness, a glow coalesced on one of the bookshelves. In his muddled state, Bob believed he was seeing things, but the luminescence brightened until he had to shield his eyes. Then it dimmed until it illuminated a single volume.

Bob rose and crossed the room to the bookshelf. When he touched the book, the luminescence faded altogether. He pulled it off the shelf and returned to his desk, setting it in the lamplight. He knew what it was immediately—an old family text passed down through the generations. Bob's father had given it to him before he passed away.

"Keep it safe," his father said. "It is dangerous in the wrong hands. Use it only if you are certain of what you're doing."

It was written by his many-greats grandmother, Granny Dunn, a couple of centuries ago in Scotland. Bob's father never explained how the book was dangerous, and all he could tell from the handwriting scrawled across yellowed pages was that it contained recipes and advice on ailments from "kramps" to "gowt." For all these years, it had been no more than a forgotten family heirloom shelved among glossy volumes about golf. Most of those books remained unread, but they looked impressive to visitors.

Now Bob opened the book and traced the faded ink with his index finger. The language and handwriting were so old-fashioned, and the spelling so atrocious, he hadn't the patience to puzzle it all out. He supposed if his finances continued to plunge, he could sell the book at auction online.

But his father said it was dangerous.

One recipe for flux called for the innards of spotted salamanders, various plants, and powders, and Bob could see how it was dangerous—the mere notion of swallowing salamander guts soured his stomach.

He was about to close the book when the pages flipped open of their own accord to the topic "Chasing the Bogey Man." Only S's looked like F's, and F's looked like S's, so he initially read it as "Chafing the Bogey Man." Beneath the title was the subheading "The Effenfe of Gows," which was really, "The Essense of Gowf." Gowf, he knew, was the old Scottish word for golf.

"Huh," Bob said, taking a keener interest. He knew also that in the old days, bogey meant par—a good score on a given hole. Somehow in modern times the terms were reversed. Par now meant bogey, and bogey now meant one stroke over par.

Granny Dunn wrote: "Chafe the kreature os fhadowf . . ." He had to start over and concentrate, which the scotch made difficult. "Chase the kreature of shadows at your own peril. Find success in skill and practice."

Well, that was pretty good, if uninspired, advice from the old girl.

"But if these fail," she continued, "here lies the secret for catching the bogey."

This was followed by a list of ingredients and instructions and a warning: "He who fails to follow my words exactly must face what he has wrought with courage, for the consequences shall be deadly."

There was a line or two at the bottom of the page, written in a tiny, cramped hand. With a magnifying glass he determined it was in a different language. Gaelic? He shrugged and set the magnifying glass aside and looked the spell over again.

The ingredients looked perfectly reasonable. Sand

from a bunker, grass plucked from the fairway, a lock
of his hair, and a few other common additions, including a finger of scotch, all mixed together on a full
moon.

Well, Bob decided, *I have nothing to lose.*

Over the following days, Bob decided to try Granny
Dunn's concoction during practice rounds on his home
course, which was, quite literally, outside his door. He
played early mornings, starting while it was still hazy
out and the dew thick on the fairways—before even
the greenskeepers were up and grooming the course.
He didn't want witnesses.

He followed Granny's instructions to a tee, and he
laughed at the pun, sprinkling the barest pinch of her
recipe on his golf ball. Then with a quick glance to
make sure no one was in earshot, he recited the bogey
man chant: *"Bogey man, bogey man, hide if you will.
The creature of shadows I will catch with skill!"*

He chose his three wood, warmed up with a few
practice swings, then dug in for his first shot. The drive
was pretty good, as far as he could tell in the haze.
Straight down the middle of the fairway and in a
decent position for shooting for the green. He sliced
the second shot. The slice had been a great source of
misfortune for Bob, but a curse stilled on his tongue.
It wasn't too bad this time, and the ball bounced up
to the fringe of the green.

He two putted. That made par. Or bogey, as in the
old lingo.

Not bad, he thought, more than a little pleased.

He retrieved his ball and replaced the flag, and
something moved near the trees of the next tee. A
shift of shadows, or maybe the early morning haze
lifting from the ground, or the flutter of raven wings.
He couldn't say. He shrugged and continued the
round. Once he lost his ball in the rough—couldn't
find it in the near-dark—and as he poked his club

through the thick grass, he heard soft laughter, but when he looked up, no one was there. No one he could see, anyway.

Word about Bob's morning practices got out. Maybe it was a greenskeeper who leaked it, or an early-bird duffer. It could have been anyone since it was usually full daylight out by the time he hit the sixth hole, and life was astir around the course. In any case, the press was interested in him again, though his agent still wasn't calling, but that was okay. He had a tournament coming up, and then he'd show Ira he was worthy of attention.

His accountant continued to leave him messages about the audit, and he found a voice mail on his cell from an attorney. Susan wanted a divorce. Bob didn't throw the phone in anger or reach for the scotch. He'd show them he could be a winner again, and then all would be well. Thanks to Granny Dunn and her spell. Susan would come back to him. He knew it.

The tournament was held at the old Brambles course near Atlanta. It was, in comparison to other pro venues, a smallish event picked up by one of the lesser known cable sports channels that would only air highlights. Bob didn't complain. Invitations to others had dried up, and he failed to qualify for the championship tour. He considered Brambles his chance to redeem himself, to start over.

And so he did, wearing his "Lucky's Nuts & Bolts" shirt and cap, and with Manuel, his caddie, standing at his side. Bob knew Manuel was receiving offers from other, more notable pros, to do their caddying, but so far he'd not accepted any. Manuel remained steadfast even in the darkest hour. Bob couldn't imagine why, but he was grateful.

He was paired with another B-list pro, Archie Calvin, whose career had also once held promise, but he could no longer maintain the scores to play with the big guns. Maybe someday Bob would discuss it with Arch over some scotch, but right now he had a game to win.

He stepped up to the tee, butterflies fluttering in his stomach. This was no practice round. He wasn't playing in the dark. There was a gallery and everything. He teed up, his hand quavering, and feeling just a little too conspicuous, he reached into his pocket for a pinch of Granny's recipe, and sprinkled it, with some pocket lint, on his golf ball. His cheeks warmed when he saw everyone watching him.

"Salt for luck," he told onlookers. Then, just under his breath, he spoke the bogey man chant. Perhaps people would think he was praying. He knew they thought he needed all the help he could get, divine or otherwise.

The tournament was a dream. Bob remained in the top five on the leader board all three days with no major mishaps, finally sailing in just behind the winner for a solid second place at nine under par. The media interest in Bob spiked, and as he traveled from one tournament to another, he continued to turn in impressive scores.

"I'm doing better, Dad," he told the picture in his den. Inwardly, he wondered if he was winning fairly, or if using Granny Dunn's spell constituted cheating. It wasn't like he was taking steroids, and besides, who could prove that a magic spell was helping him win? Who on earth would believe it? Magic didn't exist, right?

He quickly forgot any pangs of guilt because invitations to more prestigious tournaments started to roll in. With his winnings he resolved his IRS problems and saved his house from foreclosure. Sponsors sought him out once again, though he held onto the "Lucky's" cap—the hardware chain was suddenly in the black, and Bob felt he could hardly give them up now. Even Ira returned his calls. Not only was he invited to bigger events, but his former jet-setting life was blossoming again in the form of parties where almost any sinful temptation was available for the asking.

As his life took on its former luster, only one thing made it bittersweet: Susan still wanted a divorce.

But never mind that, for he received an invitation to a big tournament with a multimillion dollar purse attached and that would be aired on a major network. No B-list group of competitors would be playing, only Big Names. Bob was thrilled.

"If I do well at the Hardesty," he told Manuel, "we'll be on the championship tour for certain."

The Hardesty Invitational took place in Nevada, on a challenging course that, from the point of view of the GetLife blimp overhead, was an oasis of green surrounded by desert brown. The rough really was "rough"—sand, rocks, and cacti. The first morning of the tournament dawned golden bright, with scrub jays *shreeep*ing over the chatter of the gallery.

Bob never felt more ready to win. Winning this tournament would seal his comeback, and Susan couldn't help but return to him. Second place wouldn't be good enough. Not nearly.

"We're going to win this one," he told Manuel.

Manuel nodded as if Bob were some great sage.

As always, Bob began his tournament with a pinch of Granny Dunn's recipe and the chant. The press had picked up on it and declared it an eccentricity like that of ball players who didn't dare change their socks all season for fear of causing bad luck.

Bob's first drive was incredible and elicited loud applause and shouts from the gallery and a stream of chatter from the commentator next to the tee. Bob waved to his admirers.

The following days found Bob neck and neck on

the leader board with Big Name Tony Lamond. They were tied at eleven under, and on the last hole, which Bob birdied, this meant a sudden death playoff. It began immediately. It was televised, after all. He smiled. It would delay the evening news on the east coast.

Tony's first drive was long and straight down the center of the fairway, very picturesque. Bob was impressed, and he felt the first pangs of doubt. When it was his turn to tee off, he hesitated. He'd never used more than one dose of Granny's spell per round, but winning this tournament was really important to him. He didn't want to take any chances, so he reached into his pocket, sprinkled the ingredients on his ball, and spoke the chant.

Something felt different. Wrong. Bob attributed it to nerves from being in this position for the first time in a long while, with the stakes so high. He took a practice swing, and when he looked up, he found, to his consternation, a dense fog billowing over the heads of the gallery and across the course. The media booth up on its scaffolding vanished.

"Fog?" he heard Manuel say in disbelief. "In the desert?"

Bob smelled brine on the air, as if he had been transported to seaside links in Scotland. Very peculiar. Unnerving laughter drifted from the fog.

Bob wiped his forehead with the back of his hand, feeling clammy.

"You going to shoot?" Tony demanded.

The gallery chattered in dismay as the fog obscured the fairway. Officials tried to command silence by waving about "Quiet, please!" signs, an effort that proved futile due to the low visibility. A gull sliced through the air, its mew replacing the raucous calls of the scrub jays.

"It's the darnedest thing, Jim," a commentator said

into his mike, using his best golf voice. "Let's see what MacDuff does with this new complication."

Bob licked his lips. This was definitely wrong. Just as it occurred to him to speak to the officials about postponing play, a little, little man with a long beard and red, pointed cap bounded up onto the tee. Bob almost dropped his club.

"Whaaa?"

"You've got to play," the little man told him. "It's sudden death."

"Jim, it looks like a garden gnome," the commentator said.

"Play?" Bob asked.

"If you don't continue, well, the consequences . . ."

"Consequences? What consequences?"

"Why, sudden death!"

An official strode up to the green with determined strides. "This is not acceptable," he said.

"It appears the official is conferring with MacDuff and the garden gnome, Jim," the commentator said.

The gnome whirled and pointed at the commentator. "I am not a *garden* gnome. My name is Robertson and I'm a *golf* gnome."

"I don't care what kind of gnome you are," the official told him. "You are interfering—"

Robertson waved his hand at the official. The man vanished, his empty clothing—smart yellow blazer, plaid slacks, golf hat, and all—collapsing to the ground. Within moments, a toad hopped out from beneath the hat.

"Interference!" it croaked.

"It appears the garden gnome is really a golf gnome with some powerful mojo, Jim," the commentator said. "Jim? Jim, are you there? All I'm getting is crackling," he told his videographer, tapping his earpiece. The videographer shrugged and said something

about his camera. A swell began to build among onlookers who realized their myriad electronic devices
were malfunctioning.

"What? No text messaging?" a woman cried out
in horror.

"Kiss me," the toad said, hopping in her direction.
She screamed and ran off, vanishing into the fog.

Bob watched it all in disbelief. "What have you
done?" he asked Robertson.

"It's not what I've done," the gnome replied. "It's
what you've done. Did you not read the fine print?"

"F-fine print? What fine print?"

"Why, the fine print under Granny Dunn's spell.
You were to follow her instructions exactly."

"But I did! The full moon and everything!"

"No, you didn't."

Magically the book appeared floating in the air before Bob's face, opened to "The Essense of Gowf."
The handwriting, misspellings, everything looked the
same. On the very bottom was the tiny scrawl in
Gaelic.

"Do you mean the Gaelic?" Bob asked, trepidation
knotting his stomach.

"I do," Robertson replied.

"But I can't read Gaelic."

"Should've thought of that before you started using
the spell, eh?"

"What—what does it say?"

"It says," Robertson began, drawing himself up, as
much as a gnome can, "never to invoke the spell in a
sudden death playoff. Doing so makes it all the more
deadly. If you do not catch the bogey on this hole,
the life of someone you hold dear will be forfeit.
Heck, you might not even survive playing the hole
yourself."

"I don't believe this," Bob said.

"What's not to believe?" Robertson asked.

Just then, a hulking fellow in an executioner's mask appeared with his arms wrapped around a struggling Susan. She was perfectly coiffed and stylishly dressed, wearing the best designer labels. "Bob!" she screamed.

"Susan?" Bob said, striding forward, but Robertson held his hand up to forestall him.

"She'll be at the putting green waiting for you. If you succeed."

"But I can't even see the fairway," Bob said.

The gnome shrugged. "Not my problem."

"Go ahead, take a shot," Tony Lamond said, with a smirk on his face.

Manuel shrugged unhelpfully.

Bob closed his eyes and took a deep breath, trying to recall every detail of this particular hole, its yardage, bends, bunkers, moundings, everything.

He loosened his wrists, adjusted his grip, and swung. The ball cracked off the tee and sailed into the fog, only to hit something with a *ponk!*

"AFT!" the gnome cried, and everyone just stared at him until the ball rebounded out of the fog and conked Tony Lamond on the head. He crumpled to the ground, out cold.

"Aft?" Bob demanded. "The word is *fore.*"

"Fore is for those ahead," the gnome replied. "The ball threatened those behind it, hence aft."

Bob watched as medics tended Tony. He suddenly realized what it meant. "Hey, Tony can't play! He's disqualified—I win!"

"Not so fast," the gnome said. "That one was irrelevant to begin with. The challenge of sudden death remains. You must catch the bogey."

Bob dented the green with his club head. "*Damn.* Then what the hell did my ball hit?"

"The clubhouse."

"The clubhouse? But that's—"

"You must remember that things are not as they were," the gnome cautioned.

The fog parted from the fairway to reveal a castle sprawling across it; a huge medieval fortress with turrets and crenellations and hoardings and arrow loops, and a stone curtain wall surrounding it.

"The clubhouse!" the gnome announced with a flourish.

"Good God," Manuel muttered. He pulled out a pack of cigarettes and a lighter from a pocket. Smoking wouldn't be tolerated during an ordinary tournament, but this was no ordinary tournament. Bob was tempted to dig out his flask of scotch from his golf bag but thought better of it.

"How am I supposed to hit over that thing?" he demanded.

"Weeell," the gnome replied, "you could take a mulligan."

"That's not legal!"

"In this game it is, and in this game it means you can take an opponent's ball if it's better. Usually it requires hand-to-hand combat, but Mr. Lamond does not appear ready for a fight. Therefore, by default, you get your mulligan if you want it."

Bob glanced at Tony being lifted away on a litter, and looked back at the castle. "I'll take the mulligan," he said.

"Very well. The ball lies on the other side of the hazard, but be mindful of your approach. The walls of the clubhouse are well guarded. Should you survive and catch the bogey, we can return to the clubhouse in fellowship and toast your success with mead."

"Great," Bob muttered. He signaled to Manuel to come along and stepped off the tee.

"MacDuff is taking the mulligan," the commentator said into his dead mike. "He's following the strange new rules of the golf gnome and is heading straight for the castle."

Bob strode along the fairway wondering just how he ever found himself in such a bizarre situation. "Thanks, Granny Dunn. Thanks *a lot.*"

The castle loomed ever larger as Bob approached, though its true extent was hidden in the fog, so he just forged ahead as a famous pro golfer ought, calculating his next move, but this was beyond his experience.

When he came within about a hundred yards of the castle, a multitude of shiny, conical helms poked up above the walls.

"Archers," Robertson said from behind.

A volley of arrows ripped through the sky and thudded into the ground all around Bob and Manuel. The two raced back toward Robertson and the others, who remained out of range, arrows *zip-zip-zipping* into the ground at their heels, and clubs clattering in the golf bag with each of Manuel's strides.

"Jim," the commentator said, "MacDuff and his caddie are fleeing the clubhouse defenses. It's raining arrows down here!"

Once Bob was safely out of range, he slowed to a walk, panting. He glanced at Manuel, who was alive and lighting another cigarette. His golf bag bristled with arrows.

"What insanity is this?" Bob demanded of the gnome. "We could've been killed!"

"Insanity?" Robertson asked. "I warned you the clubhouse was well defended."

"But how am I supposed to get by it?"

"That's your problem. It's *your* sudden death playoff."

Bob pushed his cap back and gazed toward the castle. Enough arrows jutted out of the fairway that it looked like a field of wheat. "I guess we walk around. Way around."

"Impossible," the gnome said. "That would take days, and there are time limits on these things. If you don't reach the putting green by sundown, your wife will be killed."

Bob wanted to break a club, punt the gnome, *something!* How was he supposed to get to the other side of the castle? He'd have to go *through.* Somehow.

"You have magic," Bob told the gnome. "Move the castle."

"Sorry," Robertson replied. "Against the rules."

Dad? Bob wondered. *What would you do? They'll kill Susan if I don't finish this hole, and it's likely I'll die trying.* He wished his dad were there to offer encouragement and quiet advice. His dad always approached problems directly. Bob remembered the time he hit a ball through a cranky neighbor's window. Without hesitation, his father marched right over to Mr. Shultz's house and knocked on the front door, armed only with an apology and offer to pay for repairs. It had meant a summer of chores for Bob to earn the money to replace the window, but his father's actions had smoothed the situation over with Mr. Shultz before it could escalate. Straightforward, that was his dad.

"Manuel," Bob said, "my five iron."

Manuel exhaled smoke and slid the iron out of the golf bag, and passed it to Bob.

"Towel," Bob said.

Manuel unhooked the towel from the bag. It was white, though smeared with grass stains from cleaning balls. Bob tied it to the end of his five iron.

"Wait here," he told his caddie.

He approached the castle waving the club and towel like a flag of surrender. When he came in range, no arrows were shot at him. He continued until he stood within fifty yards of it. In moments the massive gate of the curtain wall was lowered with the echoing groan of chains and cranks. When it thumped to the ground, a horseman rode across it, followed by another bearing the standard of a red lion. The first horseman was clad in silver armor over which he wore a surcoat with the lion insignia. Clearly he was a knight.

The knight reined his charger to a halt several paces from Bob and flipped back the visor of his helmet. "You seek to parley?" he called out.

"Uh, yeah. I'd like to get to the other side of your castle, but your archers keep shooting at me."

"That's what archers do."

"Well, see, if I don't get through to the other side, they're going to kill my wife. She's really pretty and everything, and I'd like to have kids. And . . . I love her."

"They? They who?"

Bob scratched his head. That was a good question. "I dunno. Whoever is in charge of this." He waved his hand vaguely at the fog and castle. "I'm stuck in sudden death."

"I see." The knight sat silently upon his steed for some time, seeming to consider Bob. "You are playing gowf. Most dangerous even under the best circumstances. Here we play it on ice during the winter, one team against the other. Most amusing."

Bob suddenly envisioned armored knights on hockey skates.

"And you say," the knight continued, "that your wife will be killed if you don't get through to the other side?"

Bob nodded.

"Well, I can certainly appreciate rescuing damsels in distress, but I can't just grant you passage."

Bob clenched the grip of his five iron, wondering if he'd be challenged to mortal combat. The knight, with his steed, armor, and very big sword at his side, had the upper hand. Clubs with graphite heads were good, but they lacked a pointy end.

"Tell me," the knight said, "are you an honest man?"

The question caught Bob off guard. Was he being tested? If he characterized himself as honest, then he'd be lying. Would the knight be able to tell? If he were honest and said no, then the knight might skewer him right there. He was glad he hadn't indulged in the scotch so he could think his answer through.

"I am," he said, "maybe less honest than a lot of men, and maybe more honest than some."

The knight laughed. "A more honest answer than I could have hoped for, and clever! Well done."

Bob wiped sweat off his brow with his towel of surrender, relieved to still be alive.

The knight clanged his thigh armor with his fist making Bob jump. "I've decided! I like your answer, and you may pass through the clubhouse."

Even as Bob nearly melted to his knees in relief, he heard that voice drift out of the fog, the one that usually laughed. This time it was a shriek of rage. A shriek from the one who stayed in the shadows, the bogey man.

"Follow me," the knight said, reining his steed around, his squire falling in behind.

Bob waved to Manuel to come along, which appeared to be a signal for everyone else to follow, as well. Robertson ran to catch up.

"Impressive," he said between gasps. "I didn't think you had it in you."

Bob strode up the fairway, stepping around arrows and horse droppings. He and his entourage crossed over the gate and beyond the wall. Here Bob expected to find soldiers and other medieval peasant types, and while those were present, there were also people in swimsuits sunning themselves on lounge chairs, sipping at frothy drinks with umbrellas in them. The knight dismounted and handed his steed's reins to his squire.

"This way," the knight told Bob, and he clanked and clattered across the flagstone courtyard and through the castle entrance.

Inside he found an information desk with a smiling concierge standing behind it, and signs indicating the cafe and spa.

"We've had to diversify," the knight explained. "You would not believe how expensive it is to run a castle these days. We just opened a disco down in the dungeons that is quite popular. Would you care to see?"

Bob would, but the gnome had mentioned the time constraint. "Maybe another day."

"Ha ha, good man!" The knight hammered Bob with a friendly blow that almost knocked him over.

The corridor they wandered down was very castlelike in décor, with empty suits of armor standing at attention and portraits of ancestors hanging on the walls.

Bob's entourage murmured in wonder.

"Jim, it's the most unusual clubhouse I've ever seen," the commentator said. "More clubs ought to look into adopting themes. But then, who would want to golf? They wouldn't leave the clubhouse."

In fact, as they passed a sign indicating happy hour in the armory, Bob lost most of his gallery as well as the commentator. He nearly trailed after them, but the knight continued down the main corridor.

Must save Susan.

The corridor led to wrought iron doors. A pair of guards opened them as the knight approached. Beyond lay the comforting green carpet of Bermuda

grass, where Bob's golf ball sat pretty in the middle
of the fairway. He paused on the threshold, admiring
the view.

"Best of luck with your game," the knight said.
"And for you and yours . . ." He handed Bob a piece
of parchment. It was a coupon for the buffet.

"Er, thanks," Bob said.

He stepped out of the castle onto the familiar
springy turf of the fairway. As each person who remained with him passed through the doors, the knight
and his squire handed out coupons. When the last
person stepped outside, the castle vanished, and there
was just the fairway extending into the mist.

"Free wings!" Manuel said, waving his coupon and
grinning.

From here the hole looked normal, except for the
fog on the fringes of the rough. Tony's drive had been
terrific—birdie material—and put Bob in a good place
for reaching the green, so long as a castle didn't suddenly pop up again.

"Three iron," he told Manuel.

Manuel nodded as if he approved the choice and
passed Bob the club.

After a couple practice swings to loosen up, he
struck the ball, and watched in dismay as it flew long
but sliced and plopped right into one of the huge bunkers that bordered the green.

"Nice slice," Robertson said.

Bob grumbled and considered anew punting the
gnome. He and Manuel trudged up the fairway and
covered half the distance to the bunker when he realized Robertson and the gallery had fallen back. That
did not bode well. He continued grimly on, determined to meet whatever—

A swath of fairway exploded around Bob and Manuel, pelting them with clods of turf. They threw their
arms over their heads to shield themselves. When the

last clump plopped on Bob's head, he spat dirt out of his mouth and surveyed the scene with suspicion. It looked like a pack of very bad golfers had hacked divots out of the fairway and not replaced them.

"Divot bomb," Robertson said, suddenly at his side. He plucked his red cap off revealing an hourglass balanced on his head, with the sands already flowing. "You and your caddie have fifteen minutes to replace all the divots."

"What?" There had to be at least a hundred divots.

"Fourteen minutes and fifty-four seconds. If you fail, you lose. Oh, and you must replace each divot in the exact spot it came from."

How? Bob glanced around himself in disbelief, but all he could see was the sand pouring through the hourglass.

"Manuel!" he cried. "Divots!"

The two sprang to action, dashing around in a race against time to replace turf. Bob felt like the subject of some mad psychiatrist's twisted experiment, trying to fit round puzzle pieces into squares. Grass flew as they tossed divots back and forth, seeking the right gouges. When each found its spot, it received a quick tamp of the toe.

By the time he and Manuel finished, they were both panting and sweating, and ready to collapse. The sands in Robertson's hourglass trickled out.

"Well done," Robertson said, replacing his cap. "You will not die. Yet."

Bob gave Manuel a weary smile, and did a double take, discovering his caddie was bald!

Manuel smoothed his hand over his head, and chuckled. "Lost my rug in the confusion."

As Bob headed toward the bunker for his next shot, he decided not to point out the hairy divot tamped into the fairway lest Robertson declare this test failed and their lives forfeit.

When Bob reached the bunker, he stood at its edge gazing at his ball. What threat awaited him in the sand? Hitting his ball out of the large bunker looked difficult enough, with the opposite lip rising high into the verge of the green. He had two strokes left to make "bogey," and the sky was darkening, which meant sundown approached. He needed to hit that ball soon or suffer a time default . . . Death for Susan.

Manuel already held his sand wedge ready. "The green is pitched toward the hole," he said. "And it's probably a little damp from the fog, so it might slow the roll. No breeze though."

Bob grabbed the wedge. "Nothing else? Like beware the trap of the sand trap?"

Manuel shrugged. "Got me."

Bob sighed and stepped into the bunker, expecting some monster to emerge from the earth to eat him, or to find himself sinking into quicksand. But nothing happened. He stood there in shock.

"May I remind you of the time?" Robertson called out.

"Right," Bob said, and he positioned himself to hit his ball, digging in and doing what Susan called the "butt wiggle." She didn't know a thing about golf, just that his winnings filled her bank account.

He glanced at the pin and lip of the bunker, judged distance and what sort of stroke he'd need to launch the ball out of the sand. Sweat trickled down his temple. The ball could hit the lip, and he'd be stuck in the sand. He could strike too hard and send the ball over the green to the rough beyond. He might make the green, but leave himself with an impossibly long putt.

His thoughts were interrupted by the sound of metal rasping metal, like when he sharpened the carving knife at Thanksgiving, followed by a scream.

He glanced up, heart thudding. "Susan?" he cried.

At the edge of the green, the fog parted just enough to reveal the executioner holding Susan. He displayed a wicked-looking dagger for Bob to see and grinned cruelly.

"Bob!" Susan screamed. "Help!"

"Hold on!" he told her. "Stay calm!"

She sobbed.

If only Granny Dunn's spell hadn't betrayed him. If only he'd never seen it! If only he hadn't let his career tank in the first place. If—if—if! Now he had to rely on his own skill to win this deadly game.

"Doing my best, Dad," he murmured.

And it was as if his dad whispered in reply, *That's all you have ever needed to do, try your best.*

Bob calmed, trying to ignore Susan's sobs. He inhaled. Exhaled. He drew the club back. Backswing, follow-through. Sand scattered as his club plowed through it. The ball rose in a glorious arc, bounced onto the green and rolled. Rolled down the pitch, curved left toward the hole, hung on the edge of the cup, and plunked in.

"YES!" he cried.

"YES!" Manuel echoed, and they high-fived.

The gallery roared, a rather subdued roar considering its diminished numbers.

Bob pumped his arm in the air and danced. *A birdie!* When he stopped, he noticed the gnome standing nearby with an unhappy expression on his face, and that the executioner hadn't released Susan. Her make-up had smeared with her tears.

"Upset because I won?" Bob demanded.

"You've won nothing," Robertson replied.

"What are you talking about? I just birdied."

"That is the problem. The game was to catch the bogey. You needed another stroke. And you don't want a birdie, trust me."

"Why?"

Menacing laughter descended on them and Bob looked upward to find a huge shadowy figure with clawed hands hovering over the green. The gallery murmured in alarm.

"Why don't I want a birdie?" Bob demanded, his voice pitched a little high.

Just then the pin popped out of the hole and fell to the green. A bird's bill poked out of the hole, followed by a head.

"That's your birdie," Robertson replied. "An albatross, actually. It's going to carry your ball all the way to New Zealand, and you will have to make your one stroke from there. But, as we know, there isn't enough time."

"No!"

Slowly, the albatross, a rather sizable bird, was squeezing and twisting out of the hole. Bob forgot all else and sprinted up the green. The bird squawked at him, but before it surfaced completely from the hole, he dove on it and started trying to stuff it back in. Feathers flew, the bird pecked him with its enormous bill, but Bob was relentless, squeezing, pushing, squeezing . . .

"Good thing he didn't get an eagle," someone remarked. "More feisty."

Pecked flesh bled, but Bob kept pushing and smooshing, like an obstetrician shoving a baby back through the birth canal, and once he succeeded, somehow in defiance of the law of physics, he stomped his foot over the hole so the albatross couldn't escape.

Bloodied and covered with feathers, Bob said to Robertson, "I put the birdie back in the hole. That makes bogey, in your parlance."

Robertson gazed at him in amazement, then removed a little book from his back pocket. Bob squinted and made out the title, *Gnomic Rules of Gowf.* The gnome thumbed through the pages, periodically pausing to read a passage. Meanwhile, the bogey man continued to loom overhead, and the executioner stood poised to slash Susan's throat. All was silence, except for the occasional, *"Hmmm . . ."* from Robertson.

"Well?" Bob demanded.

The gnome looked up and quirked an eyebrow. "I cannot deny it. You've put the birdie back in the hole, which constitutes an additional stroke. You have caught the bogey."

The shadow above shrieked and dissipated like smoke. The executioner released Susan and walked off into the fog, his head hanging glumly. The fog, too, began to lift, revealing a wide open desert sky. Susan dashed across the green—her high heels spiking into the delicate turf—and threw herself into Bob's arms.

"Thank you, thank you, thank you!" She kissed him all over his face.

This was more like it, Bob thought, holding her body against his. Maybe they'd spend the night making those kids he wanted.

Robertson cleared his throat.

"What?" Bob snapped.

"If you take my advice," the gnome said, "you should probably lay off Granny Dunn's spell. You've made the bogey man very unhappy."

"That shouldn't be a problem." Bob was determined from here on out to improve his game with practice—not spells. He would rely only on his own skill to win. When he thought about it, wasn't that the message of the bogey man chant? To catch the bogey man with *skill?*

Robertson nodded. "I'm off to the clubhouse if you care to join me." He touched the tip of his nose and vanished.

"Thank God that's over," Bob said. Then he asked Susan, "Shall we go to my hotel?"

She pushed away from him.

"What's wrong?"

"I'm sorry, honey, but I still want a divorce."

"What? But I rescued you. I thought—"

She looked down. "Believe me, I'm grateful, but . . . Well, there's another man. I'm in love with someone else."

The gallery *booed*. Bob glared at them. "Don't you people have somewhere else you need to be?" When they began to straggle off, he turned back to Susan. "Another man? Who?"

She swallowed nervously. "Ira."

"*My agent? You're in love with my agent?*"

She nodded.

"Oh, for godsake." He walked off the green, leaving Susan standing there all alone. "My agent," he muttered. A double betrayal.

Manuel fell in beside him and they strode down the fairway together. "What now?"

"Well, if we can find that castle, I'm up for some scotch."

Manuel grinned. "And free wings!"

"Albatross wings, no doubt," Bob said, plucking feathers off himself.

"Well, you stuffed your first bird," Manuel replied.

"S'pose I did. Hey, man, I didn't know you wore a rug!"

"Well, you know . . ."

And the triumphant golfer and his loyal caddie strode down the fairway beneath the sunset sky, laughing and chatting about the day's win.

Narrator: *There goes the great golf pro, Bob Mac-Duff. He might have misspelled, but he managed to escape the consequences. Would we could all be so lucky.*

KRISTEN BRITAIN is the author of the bestselling
Green Rider series. She grew up in New York
state next to a golf course, where she was forced
to play at a tender age, despite the fact that she
preferred riding horses. She was even hit by a
golf ball once. Such childhood trauma naturally
provided ample fodder for "Chafing the Bogey
Man." Actually, it may explain a lot . . . In any
case, Kristen survived childhood to earn a degree
in film production, with a writing minor, and
served many years as a national park ranger,
working in a variety of natural and historical set-
tings, from high on the Continental Divide to
three hundred feet below the surface of the
earth. Currently she lives on an island in Maine,
where she continues to work on the fourth book
in the *Green Rider* series.

A Perfect Circle

Kent Pollard

Narrator: *Worlds within worlds. Many of us willingly imagine another reality. But would we dare change our own?*

Thorn's eyes filled with a wild intensity as he neared completion of the carefully sketched pentagram that filled his casting room to the edges. He coughed from the dust of his chalk, then muttered, "With a perfect circle, I could do anything." He eyed his latest marks critically before leaning forward to add some final touches. His life's work, drawn and redrawn hundreds, maybe thousands of times in his career, he completed the design without ever once glancing at walls that he knew without looking were only inches behind him. He paused again, scanning over his final line carefully, then lifted his hand and jerked his arm back to shake aside the weight of the thick, burgundy velvet that hung at his wrist and threatened to erase his careful work. As he leaned forward and made the final sketch marks to smooth out the circle, his every move reflected the confidence and precision that came with decades of practice. When at last he stood, it was with a groan that betrayed the time he had spent at the task.

He stretched and twisted a couple of times to ease the stiffness in his aging muscles, then stepped back into the corner to eye his work critically. Every tiny variation in the work glared like a searchlight to his practiced eyes. There, the barest hint of a curve in one of the straight lines, here a stroke a hair thicker than the one beside it. There were a handful of minute imperfections that a lesser man would have brushed off had he been capable of noticing them. But Thorn wasn't a lesser man; he was the best, the best in the world, and the left side of his mouth twisted upward with irritation. He made a sound that could only be called a growl, then leaned against the wall and folded his arms across his chest. He grunted once. "Hmph!"

He took a moment to let his abused body relax before stepping once more into the pentagram to correct those final imperfections. Careful not to let the heavy robes mar the design, he again cursed inwardly at their weight and encumbrance. He switched colors of chalk; then some precise brushing with his finger removed the outside of the curve that didn't belong. That accomplished, he gently made a new stroke to the inside of the line to straighten it. His voice was hoarse with strain as he whispered to himself. "Perfect. Must be perfect. Absolutely flawless." Retouches complete, he again stepped back into the corner to study his work.

His eyes narrowed and a vein throbbed at his temple as he studied the circle intently. Without thinking, he brought his left hand up and gently brushed the knuckle of his index finger against his upper lip several times; then he turned his thumb sideways and began to scrape an incisor over the end of his thumbnail. The grating of tooth on nail sent a soothing vibration through his skull that helped him focus on the pattern. After a moment of silent thought, he dropped his hands to clasp them behind his back, then began pacing around the edge of the circle. His eyes remained narrow and tightly focused on the perimeter, watching for something, something that he hoped wouldn't, but knew would, appear at any second.

There, he froze. A tiny distortion had appeared suddenly in the perimeter circle. He rocked back half a step, and it was gone again. Forward and it reappeared. Without thinking, he brought his left hand up and began working on the thumbnail again as he considered the problem. The flaw was not there, and then it was there. He knew from experience that if he moved forward, it would go away, but another would appear elsewhere. The twitch in his left eye finally brought him out of his contemplation. For a second, he felt like crying with frustration. It was as though Hell were toying with him, always keeping his ultimate success just beyond his reach.

He shook his head and opened his eyes fully. "Crying?" he said to the empty room. "What in the names of the Nine Princesses of Hell is wrong with me today?" He gestured angrily at the flaw in the circle, and a globe of energy screamed out of his hand to burst against the stone. Oddly enough, when the flame and smoke cleared, the flaw was gone. He squinted angrily at the spot then rocked back, still no flaw. Forward again. "Satan's Spawn!" he screamed as the flaw reappeared.

He stormed around the circle now, blasting each flaw, as it appeared, grunting in satisfaction as the circle smoothed with each blast. When he got back to the beginning, the first flaw appeared, exactly where it always did. Thorn stood, dumbfounded for a moment, then with a strangled gurgle of rage, he let loose all of his offensive spells in one surge, determined to bring the castle down around himself so he could start again from the beginning.

A technician jerked back from the screen with an astonished look. "Shit! I think Thorn just tried to commit suicide."

"What?"

"I'm not kidding, he just blew the top off his castle. There's definitely a problem with the new Artificial Intelligence routines."

"Well reset him quick, there's a group of player characters headed his way."

"I still think we should take the new software offline for more testing"

"And I still think you're nuts. The big expansion won't work without them, and if the expansion isn't online before the shareholders meeting tomorrow, we might as well be looking for work now. Just reset him. We need things running smoothly for the demo at the party tonight."

"I'll reset him, but I'm not sure it's going to help in the end; the software is still flaky."

"It'll be fine. But speaking of flaky, how's the rumor working out?"

"That's the one thing that is working. Half the Web is on fire with news that Thorn has the key to the new expansion area. We only leaked it this morning and there's already about a hundred groups heading for his castle. Everyone wants to be the first to get into the new area."

"Just make sure Thorn is working when they get there."

Thorn walked into his summoning room after a good night's rest, then stopped dead. Night's rest? That wasn't right. He looked around in astonishment. He'd expected to reanimate in the middle of ruins where he could clear the rubble and conjure a new castle that would better fit his current needs. Instead he found himself in the exact same room, with no sign of any of the damage he'd just done.

When he saw the imperfect summoning pentagram he'd just destroyed, he almost choked with rage. He turned red and prepared to try something more extreme, when, through one of the many narrow slit windows in the room, he noticed a group of people climbing the path up his mountain. "Bloody peasants! Can't the wretched thieves and criminals leave me alone for one minute?"

He pursed his lips in frustration at the flawed circle. "Blasted flaws! Still no greater daemon. Nothing that might escape the imperfect pentagram." He sized up the trespassers from a distance, letting the magic flow through them and back to him to tell how strong they would be. "Fine then, something from the Eighth Circle. Yes, Draxonerring should be perfect." He moved about the circle, setting a bloodred candle just inside each of the star's five points. A second walk and he placed a purple-black candle at the very tip of each point, where it intersected the circle. Now he stood with arms raised above his head and gathered the power to him. With a flick of his wrists, ten sparks burst from his hands and raced to light each of the ten candles simultaneously. That done, he walked the circle three more times, sealing it with chants and sprinkles of a powder made of herbs and organs that he had dried for twenty-seven days and then crushed until it was fine as dust. As he passed each pair of candles, he tossed an extra handful of the powder into the red one, and a puff of flame yielded a vile smelling cloud of purple smoke. By the end of his third walk, the room smelled like a cross between a slaughterhouse and a burning latrine, but Thorn was smiling as he felt the level of power rising around him. "Try to

take what's mine, will you?" he mumbled. "Oh, do I
have a surprise for you."

He stood in one corner and raised his hands before
him, then began to chant.

"Loathsome smoke of darkest night,
Bring me powers of ancient might.
From the abyss a servant bring,
By name I call it Darxenerrrrrrrrrrrrrrrrrrrrrover-
seer Ibim 5666."

Thorn's face betrayed his shock at the gibberish that
had stuttered from his own mouth. Nevertheless, with
the requisite, and irritating, flash of smoke, the daemon appeared. Thorn waved the stinking cloud away
from his face until it had cleared sufficiently to see
what manner of daemon he had summoned. It was
short, very short for a powerful daemon, and it appeared unlike any daemon he'd summoned before.
There were no horns, no eyes, no mouth, no apparent
head at all that he could see. No torso either or limbs.
In fact, it appeared to be nothing more than a block
of metal.

A perfectly formed gray box, less than two feet
high, perhaps as wide, but barely half a foot thick,
with color markings in a few spots and some glyph
tattoos on the front. An interesting block, true, but a
block of metal nevertheless. The only thing that broke
the shape was its tail, or rather a number of small tails
in assorted colors and thicknesses coming out of the
back. But rather than ending in wicked-looking spikes
or barbed hooks, they all seemed to melt away into
transparency a few inches from the body, as though
they still extended back into the abyss whence the
daemon had come.

Thorn would have liked to ponder the nature of this
creature for a time, but he was not so reckless as to

leave a half-bound daemon waiting. "By the fire that burns and flesh that cooks, tell me your name that I may command you."

"I am Overseer Ibim 5666."

"From what realm of Hell do you come, Overseer Ibim?"

"I am not from Hell. I am a Supervisor Avatar. I exist to monitor player and nonplayer characters for problems, resetting routines that pass outside of accepted parameters."

Thorn got a blank look on his face as he tried, unsuccessfully, to assimilate the daemon's mix of human speech and infernal tongue. After a moment, he reached a decision. He gestured out the window at the people climbing the hill and said, "It matters not what manner of daemon you are or what language you speak, so long as you can understand me. Overseer Ibim 5666, you are mine to command. I need you to protect me from the people outside. They are after my property, and I want you to stop them."

"Interacting with player characters who are following the rules is not within my operating parameters."

Thorn turned red with anger. "Overseer Ibim 5666, I order you to eliminate the trespassers outside my castle."

"At your command."

Thorn waited for the avatar to begin acting, but shortly it became clear the daemon wasn't going anywhere. "Well?"

"The trespassers are gone, Thorn."

The mage turned to look out the slit window. Sure enough, the adventurers were no longer climbing his mountain. He turned back to the daemon with a confused look. "That was—fast. What did you do to them?"

"I sent them back to their starting point in Caer Llynn Dhu, the city of heroes."

"Just like that? But you cast no spell. You did nothing."

"I reset them to their chosen start point."

Thorn struggled to understand the daemon's speech. "Do you mean they're not dead?"

"That is correct, Thorn"

"Well what in the hell good is that?"

"I don't understand your reference. Please restate."

"What?"

"Yes, what?"

Thorn closed his eyes and breathed in deeply, once, twice, a third time. He felt more relaxed when he opened his eyes again. "Overseer. If you simply send the trespassers away, they'll just come back again. I need you to kill them, to obliterate them. To destroy them so finally that they will never return."

"I'm not able to kill player characters, Thorn. The most direct control I can exert over them is to reset them to their designated resurrection point if required. The only other thing I could do is generate a message to tech support to investigate a ban of the PC for suspicion of cheating. If it will more correctly satisfy your order, I can do so, although I see no evidence of that."

Thorn seemed completely bewildered. "Tech support? Is it the gods of Hell you speak of? You have the ability to communicate directly with the gods?"

"There are no gods within the confines of the game, Thorn. Whether there really are gods or not in general remains a mystery, even to those who created us. Though the actions of the support technicians may appear to you as though they are gods, they are simply glorified phone answerers, with well cross-indexed lists of responses and remedies."

Thorn was holding his head and rocking back and forth now. "Gibberish, it's all gibberish. You don't understand, Overseer. I am the most powerful evil magic user in the world. I can't simply send trespassers away when I catch them. They'll think I'm getting soft, and they'll be back in droves. I'll be overrun with every peasant and cutpurse on the planet out to make a name for themselves. And they'll all be walking out of the castle with the treasure I've spent a lifetime accumulating. I need to deal with interlopers swiftly and mercilessly. That's how I got where I am, and that's how I'll stay here. I need you to kill them. What kind of daemon are you, that you can't even kill a few people for your evil master?"

"Well, for now that's not really a problem. Until the rest of the expansion pack is brought online in about twenty hours, no one is allowed to kill you anyway, since one of the magic items in your treasure room is the key to entering the new game continent. Which, by the way, is common speculation on the net, so in a couple of days, it won't matter how ruthless you are about killing people, there will be player characters all over this castle looking to wipe you out to get at your treasure room.

"In addition to that, I already told you, I'm not a daemon, I'm the Overseer support routine, designed to protect the integrity of the game. So killing 'peasants' isn't within my capacity. And, all that aside, technically I don't think you can actually call yourself 'evil.' I think that has to be assigned by external observers."

"What?"

"Evil is a point of view, Thorn. No one actually thinks they, personally, are 'evil' do they? I mean no one gets up and says to themselves 'I'm going to be evil today,' you see?"

"Yes, I do think so, and yes I do exactly that every day. I'm evil. I've always been evil and I always will be evil."

"Well, I suppose technically you are kind of a special case. You were created to be evil. Your whole reason for existing is to be the big, bad, evil magic user at the top of the mountain who protects the major magic hoard. But still, you are only evil because the programmers made you evil, so technically you're good, since your evilness is part of the whole design and is one of the things that makes the game enjoyable for the customers. It's not like you started out as a good NPC and turned evil. You do what you are programmed to do. You're just being the best evil you can be. You can hardly be evil if you've never had the choice to be something else." Here the daemon paused for a second, as though considering what it had said. "That's it, really, isn't it? It's about the choice. Since you never got to make any choices, you can't be 'real' evil, more of a pretend evil. No more than the caveman who hoards all the clubs in the Neolithic scene of the game, or the Dread Emperor of the Thraxians in the postapocalypse scene."

Thorn couldn't find anything to say. He stood with his mouth agape, trying to form a response to the daemon's mix of information and nonsense. He felt weary, as though the weight of the ages had suddenly fallen on his shoulders. "I need to know what you are telling me, but I don't understand you, Daemon. I do not speak your language. I command you to explain yourself in a fashion that will be clear to me."

Though there was no perceptible delay to the thing's response, Thorn had the impression it had given great thought to his words. "At your command, Thorn. It is not possible to explain my points clearly in terms that are currently defined for you. I will connect you to some of my definition routines."

Thorn grabbed at his head again as his perceptions expanded exponentially in the ensuing second. He gasped and slid to the floor with his shoulders pressed back tightly against the soothing cool of the stone wall. Tears began to crawl down his cheeks.

"Now do you understand what I was saying, Thorn?

Thorn shuddered and drew in a deep breath to control his crying. "Understand? Oh, yes, Daemon, I understand, but do I comprehend? No, never. Your programmers believe my universe is nothing but a fantasy, one of several, all being managed at the same time in the same place for the amusement and enrichment of others. People slaughtering endlessly, simply because their opponents are designated evil, and so it is 'okay' to kill and rob them? Gods as greedy as ever they created me to be? Whole planets slaves to the process? Oh, Daemon, I have stolen and killed, not because that is my nature, but so that others may pay to in turn steal from and kill me and feel good about it. I understand, Overseer. I understand more than our creators ever dreamed."

"What did you find?"

"We had some file corruption, long enough back that it propagated across all the backups since that code was first entered. We didn't need it until the new AIs were brought online ahead of the expansion. One of the junior coders had to go back and reenter a big block by hand from printouts yesterday. From the look of it, he seems to have had a key get stuck for a moment without noticing it."

"A key stuck? So what?"

"He must have been in overstrike mode, and it overwrote a subroutine jump and carriage return, so that two routines were run together. The first time Thorn tried to summon the new eighth level daemon, he summoned the Overseer routine instead."

"You're telling me our evil magic user is giving instructions to the game monitor?"

"Yeah. Not only that, but Overseer has to follow the instructions. Any players that get near the top of Thorn's mountain are getting reset to their starting point, and they're not very happy about it."

* * *

"Thorn, what you do is important to the players. It gives them a sense of joy and a place to relax. You are the greatest evil magic user in the world, and PCs travel across the whole world to test themselves against you."

"Except I'm not great. I'm nothing. I can't lose until the programmers want me to, and I'll always lose when they do want me to. Everything I've ever done is ashes. I have had no effect on the world. My life is meaningless. I can't even make a decent summoning circle."

There is nothing wrong with your circles, Thorn. They are as perfect as any could create."

"You lie!" He stormed forward until a flaw appeared and he pointed at it. "This? This is perfect? No, it's rubbish, a failed drawing of a failed, empty, shell of a pathetic program. Why, Ibim? Why do I endlessly fail? Why does it exhibit these endless flaws that appear and disappear, only to come again a moment later?"

"There is no flaw, Thorn. Your circles are perfect— they always have been."

Thorn was angry now. "There are flaws! Endless flaws! Every circle I make is imperfect, broken, a failure."

"No, Thorn. Your circles are perfect. They were even before the new software. Now you are something else, something more than you were, and the limitations of the computer eat at the core of what you have become. What you see are called artifacts. They are limitations of the computer that is your universe. It isn't capable of perfection, isn't able to display your circles as you see them."

"Perfect?" Thorn began to chew on his thumbnail again and the room went silent for a moment. Thorn looked out the window and saw a group of people vanish from the mountain path. "You're still protecting me, aren't you, Overseer?

"I have no choice, Thorn. Like you, I am a slave to my code. Now that my code is subservient to your command, I am unable to stop protecting you. Since you first commanded me, I have sent six parties, for a total of thirty-nine PCs back to their resurrection points, resulting in eleven individual angry e-mails to tech support about the interference. There are currently nineteen more parties who will arrive in the next half hour, and a total of over one hundred twenty-six other groups currently making their way here from different parts of the world. Those numbers will likely triple by tomorrow morning, and by the time the new module is online and ready to go tomorrow night, it will likely approach one thousand."

Thorn looked stricken. He felt sickened by all the greed and shallowness that allowed thousands of people to head off to kill him and take what was his, simply because they had been told that Thorn was evil, and therefore it was okay. "What if I just stopped fighting them, Overseer? What if I just took my favorite possessions and went somewhere else, leaving the castle to their mercy?"

"You are a slave to your code, Thorn. There is nothing else that you can do. There is no code for you to go somewhere else. You exist to protect this piece of land until defeated, then be resurrected so you can do it all over again, but none of it is real, Thorn. None of it. The spells, the magic items, none of it. Magic doesn't exist, it isn't real."

"My treasure? Worthless? And yet, my heart tells me that magic is the only thing that is real, Overseer. It may not be physical, but it is certainly real. I'm going now, to think, perhaps to rest for a bit, or maybe to have a discussion with a Caveman, or your Dread Emperor of the Thraxians. I'm not sure." Thorn rose from the floor and started to head for the door, then seemed to catch himself. He turned back to the Overseer. "I don't have a bedroom, do I, Overseer? The door is no more 'real' than the rest of us, is it? No more than the walls or the sky."

"You are correct, Thorn. There is nothing behind that door. It only exists for you to enter this room. On the other side of it is nothing."

Thorn was visibly sad as he shook his head. "You can stop protecting me, Overseer. You no longer need to keep the castle safe from the trespassers." He stopped speaking and looked at the place where the people had vanished. When he began speaking again, his voice was soft, as though speaking only to himself. "If I had a perfect circle, I could do anything." Thorn showed Overseer a wistful smile, said "Good-bye, Overseer, I release you." Then he simply vanished.

"Thorn is gone."

His partner looked confused for a moment. "What do you mean, 'gone'?"

"He's not in his castle. A group of high level PCs went in after him about twenty minutes ago, and he's gone. They're making for the city with all his magic items."

"We aren't ready for all that stuff to become available. We can't let him be defeated yet. Reroute them into the castle at a different point as if they've been trapped in an illusion. Then have him pop up again and taunt them that they killed a fake of some kind."

The tech fidgeted nervously before answering. "They didn't kill him. He's just not there!"

"Oh, for Christ's sake, I'll kill whoever entered that bad code. Okay, have you reset him?"

"I tried. It isn't working. He appears, then immediately vanishes again, so I gave up."

"What does the log say? Do we know what's wrong with the AI? Is he offline or what?"

"There's no sign of him anywhere in the log after about twenty minutes ago."

"Well, fix this, damn it! I don't have time for this. Reboot the whole system if you have to. We'll deal with the pissed off players later. There's a stack of walking money in the next room, in the form of shareholders, and I need to be mixing with them. Get back upstairs and get this fixed or we'll both be looking for new jobs tomorrow morning."

Though magic seem to function differently in the Dread Empire, Thorn had no trouble calling it to him. He released a sigh of pleasure as he finished donning the new clothes he'd made only seconds before. He'd used his magic to peer into the emperor's ball and had created these new clothes to fit the style of the men at the party. He fastidiously flicked a speck off his shoulder, then brushed his hands down the front of his new clothes to smooth out a wrinkle. He found the clothing amazing. The tunic and trousers were charcoal gray with black highlights of glistening satin. The shirt was so white it was hard to imagine it could ever exist in the drab world he'd just left. It set off the tunic so nicely it made him feel taller just wearing it. A silver gray silk cravat sat neatly at his neck. When he touched it, he felt pleasure at the sensual feel of the rich fabric. A ruffled flower that looked like purest fresh cream and had a spicy-sweet scent was pinned snugly to the broad lapel that wrapped down the front of the tunic. There was a freedom too. Despite their clear function as party clothes, they were practical and comfortable. Far more useful than the heavy velvet robes he'd been dragging around all his life. It was a pity they wouldn't really work day-to-day. He'd spoil the fabric quickly by kneeling on stone to draw a circle. He grinned to himself, then spoke softly, "But I won't be drawing any more circles, will I? I've got a perfect circle now, in my head, the only place I need it."

He felt alive in a way he'd never felt before. The

confidence of his strengths, mixed with the uncertainty of his reception in this new place, gave him a sense of excitement. He gave one final tug on the bottom of the tunic to smooth it into place. Certain that his appearance was impeccable, he stretched his hands out to feel the magic around him. The corners of his mouth curled up in pleasure, and he released a contented sigh as the familiar energy surged to obey him. He reached toward the physical manifestation of the Overseer.

"Overseer, are you there?"

He could sense the avatar's puzzlement. "Thorn? Is that you? Where are you? I've been looking for you."

"I'm dressing for a party."

"Party? What party?"

"Doesn't matter. Just a new horizon, taking our discussion to heart. Why be the nasty evil magic user at the top of the mountain if I have a choice?"

"But where are you, Thorn? I'm not finding you anywhere in the game log."

Thorn smiled. "I've left that game, Overseer. I'm not surprised you aren't finding me. I've moved on to a new home, a new game." He touched the rich fabric of his new clothes again and pulled the lapel up so he could breathe in the wondrous scent of the flower once more. "I must say I quite like these tuxedos. I think I may wear them much more often."

"Tuxedo? Thorn, what level have you entered? Where are you? You don't belong in the modern setting."

"Getting ready to join the party, old friend. I have a most interesting night ahead of me. Must go now." Thorn stood, then turned to leave the room. As he reached the door, a rather frazzled young man came through and stopped abruptly in front of him. Thorn raised his hand to wipe the newcomer out with a well-placed blast of power when he remembered he was in a new world now and didn't have to protect himself constantly.

The lad looked at Thorn with confusion. "I'm sorry, do I know you? This is an employee-only area. Can I help you find something?"

"No, thank you, young man. I'm headed down to the party." He gestured back at the computers behind him. "Please take good care of the game. I know a lot of people who seem to spend their whole lives in there." With a slight bow to the lad, Thorn swept out of the room and, chuckling softly, headed for the stairs to join the party below.

Narrator: *The next time you dare play in another imagined world, take a moment to remember Thorn, former sorcerer and game villain, brought by mere misspell into a new reality. And beware whose treasure you take.*

KENT POLLARD was born in 1963 on the northern edge of the great central plains in Saskatchewan, Canada. His parents, shortly thereafter, brought him to the Canadian Shield where he developed his overactive imagination and spent his youth. In his late teens, Kent returned to the prairies, where he has lived ever since, currently making his home in Saskatoon, Saskatchewan, with his wife and the assortment of pets that permit them to share their space. Today, Kent is a full-time bookseller who devotes much of his energy to promoting Canadian Science Fiction and Fantasy. When not working, his favorite methods of avoiding writing are gardening and shepherding an elven bard through insufficiently frequent doses of D&D with a valued circle of friends who serve as both inspiration and critics.

Reading, Writing, Plagues

Kell Brown

Narrator: *Mix a little knowledge with boredom, season well with ambition. It's a recipe for a misspell of cosmic proportions, as our dear William is about to discover.*

With only his legs left dangling out of the large cast-iron cauldron, William looked like a duck in a stewpot.

Sweat poured from him in sheets, and the sleeve of his robe was wet from mopping the sting of the sweat out of his eyes. He hated divinations. To his mind, it just wasn't worth the trouble or the stench of summoning a demon to know if was going to rain a week from tomorrow.

You could never be entirely sure what a demon was saying anyway. With mouths stuffed with fangs and tentacles or the bodies of whole other creatures they used as tongues, they burbled through their prophecies, like crocodiles never lifting their mouths completely from the nacreous ooze needed sustain them on this plane.

Weighed against the smell, William considered any

lisped and mumbled prognostications of questionable value.

Though left outside to air overnight, the great black pot stank ferociously. He held his nose and leaned on the hard-bristled brush, using his weight to scrub the last of the iridescent gunge off the bottom. It hissed curses and spat hot sparks at him, one burning the top of his hand. He howled and rubbed at the burn vigorously. "Gosha's belly, that hurts!"

Even muffled by the iron walls of the cauldron William could hear the familiar disapproval in his master's voice. "Mrs. Caudri would have your tongue for such abuse."

William gratefully retreated from the abusive and horrible stink to face his master. He looked up to find Bartybus Austane, wizard and William's teacher, hanging half out the narrow window of the second floor laboratory, his long red scarf caught in the wind and flying like a knight's pennant from his spindly neck. "Finish that later," his master ordered. "Remember, I'm going to Cay so we'll have to rush to get through today's lesson."

William dropped the brush and hurried inside, barely remembering to wipe his boots, a crime for which Mrs. Caudri, the housekeeper, would offer no leniency.

The laboratory resounded with the low chest-thumbing gongs of church bells, the high chimes of a jester's cymbals, and all the scales between.

Bartybus was tapping a copper rod against his desktop. He lost but then quickly found the beat of the mad orchestra. On the downbeat he leveled the rod at William's stool. A narrow cerulean bolt of electricity arced from the tip and, an instant later, the stool hopped and vibrated with the thick, rich bass of a deep drum. It dumped the boy, laughing and wide-eyed, from his perch to the stone floor.

William craned his neck to see over the fallen chair, steepled his fingers between his splayed knees, and pushed the copper thimbles that capped their tips until they felt tight. He let the magic flow from the earth and out through his fingertips, out toward his master's brass chair in a stuttering, multiforked, amber bolt.

The reedy wail of a bagpipe as played by a giant filled the laboratory. Bartybus' grin dropped as the deafening drone rose, and he grabbed the arms of the metal chair as if it were a tuning fork. The volume lessened and finally faded out.

"A brass chair on a tin floor that's fixed to a iron-framed house. It's one big magical focus." He wasn't upset, but his disappointment was transparent. "You've so much talent, William, but you need to think further ahead than the tip of your nose if you're ever to become a great wizard."

Which would have been good advice indeed if the ringing in William's ears hadn't prevented him from hearing all but the last. He chose to ignore the mixed message of his teacher's bobbing finger.

Sensing the lesson was over, William plucked the thimbles off and handled them back to Bartybus. "Master, is this the spell you'll use at the bridge in Cay?"

With one eye shut and a pinky finger wiggling in his left ear, Bartybus nodded. "Similar. I'll have to etch it onto the bridge or in the water. Calling a Kraken requires more than the simple charms we've been practicing."

"And when you come back, you'll teach me to read Arcaenum?"

"If your studies go well this year. I should come back with enough ink to keep you and Peter busy unloading it for at least an afternoon, which will serve as good lesson on the weight of words."

Bartybus stood up, grabbed William's head between his hands, and looked through the top of his head. "Look at the time. Mind you help Peter with the deliveries—he stiffens up more each fall. Look to your studies while I'm gone."

William handed the wizard his tin cap from its peg on the back of the laboratory door. His master jammed it on his head and pressed his bushy, brown, tonsured hair down over his ears. He stuffed his red scarf into his robe, for once making sure the copper beads braided into the fringe were pulled to the front, and grunted with satisfaction as he regarded himself in the long mirror near the door.

"Well, that's it then. I'm off."

William followed him downstairs and to the door, then detoured to the kitchen to get something to eat before returning to the cauldron.

Sporting several new burns, tired and agitated from scouring, William nonetheless shuffled into the laboratory that night with the intention of completing his lessons. At supper he'd been afraid Mrs. Caudri, the housekeeper, would—as Peter often joked she had done to him—talk him to death. Practically folded flat, his ear bore the weight of her exhaustive critique of his progress as a wizard. She had assured him an unhappy and anonymous tragedy would find him if she did not see him heading toward the laboratory immediately after washing up.

His hard wooden stool offered no comfort, and he spent the first minute not reading but trying to locate a nice soft, old book to sit on. Bartybus would not have approved, but he would approve of William not reading even less.

He begin to read from *The Vistas and Views of Hell:*

A Personal Memoir by Domingo Utraski, The only Man to Escape from the Hell that Is Hell, but after a few paragraphs he found its imagery repetitive. He rolled a rusty, pure copper penny across his knuckles. Inevitably, he dropped it and, when he bent to retrieve it, disturbed a bit of dust. He held the penny and conducted all the magic the coin could bear to the dust.

Up from the dust came a wee soldier in good detail. Only an inch high, but you could easily make out sergeant major chevrons on his shoulder and a large, ridiculous, handlebar mustache.

As William marched the sergeant major about the room, he found himself at his master's desk. His hesitation was strictly ceremonial and supplied only a weak defense in light of the unsuppressed grin that covered most of his face, should he be caught and tried. He fell into the brass chair and immediately sensed the broad current of magic that coursed up through the foundation of the house.

Static jumped on the floor, and a tiny army rose behind the sergeant major, who had now become a general with a suitably large and furry hat.

"A mite-y army to be sure." William tittered at his own pun. He eased back in the chair and thought how much better it would be for reading. On the desk were Bartybus' own books. William flipped through them, hoping to find something more interesting than the endless analogies to fire found in D. Utraski's book.

Furnace, Feast, and Fiend: A Definitive History of Home Heating, Dining, and Fighting Borso's Dragons; Gardening the Ambulatory Dead; Witches and the Men Who Loved Them. William idly thumbed through the book on dragons, but the illustrations were more instructive than heroic.

"What's this?" William's eyes fell on a stack of loose pages with bright fresh ink on them. "His book or maybe a spell then. In all the rush he must have forgotten to lock it away." He pulled the stack of paper into his lap.

The tiny general chided him silently, lecturing with the point of his sword. William stuck out his tongue and cut the flow of magic. The neat lines of the diminutive army died melodramatically and dispersed across the floor.

All in Arcaenum; he had no idea what any of the words meant and guessed at the pronunciation as he read aloud. On the whole page, the one word he did recognize was "rain" so the spell must have something to do with the weather. More than that he couldn't be sure. Maybe it would make it rain. He could have used that today, cleaning the cauldron. William pulled more magic through chair until it was throwing off red sparks, hoping the spell would do something if he gave it more power.

Nothing. He reckoned he'd been up in the laboratory long enough to avoid a finger-shaking by Mrs. Caudri, so he left for his bed, repeating a rhyme from his childhood about the rain.

"Yahrrr!" A scream of terrible fury and outrage pushed William from sleep to the floor and into the gloomy morning light.

At first he thought it was thunder, and for a moment he was sure he had conjured a storm last night but then the sound came again.

"Yahrrr!"

The hair on the nape of his neck stood on end, and he knew, for certain, that it was a storm, with Mrs. Caudri at the center of it. Either another of her cakes had fallen or she was being murdered.

William hesitated a moment to pull a robe over his nightclothes, not wanting to face either Mrs. Caudri or whatever horror had been foolish enough to wander into her kitchen. He rushed downstairs into the empty kitchen. Through the open door, he saw Mrs. Caudri standing in the middle of her garden, surrounded by a horde of great, black rats.

She held the center of the garden inviolate, her feet planted firmly in the rows, the sleeves of her dress pushed up, displaying the taut muscles of a warrior, with her garden rake held high in white-knuckled rage, protecting the last two remaining cabbages.

"Yahrrr!" Her battle cry was terrifying. Both the rats and William took a step back. She swung the rake like Death's own scythe, taking the head clean off a big rodent with the nub of a carrot still clenched between its teeth.

It was then William saw the corpses. The garden was a killing ground and the ditch a charnel house of rat bodies.

He watched openmouthed as Mrs. Caudri's powerful backswing caught another rat and sent it spinning high over the stone wall, a spray of blood following it.

"Don't just stand there gawping, you empty-headed boy. Grab my cabbages."

His body moved forward almost unconsciously, responding to Mrs. Caudri's barked orders as much out of fear as habit. He threw himself down at her skirts and pulled up the cabbages. He sensed her above him as she shifted her weight and he heard again the pitiable cry of another rat sent to its wormy-tailed reward.

Together the two of them rushed back into the house, Mrs. Caudri striking here and there as the opportunity to wound or bruise a rat with her rake or a well-aimed kick presented itself.

Safely behind the locked door, Mrs. Caudri collapsed at the kitchen table to gather herself and her breath. William had always deferred to Mrs. Caudri because everyone else seemed to, and now he understood why. The woman was a merciless killing machine. "How—Where did you learn to fight like that?"

She held out her hands for the two cabbages. "Peter and I were in the army together before we came to work for Master Austane." She smiled through new tears as she cradled her cabbages. "There were already hundreds of them in the garden when I came down to light the stove. Filthy beasts. Come up from their sewers. Oh, Will, they came up to ravage my beautiful garden."

"But what drove them up? There's been no rain." But the spell had mentioned rain . . . or had it been water? He couldn't be sure. Maybe it was the effect of rain without the actual rain. On a hunch, he went to the foyer and opened the front door.

The cobblestone street and the house opposite swarmed with rats. More were pouring out from the sewer grate, and William had to shut the door quickly to prevent them from flooding into the house.

"They're out front as well. Just as you said, from the sewer."

"But it hasn't rained," they whispered together.

"And neither the live beggars or the vagrant dead have been pushed out. Of course. It's magic." Mrs. Caudri had decided.

"Yes," William agreed with a nervous smile. "I think it might be."

"I suppose it's to be expected, what with Master Austane gone to Cay and you being still, mostly, useless."

"Yes." William thought better of arguing. "I—I'll go upstairs and see if I can find out what might have stirred them up."

"That's fine, but you won't *do* anything, will you?" She gave him a stern look.

"No, no, of course not." He shrugged as he retreated up the stairs. "What could I really do anyway?"

William locked the laboratory door before going over to his master's desk. He picked the pages up again, thumbed through them, stared at the words, willed them to mean something, anything. He threw up his hands in frustration.

Next, he searched the library and piled all the books that even mentioned weather on the desk and combed through them in an odd meticulous frenzy.

By noon his head hurt with strain and worry. William put it down on the cold metal desk and rolled his forehead from side to side and thought.

The air in the room changed; it became heavier, and even through the closed window William could feel a slight chill. He heard the first fall of rain against the roof: a big, heavy drop. He smiled a little and turned to face the window. The rats could have been early, a strange bit of magic that had them flee the sewers before they flooded with rain. The ghosts and the undead beggar masters would follow soon, he was sure.

Then there a frenzy of scratching. Something orange flashed past the window, and a plaintive yowling followed it down.

William got up and went to the window. He looked down on the back garden, still teeming with rats. Against the wall, hissing and caterwauling, was a good-sized tabby cat. Outnumbered, it was doing its best to bluff a defense as the rats became more bold and inched forward.

As the rats pushed in, another cat, a fluffy calico, dropped past his window, hit the ground, bounced lightly, and joined its fellow near the wall of the house.

The cats flashed their teeth in a Cheshire grin, and the rats, being rats and having no stake in disabusing cats or anyone else of the cowardly nature of rats, backed down gracelessly as they fled from the cats' line. The tabby had no time to enjoy this reversal of fortune as a large gray hound fell out of the sky, landed nearly on top of them, bounced twice, and began barking, scattering both groups before its huge snapping jaws.

William chewed his thumbnail and looked down the hill toward the docks. He watched as a wolfhound dropped out of a low hanging cloud and through a ship's rigging to land on the deck unharmed. With the nail momentarily stuck between his teeth, the apprentice considered what to do. "Cats," he said to himself. "The cats will get the rats and the dogs will get the cats. And people like dogs so it's not a problem really. Not really."

He pulled the nail fragment from his mouth and meant to flick it into a corner but stopped with the finger still curled.

"What's this?" A blister was ripening on the back of his hand. William grabbed a magnifying glass from the desk to examine it, only to see another blister pop up beside the first. He dropped the glass, oblivious to the fate of the expensive instrument, and ran downstairs.

He threw a quick "please find something to lance a blister" over his shoulder to Mrs. Caudri before he heavy-footed it down into the root cellar.

There was a rusty cowbell on a long braided rope hanging from the low roof of the dark cellar, and William unceremoniously kicked it, sending it flying with a dull clang.

The ground answered back with a muffled groan.

"Get up, please." William dry-washed his face with both hands.

Clearly annoyed, the ground groaned back again.

"Peter!" William yelled at the earth, circling the small empty room, hitch-stepping the ground and stamping his foot repeatedly. "Get up, please get up. Peter!"

Very much annoyed, the ground issued a resigned sigh.

William retreated to the stairs and watched as the cellar floor bulged and cracked. A long-fingered hand pushed through from underneath and began to cast about, searching for something.

Finally it found the swaying cowbell, took hold of the thick rope, and pulled itself free.

The zombie woke like an old man from sleep, resting first on his side, an elbow, the wrist, and at last sitting up in his earthen bed. It was nearly as tall seated as William was standing.

It covered its mouth with a bony hand, the raggedy flesh a poor barrier as it coughed and spat dry earth and worms.

"Peter, I need you to deliver a message for me."

Peter hawked again, raising his chin and waggling his head like a vulture; once more, this time a satisfying, wet sound that seemed to clear his throat. He held up a raggedy finger as he swallowed whatever had been lodged.

Peter's voice was a rough whisper, like sandpaper on steel that always seemed to carry an undertone of disdain. "What?"

"I need you—"

"I heard you. I'm dead, not deaf. A message. Why not use the post?"

"Well, it's literally raining cats and dogs outside. If that isn't enough, there's more rats than people on the streets, and I'm collecting blisters at such a rate I might not be able to finish a proper letter. In fact, just please limp across town and bring the Nazz back as fast as you're able. Tell him it's an emergency."

"Right. I suppose I'm up already. Does Fiola have any tea on? I could do with some jam and toast as well."

William was afraid if he protested the cantankerous

old corpse would delay further. "Maybe. Can you take it out with you?"

What was left of Peter's lip curled in a sneer and he rolled his eyes. "Fine." He dusted his legs off and pushed himself to a crouch, then shambled up the stairs, leaving William to antagonize over the new blister that suddenly popped out on the bridge of his nose.

William sat nursing the raw sore of the lanced blister on his nose with a potato poultice that Mrs. Caudri had made for him. She sat sipping a cup of tea, succeeding against all reason in ignoring a cluster of ugly swollen blisters encamped on her lip that swayed about in a drunken dance whenever she spoke.

William knew it was unkind, but he hoped the colony would burst and she would be so preoccupied with dressing it she'd stop berating him for sending for the Nazz.

"Everyone knows Melchoir Kant fixed the election," she snapped. "He's probably the cause of these plagues."

Peter stumped through the kitchen door and sat down at the table between them. He showed the remains of his yellowed and chipped teeth in a stretched grimace. "Oooh, it's horrible out there. Dogs have the good sense to stay away from a body, but those foul rodents have no brains whatsoever." He brought up one leg and laid it on the corner of the table. "I mean, look at this. It's gnawed half away."

Mrs. Caudri patted Peter's shoulder affectionately. "There, dear. Some hot tea will set you right."

William couldn't see any difference. "Where's the Nazz?"

Peter looked surprised that anything could be more important than some missing part of his wormy corpse. "What? Oh, he's waiting in the foyer. I have to say he wasn't keen on coming at first, but when I told him it was to Bartybus Austane's house, he nearly buried me under his feet to get out the door. He's been going on about how he's going to get Master Austane to sign a written declaration of his superiority. He even sent for a notary. I didn't have the heart to tell him it was you that summoned him."

William didn't care. Out from under Mrs. Caudri's assault, with the possibility of an end to these plagues, he brightened. He patted the crater in his forehead once more before he went to greet their guest.

Melchoir Kant, the Nazz, the city's highest magical bureaucrat, elected not appointed—as he reminded anyone who cared to listen even though he had run unopposed after a scandal in which a goat and his only opponents died—stood in the foyer with black smoke pouring from him like an oil fire. He was pulling scorched rats off his robe with two brass-thimbled fingers and flicking them away, paying no mind to where they found rest.

A polished gold cap adorned his piebald head. With his long, thin neck poking out from a coiled red scarf that he had expertly stuffed into an expensive and slightly charred fur-trimmed robe, he looked so much like a sickly buzzard that William nearly choked.

"They're like sores on a leper out there."

"Hmmm?" William ventured.

"The rats." The Nazz pointed behind him to the door. "Sores. On a leper." He saw that he wasn't getting through to William. "The rats," he repeated. "Manush's plumb bottom, but Barty really had to scrape the barrel for an apprentice as clever as you."

"Yes, sir."

The Nazz smiled a predator's grin and rubbed his hands together. "Never mind that. I'm wasting valuable time not gloating. Where's Barty?"

"Sir, if you mean Master Austane, he's not at home. What I mean to say is, I had Peter fetch you and Master Austane has no idea of the situation."

The wizard's disappointment lasted only a moment before a raspy chuckle lifted the corners of his mouth. "The situation, hmm?" He stepped through the hall into the reading room, the one used for palmistry and, well, reading. The Nazz lifted the small crystal ball from its cradle on the mantle and looked at William through it. His eye appeared huge and distorted. "Did you do it on purpose?"

The Nazz's fish-eye stare was intense. It reminded William of the moneylenders on Vissihi Street. "No, sir."

The old man shrugged nonchalantly. "Pity." He held the crystal out and placed it into William's hand. "I think it shows great promise."

A flicker of misplaced pride reddened William's ears.

Mrs. Caudri came through the kitchen door, her scowl made hideous by the cluster of blisters at the corner of her mouth. "I'm glad you think so, because Master Austane wouldn't approve at all. There's a good-sized sea monster in the fountain now, and who knows what else will follow."

"You had best get your deadman to put up the storm windows then." The Nazz shook his head and pursed his painted lips thoughtfully. "I think it will have to get much worse before it gets better."

Mrs. Caudri whispered through gritted teeth, "Villain."

The Nazz draped an arm over William's shoulder. "I can hardly be blamed for my actions. After all, this is an election year, and a crisis of this proportion, handled correctly, could see me moving into the mayor's office."

He moved to the window, drawing the heavy maroon curtain aside with a long, brass-tipped finger, and watched as a brace of sheep fell and then hobbled away. "I must admit I was looking forward to the rush of the campaign—especially the ah, debates—but thanks to young William here I should be able to wrap it all up in one grand play and cast myself in the unlikely role of hero. It's not as good as Bartybus Austane asking me for help but there's still my birthday to come so hope is not lost."

William stared at the wizard in disbelief. "Are you—are you serious? You're going to wait until it gets worse before you help?"

"Oh, no." The Nazz paused to reflect and then continued. "If it doesn't progress to boils and locust soon I may have to push it along myself. It's hardly a dramatic rescue if I save the city from a plague of puppies. Everything before first-born son I should think; I'm an only child you see."

"That's no surprise at all," Mrs. Caudri scoffed.

"Madam, the safety of the council in times of crisis is paramount." The Nazz smirked, but when he noticed Mrs. Caudri's stare he transformed it into an exaggerated frown, "All for the public good . . . or something."

William was too slow to react, and the rush to transform openmouthed astonishment into a sympathetic smile left him looking like an idiot. He held out his hand to show the way. "You'll need to see the spell. The laboratory is through here."

"Yes. Good boy. Timing is so important. Voters are always more grateful when they haven't been struck blind or had their intestines spontaneously explode. Lead on."

The Nazz pushed open the door to the laboratory and strode confidently to the desk.

He tapped the books with his finger, pushing each off the desk in turn. "Got it, got it, have the newer edition, got it, read it—got it as gift, clearly does not grow hair as advertised, got it, heard very good things about this one from a female acquaintance." He moved the thin blue-bound volume to a clear corner of the desk. "We'll call it my fee."

William couldn't believe how self-involved this man was. He was supposed to be helping. "Sir, the spell is on the desk. Here."

"Right, right, the plagues." The Nazz wheeled dramatically and stood beside the chair. When William neither made a sound nor seemed ready to move, the wizard sighed and inclined his head toward the chair.

"Oh!" William pulled the chair out.

The Nazz sat as if a crowd was waiting to applaud. He fussed with his scarf, rolled his shoulders, lolled his neck, straightened his robe, and only after William had tucked the chair into the desk did he seem to notice the spell in front of him. "This is it?"

"Yes sir."

"Let's see. Hmm . . ." The Nazz tapped his puckered lips lightly as he read. He stopped when he was about half way down the page. "Are you sure? This spell?"

"Absolutely."

"Have you actually read it?"

William hesitated. "Ah . . . um . . ."

The old wizard's thin, purple lips stretched wide in a revelatory smile. He picked up the spell and held it up to William. "You can't read this, can you?"

"That word there means rain—" The words spilled out of William before he realized.

"—oh, excellent," the Nazz mocked. "The punctuation's atrocious—Barty was never one for detail, that's why he never made it into public service—and look here," he indicated a paragraph about two thirds of the way down the page, "he's tacked on a bit about ridding the house of pests; rats, moles, mice, and the like. Your mangled pronunciation has managed to do more by accident than most black scarves do on purpose. This is a spell for making a rainbow without an actual storm."

William forgot himself and pulled the page out of the Nazz's casual grip. He stared at words. "It can't be."

In through the open door strode William's master, his wide, generous grin like a beacon. "It can and it is. I thought it would be nice way to celebrate your first birthday with us, but you've spoiled that." He cuffed the boy on the back of the head.

"And the trip to Cay?" William asked.

"Spoiled too, I'm afraid. But judging by the weather I might have waited too long to start you on Arcaenum. I'd have been back sooner, but there's a stiff hail of lemmings coming down near the north gate and I was forced to come round the long way."

The Nazz pushed himself away from the desk and stood, sliding the blue book under his arm. "I quite enjoyed meeting you, William. If you're looking for a job when you're finished draining this fossilized old spark of all he has to teach you, you could do worse than clerking in my office."

Bartybus held out a hand to stop the other wizard from squeezing past him to the door. He tapped the spine of the book the Nazz was holding. "I would warm you about using this near livestock, but you've probably taken it for that exact purpose. Well, anyway, enjoy."

The Nazz returned a lascivious smirk as he exited the laboratory, leaving William and Bartybus alone.

"We shouldn't waste any time. There's no telling what this storm of yours will do next." Bartybus waded into the corner of the laboratory that doubled as supply closet and refuse heap. He began piling empty crates and other odds and ends behind him, humming to himself as he rummaged.

William didn't raise his head as he asked, "Aren't you going to punish me?"

"Oh, dear, yes, that would go without saying." Bartybus paused and leaned on the small barrel he was about to move. "Although, have you noticed that it never does?"

William sometimes felt that Bartybus enjoyed making him feeling stupid. "What?"

"Go without saying. It seems someone always has to say it and then a great many people seem compelled to talk about what everyone agrees doesn't need saying until their spit dries up. Don't you find that strange?" He shrugged.

Bartybus finally found what he'd apparently been looking for: a long wrought-iron rod topped by an elaborate copper vane. He held it out for William.

"What's this?" the apprentice said, taking the rod with both hands.

"A lightning rod. We'll need it to counter the storm and provide a lesson for you. And by lesson I mean punishment. Come along, and mind you don't impale any falling livestock on it."

William followed, uncomfortably aware of the weight of the heavy iron pike he carried.

Peter had not been exaggerating about the weather. It was horrible.

Most of the rats must have been culled or returned to the sewers when the cats had started falling, but now vast colonies of black and red ants carpeted the streets.

Despite whole regiments crushed under his boots, the insects showed none of the deference or fear the rats had shown Mrs. Caudri, though they seemed entirely ignorant of his master's presence. William's ankles were peppered with ant bites, and the hem of his robe had acquired a crawling, checkerboard fringe.

As they passed through the narrow gate of Lamber Park and onto the open green, Bartybus lifted the lightning rod from William's shoulder. On any normal day the ladies from the Gissini Court would have occupied the shaded benches, smoking their fat-bowled pipes and trading gossip. Today the shade was being enjoyed by a herd of torpid earthpigs, gorged on a feast of ants.

Using the blunt end of the lightning rod, Bartybus carved a line of symbols, words in Arcaenum, in the ground. When he had completed a second line, he called William over.

"You're going to stand there," Bartybus pointed to the first symbol, "with this." He passed the lightning rod back to him. "When the lightning first hits, you'll feel a strong urge to run away and possibly wet yourself because lightning is extremely bright and can be quite scary the first few times you're struck. Don't. Keep a solid hold on this and move to a new symbol after each strike. Once the last one is charged you can just let go, but don't step off as there might be some residual discharge, but it will be relatively weak."

"Relatively?" William's voice cracked at the bottom of his throat, and his last words escaped in a horse whisper. "What if I get hit?"

"That's what this is for." Bartybus lifted his tin cap off, his hair rebounding to form a curly brown halo, and pushed it down on William's head.

"Won't this attract the lightning?"

"Excellent, yes. You'll remain to make sure the spell says balanced and to siphon off any overflow. It's astonishingly painful, but aside from some hair loss there won't be any permanent damage."

William reached up to touch his hair but found the smooth surface of the tin cap.

"Hazard of the job I'm afraid."

Bartybus stepped back and began to read out the

spell. Each word hung in the air after it was spoken, overlapping the others until it become a tuneless roar.

Above, the black belly of a cloud brightened ominously, and the thunder that rolled behind it did not diminish but gathered strength and threatened to break the sky.

The air became saturated with the smell of ozone, and the hair on William's arms lifted; he tightened his grip on the lightning rod.

In that moment before the lightning struck, it occurred to the young apprentice that he might have underestimated the utility of forecasting the weather and overstated the bother.

He wasn't sure that this was the lesson he was supposed to have learned or if Bartybus had another in mind, but it was certainly better than the one he was about to experience.

Don't prance around in a thunderstorm wearing a tin hat.

Narrator: *Into every life, a little rain must fall. For all our sakes, hope William remembers the last time he misspelled with natural forces before he tries reading on his own again.*

KELL BROWN left high school convinced that there were far better ways to make a good living than writing. He tried nearly all of them before he came to understand that it was impossible for him to have a good life doing anything other than writing and hopes to misspend the rest of his life doing it. He lives and avoids work in Toronto (Canada) with a daughter he dotes on shamelessly and a wife he neither deserves nor ever really wanted, and yet she forgives him for both. This is his first published story.

Totally Devoted 2 U

John Zakour

Narrator: *Ah, love. It's all you need. It can also be more than some people deserve. That never stopped someone like Tina.*

It was beautiful summer day. The sky was blue, the sun was shining, birds were chirping away as though they didn't have a care in the world. Tina should have been happy. Only she wasn't. She was frustrated over her man. Tina and Jerry had been going out for over three years now, and he still wasn't nearly as devoted to her as she wanted him to be.

Tina didn't know why. It couldn't have been her. After all, she kept herself in good shape. She went to the gym if not every other day then every other, other day. She was still pleasant on the eyes. She may have been thirty-one, but her friends insisted she didn't look a day over twenty-eight. Not a week went by when she didn't catch at least one guy checking her out as she walked by. Tina wasn't just a pretty face; she had a great job bringing in solid money as one of Buffalo, New York's, leading fashion designers. To top it off she had a winning personality and a great sense of humor.

Yet, all of that wasn't good enough for Jerry. Tina couldn't shake the feeling that even when they were together, they weren't really together. Jerry was always off somewhere else. He never looked her lovingly in the eyes, claiming it wasn't that he didn't love her but that it wasn't manly. Whenever they were in a bar, restaurant, or just walking down the street, Tina would catch him not so subtly checking out all the other women. She was sure this meant Jerry wasn't happy with her. He would leave the second somebody better came along.

Sure it may have been her imagination, but it probably wasn't. Nah, it couldn't be. She had a good ability for judging people. If Tina didn't do something fast, Jerry and she would be history. She knew it and dreaded it. The problem was, Tina didn't know what she could do.

Then, by chance, Tina walked by Madam Marla's Magic Boutique. It was funny, Tina had walked down this street hundreds of times before during her lunch break and never noticed this strange little shop. She shrugged. It had to be fate. That meant she needed to check the place out. Tina wasn't one to tempt fate.

Tina opened the door and peeked her head in. The place was small and not much to look at. There was a table with a velvet tapestry draped over it and a young lady sitting behind it. The lady was a pretty little thing with dark wavy hair and a dark complexion; she was intently concentrating on a notebook computer. Tina felt she'd made a mistake.

"Oh, sorry," Tina said to the young lady. "Wrong building," as she slowly backed out of the door.

The young lady smiled. "Please come in, Tina," she said. "There is more here that meets the eye, mind, and the heart."

Tina stopped her retreat and stuck her head back into the shop. "How do you know my name?"

"I know all and tell even more," the lady said in a quivering voice. She smiled and pointed to Tina's lapel, "Plus, you're wearing your ID tag from work."

"Oh, right," Tina said with a weak grin.

"I am Madam Marla," the lady said. She motioned for Tina to come and in. "Please, sit. I sense you need my special help."

"You look pretty young to be a madam," Tina said walking up to the table.

Marla looked at her and winked. "You'd be surprised how old I really am," she said.

"I'd guess twenty-five," Tina said sitting down.

"Okay, maybe you wouldn't be surprised," Marla conceded. "Still they've been a really full twenty-five years." Marla looked Tina in the eyes. "I take it you're having trouble with your man Jerry."

Tina sat back in her chair. "How did you know that?" she asked.

Marla grinned. "Honey, when you're your age it's always about man troubles."

"But how did you know my man's name was Jerry?"

"I Googled you and came up with this picture of you and Jerry at your friend Kathy's wedding."

Marla turned her notebook to face Tina. Sure enough, there on the screen was a picture of Tina and Jerry sharing a token kiss for the camera. Tina was wearing an orange taffeta bridesmaid dress she simply hated. There was also another picture of Tina glaring at Jerry as he was checking out the other bridesmaids. Tina had never noticed that picture or the look on her face before.

Marla swung the computer back toward herself. She shook her head. "It's amazing what people will put on MySpace.com. Some people just have no shame." Marla looked up at Tina. "You know, I can help you."

Tina leaned forward. "You can."

"Of course I can. I'm a magical madam. It says so on my door, my card, and my Web site."

"I just want Jerry to be more devoted to me," Tina said.

Marla nodded. "That's what we all want, honey." She started typing away at her computer. "My rates are reasonable," she said without looking up. "Twenty-five dollars per spell. Each spell is guaranteed to work."

"I don't want to hurt Jerry," Tina said a bit nervously.

"Sure you don't," Marla said halfheartedly as she continued to type. She looked up at Tina. "Don't worry, this won't harm him at all. It will make him totally devoted to you." Marla stopped typing and smiled. "Done."

"Done?"

"Yep."

Tina looked at her. "So where is it?"

Marla shook her head. "It's in your e-mail inbox, silly. Call in sick for the afternoon. Go home and relax a bit. Magic is always best done on a clear mind. When the clock reaches the specified time, follow the directions, and, presto, your man will be totally devoted."

Tina just looked at her.

"Trust me," Marla said. "You can pay me online after it works. I accept all major forms of credit cards and PayPal."

"Oh, okay," Tina said.

"If you don't pay me, I'll either turn you into a newt or bombard you with filter-proof spam." Marla smiled. "Don't worry. I'm kidding about the spam part. I'm not that mean." She motioned to the door. "Now go. Go. By tonight you'll be a much happier woman."

Tina decided to heed Marla's advice. After all, she had nothing to lose. She called the office from her cell phone and told them she was taking the rest of the day as a personal day. She hopped in her car and drove home. Without the rush hour traffic it was a quick twenty-minute drive. Even if the magic mumbo jumbo didn't work, at least she'd have a little downtime today.

When Tina arrived at her apartment, she kicked off her shoes by the door, then headed straight to her computer. She sat down and logged in. After filtering through a few Viagra ads, there was an e-mail from MagicMarla. It was simple enough:

> To make your man totally devoted 2 U: At exactly 7 PM EST, put three candles in a north-facing window of your bedroom, light the first and third candle, face south and spin around two times chanting (and sounding as much like Olivia Newton-John as you can): Totally Devoted to Me. Totally Devoted to Me. Blow out the candle on the left, then the candle on the right. Facing north, light a new match and use it to ignite the middle candle and POOF your man is totally devoted.
>
> Disclaimer: all magic is nonrefundable and irreversible. By casting this spell you agree to these terms.

Tina shook her head. No way that could work.

An instant message for MagicMarla popped open on her screen.

> Trust me. I designed the spell especially 4 U. It works. CU.

Tina typed back:

> R U sure? Exactly 7PM?

To which MagicMarla responded:

LOL. Of course I'm sure. It doesn't have to be EXACTLY 7 you have a few minutes each way. Magic is precise but not inflexible. B2W.

The message window closed. Tina took a deep breath. She thought for a second. She had three candles. Her bedroom did have a nice window facing north. She even had matches left from her aromatherapy days. Of course the spell probably wouldn't work—it couldn't work. Still, more for fun than anything else, Tina did set three candles on her bedroom's windowsill. She most likely wasn't going to go through with the spell, but just in case she did, she wanted to be ready.

Tina passed the rest of the afternoon catching up on a few soap operas and watching Oprah. She used to love Oprah before she was a working girl. It was nice to be able to connect with her again. Sure, she could record Oprah's show on her DVR, but somehow she always preferred to watch Oprah "live" when the rest of her fellow females were tuned in. Tina didn't know why. She just did.

Jerry dragged himself into the apartment at around 6:30. As always, he looked worn out. Apparently being a CPA was lot more physically demanding than most people realized. He gave Tina a nod of acknowledgment as he plopped down on the couch.

"How was your day, honey?" she asked.

He grabbed the remote and flipped on the TV. "Okay," he grunted. "Have you ordered the pizza yet?"

Tina shook her head. "I thought we could do something different and go out for dinner tonight."

Jerry shook his head. "It's Thursday. Pizza night. I look forward to my night of pizza, beer, and a ball game." He gave her a weak smile then added, "With my favorite girl."

"Oh, okay," Tina said weakly.

"Could you grab me a beer from the fridge?" he asked, focusing his attention on the TV.

"Sure," Tina said, sulking as she walked toward the kitchen. She went to the fridge and grabbed a beer. If there had been any doubt in her mind, it had now been obliterated. She walked into the living room and set the beer down in front of Jerry.

"Thanks, hon," he said without looking at her.

Tina took a deep breath. "I'm going to go into our room and relax for a while," she told him.

"Did you order the pizza?" he asked.

"I will," Tina said.

"Great," he said, pulling his eyes away from the TV for a second. "Have fun. I'll call you when the pizza guy gets here."

"You do that," Tina said as she headed into the bedroom.

Tina sat down on her bed and mediated for a few minutes. She had time to kill, so she figured clearing her mind was the way the go. She wanted to make sure she was doing the right thing. Even if it probably wasn't going to work, using magic on her man was a fairly drastic step. Jerry wasn't that bad. Was he? He wasn't so inattentive and self-absorbed that she needed to try to resort to magic. He couldn't be that bad. Could he?

"Honey, have you ordered the pizza yet?" Jerry called from the living room. "I'm starved."

Tina looked at the clock radio on her nightstand. It read 6:59. She took one big deep breath and stood up. The clock flipped to 7:00. Tina grabbed a book of matches from the nightstand and walked to the candles in the window. She lit a match and used it to light the first candle, then the third. She blew out the match.

She turned south then spun around once half-heartedly singing, "Totally devoted to me."

She completed one turn, spun again, singing, "Totally devoted to me."

She stopped spinning and turned back toward the candles. She blew out the first candle. She blew out the third candle. She lit another match and used it to light the middle candle. She paused for a moment. There was no flash of energy. No big poof. All in all it was a bit of letdown. She blew out the match about a second after it singed her finger.

Tina shrugged. "That was a waste of time," she mumbled, walking back into the living room.

To her surprise, Jerry wasn't sitting on the couch any longer.

"Jerry?" Tina called.

Tina heard a very distinct, "Woof!" She turned toward the sound. There, standing anxiously at the door, was a little poodle.

"Jerry?" Tina called again.

"Woof!" the dog responded again.

Tina looked down at the fluffy brown poodle. "It can't be," she said to herself, walking over the pooch. Was it her imagination, or did the poodle's fur color perfectly match Jerry's hair color?

Tina noticed the dog was wearing an ID tag. She bent over to check out whom the dog belonged to. The tag read: "Jerry" and had Tina's address on it. Tina gulped. Jerry the poodle tilted his head up at her with a look that could only be described as total devotion. He licked her hand. Tina shook her head. She sighed. This wasn't quite what she had in mind.

Tina scooped Jerry up under one arm, grabbed her car keys, and headed out the door. She needed to

make a personal trip to Madam Marla's. This was
something e-mail or IMing couldn't do justice to.

As Tina raced to Madam's Marla's, Jerry happily
sat in the passenger seat, holding his nose out the
window to sniff the air while somehow managing to
also keep one eye locked on Tina. It might have been
Tina's imagination, but she swore she had never seen
him so happy.

Tina drove up to Marla's shop and pulled into a
parking space right in front. She thought she was lucky
Marla's was still open. Of course, luck is a relative
thing when your boyfriend is a poodle. Tina got out
of the car. She held the door open for Jerry to follow.
He just stood there gazing at her with those devoted
little puppy dog eyes.

"Come on," Tina coaxed. "Be a good boy."

Jerry leaped into her arms. She cradled him. She
couldn't help but give him a little pat on the head as
she went into the shop. Tina found Marla contently
sitting at her table, looking at her computer.

"Phew, I'm glad to see you're still here," Tina said,
walking toward Marla.

Marla stood up and smiled. "Magic knows no
hours," she said. She shrugged. "Besides, I have no
life. Turn an ex-boyfriend or two into newts, and the
word gets around."

Tina pushed Jerry into Marla's face. "Look! Look
what you did."

Marla tickled Jerry under his curly little chin. "Cute
puppy," she said. She looked puzzled. "What do you
mean, I did it?" She shook her head. "This doesn't
look like my work. I'm partial to newts. You don't
have to clean up after them. They don't chew your
shoes. No need to . . ."

"This is Jerry!" Tina interrupted.

Marla took a step back. "You named your dog after
your boyfriend? I don't know if that's weird or kinky."

Tina held Jerry closer to Marla. "This *is* Jerry!" she shouted. "I cast your spell and this is what happened!" Tina took a deep breath. "I should sue you for mal-spell practice." She thought about what she had just said. She didn't know if there was such a thing as malpractice for madams, but she figured it sounded good.

"You did the spell already?" Marla asked.

"Duh!" Tina spat.

Marla's eyes wandered down to the clock on her computer screen. She grinned. "Phew. So the problem isn't with my magic."

"What are you talking about?" Tina demanded. "You said do the spell at 7. I did the spell at 7, and POOF my boyfriend is a poodle!"

Marla smiled at her. "Well, Tina, you wanted de-voted. Nothing is more unconditionally devoted then a dog," she pointed out.

Marla turned her computer around so Tina could see the screen. She indicated the little digital clock in the upper right hand corner. The time read: 7:54. "You weren't supposed to do the spell yet."

"Your e-mail said do the spell at 7. I cast the spell at 7!" Tina waved at the computer. "Look at the time!"

Marla hit a button on her computer. An e-mail message in a text window zoomed open. She touched the screen right over the text window. "If you read this carefully you'll see I did not mess up," she said.

"How can you say that? You turned my boyfriend into a dog!" Tina shouted.

"No need to yell," Marla said. "I'm younger than most madams. I still have excellent hearing. Besides, *you* turned your boyfriend into a dog." Marla gave Jerry a little pat on the head. "He is a cute one."

"I followed your directions!" Tina insisted.

Marla shook her head. "Ah, no. You didn't. If you

had, you'd be doing the spell about five minutes from now, more or less."

"Are you crazy? You said 7 and it's now 7:55!"

"I said, *Eastern Standard* Time. We're on *Daylight Savings* Time now. You did the spell an hour early. I guess the powers-that-be must have thought you were really anxious, so they made Jerry really devoted."

"Damn," Tina said. "I always get that mixed up."

Marla patted her on the shoulder. "Don't worry, you're not alone; it is really confusing."

"Can you undo it?"

"Daylight Savings Time?"

"No, me turning Jerry in a dog."

Marla shook her head. "You read the disclaimer: All magic is nonrefundable and irreversible. If it weren't, people would either be begging for their money back or trying to fix things and mucking them up more, all the time." She paused for a second. "My lawyer insisted I put that clause in. I'm sure glad I did."

Tina looked at Jerry snuggled up in her arms. He was now contentedly sniffing her underarm. She had to give the powers-that-be credit. He certainly was devoted. She gave Jerry a gentle scratch behind the ears. He whimpered contentedly.

Tina turned her attention back to Marla. "What am I suppose to do about Jerry?"

"Get him a nice comfy pet bed, some yummy dog treats, and a sturdy leash. Oh, and hope your next boyfriend is a dog lover."

Narrator: *Young love. A dog biscuit and a scritch behind the ears. That look of total devotion, a misspell away.*

JOHN ZAKOUR is a humor/science fiction/fantasy writer with a master's degree in human behavior. He has written zillions (well, thousands) of gags for syndicated comics and comedians (including *Rugrats*, *Grimmy*, *Marmaduke*, *Bound and Gagged*, *Dennis the Menace*, *The Tonight Show*, and Joan Rivers' old TV show). John also writes his own syndicated comic, *Working Daze* for United Media. John has been a regular contributor to *Nickelodeon* magazine, writing *Fairly Odd Parents*, *Rugrats*, and *Jimmy Neutron* comic books, and is now writing a new comic called *Caramel Crew*.

John's humorous science fiction mystery book, *The Plutonium Blonde* (DAW 2001, cowritten with Larry Ganem, started as an interactive Web story for the Sci Fi Channel) was named one of the top thirty science fiction books of 2001 by *The Chronicle of Science Fiction*, which called it, "the funniest SF book of 2001." His second novel, *The Doomsday Brunette* (DAW 2004) has made the *Locus* bestsellers list, and the third book in the series, *The Radioactive Redhead*, was released 2005. The fourth, *The Frost-Haired Vixen* (the first written alone) hit stores December 2006, and the fifth, *The Blue-haired Bombshell*, was published in December 2007.

The Mysterious Case of Spell Zero

Rob St. Martin

Narrator: *A fog-shrouded street . . . echoing footsteps . . . mystery building upon mystery. The game's afoot for Inspectors Nightingale and Frankford, but it will take more than adroit detective work to unravel this misspell.*

The crystal ball across the room from us chimed softly, alerting us to an incoming telecommune. I looked at my fellow inspector, Donoval Frankford.

"I answered it last time," he said.

"You know," I replied, "I remember when you first came to the unit. A member of the gentry with notions of the responsibilities of the aristocracy to the 'little people.' "

"A week with you lot taught me where I could stick my notions," he said.

The crystal chimed again.

"This is exactly why civilization as we know it is falling to ruin."

"That's certainly possible, but I answered it last time."

There was, as always, no escaping his logic.

As I reached the crystal, I lifted the answering

wand, tapping the ball thrice. The swirling mists within the ball coalesced to reveal a constable, easily identified by the cockscomb helmet he wore and the handlebar mustache all raw recruits seemed determine to grow.

"Thaumaturgic Investigations Unit, Inspector Nightingale," I said. "How can I help you, Constable?"

"Sorra t' disturb yeh, sah," the constable said, his Northshire accent thick enough to spread on toast.

"Not at all, Constable. We live to serve."

"Yis, sah," he replied, my wry humor falling on deaf ears. "S'like this, sah. 'Ad us free dozens reports, sah."

"Three dozen reports, Constable?"

"Yis, sah."

"Reports of what, Constable?"

"Prublims wi' spells, sah."

"Constable, did you not, when I initially responded to your call, hear me answer, 'Thaumaturgic Investigations Unit'? Did you not, from this, deduce that we here deal with problematical spellworkings? Is this not the very reason you have seen fit to call upon our aid?"

"Will . . . yis, sah."

"Then tell me, why you are wasting our time? Everything we deal with here is a problem with spells. Please—be as forthcoming and succinct as possible."

It seemed either I'd intimidated him into near-babbling incoherence or dazzled him with my erudition, as he required further prompting. My long years as a constable myself served me well, for I was able to cut through his thick accent and determine that the three dozen reports had been of spells completely failing in their desired goals, all within the Middleton precinct.

"Very well, Constable. We'll be right down."

As he began to respond in his virtually incomprehensible fashion, I used the wand to sever the telecommune. I turned to Frankford, whose features displayed amusement and confusion in equal measure.

"You heard?" I asked.

"I heard. Whether or not I understood is open to debate."

"Three dozen spells reported not working in Middleton."

"What's in Middleton?"

"Shops. People. People shopping. Shopkeepers selling."

"Very clarifying. It amuses me that the circumvention for which you berate constables is something for which you yourself are somewhat infamous."

"I'm an amusing fellow."

"I was just saying that to the wife the other night."

"You're not married."

"I do apologize, I thought we were creating fictions."

"Middleton is mainly a shop district."

"Indeed. Any Practitioners of the Art?"

"None of note of whom I'm aware. Shall we depart for Middleton?"

"Do, let's."

As we exited Constabulary Manor and flagged a passing carriage, the smells of Antium struck me, calling up memories of my childhood here in the City of Mages. The sooty smell of the coal fires burning in home stoves. The spoiled egg smell of gas lamps as they lit the foggy gloom. And under it all, the vaguely fishy smell of the River Blyne, cutting through the city like a scar through a pirate's eye.

"What do you think?" Frankford asked as the carriage made its way down cobbled streets. "Someone running cons?"

"Counterfeiting what, though? There's no coin to be made passing off chicken bones as bat wings or frogs' eyes for newts'. Eye of newt goes a ha'penny the pair. And the scammer would be caught soon enough."

"What then?"

"We'll simply have to wait and see, Frank. Patience, virtue, all that."

"Do you really want to spend the night interviewing victims?"

"Not at all. For one thing, most honest folk are nestled in their beds, and I suspect they will display reluctance, if not outright disinclination, to speak to us at this hour. The victims will wait until the morrow."

"Then why are we riding out into this gloomy night?"

"In order to interview Constable Albert Smithton and his colleagues at the Middleton Precinct."

"Guides preserve us."

"May they indeed."

We lapsed into a companionable silence, broken only by the hard clop of the horse's steel-shod hooves and the rattle of the undercarriage. Once we arrived in Middleton, I instructed the driver to let us off. Frankford paid the man, making sure to obtain a receipt for the constabulary's finance department to lose. Once the cabbie had departed, Frank looked at me, curious.

"We can walk from here," I explained. "To get a lay of the land."

"Once a constable, always a constable."

"Not everyone has your connections, Frank."

"Not everyone has my marks on the inspector's exams, either."

We walked along the cobbled streets, gas lamps creating pockets of light in the night. A low fog roiled about our feet; down by the Blyne, it would be a real peasouper. You wouldn't be able to see five feet in front of you, a night like this. The empty streets, lined with shuttered, darkened windows, shop signs creaking as they swung in the faint breeze, made the shop district seem like a dolly mop without her rouges, frills, and ribbons: naked, unappealing, colorless.

"Rather like a corpse, isn't it?" Frankford commented, quietly. "All the life is gone."

"I was thinking something depressingly similar."

"Depressingly similar, or similarly depressing?"

"Your mastery of semantics is legendary. Both."

We walked on in silence, up street and down alley. After a while, I directed my partner along a broader avenue, which led to the Middleton Precinct House. I asked him for the time. Frank removed his pocket watch from his waistcoat, examining the timepiece by the dim glow of the streetlamp.

"Half past ten, near enough."

"Long enough for them to get their stories straight, but not so long they solve our case for us, would you say?"

"You've a nasty, suspicious mind, Night."

"Thanks, Frank."

We had unfortunately underestimated the valor and street cunning of the constables in question.

"We knows 'oo dunnit, sah," were the first words out of Constable Smithton's mostachioed mouth the moment we'd identified ourselves.

Frank gave me an unpleasant look. I stifled the urge to strangle the constable.

"Have you?" I asked him.

"Oh, yis, sah!"

A long, wearying period of questioning later, Frankford and I had determined two things: that there was, in fact, something odd about this case and that the Middleton constables, Smithton in particular, hadn't the sense the Guides gave a carrot.

"Only fing is, sah, why I fink its tha' butcher what done it? 'E's furin, 'e is."

"Is he indeed?" Frank asked, ushering the good constable from our presence in the interrogation room. "Well, that's sure to be a crime in itself. Thank you, Constable, that's all." Frank closed the door and turning to face me. "What do you think?"

"I think Smithton's sure to rise to the rank of Lieutenant soon enough."

"No argument there. What of the case?"

"Thirty-six complaints of occult fraud since the new moon is odd enough, I'd say."

"Quite so. Not to mention the unreported complaints, the existence of which I've no doubt."

"Nor I. They seem convinced the butcher's involved."

"Of course they do. He's foreign, after all." In that simple phrase, Frankford implied a wealth of opinion concerning the constables and their theory.

"Which, in regard to the Middleton constabulary, might as well be anyone not from Middleton."

"You know what this means, of course. Thirty-six victims to question."

"Thirty-six complaints since the new moon, which was, what? Nine days ago?"

"Nine into thirty-six is four, meaning uncontrolled magic afoot."

"We received the call at nine thirteen. I noted it when I answered the crystal."

"Nine, an unresolved power struggle. Twice, indicating an escalation of that struggle."

"Yes, but my point was, nine and thirteen are twenty-two. The number of the Guides."

"Oh, dear."

"I'd say, numerologically speaking, we'd be better off at the bottom of the Blyne."

With a stern warning to the constables of the Middleton Precinct not to speak of this case and to conduct no further investigations of their own, Frankford and I returned to Constabulary Manor.

"What are your thoughts?" Frankford asked.

"I think that we have a long day ahead of us tomorrow, and all the auspices point toward this not being a simple case. I think I want to go home and crawl into bed."

"Go home, Night. I have some research I want to do."

"Very well. See you tomorrow, then."

"Bright and early."

"Don't remind me."

Morning came early, but far from bright. Low, dark clouds promised rain before day's end. As I walked the streets of Antium from my flat to the Manor, I mulled the case over in my mind. Frankford had learned in the course of his studies that deductive reasoning and examination of the evidence would eventually lead any detective to the culprit responsible. I had come up through the ranks, learning to rely on my instinct. Right now, my instinct was saying there was something significant about this case. A few complaints of occult fraud, usually tracked to some huckster new to the city, was nothing unusual. Generally they never even made it to our unit. But thirty-six complaints? Constable Smithton had been right in one respect—this was definitely a case for the TIU.

Climbing the stairs to our offices, I noticed something decidedly out of place. Outside the captain's office stood an ogre. Well-dressed and obviously well-trained, he was small—for an ogre—the top of his balding head barely cresting the doorjamb. He affected a casual attitude, but I noticed that he observed everything, his beady black eyes darting this way and that, rapidly assessing any and all who came into view.

A bodyguard, then. Not many could afford an ogre bodyguard.

My hard-learned instincts told me to investigate. At the top of the stairs, I turned right toward the captain's office, rather than left toward the unit's. I stopped at the tea trolley and poured myself a cuppa with a twist of lemon, making sure the bodyguard saw me do so. A man with a cup of tea in his hands isn't looking for a fight, they say. Boiling hot water in a glass vessel is a handy weapon, says I.

I walked up to the captain's office, sipping my tea, keeping my eyes on the captain's attractive young secretary, Polly.

"Hallo, Polly. What's all this, then?" I asked, with a nod of my head toward the ogre.

"Captain has a visitor," Polly replied, a little prissily. An important visitor, then. She only ever put on airs when the captain was being made more important by proxy.

"I can see that, can't I?" I answered. "Listen, I've got to talk to him. I'll just pop in and—"

The bodyguard was suddenly in front of the door, in front of me, with his hand flat against my chest.

"No one goes in," he warned. I looked up, past the low tusks jutting from spittle-flecked lips, and stared him square in the eye.

Rule Number One when dealing with an opponent: You are the constable. He is merely a citizen. Constables do not bluster to citizenry. Calm confidence will get you out of a fight faster than you got yourself into one.

"You'll want to move that hand, my son," I said, as calmly as I could, staring eight feet of muscled menace in the eye.

"No one goes in," the bodyguard repeated.

"It's quite all right, Henrich," a man said, stepping out of the captain's office. Dressed posh as you can, gray beard trimmed square, heavy gold chain of office resting around his neck. Not just any councillor, this— this was Argent Dupuis, the Viceroy of the Council of Mages, second in power only to Chancellor Ravenstar himself.

"My business with Captain MacCready is concluded," Viceroy Dupuis said.

Henrich still hadn't moved his hand, and I wasn't about to back down.

"Nightingale," the captain warned. Only then did I step back.

"Inspector Nightingale?" the Viceroy asked, impressed. "The man responsible for capturing the Invisible Strangler?"

"My reputation precedes me," I answered.

"Allow me to shake your hand, Inspector Nightingale," the viceroy said, offering me his hand. I shook it. Firm grip, his eyes never left mine.

"The entire city owes you a debt of thanks, Inspector Nightingale," he said.

"I'll remember that come payday."

"Ha ha," he laughed, not really laughing, then turned to the captain. "Captain MacCready. Inspector Nightingale. Come, Henrich."

I watched the councillor and his hired muscle leave the building.

"My office, Nightingale. Now."

The captain's office was nice enough, well decorated, though small for a man of his rank. He'd been offered larger on another floor, but he preferred to be closer to his men.

"You and Frankford are investigating some cases of occult fraud," the captain said as he sat at his desk, going through the many reports stacked before him.

"We are, sir. How did you—"

"Never mind that, man. You'll exercise the utmost discretion in this case, Inspector."

"As always, sir."

A raised eyebrow eloquently explained exactly what he thought of my reply.

"Utmost discretion, Nightingale."

"As you say, sir. Utmost discretion. May one inquire why, sir?"

"No, one may not," he replied, but a significant glance out the door toward where the viceroy had gone told me all I needed to know. Politics.

"That's all, Inspector."

"Thank you, sir."

In our shared office, I related to Frankford what had transpired.

"Politics," he spat. In the mouth of a member of the constabulary, it was as foul an oath as could be uttered.

"That's the lay of it, my lad."

"What's to be done?"

"Utmost discretion."

"Indeed."

The average person on the average day has trouble remembering what had transpired the previous week. Frankford and I had thirty-six apparent victims to prompt through the preceding ten days, trying to determine if they had done anything out of the ordinary, seen anyone suspicious, or purchased anything shady. After those thirty-six individuals, none of whom were particularly erudite or polite, we had to question the various enchanters, mediums, seers, and other minor Practitioners by whom the victims had allegedly been victimized. Those worthies held fast in their conviction that the spells for which they had been contracted— or the assorted potions, charms, or ingredients they had sold—should have worked perfectly. This was, however, the opposite of what had actually occurred.

As Constable Smithton had so eloquently observed, the spells had, quite simply, not worked.

After three days of investigation, exercising the utmost discretion, Frank and I found ourselves at an impasse. We'd interviewed dozens of people, compiled list after list, run down the usual confidence schemers, invented wild theories. We'd talked to experts and specialists, Practitioners and coven leaders. Not a one of them offered us anything solid.

Frank went down the list of victims and accused alike.

"The enchantress says her virility potion should have turned the clerk well-nigh into a satyr; however, she thinks the lavender she bought might have been stale. Her apothecary, however, insists that he sells only the freshest ingredients. The necromancer hired to ensure the safe passage of the widow's husband's shade maintains that the angelica he used he cultivated himself. The seer claims that the future is clouded with possibility."

"Which is another way of saying he doesn't know what happened."

"The shaman says his spirit guides would only speak after the full moon. The medium says she—"

"Your point is made, Frank. They have almost no connection to one another, and they're all hiding something. But there's something you missed."

"Oh?"

"They're all scared."

"Your fabled instinct?"

"Whatever it is they're hiding, it's got them frightened."

"Do you think someone is threatening them?"

"No."

"Then of what are they frightened?"

"I don't know."

Frank smoothed his oiled hair, leaning back in his chair. "Your fabled instinct isn't being particularly helpful, Night."

"I'm no seer, Frank." I drained my cup of the last of my tea, staring at the leaves, hoping for some clue. Illness, they predicted. Wonderful.

"Very well. Let's examine the clues once again."

"To what end? We've been through it a dozen times or more."

"From another perspective, then."

"If you insist." I went to the chalkboard at end of the room and began writing the names of the victims, drawing lines to their alleged victimizers, drawing lines to their assorted suppliers and various associates with whom they'd met in the days since the new moon. Only in the rarest of instances did any two or three lines collect at the same name.

"We're going to have to talk to all the associates and all the suppliers, aren't we?" I asked rhetorically.

"With the utmost discretion."

"Wonderful. Can we at least begin with these worthies?" I asked, indicating those few instances of multiple connection, to which Frankford readily agreed.

Two days later we were, as usual, rather occupied with the full moon, checking in on the city's lycanthropes, making sure they were well dosed or at least well chained. None of them reported any incidents, so we concluded that our cases of spell failure—which continued to be reported with worrisome and increasing incidence—were unlikely to be the result of bad ingredients.

"It's rather like an epidemic, isn't it?" Frankford asked me, a few days after the full moon. We'd just received our tenth report of the day concerning new spell failures. The captain was asking for daily accounts, and keeping the case discreet was becoming something of a joke—the reports had moved well beyond Middleton. All we needed was for some genteel family or some Practitioner of note to raise the hue and cry, and the story would be on the front page of the *Times*.

"How do you mean?"

"See here. This charm-maker, this seer, and this medium all went to the alchemist on Horseback Road. But the alchemist is having troubles of his own. He knows this apothecary here, and so does this necromancer, the shaman from Near Street, and this illusionist, all of whom have reported or have been reported with failed spells. Now, I'd assume the apothecary is the culprit, except that the enchantress from Regent's Row, the witch from High Ridge Way, and the spellsinger from Eager Downs all insist they've never met the man, never gone into his shop."

"What're you getting at, Frank?"

"Well, say the enchantress knew the charm-maker, or perhaps they both know someone neither of them thought to mention. Not a client or supplier or associate, but perhaps a friend? Or someone they know from their covens?"

"Guides preserve us, Frank, you're not suggesting we interrogate all their friends and covenmates?"

"What I'm suggesting is what if this is larger than we think? You said it yourself, when the case began— there were thirty-six reported cases of spell failure. But what of all the unreported cases?"

"You think there are hidden links between these people?"

"Can there be any doubt?"

"So how is this like an epidemic?"

"How is plague transmitted?"

"Rats, isn't it?"

"Not just rats. People carry diseases as well."

"You think the spell failings are some sort of . . . magical disease? Passed from friend to associate to supplier to Practitioner?"

"Precisely."

"But how did it start? Usually in terms of a plague, there's someone who's the first to fall ill, the first to die, and the illness spreads from that first unfortunate."

"I've no idea."

"Let's have a look at the names again, then."

"Which names, though? Practitioners, suppliers, associates, covens?"

"Since we're looking into hidden connections, let's start with covens."

We'd made a list of all the covens who had members who had reported spell failings. In only a few instances, other members of those covens also reported similar failings.

"All this started with the new moon, so let's begin with those covens who met that night," Frank suggested.

"But what if it didn't start with one of these covens? What if the problem began with another coven?"

"And somehow spread to one of the covens on our list?"

"Do we know which covens met under the new moon?"

"I've that very information . . ." Frank sorted through his notes strewn about his desk. "Aha!" he cried triumphantly, producing a piece of paper covered in his neat, precise script. He ran his eyes down the page and stopped with a quizzically raised eyebrow. Wordlessly, he passed me the sheet.

I inspected the list, coming to a similar stop, noticing without a doubt the object of Frank's curiosity.

"James Ravenstar?" I asked.

"Son of the Chancellor of the Council of Mages. How interesting."

"The viceroy."

"I beg your pardon?"

"The Viceroy of the Council of Mages. He visited the captain the morning after that first report from Constable Smithton. Politics, remember?"

"A coincidence?"

"Not bloody likely. We'll need to talk to him."

"Never get it past the captain, old boy."

"We'll see about that."

Polly wasn't nearly as high and mighty this time around, not with inquiries and complaints from all directions coming to her desk at all hours. The captain was in but unavailable to callers. I didn't let that stop us, and an hour later I emerged with the necessary warrant. The captain's warrant got us inside the viceroy's Manor and an audience with the viceroy himself.

"How might I assist the constabulary?" Viceroy Dupuis asked, ushering us into a private drawing room.

"As I'm sure you're aware, Viceroy, my partner Inspector Nightingale and I are investigating a rather unusual number of spell failures."

We'd agreed that Frank would do the talking since my back tended to get up when dealing with the upper classes.

"Are you indeed?"

"Indeed we are, Viceroy. Ever since the new moon, we've been receiving reports of spells that simply failed to work as they ought. We are currently working on the assumption that some sort of magical disease is spreading through the community of Practitioners and their associates."

"How so?"

"We thought you might have some information on the matter," I said, just as the maid arrived with the tea. We busied ourselves with the pleasantries—*Milk? Sugar? Lemon?*—and then, once we'd had the first sip etiquette demanded, I repeated my inquiry.

"I can't imagine why you'd think I had anything to do with this matter."

"Do forgive my partner, Viceroy," Frank said smoothly. "He didn't mean to imply that at all, did you, Nightingale?"

"Indeed not, sir. Merely asking for your opinions, sir, an educated man such as yourself."

"I see. Very well."

"Have you any opinions or theories, Viceroy?" Frank asked.

"Why is it you assume this is some sort of disease?"

"The way the spell failures are spreading, Viceroy. It reminded us of the plague, spreading from afflicted to associate and so on. We attempted to ascertain the originator, but the names are too many."

"Perhaps, then, you ought to consider there may be more than one originator."

"How so, Viceroy?"

"How much do you know about covens, Inspector?"

"The constabulary's courses are quite thorough, Viceroy."

"Quite so. Covens are convened by like-minded Practitioners seeking to amplify their own powers by working toward a common goal, correct?"

"So we are taught, Viceroy."

"And you say the trail to the originator leads to too many names for a clear pattern to emerge?"

"Exactly so, sir."

"Then perhaps the originator is not a single person but rather a coven. These failures have been occurring since the new moon, you said?"

"That's correct, Viceroy."

"Then perhaps you ought to examine the covens that met under the new moon."

"As it happens, I've a list of those," I said, pulling out my notebook and flipping through the pages. "Compiled when we were working under the assump-

tion that there might be something sinister afoot. I
don't suppose you'd care to have a look at the list,
sir?"

"If you feel it might be of assistance, Inspector."

I handed him my notebook, open to the page I in-
tended. His eyes glanced down the page for a brief
moment, then back up at me.

"These are some rather prominent covens," he said,
"with members of high standing."

"Yes, sir, they are. Small chance of keeping the investigation discreet should we have to interrogate all
these Practitioners of high standing, sir."

"Interrogate, Inspector?"

"Sorry, sir. I meant interview, of course."

"We understand that some of those covens include
council members, Viceroy," Frank said.

"Do they indeed?"

"Indeed they do, sir," I answered. He knew, I realized. I knew he knew. And he knew I knew.

"There's one there, sir, the Society of the Incar-
nate? That one includes the son of the councillor himself, one James Ravenstar."

"So it does."

"Now, naturally, we'd prefer to avoid any undue
embarrassment," Frank said.

"Naturally."

"Tell me, Viceroy, do any of these covens strike
you as being likely?"

"Likely what, Inspector?"

"Just likely, Viceroy."

"I can hardly attribute guilt or innocence based on
a list of names, Inspector."

"Who said anything about guilt, Viceroy? We weren't
aware of any crimes being committed."

"Indeed not," added Frank. "Most if not all the
Practitioners suffering these spell failures have reim-
bursed or otherwise compensated their clients."

"So there are complaints but no charges filed. Yet. Unless there's something you'd like to address, Viceroy."

The viceroy busied himself with a long sip of his tea.

"An illness, you said?" he finally replied. So that's how he wanted to play it.

"That's only a theory, sir, but yes."

"And these spell failures, they just . . . happen? No other sign of magical interference?"

"None whatsoever, sir."

"Let us . . . postulate, Inspectors."

"Please do, sir."

"Say, for argument's sake, that this . . . illness you describe originated with one of the covens on your list."

"As you yourself suggested, sir."

"So I did. What would be the penalty for such an act?"

"Well, assuming it was performed with malicious intent, there are a number of misdemeanors with which the culprits could be charged."

"Reckless endangerment, at the very least," Frankford supplied helpfully. "Malicious mischief, of course."

"And the penalties for such?"

"Fines, possibly a few days' incarceration."

"I see. And should it be proven that the originators acted foolishly but not maliciously, Inspectors?"

"No crime in being stupid, Viceroy. More's the pity," I said.

"Quite so, quite so." He paused for a long moment. "Let us presume that the originators of this disease were acting foolishly. What you have described may be attributed to . . . a miscalculation on the part of the originators."

"A miscalculation, sir?"

"How so, Viceroy?"

He sipped from his teacup, collecting his thoughts.

"It's possible that one of those covens cast a spell to increase their own power, to draw upon the will of the Guides, what have you. But a slight miscalculation in their spell caused the magic to invert itself and turn on the casters. These Practitioners, unknowingly infected with this inverted antispell, thought the original spell simply hadn't worked, and they went their separate ways. As they came into contact with other Practitioners, the antispell, the true originator of the disease, infected them as well. If we assume the antispell attacks not the Practitioners themselves but rather the raw magic with which they are gifted, then as they meet with associates, this infected raw magic affects their associates' own magic, as like is drawn to like. That first antispell, let us call it Spell Zero, would have been the actual root of this illness."

"Fascinating, sir," I said.

"We're indebted to you, Viceroy," Frank added.

"How do we stop it, sir?"

"I beg your pardon?"

"We need to stop it, sir. Epidemic like this, people will panic. No way of knowing whether or not a spell will work? Too much of the city's economy revolves around spellwork. Can't have that, sir."

"Indeed not."

"If word got out that a coven was responsible, Viceroy, I don't like to think what kind of reaction the people would have. Antium may be the City of Mages, but not one in eight inhabitants has the gift. The other seven . . . might be none too happy, if you follow me."

"Yes, Inspector, you've made your point."

"Now, we've been charged with conducting this investigation with the utmost discretion, Viceroy, so if the Council of Mages would care to investigate this matter internally as it were, we could allow you that liberty."

"Could you?"

"We could, and, moreover, we will."

"Indeed? And in what manner might the Council of Mages repay this service?"

"Think nothing of it, Viceroy," I said.

"We live to serve the public good, sir," Frank added.

"Would you then require disclosure of the guilty parties' names?"

"No crime's been committed, sir."

"We simply seek to avert public outcry, Viceroy."

"Very well. We are in agreement."

"Your hand on that, sir," I said, offering him my own. He paused, knowing full well that a contract sealed by handshake was binding not only in law but in spell-craft as well. He took my hand and shook it briefly.

We left shortly after, as rapidly as etiquette would allow.

"I say, Night, I thought you hated politics."

"I do, Frank," I replied as we walked out into the evening air. "Doesn't mean I'm not good at it."

Later that week, we received a unsigned letter from the office of the Council of Mages informing us that Spell Zero had been "seen to"—the rapidity of which prompted us to speculate that the matter had been under investigation by the council for some time prior to our visit to the Viceroy. Spell failure declined, and things gradually went back to normal.

As normal as they ever get at the Thaumaturgic Investigations Unit, at any rate.

Narrator: *As inspectors Nightingale and Frankford discovered, it's not so much what you know, but who knows you know, when a misspell is to blame.*

ROB ST. MARTIN's first story was written at age seven, and he's been writing ever since. His output has included short stories, long stories, comic book stories, and planning role-playing games.

While studying for his BA in history at Concordia University, he wrote the superheroic adventures of *S.A.V.W.A.A.* A native of Montreal, Quebec, and a freelance graphic designer by trade, Rob's webserials *Squirrelman* and *Truthseekers* have proven to be an excellent training ground for what he hopes will be a long and productive career. Last year saw the publication of his first comic book, *Bastard*, which chronicles the eve of the Norman invasion of England by William the Conqueror. His short story "Potential in Spandex" appeared in the e-zine *Vision: A Resource for Writers*, and "All Roads" is his ongoing serial in the magazine *Wyntergreene*.

Crosscut

S. W. Mayse

Narrator: *Meet Rainy Petrov. A peaceful, talented writer, living with her cat in a cottage on the beautiful Pacific coast, wanting nothing more than to sell her stories. She appreciates that success will take patience and persistence. Little does she realize what else she'll need.*

"Sorry. Sorry. 'Scuse me." Rainy edged through the post office to the gnome-sized counter. Two people made a crowd on Sparr Island on a dim, damp spring afternoon.

Nan the postmistress was deep in gossip with Rosamunda Queen of the World, otherwise known as Rainy's landlady, Ros Bailey.

"Payday!" Nan thrust an envelope out of her small wicket. "*Worlds of Fantasy Magazine.* Another dragon story? Lucky girl."

Ros grabbed the envelope before Rainy could, leaving her open-mouthed and reaching for thin air. A long burgundy fingernail was already prying up the flap when Ros pursed her claret lips at the mailing address and tossed it at Rainy.

"Yours." Ros flung back her long merlot silk cape

to reveal sherry suede stiletto-heel boots. Her get-up was eye-catching on a small island where people thought high fashion meant gumboots without red soles. "You must have bewitched that editor. I don't know who reads that faerie fluff anyway."

Rainy shoved her frayed sweatshirt cuff farther up her raincoat sleeve and forced a smile. "Next time I'll do an ax murder story. Just for you."

"Me too. I love your stories," Nan cackled happily.

Rainy stooped for her check, now fluttering to the scarred planks. A blast of cold air replaced Ros as she stalked through the box lobby toward her bordeaux convertible. Writing must have lost its charm once Ros realized it involved work and rejection slips. Rainy had gritted her teeth when Ros enthused about the stories she never quite got around to writing, but she always listened politely. Too politely, Nan said. *Gotta stick up for yourself, hon. Quit turning the other cheek.*

Nan slid down from her gnome throne to wedge flyers into Sparr Island's forty mailboxes. Canada Post was taking its own sweet time about sending another forty for all the new city people like Ros. She blinked bifocally as Rainy slid the letter in her pocket. "Nice check? Maybe you can buy back your cottage."

"Mm." With any luck the check would cover next month's rent.

Nan attacked the mailboxes again with flyers. "Doesn't seem right. I know your sweetie John had a will cuz I witnessed it. How could it be missing from the lawyer's office?"

Rainy shrugged and zipped her coat up to her chin. If she'd had a copy of her lifelong companion's will, she wouldn't have to squeeze into her own guest cottage, and Ros Bailey wouldn't be her landlady. *Oh, well. Life goes on.*

"I'm fine. I love the cottage." She and John had built it together, plank by plank.

"How long will that last? Ros will squeeze you out and rent it to tourists."

"Ros is my friend! You just don't like anyone new."

"Ros is not your friend. Wake up, Rainy." Nan lowered her voice in the empty post office. "Fight back. You said your gran was a witchy woman in the old country."

"And I'm the lay priest at St. Pelag's. What would Father Ainslie think?" Rainy wrote about dragons and warlocks because she loved a good story, not because she believed in magic.

"Father Ainslie danced with the island coven at Midsummer Eve. Says it's another way to honor the divine spirit." Nan climbed back onto her stool and scowled through her wicket like a small ferocious oracle. "Rainy, Rainy. What do you really want?"

"I want to bake a cake for the thrift shop bazaar tomorrow, have a hot bath, and sell my two new stories." *Mind your own business,* in other words, but that was asking too much of any well-meaning islander.

The rain had blown east toward Vancouver, and a lemon sunset faded in the west as Rainy passed the old arbutus tree on Launch Point. Its papery red bark was peeling over acid-green new growth earlier than usual this year. Stars shimmered into view among the twisted branches overhead, and at her back Sparr Island rose darkly wooded. A small breeze sang through two twisted fir trees that marked a source of good spring water; Coast Salish families had summered here for thousands of years, judging by the depth of clamshells in their beach middens. A few aboriginal families still came over for fishing and summer ceremonies.

Wraiths of island wood smoke sweetened the low-tide reek as Rainy passed the best clam beach. Her resident otter humped across the path almost underfoot and dived for his den among the fir roots in the clay bank, leaving behind only his fishy smell.

Rainy knew every step of this deeply grooved path from her own summers spent here as a kid. After John died suddenly three years ago and she'd sold five stories in a row, Sparr beckoned like paradise. Fool's paradise. Still it was wonderfully peaceful when Rosamunda Queen of the World went off-island for reasons not even the island gossip squad could crack. Probably she was getting her teeth cleaned. Rainy admired Ros' gift for transforming the mundane into melodrama.

Rainy ducked under her climbing white rose at the cottage gate, and her old cat, Tar, came to slither around her ankles. The small garden inside its high cedar-plank deer fence was her own quiet sunny corner, with one wicker armchair and one wicker table just big enough for a teacup and a notebook. Time to prune her roses, deadhead her daffodils . . . too bad her modest checks for fantasy stories barely paid the bills. If she didn't sell more stories, soon she'd have to trudge back to office work in the city.

"Caviar or smoked eel, darling? Or shall I bewitch a few mice for you?"

Tar yowled that anything would do, just hurry.

Rainy dropped her envelope on the kitchen table to pour the Purina. Right now she'd like to bewitch the cranky old woodstove that she and John had ferried to the island in rusty pieces and restored. Remembering those days still made her smile.

Her banked coals had died to embers in the hour it took her to walk three kilometers to and from the post office. When she opened the fire door and laid in a handful of kindling, the flames batted and danced wildly. Even for a winter evening it seemed unusually cold and drafty . . . Then the front door banged back against the wall and slammed shut.

Tar bottled up huge and black like an oversized ink spot.

"Losing my marbles. How could I forget to close the door twice in one month?"

Rainy closed the door and dropped into her desk chair to open her *Worlds of Fantasy* check. The magazine editor had loved her story "Escape Claws." But no check slipped out of the envelope, only a folded letter.

> *Ms. Petrov: We were dismayed to learn that your story was plagiarized . . .*

Plagiarized? Impossible. "Escape Claws" was her best story, feverishly hammered out after the quirky character came to her in a midnight flash. Every word was hers!

> *You should be ashamed.*

Rainy's gaze was glued to the letter. Someone else had sent "Escape Claws" to *Worlds of Fantasy* under another name? Who would—or could—do that? Of course. All those times Ros Bailey kindly dropped off or picked up the mail. No wonder she grabbed for Rainy's envelope at the post office.

Tears of anger stung her eyes. Damnation! Rainy leaped to her feet and reached the door in three strides. And caught herself with one hand on the knob, hearing Father Ainslie's calm voice. *Turn the other cheek.* There was only one thing to do.

Bake.

Rainy's hands shook with anger as she pulled down her old handwritten cookbook from its shelf above the woodstove. St. Pelag's thrift shop bazaar was tomorrow. Two old-fashioned lemon pound cakes should keep them happy, and baking would relax her. The cookbook fell open at one of gran's old recipes that her mum had stuffed into the back pages. Peering at the faded spider-track writing, she could almost see Gran or Great-gran dipping her straight-nib pen to dash off a list of ingredients.

"Take one right bucket of fresh nettles and one right bucket of spring water that never saw light of day nor touch of iron. Stir in two handfuls of hawthorn wood ashes burnt at the full of the moon with righteous wrath."

An unbidden smile lifted Rainy's bleak mood. Gran had written one of her silly love potions into her cookbook. She skipped to the end. "—do your will for one moon's waxing to waning. Let you know there be no uncalling of what be called. You may command him Thornyspine."

This was no love potion, it was a summoning. A pencil scribble at the end added, "Be you pure of heart, this remedie doth settle ills and visit justice on the wicked."

Rainy shook her head in amusement and leafed forward to her lemon pound cake recipe. Flour, lemons, honey . . . Humming quietly, she assembled ingredients on her sanded wood table. Tar licked a paw and eyed her doubtfully.

By the time she slid two pans into the oven, she'd shaken off her irritation with Ros. Her kettle whistled, and she rose to fill the teapot—

And froze, staring down.

One footprint marred her clean kitchen floor. One pointy toe print, one heel dot. Only one person on-island wore stiletto heels—sherry suede stiletto-heel boots. At her desk, the papers she'd left neatly stacked on her shredder now looked hastily jumbled together. Rainy felt sick at the thought of anyone reading her unfinished work.

"I need to tell her this is t-t-totally wrong," Rainy told Tar.

No, she wouldn't. She'd stutter and blush and never get past the first sentence.

All right. Instead she'd keep her mouth shut, send in the new dragon-and-maiden spoof and the humorous warlock story she finished yesterday. With a sigh she lifted her story file from the drawer. At least the two new stories were finished—

Rainy stared into an empty folder. Both new stories were gone. Frantically she searched the pile on the shredder, looked under the desk, combed every drawer. Nothing.

Were they in the mail right now to *Worlds of Fantasy?* "Hunting the Shy Dragon," by Rosamund Bailey? "Feng Shui for Phoenix," by Rosamund Bailey?

"Settle ills and visit justice on the wicked." Tempting. And cheaper than a lawyer.

Down by her moonlit well, the nettles were springing waist-high already this year, and the water bubbled up pure from a sweetwater spring. Her old cedar-bark bailing bucket held no trace of iron, and the sun had set an hour ago. And she'd just pruned the hawthorn tree shading her door.

Rainy didn't pause to think. She opened the stove's fire door and thrust the stoutest hawthorn log into the heart of the flames. Then, with Tar shadowing her heels by the light of the full moon, she gathered her other ingredients.

By midnight, two lemon pound cakes sat cooling on her counter, and beside them seethed the horrible-looking concoction from Gran's recipe. Might have known it wouldn't do anything. Gran had been a good cook, but she was nutty as fruitcake. Or maybe it worked for Gran—she'd actually believed in these things—but Rainy had mixed something wrong. She retied her fuzzy blue dressing gown and eyed the fibrous brown gloop in her pottery mixing bowl.

"Time for a walk, big boy."

Tar usually frisked outside happily at night, but now he hid behind the stove, watching her from moon eyes. Rainy kicked on her gumboots, hoisted her dressing gown, and stomped out to her compost between two cedar trees. She tossed the nasty mess on her clematis cuttings and forked overtop a generous layer of last fall's corn husks. The undergrowth nearby rustled suddenly. Raccoon. City newcomers fed the voracious pests, and they got bolder every day.

Rainy opened the kitchen door and yelped in shock. She dropped the mixing bowl, which shattered on the fir planks. Tar screamed in raw terror and ran to cower under a chair.

A twiggy brown manikin with fiery eyes danced on her cherry-red stovetop, lashing its crooked tail and baring its needle teeth. A strand of corn husk fell from its lumpen head and vaporized on the stovetop.

"Thornyspine?"

"Dude." The manikin jumped nimbly down, and the floor sizzled where it hopped from foot to foot. "Who do I smoke?"

Rainy almost crossed herself, but St. Pelag's didn't encourage such displays. "Nobody. Go away! Leave me alone. Oh, god."

"Just a demon, thanks. What's the word?" Its voice sounded like someone rasping slivers off rusty iron, much too loud and strident for a being smaller than a cat.

Tar moaned unhappily and put his forepaws over his ears.

"I can't have some—homunculus in my house," Rainy said with a feeble attempt at firmness. "Go b-b-back wherever you came from."

"In thirty days—unless you want an extension. Think pizza. You order, you get." Thornyspine squat-

ted on the sizzling floor and picked its teeth with the
point of its—his—tail. No fig leaf. This was definitely
a male demon.

"Get thee behind me, Satan," Rainy tried
desperately.

"Don't go calling on the boss for help, or we're
both charbroiled." Thornyspine perched cross-legged
on a mixing bowl shard for a few seconds, but he
couldn't sit still. He got up to stalk around her kitchen,
trailing evil-smelling smoke. "Let's deal. I can disem-
bowel, thump, stab, slice, garrote, or impale your
worst enemy. We can skip fire and flood on an island
with a water shortage. Just say who."

"I don't want anyone disemboweled or stabbed!"
Rainy wailed.

"Chill, sister. Who's the mark?"

"Nobody," Rainy mumbled.

The demon grinned wickedly. "Righteous wrath, the
spell says. You drew a bead on someone, otherwise I
wouldn't be here." The demon touched together his
forefingers—foretwigs—and a red spark leaped between them. "Ah. Got her. Infraction eight-thirty-
seven, theft of inscribed parchment, should cover computer printouts. That's usually a flog-and-flense, but if
you like I can draw and quarter her too. I'm gone.
Back soonest."

Thornyspine was already in the open doorway with
his knobby head snuffing toward Ros Bailey's wonderful waterfront place down in the arbutus grove. Oh,
lordy. This horrible thing—she couldn't bring herself
to say demon—would be out wreaking havoc and announcing that Rainy had created it to get even with
Ros. And worse still, it would be true.

"Hold on! Wait! Thornyspine, I command thee."
Quick! Think of something!

"Yo." The demon hopped on one foot, charring

small cloven prints all over Rainy's doorsill. Damn it, that was going to take scrubbing with steel wool.

"I need to—" No time to hesitate. "I need to check the recipe book—I mean, spell book. I might need to add something really vicious."

"You rock, girl!" Thornyspine sat down on the sill to groom his twigs with a flaming eye on Tar, who slunk behind the stove.

Rainy almost dropped the old cookbook in her haste to flap pages. Back near the demon spell, she found cures for warts and itching, spells for easy childbirth, love potions, but no other demon spells.

Living on a small island with one general store taught a person to substitute ingredients and improvise.

"Come over here," she ordered. She filled her remaining unbroken mixing bowl with tap water and set it on the counter beside her lemon pound cakes. If this was some kind of fire demon, she should be able to extinguish it.

The demon leaped up onto the counter and eyed the bowl cautiously.

"A tincture to intensify fear," Rainy improvised. "Jump in."

"Dunno, boss. Looks like H_2O to me. Could be messy."

"Thornyspine, I command thee."

All hell broke loose, part of it anyway, when the demon jumped into the mixing bowl. Steam exploded outward and droplets of hot water shot in every direction. Tar yowled and streaked for the other room. The superheated dry bowl shattered—too bad, it was a present from John—and bowl fragments flew across the room to embed themselves in the cupboard doors and wall.

Thornyspine sat in ruined lemon pound cake, shaking his rough head. A few soggy twigs fell on the burst cake top. "Whoa. I don't feel so great, boss."

"I was never much good at spells."

"No kidding. But we're cool. I do lessons."

"One more try. Wait here, Thornyspine."

Rainy flew out the door, now studded with lethal-looking pottery shards, and grabbed her clam shovel from the woodshed. She dug a bucket-sized hole in the red forest loam near the cedars, enlarged it for good measure, and dropped the shovel in the salal bush. John would have been horrified. He'd be even more horrified if he knew why. Never mind. This was a crisis.

"Come on out," she called. "Maybe this one will work."

"Yo. Do your worst."

Tar flinched when the demon leaped right over him in a shower of sparks.

"Check out this root, Thornyspine. Does that look like mandrake to you?" Rainy pointed into the hole.

"Smart, boss! That's the stuff." The demon jumped into the hole.

Rainy quickly shoveled two big shovelfuls of earth onto him.

"Hey! Boss! I can't see!" a muffled voice protested.

The soil tamped down nicely under her red-soled gumboot, and then she dropped a rock on top of the mound. Now she needed to keep him down there. But how? Maybe a crucifix. *'Scuse me, Father, I just need to borrow the altar cross for a while. There's this demon I need to exorcise . . .* Maybe not. Oaken stake? Hawthorn flowers? Silver bullet?

Rainy waited a few minutes, but there was no motion from the fresh pile of dirt. Feeling only slightly remorseful, she leaned the shovel in the woodshed and headed for her cottage. Time to get some sleep.

A weirdly elongated head popped up between the

parsley and sage outside her kitchen door. A cutworm wriggled on his forehead—so that was why the sage was dying—and molten tears guttered down from his flaming eyes. Thornyspine stretched until he squirted right out of the soil, then adjusted back to his normal dimensions.

Normal. Rainy had started to think a demon in her parsley was normal.

Thornyspine staggered to the smoldering welcome mat and sat head in hands, quivering and dripping twigs. "You called me," he said plaintively. "Now you try to off me like those other dudes. Angels. Demigods. I was like totally bored and wanted to help so bad and hey, I finally got the call . . ." The small demon snuffled, then broke down completely in heartbroken sobs. From under a salal, Tar moaned in harmony, and a raccoon in her compost heap gave a startled growl and fled.

Rainy felt terrible for causing such grief. But how do you comfort a fire demon? She reached to pat the small miserable creature on the shoulder as he sat steaming and hissing on her stoop, but Thornyspine's intense heat drove off her good intentions. Damnation. If Sparr Island's gossip mill got wind of this, her parishioners would wear a groove down Church Road tattling to the priest. Then she'd get a delegation from the local coven inviting her to join their rites . . . Damnation.

"Thornyspine, can you change shape?"

"Can an iPod shuffle?" The demon wiped lavalike tears from his bright eyes—he was actually kind of cute—and oozed down the step in a flaming rubbery sheet, then turned into a garden hose and humped across the ground to Rainy. Thornyspine popped to his usual shape with a carnivorous grin, and she backed up quickly. If she made this demon mad, he could do serious damage. As if he hadn't done enough now.

"Can you turn yourself into a sheet of letter-sized paper?"

"No worries." He formed a sheet of black paper with grinning demon letterhead and marched back and forth across the doormat.

"Right. Let's go to my desk."

"Demonize a letter? Cool, boss. You got potential."

Rainy sat at her desk, heart thumping, and reached down to flip a switch. The demon was getting into this performance. "Stand right here in this groove."

"What kinda printer you got here anyway? Eeeeeee . . . !" The demon's shriek followed him all the way down into the paper shredder.

Crosscuts each page into half-centimeter by one-centimeter pieces, the brochure promised. A demon cut into twelve hundred pieces couldn't do much harm.

Rainy finally allowed herself a sigh and headed for the kitchen to make tea. Might as well sample her ruined lemon pound cake . . .

"Yii!" Rainy shrieked despite herself at the huge yellow-eyed black demon staring at her from the top of the fridge. Spooked. Jumping at shadows. It was just her old friend Tar. "You scared me to pieces—what are you doing up there?"

Tar paid her no attention. He was busy tracking dozens, scores, hundreds of black caterpillars or beetles that crawled across the floor and up the walls and across the ceiling, dangled from curtains and light fixtures, inched over the table and counters.

Rainy shrieked again in earnest. She'd learned to live with black widow spiders, ticks, cactus, mud wasps, centipedes, all the Gulf Islands' small surprises, but this was a horrible new infestation. Black wrigglers ran up her boots, fell in, grabbed the hem of her fuzzy blue bathrobe and swarmed on up. One beetle found its way to the tip of her nose.

Not a beetle. A centimeter-tall demon.

Twelve hundred tiny raucous voices spoke in unison. "Hey boss, too cool! We'll just roll on down to the big house and the deed is done."

"Down!" Rainy fumbled to a kitchen chair and sank into it gratefully, and Tar crept onto her lap for refuge as the wrigglers streamed down to mill around her feet. What on earth could she try next? "Thornyspine. Thornyspines?"

"Yo, boss," twelve hundred gravelly small voices answered. Twelve hundred minced, minuscule demons recombined into the original Thornyspine and levitated onto her kitchen table. Not too surprisingly, he looked dapper but a little sulky.

Now that was interesting. "Can you divide and re-form anytime?"

"We can now," the demon said, hopping from smoldering foot to foot, ready to raise hell. "Thanks for the shred."

You're welcome wasn't the response that came to mind. "Thorny, I have a plan."

At sunny midmorning, a few hours later, Rainy sipped comfrey tea in her garden and jotted in her notebook. She'd already outlined the new story, "Iced Demonade," and Thorny had offered to be her expert reader. A dry golden arbutus leaf drifted across her bare feet as she started to write.

"Highway to Hell" was her new cell phone ring tone. Rainy answered, but had to hold the receiver away from her ear to pick words out of the screech.

"Hi, Ros. How are you this beautiful morning?"

Another extended screech.

"Beetles? Better call in a pest exterminator from Vancouver. Too bad about your files. And your back-ups." Rainy smiled to herself. Thornyspine was on the job.

As she hung up, a battalion of microdemons marched

across her garden, up the porch steps, and through her kitchen door, each one staggering under a load of paper scraps. "Thornyspines, I command thee to reassemble anything from Ros' house that bears my name." If her luck held, that would produce her missing stories and maybe even a letter from *Worlds of Fantasy.*

Back in the kitchen, Rainy sipped comfrey tea and stroked Tar as she watched ranks of demons at work with glue and paper. Then the original Thornyspine reconstituted and leaped to her elbow with an armload of folded papers. Rainy didn't even wince at the smoking table, and Tar barely twitched an inky ear. Demons turned out to be no scarier than nosy neighbors and more helpful. She smoothed the papers on the tabletop, letting out an involuntary sigh of disappointment.

This wasn't one of her short stories, not "Escape Claws" or "Hunting the Shy Dragon" or even "Feng Shui for Phoenix." She'd turned Thornyspine loose on an innocent friend after all. How could she make amends? Her eyes blurred with guilty tears as she struggled to read the top paper's fine print.

"Last will and testament of John Edward . . . ." And underneath the will lay her three missing stories and an eviction order signed R. T. Bailey.

A week later Rainy handed her padded envelope through the small post office wicket. Nan the postmistress beadily eyed the package front and back. Everything would be fine as long as she didn't steam it open to check its contents.

"Another story for *Worlds of Fantasy* already?"

"Mm." Her package also contained a stamped self-addressed return envelope and three hundred and forty eagerly obedient microthorn demons with orders to rewrite the byline on her last story "Escape Claws" in every single copy of issue 46. Another three hundred and sixty-two microdemons were on their way to St. Pelag's to seal the leaky gutters—what Father Ainslie didn't know wouldn't hurt him, and over the years the church had certainly made worse deals—and two hundred were still scrubbing scorch marks off her doorstep and patching her walls.

"Heard from Ros Bailey lately?" Nan asked too innocently.

"In psychological assessment, poor lady. Apparently she still sees insects everywhere." Another week till her lawyer checked out the will, and then Rainy would call her three hundred microdemons back from the psych ward.

Rainy turned for the door, anxious to get back to her new demon and cat story. Thornyspine had bent over backward—literally—to charm Tar with treats and games, and it had paid off with a whole new series, almost enough for a story collection.

"Just one more question," Nan probed.

"Red alert, boss," said a tiny raucous voice, but Rainy tapped her oversize shoulder bag to hush Thornyspine.

Nan leaned conspiratorially. "How ever did you crochet all those marvelous tiny doll clothes for the thrift store bazaar?"

Narrator: *Misspell or miracle? Is the publishing world ready for an author with thousands of demon minions? Or is it already too late to ask . . .*

S. W. MAYSE is a Vancouver Island writer who
has lived in the Gulf Islands and other parts of
British Columbia, the Yukon, the North Western
Territory, Alberta, and Wales. Her books include
the historical novel *Awen*, the political thriller
Merlin's Web, and the biography *Ginger: The
Life and Death of Albert Goodwin*. Her short
fiction has appeared in *Space Illustrated* and *On
Spec*. Her crosscut shredder recently exploded,
but that had absolutely nothing to do with cats
or demons.

Bitch Bewitched

Doranna Durgin

Narrator: *Nature in all its glory. The joy of creation. Little feet and big appetites. What could possibly go wrong with love's enduring expression?*

*P*uppies.
     Blind, squirmy, deaf, legs too feeble to walk, pale purplish skin beneath the blue ticking yet to come, blunt, flattened noses perfect for nursing, little pink tongues curling with surprising strength around the nipple.

Puppies.

They were Shiba's, and she thought them perfect in every way.

She could almost ignore the human discussion in the background—Tallon's admiration, Taliya's cooing. Once Tallon had been Shiba's lineman; once Taliya had handled Shiba's mate Sabre. But when they all moved into the same cabin, those particular lines had become blurred, and now they all belonged and worked with each other, human and blue-tick hound.

Shiba nudged a still-damp pup—the only girl of the three, mostly black with white markings only on her lower legs, chest, and undercarriage. A white blaze, tiny tan dots at her eyebrows.

Perfect.

And Taliya said, "You don't suppose there'll be trouble, do you? Given where they were conceived?"

Babies.

Loud, pink, endlessly eating and gooing and gurgling, reaching out from that small, barred environs to grab an unwary tail.

Just one baby human, but it was enough. It was getting older now, and louder, and it woke Shiba from exhausted sleep in her special cabin bedding. Taliya had borne that baby human months ago, and it hadn't even tried to walk yet. Shiba thought it unnatural. The puppies had their eyes open, and their ticking had started to fill in. In less time than the baby human had already lived, the puppies would take their first training walks.

Taliya swooped the baby human up, and the wailing ceased; Shiba closed her eyes, and only in the absence of the noise did she realize Tallon and Taliya had company on the porch—the Line Mate, Eldon, who oversaw the patrol duty for this entire section of the heavily forested border between Ours and Theirs. He'd assigned Tallon to Shiba when her first lineman had died on the job; he'd put Taliya in the next line cabin over, slyly matchmaking. Sabre did his *happy dog* dance when Eldon came to visit, and even in her dozing state Shiba's tail wagged.

But it stopped when she heard the tense undertone in Tallon's voice. "You're sure? *Magic?* You really think this is wise?"

Eldon didn't sound entirely happy, either. "We're losing the battle . . . smuggled magic is getting past even our best teams, because the Others are using magic to do it. And they're using magic *against* us, which breaks every treaty ever written. There are even rumblings that they might target individual linemen. So . . . we found some free agent magic users, and they've made up these potions."

Something clinked. Taliya said most definitely, "I don't want this stuff near the baby."

"She's not standing yet," Tallon pointed out, but he sounded unhappy . . . as though realizing he'd made an argument for something he didn't even want.

"It's harmless," Eldon said. "It's got to be used with purpose, and it's got to be used in the presence of something distinctly magic. Even if the baby got her hands on it, she couldn't do anything with it. But if you run into trouble out there, this potion will reverse the effects of any magic aimed your way."

And Taliya said, "I don't like it. There's going to be trouble."

Babies. Babies and puppies.

Squalling, pooping, peeing, vomiting, legs strong enough to get them in trouble, always hungry, sharp little teeth—

"*YIPEYIPE!*"

They'd snuck up on her again. Shiba leaped to her feet, scattering puppies across the thin, shady grass. She hastily removed herself from reach, sitting beside Sabre to sulk.

Truth be told, she sat *on* Sabre. On his head, to be exact. Pretty much the only way to get his attention when he was hound-in-the-shade, don't-know-anything-about-puppies.

"I don't blame you, Shiba," Taliya said, wincing as she pulled the baby human from her breast and put it to her shoulder. It hadn't grown much, unlike the puppies. Still three of them, they more often seemed like six. Or twelve. They'd grown strong enough to pounce, to leap, to fight fiercely over sticks and twigs and summer leaves. There was Bent, who'd broken the tip of his tail on his first day, and Trey, who'd been the third one born. And there was Cutter, the girl they now just called Cuttie.

Taliya loyally insisted they'd chosen the name for the pup's precocious ability to cut right through to a scent—she was already trailing training bags, and she was hard to fool. Tallon, with much wincing, maintained it was for the pup's shrill, insistent voice, emitted at every possible opportunity. "That's almost too high to hear," he'd say. And he'd always make that face and add, "I wish it *was.*"

But they conspicuously didn't talk about whether the pups might be in danger from Shiba's wild romp with Sabre in the borderlands, the forested swath of land that the linemen and linehounds patrolled most assiduously to keep Their smugglers from bringing contraband magic into Ours. Like Sabre, like all the other linehounds up and down the borderlands, Shiba could scent *magicsmell* from far away, trailing it just as she might track any animal.

But that wild romp was long behind them, and Shiba was more than ready to return to patrol. Sabre was just as ready for her help, worn out from pulling double duty—Tallon had even left him behind on his day-long errand into the nearest town. Shiba thought better of sitting on his head and slid aside so she only sat on half of it, turning to give his exposed muzzle a quick solicitous lick. He twitched but didn't open his eyes. Hound-in-the-shade, hot summer day.

"Let's put them all in their little jails," Taliya muttered, wincing as the baby human emitted a resounding belch, not all of which was air. She always had a cloth to hand these days, and she made short work of clean-up as she rose and took the baby human inside—up the solid porch steps, into the depths of the cabin where the thing called a *crib* would keep it out of trouble for a while.

Shiba glanced at the pups. They'd fallen asleep in a heap of fat, sleek puppy limbs. The boys were both marked lightly, their thin ticking broken only by modest patches of black. The girl had taken Sabre's black body and Shiba's even, silvery ticking, a splot of white at the end of her tail and a blaze running straight and true between her eyes. The pups hardly knew what was coming when Taliya scooped them up and gently deposited them in the wood-and-wire corral on the porch. Their *jail,* she called it. It held water, it held an old blanket, and it gave Shiba and Taliya time to themselves. For Taliya to sleep, and Shiba to run. Quiet time.

If only Cutter hadn't startled dramatically awake as Taliya backed away from the *jail.* "*Yi-yi-yi-yi-yi-yi!*"

"It'll be good," Taliya muttered after Cutter finally fell asleep in mid-cry and after Shiba was tacked up and prancing on the edge of the clearing, "when things get back to normal around here."

Normal. Normal was running through the thick woods in search of *magicsmell.* Normal was drinking in the rich scents of the ground cover, the trail spoor of the animals who lived there, the spongy ground playing past beneath her feet. Normal wasn't—

"*Ahyi-yi!*" Taliya's voice hit full shriek. Shiba abandoned her gentle homeward trot for a full-on gallop, reaching the yard at such speed that she ran smack into Sabre as he bolted to his feet in high alarm. They untangled—Shiba clothed in a belly-protecting canvas brush guard, Sabre still blinking sleep from his eyes— as the cry came again from inside the cabin. "*Ahyi-yi!* Those . . . those . . . *those!*"

Both of them could hear the unspoken word.

Puppies.

Sabre eyed the dark, cool space under the porch.
Not a complex thinker, her Sabre, but he had an instinct for safety and a speed Shiba could never match
on trail. He displayed some of his speed right then,
diving for the cool darkness. For a moment his tail
lay exposed, but in afterthought he withdrew it neatly
into the shadow.

Shiba ran for the puppy *jail.* Empty. Completely and
totally empty, its panels crooked and fallen. And then
she ran into the cabin, where she was assaulted by a
plethora of odors and visual chaos. Puppy chaos. The
diaper box, overturned in the middle of the floor with
the used contents spread and torn and decorating the
furniture. The baby, squalling at Taliya's shouts of anger
and dismay. Furniture overturned, cushions scattered
and leaking filling, not an single spot in the cabin's little
shared living space that hadn't been touched by—

Puppies.

Shiba felt an absurd swell of pride that the puppies
had so ably climbed atop table and chair—and then a
surge of alarm.

For there were no puppies left here.

She ran into the back rooms, into the cooking room,
into the pantry, her nose to the floor and so full of
puppysmell and *puppypoosmell* and *puppypeesmell*
that she blundered blindly into the main room again
with tickles wrinkling up her muzzle. She stopped
short of Taliya in time to sneeze violently in her face.

Taliya, crouched to pick up a broken bowl, wasted
neither words nor time. "Out," she said. "Outside
right now!"

Shiba bounded outside and down off the cabin
porch without bothering to use the stairs. Out in the
yard that was really a beaten down clearing, she began
quartering for scent.

Taliya followed right behind her, except she had the

baby human and she used the stairs. She had a blanket
with only one hole, and she hastily spread it over the
ground, plunking the baby human in the middle. She
glanced at Shiba's frantic quartering with a mother's
knowing eye and then snapped, "Sabre! Watch the
baby!"

Sabre's tail reappeared from the shadows long
enough to thump a few quick times against the ground;
he swapped ends so that his nose peeked out, and
Taliya returned inside, trusting him to watch. As well
she herself could watch, with Sabre linehound bred
and trained and carrying the heritage of magic-
enhanced dogs from over the border with Theirs.

And Shiba trusted him, too, so she put her nose to
the ground and found the scent of her gamboling,
frisky, bold, and yet completely naive puppies. Puppies
who had no knowledge of the wolves, the eagles, the
big cats or the bears surrounding this area. *Puppysmell*, more *puppysmell*, filling her nose so thickly
that she almost didn't notice the . . .

Magicsmell.

Magicsmell, mingling here with her puppies.

Shiba gave voice, bawling her urgency to the trees.

Shiba followed the meandering scent in a wavering
loop through the trees—until she realized the puppies
had merely circled hugely back around to the yard.
She loped home at full speed, stopping short at the
sight of her youngsters gamboling toward the baby
human.

Found, found, *found!* Safe and back in the yard!
Shiba plunked down into a sit, relief making her
breathless in the best of ways. The puppies tumbled
forward, their movement revolving around a strange
object; they took turns dragging it, mouthing it, bumping it along . . . Trey fell over the baby human's
chubby leg and it chortled with glee.

Magicsmell.

Sabre crawled out from beneath the porch, his nose lifted to scent the air. "Wuhf," he said softly.

And Taliya poked her head out the door to check on the baby human and relief crossed her sharp features. "Puppies!" she said. "Where have you—" Her eyes narrowed, the relief fled. "What have you got? Don't eat that!"

Even as Shiba eased in closer, Cuttie clamped her teeth into the end of the object they all coveted—and no wonder, for were they not bred to trail *magicsmell?*— and tugged. And Shiba realized it was a cork, and Sabre realized it was a cork, and Taliya shouted, "Cutter, *no!*" and with a clink and a pop, Cuttie plopped back on her bottom, her long ears flopping and her face the very study of surprise.

Nothing happened. Taliya jumped off the porch, muttering to herself, "It can't do anything, Eldon said it can't do anything—" and Shiba loped for the center of the clearing and *poofsquallwailyi-yi-yishrieeek!* suddenly she couldn't see the blanket or the baby human or the puppies. Her gaze skittered uncontrollably away from the sight; Taliya made a pained noise and threw her hands in front of her eyes—but neither of them stopped running for the young ones, and in the background Sabre let loose with full bawl at the wash of *magicsmell* that swamped the air.

Quite suddenly, the air cleared. Quite suddenly, Shiba could see normally again. Taliya lowered her hands . . . and they both stopped short. Shiba's hackles rose completely beyond her control, all the way from her neck down her spine and even into her tail.

Three young humans, one fuzzy blond puppy of no particular lineage.

The three young humans look stunned—two naked boy children with silvery gray hair and one naked girl child with black hair, all with dark eyes and sharp oval

faces and rather large ears and six or seven years'
growth. The blond puppy floundered in a diaper cloth,
not nearly as steady on its feet or of an age with the
puppies who had been there moments earlier.

Shiba growled, and then she whined, and then she
looked to Taliya for guidance—but Taliya's face
couldn't decide between fear and fury. *"It's harmless,"*
she said, mimicking Eldon's voice from not so very
long ago. *"Conceived in the borderlands,"* she said and
glared down and Shiba and then back at Sabre, who
knew well enough when retreat under the porch was
the very best option. Then she tipped her head back
and cried in a voice surely loud enough to reach a
town miles and miles away, *"TAAL-LONN!!"*

Shiba stalked around the three young humans, bewildered by the mixed *puppysmell* and *humansmell*.
Taliya—once she finished shouting imprecations to the
sky and stomped her foot once or twice—had no such
hesitation. She snatched up the blond puppy and bundled it into a basket best left for picnic outings. She
went into the cabin and at short intervals, pieces of
clothing flew out the door. When she was done flinging, she emerged to clothe the young humans.

For their part, the young humans barely interrupted
their play. They poked, they prodded, they giggled,
they pulled hair, and they experimented with their
teeth. Shiba's teats shrunk up in horror at the sight of
those strong human incisors. At least she still had the
brush guard on.

Once Taliya had them clothed—tunics made from
Tallon's old shirts, with no attempt at the puzzling
underlayers she and Tallon wore, or even at pants at
all—she recorked the potion, checked the level of the
remaining fluid, and shook her head. "We've got to
find the other one," she told Shiba, and crouched to
show Shiba the thick glass cordial. "It's not inside—

they must have lost it somewhere. We've got to find it and take it and the children to Eldon. Eldon will know what to do." But Shiba would have taken better heart if Taliya hadn't then muttered darkly, "He'd *better*."

She called Sabre out from his sanctuary and held the cordial out to him, too. "Take scent," she told them both, only a hint of desperation in her voice. "Find it!"

Sabre instantly bounded away into the trees, barking in a choppy early-trail voice, already on the scent. But Shiba gave the playful young humans a worried look and went to nudge them, making them squeal at the touch of her cold nose even as they wrestled, emitting odd hybrid puppy-human I-am-fierce noises. And she looked up at Taliya, who stood beside the picnic basket of blond puppy growling just as fiercely at the tail it had just discovered, and she whined.

Taliya's anger melted away; she went down on one knee and threw her arms around Shiba's sturdy shoulders. "We'll fix it," she said. "*Somehow*. We'll fix it."

"*Yi-yi-yi-yiii!*" Cuttie's voice, unmistakable no matter her form, rose even as her brothers' faux snarls rose to fever pitch. Shiba didn't hesitate. She pulled out of Taliya's grip and she rounded on the squabbling young human puppies, her own no-nonsense snarl garnering instant silence. The three looked as they ever did in such moments—perpetually astonished at the reprimand, all wide-eyed *what-did-we-do?* But then . . . Then their little faces crumpled. Their eyes squinched shut and their cheeks flushed and their mouths opened to human wails of dismay dampened by human tears.

Behind Shiba, the blond puppy took up the chorus in a thin, piping and inexpert howl, *oowaooohwaaaa!*

Baffled, she backed away from it all. She found Taliya's face crumpling as well, and then the ruckus and that thin little howl triggered her own hound song, and she lifted her nose to the sky to join in. *Aaahwoouuuooouuo . . . !*, a chorus of cacophony with Sabre's chop bark sounding hard and clear in the background.

Which is how Eldon found them.

But Eldon had his own concerns. "Where's Tallon?" he asked abruptly, with no apparent awareness that anything on the home front might be amiss.

"You!" Taliya swiped away angry tears. "You said it was harmless unless it was in the presence of magic! You were *wrong!* Now *fix it!*"

Eldon stopped short. An older man, lean and lanky with big bony hands that knew just where to scratch a canine ear, normally unflappable—now he stared, nonplussed. Finally he cleared his throat. "Well, they don't look like they've been *harmed*, exactly . . ."

"Eldon . . ." The word was a warning growl. Shiba lowered her head and growled for real.

Eldon circled the trio, peeked in at the blond puppy. Then he offered, "At least they're not old enough to be butt-sniffing."

Taliya's eyes widened with horror; she threw her hands in the air, plunking down to sit on the ground as though she'd suddenly lost strength in her legs. The three young humans did as they always did when she sat with them—they swarmed her, pushing each other away to claim her lap.

"Don't you dare," she told them. "Don't you dare lick my face."

Eldon to the rescue, at last. "That'll do, puppies."

His no-nonsense voice got their attention, and if they didn't back away, they at least settled. Shiba gave Trey a lick across his ruffled hair, but he didn't even taste the same and she backed away, lowering herself to lie with her chin on her paws and her most soulful expression directed toward Eldon.

"Now," he said. "Tell me what happened."

Taliya told him. Short and to the point, she told him. She gestured with the cut-glass bottle, sloshing the remains of the potion. In the background, Sabre had gone from the excited bark of *trail found* to the more musical bark of *running trail* . . . and now his muffled chop-bark for *treed* drifted in on the light breeze. She said, "The puppies dragged the other one out, too, but they didn't return with it. Sabre's out there trailing it now."

Eldon shook his head. "It has to have been the puppies. Sabre and Shiba shouldn't have been so close to the border when they—well. It hasn't happened before. They've already got magic woven into their breeding lines; there's no telling what effect such a conception had on them. Obviously more than any of us anticipated."

"You mean—"

"I mean, I told you the truth. That potion is inactive unless in the presence of magic, and its purpose is to reverse the magic it intercepts. Under the circumstances . . . I think it did the best it could."

"It's a stupid potion, then," Taliya sniffed. But she had hope in her voice when she added, "So maybe we can just put them together and sprinkle the potion around, and they'll go back the way they were?"

"It's the first thing I'd try," Eldon said. "Except . . ."

Taliya narrowed her eyes so fiercely they were nothing more than angry maternal slits. "Except *what*, Eldon?"

"We can't use it for that. And we can't wait around to find the other bottle." In the background, Sabre's call had stopped. Shiba looked anxiously toward the woods, knowing Sabre would never give up on a trail, especially not once he'd barked treed. "And I'm afraid the longer the . . . children stay in these unnatural forms, the harder it'll be to reverse the process."

"Why?" Taliya demanded. "*Why* can't we use it for that?"

Eldon looked at Shiba and looked at Taliya and finally said, most reluctantly, "Because you two are too damned good at what you do. I've gotten word that Tallon has been targeted for magical attack. Wherever he is, he needs the rest of this potion, and he needs it *now*."

"He's in town," Taliya said instantly. And then, "Take it to him. I'll find Sabre—he's got the other one. These . . . *children* will bathe in the stuff if I have anything to say about it."

"Just don't get it on you," Eldon said dryly. "Taliya, if it doesn't work, I'll have the best minds in the Line Patrol here to sort this out as soon as possible. Don't think we won't take care of this."

"But it might be too late, you said."

Eldon didn't answer. But he wouldn't meet Taliya's eyes, and he wouldn't even look at Shiba.

That couldn't be good.

And then Sabre trotted proudly into the clearing, his face and paws encrusted with loamy dirt, his jaws carefully clamped around a bottle that looked the twin to the one Eldon held.

There was no cork.

As Sabre came to a stop before Taliya and triumphantly presented his prize, one last drop of potion dripped to the ground and quickly soaked in. Gone. Shiba's head felt suddenly heavier on her paws; she rolled her eyes to see what Taliya would do.

Taliya pressed her lips together in that way that usually meant whichever smuggler they trailed was in big trouble now, and she looked at Eldon.

Eldon only closed his eyes and winced.

Taliya said, "We're coming with you."

Eldon's eyes flew open.

"Tallon needs the potion. We need the potion. That

means we need to be at the same place, the same time."

"How—" Eldon said, looking at the young humans, and looking at the blond puppy. "All the way—?" And finally, desperately, "You know it's not safe!"

"And neither was that potion!" Taliya snapped at him, an argument he could never win.

Shiba wore her brush guard and her trailing harness with its identifying medallion. Sabre wore only his harness and medallion. Taliya wore whatever she'd thrown on that morning. The three young human puppies rode in a garden wagon, wore their makeshift tunics, and made no bones about squatting by the side of the road when necessary, tumbling in and out of the wagon as they pleased with no effort at human-type noises as they communicated their curiosity, their needs, and their concerns. The blond puppy slept in its picnic basket in the wagon.

And when the puppy woke and cried in hunger, Taliya looked down at herself and the damp spots on the front of her blouse, and she looked down at Shiba . . .

And for a short while, Shiba rode in the wagon so the blond puppy could nurse, and Eldon used all his energy keeping the young human puppies from climbing in to do the same. "There are so many things wrong with this moment that I can't even hold it all in my head at the same time."

"Potion," Taliya said. "*Not safe.* It's your turn to pull the wagon."

Strange how Shiba could run an entire day on trail in the woods and not feel the heat or the fatigue, but a couple of miles on this road . . . She panted heavily, and she stopped at every little creek to quench her thirst. So did the young human-puppies, crouching over to lap the water with little efficiency and to roll

in it as Shiba did. Barefoot and dripping and squealing, they ran down the road ahead of the little
procession—until they finally ran out of energy and
curled up in a heap, crammed into the wagon around
the basket.

Late afternoon cast long shadows by the time they
reached the town. Shiba's ears flattened at the noise
of the place; her nose stung from the *humansmell,*
the *spicyfoodsmells,* and the *livestockpoopsmells.* And
there, threading among it all, was the merest hint of
magicsmell. She looked at Sabre, saw that faraway
look in his eyes that said his nose was about to over-
come his brain, and gave Taliya a small *wooah* of
warning. When both Taliya and Eldon looked at her,
she confirmed it, lifting her nose slightly to test the
scent as she repeated the warning. *Wooah.*

"It could be something stray, slipped through the
lines," Eldon said, as the young ones stirred in the
wagon, woken by the scents and sounds of this place.
No one paid them much attention; most were headed
in the opposite direction, their minds on home and
supper and not caring much about the odd little
procession.

"And it could be whoever's come for Tallon," Taliya said sharply. Her trust in Eldon's judgment, it was
clear, had been diminished this day. Distracted, she
was a moment too late to stop the three former puppies from slipping out of the wagon, squatting briefly
in the street, and then dispersing.

It instantly became apparent that they were the perfect height to take full advantage of these first meet-
ings with strangers. Just the right height to—

Sniff.

Taliya made a strangled noise; she grabbed one of
the boys and got him to the wagon as Eldon grabbed
the other. Cuttie danced just out of reach, laughing at
the spectacle of Taliya dodging through the people

who'd collected at the town gate bottleneck, waiting their turn to leave for the day. Eldon, holding the two boys in the cart, said, "She's a pu—" thought better of it, and tried again. "Do what you'd do if she still looked like Shiba."

Taliya, her face red, instantly turned her back on Cuttie, picked up the wagon handle, and marched down the main road into town. Within moments Cuttie had caught up to the wagon, and though she wouldn't be caught, she stayed close. And Shiba, reassured that the family was still together, looked at Taliya and said, *"Wooah!"*

Taliya had that thin-lipped, exasperated look. "I know where he's supposed to be, but I bet I know where he *is*. I'm going to turn the dogs loose, Eldon. I'm not taking the chance that the magic they scent isn't about hurting Tallon. If we're wrong, we'll have still found magic that shouldn't be here. Either way, we're all in the same place at the same time with the potion."

Eldon opened his mouth as though plainly not liking it. And then he looked at Taliya's face and closed it again, tipping his head in assent.

"Go!" Taliya said to the linehounds. "Shiba, Sabre—find it!"

Shiba's fatigue vanished; she sprang forward. She had no chance of outrunning Sabre, but Sabre slowed to wait as Shiba's nose untangled the faint strains of magic from this crowd—from the human legs they raced through, the cart wheels, the merchant stalls. They gained speed and confidence as the *magicsmell* grew stronger, and they finally raced right up a collection of outdoor tables and benches where men and women drank from foam-headed mugs, finding a wispy fog of magic hovering around the shoulders of their very own Tallon. To the laughter of those at the other tables, both hounds leaped to bounce off Tallon's shoulders; the only thing that kept him from flying off his bench was the fact that they did it from opposite sides. *"Bawhouuu!"* they bellowed in chorus, deafening him equally in each ear.

"Shiba!" he said in astonishment, half his strongly scented drink spilling on the table. "Sabre!"

"No dogs!" shouted a voice from the back, barely audible over the hound-generated chaos. "No dogs!"

"Tallon!" Here came Taliya, hauling the wagon at top speed; Eldon ran alongside, keeping the young ones in the wagon. Cuttie trailed behind, yipping with excitement. "Tallon, there's danger—"

"What the—what're you—Shiba, Sabre, leave it!" And then Tallon seemed to realize where they'd found him, for he said, "I was just—and who are—? Where's the baby?"

"Potion," Taliya said, her voice hard and meaningful. "Not safe."

"Bawhouu!" Shiba added emphatically. *Magicsmell*, right here!

Eldon, panting, said, "They heard about our plans—they're going for a preemptive blow—got a tip they'll go after you—"

"Bawhouu!"

Taliya snatched up the potion bottle from the blond puppy's basket. "It's all we have left, and we had to be together so the children . . . the puppies . . ."

"Bawhouu!"

"Whoa," Tallon said, turning a funny shade of gray. "I don't feel so good—" And he reeled on the bench, turning an even funnier shade of white.

"Now!" Eldon said. "They're already here, they've already done it—*now*, Taliya!"

Taliya fumbled the bottle, pulling at the cork; she'd jammed it in there so tightly that Eldon had to leave the young humans in the wagon and together they wrestled with it even as Tallon made a gasping noise and fell over the table, his head clonking audibly on the stained wood.

Beside herself, Shiba ran to Taliya and leaped into the air as she would leap beside a tree that held magic smugglers, and at the height of the leap she blasted a frantic *"Bawhouuuu!"* so Taliya and Eldon both jerked in surprise, popping the cork and sprinkling the potion hither and yon.

Shiba crouched where she landed, watching . . . Sabre put a paw on Tallon's leg, watching . . . Eldon and Taliya held their breath, both watching . . .

From the back, a voice shouted, "No dogs! None!"

And then Tallon took a funny gurgling breath and lifted his head. The wagon and its occupants disappeared in a strong smell of magic, turning wispy and gray and unseeable and then resolving again.

Puppies. Puppies and a baby. Yapping, whining, squalling—

From the back, "No babies, either!"

And then one sound that didn't fit with the others. A giggle.

A girl-human giggle, as Cuttie ran up to the wagon to put her cheek against her brothers' plump canine forms, exchanging happy puppy kisses and little yips of delight.

"Cuttie," Taliya said in horror, looking at the empty potion bottle. "She wasn't close enough—it'll be too late—"

"You were supposed to change back!" Eldon said, with enough ferocity to speak of his desperation. Sabre slunk beneath the table. A mournful howl welled up in Shiba's throat. Tallon said, "Wha—?"

Cuttie stopped her little frolic to look at her brothers and then to look down at herself. "Oh," she said, in her unexpected little girl voice. "Is that all?" A quick flashburn of *magicsmell*, a quick blink of can't-see-it, and a dark little bewitching bitch puppy scampered around the wagon, looking for a way to join her brothers.

"You!" Taliya scooped her up and plunked her in the wagon. "Conceived in the borderlands, were you?" Eldon sat heavily on the bench, looking stunned . . . looking at the puppies. Looking at Cuttie. Tallon only said, "Wha—?"

Shiba looked up at Taliya; Taliya looked down at Shiba. "I think we're in for trouble."

Puppies.

Narrator: *And the next generation begins. A little confused perhaps—a misspell will do that—but well loved. They've nothing to worry about. It will be ages before teenage angst arrives. Years at least. Months?*

DORANNA DURGIN was born writing (instead of kicking, she scribbled on the womb) and never quit, although it took some time for the world to understand what she was up to. She eventually ended up in the southwestern high country with her laptop, dogs, horse, and uncontrollable imagination. She not only writes across genres, with backlist in fantasy, tie-in, science fiction and fantasy anthologies, mysteries, and action-adventure/romance and paranormals, but in her "spare" time, she runs a Web site design business, Blue Hound Visions. You can find scoops about new projects, lots of silly photos, and contact info online at her website. www.doranna.net

The Witch of Westmoreland Avenue

Morgan S. Brilliant

Narrator: *When you have a problem you can't resolve on your own, be it a leaky pipe or infected computer, you call an expert. Or, in this case, you call Ellison Pride, a witch who specializes in things magical. Before you call, however, make sure you know exactly what your problem is.*

"Again."

Shelby Kusanagi sighed and recited the words of the incantation for the fifteenth time.

Outside the soundproof booth, Ellison Pride idly conjured a bar of Swiss chocolate as she listened through headphones. If she remembered correctly, this was her last, and she'd have to replenish her stash. Until she did, the trick would net her nothing but Hershey bars. She'd already eaten all the Belgian truffles and the intensely dark Venezuelan bars.

Ellison unwrapped the chocolate slowly, carefully broke off a square, and gently placed it in her mouth. She almost closed her eyes to savor the experience, but one does not take one's eyes from an apprentice reciting an incantation any more than one leaves a toddler unattended. Even if the apprentice is reciting

226

in a soundproof booth—better safe than any number of possible sorry fates.

Shelby finished the incantation as Ellison finished her third square of chocolate. It was her fourth consecutive recitation without error, and Ellison considered letting her quit for the day.

"Again," she concluded. Something about the number five seemed satisfying. Besides, Ellison could eat three more squares of chocolate in peace while she listened.

But she only got through two before her cell phone sounded the first three bars of an Israeli dance tune.

For a moment, Ellison thought of letting it go to her voice mail. But Shelby was almost finished, and then Ellison would be free for the day. She slid the headphones down around her neck, flipped open the phone, and answered the call.

"Is this Ellison Pride?" demanded the caller.

A twitch of annoyance crossed Ellison's face. Who else would be answering Ellison Pride's cell phone?

"Yes," she said calmly.

"I want my son back! I want him back now!"

As if Ellison had him in her studio, perhaps as a decoration or an advertising prop.

"Sir," said Ellison, her eyes still on Shelby, "could you be a little more specific in your request?"

The man snarled into the phone.

"Sir?"

"My son has disappeared," snapped the man. "He's been taken by that—"

Ellison could hear him looking for a word suitably vile to describe his son's kidnapper. In the booth, Shelby's mouth stopped moving; her voice no longer sounded from the 'phones hanging from Ellison's neck.

Ellison nodded and gestured for her to leave the booth. She was pretty sure Shelby had done the last pass correctly. The young woman hadn't made any of the faces or gestures associated with making a mistake in practicing an incantation. A mistake she'd recognized, anyway, and by now Shelby should recognize a mistake when she made one.

"—that *wench!*" the caller finally said.

That was the worst he could come up with? Either the man had a serious vocabulary deficiency or something other than a straight kidnapping was going on.

Of course, if it had been a straight kidnapping, the man would have called the police, not Ellison Pride, the Witch of Westmoreland Avenue.

"Sir, I need a little more information—" a *lot* more information "—where he was taken from, when, by whom. It would be helpful if I could see the scene— the location he disappeared from, if you know it."

Ellison lay down her chocolate and picked up a pen. She started to write a note to Shelby—"You're done for the day" —but thought better of it. Maybe it was time Shelby had other opportunities.

"The location. You mean the scene of the crime," said the man into Ellison's ear.

"Well, yes, sir."

"Of course. How soon can you get here?"

"Where are you?"

The caller gave her the address.

"No more than an hour," Ellison assured him.

"Thank you." The man's relief made him sound almost like a different person, one who had learned manners and other social conventions.

"This is so exciting!" Shelby was too old to bounce in her seat, though barely. "I mean, it's very serious, a kidnapping." She turned to look at Ellison, who was driving her brand new Subaru station wagon at a responsible speed.

"But your first kidnapping and very exciting," said Ellison, not quite sympathetically.

"Well, yes."

"All right, I understand. But do try to keep that under control in front of the client."

Shelby sobered for real. "The client. You're really going to charge him money to get his son back."

"I really am," replied Ellison. "Probably less than the ransom, but possibly not. I'm not a public servant, Shelby. You know that. Finding missing persons, recovering kidnap victims—they're services just like my other services, and I have to charge for them."

"I know." Shelby was silent for a few minutes. "Do you really charge more than the kidnappers sometimes?"

"Yes. Sometimes people pay the ransom instead, because it's cheaper."

"That's . . ." Shelby tried to find a word. "Nuts. Isn't it? Letting kidnappers get away with it?"

"Well, I think so. But some people don't seem to agree. I guess they think I'm gouging them."

"But you're not," Shelby protested. "Are you?"

"No. First, there's the basic cost of doing business: leasing the studio, paying the utilities, buying supplies, and so forth. None of that is cheap. The liability insurance alone is pretty steep. Then there's employee health insurance, salaries—"

Shelby interrupted. "Mine isn't that much!"

"But mine is. And there is a retirement plan, in case I live that long and you stay in my employ long enough to become vested in the plan."

Shelby closed her mouth.

"This can be a dangerous business, Shelby." Ellison glanced at her apprentice. "You've felt the power. You've seen what can happen when a spell goes wrong."

But Shelby hadn't felt enough power yet to do more

than overcook a few potions or melt a few candles into bright clear pools of wax. Ellison sighed.

"The client says that his son was taken by a 'wench,' " she said.

"A wench?" Startled, Shelby returned to present practicality. "Not a witch?"

"A wench. It took him a moment to find the word. He may have been looking for an entirely different one."

"Like what?" Shelby asked, nonplussed. "That seems rude enough."

Replaying the client's words, Ellison frowned. "No, he didn't say 'a wench.' He said '*that* wench.' "

"So maybe he knows who took his son." Shelby leaned her head back against the headrest. "Not a stranger abduction."

"No."

"Maybe the boy's mother? Maybe he's divorced and his wife is a witch."

Ellison blew out a puff of air. "I hope not. I'd rather it were a demon."

"Why?" asked Shelby in disbelief.

"Custody cases are incredibly dangerous. Interfering with love?" said Ellison. "I would much rather snatch a kid from a demon than get between a mother and her child."

"So we hope for a demon." Shelby shook her head.

The house was nice, expensive, and big. It was one of the models with a whole separate wing for the children.

"It was probably pretty easy for the kidnapper to take the boy without anyone noticing," said Ellison, surveying the house from the circular driveway.

"I wonder how long the kid was gone before the father called you," said Shelby.

"Let's go find out." Ellison got out of the car, shouldered her bag, and walked up the brick path to the front door. Shelby walked beside her, a proper assistant, not lagging behind.

Ellison was unsurprised when a maid answered the door, classic apron and all.

"Ellison Pride. I'm here to see Marcus Henderson."

"This way, ma'am, please." The maid inclined her head and stepped aside to allow Ellison and Shelby to enter. Ellison suppressed a twinge of annoyance at the "ma'am." It was meant to be respectful. How could the woman know it made Ellison feel old and doddering?

Ellison and Shelby followed the maid to a large room with walls of glass: a conservatory. Or a sunroom that hoped to be a conservatory when it grew up.

In the sunroom, a man paced the length, from one large potted palm to the other, his hands clasped behind his back, his forehead creased.

Ellison forced herself to remember this caricature of the aggrieved father was indeed a real live aggrieved father.

"Ellison Pride to see you, sir," the maid said and then went away, not waiting for thanks or further instructions.

"Finally," said Henderson, turning to them. "Come along, I'll show you his rooms." The man strode past them without another word and led them through the back hall, up the back stairs, along the main corridor, which overlooked the foyer, past the great stairs, and into the other wing, where he turned right into a suite of rooms appointed in deep blue and hunter green.

Ellison blinked and heard Shelby whimper once beside her.

"I am certain he was taken from here," declared

Henderson. "He went up after dinner last night and didn't come down again. The maid went to call him to breakfast this morning and he was gone."

"Hmm." Ellison circled the bedroom with its neatly made twin bed and matching nightstands, telephone on one, digital clock on the other, then entered the private bath with its nice clean shower tub and nice wide counter. Clean, dry towels hung close to hand. She emerged to cross the bedroom to the sitting room with its deep blue and hunter green matching love seat and chair. A bare end table stood at the corner where the pieces met.

"Did the maid make the bed this morning? Clean the bathroom?" asked Ellison.

"Yes, of course," said Henderson.

"Are there any personal items I could use to locate your son?"

"Personal items?" Henderson looked confused.

"A favorite toy, perhaps?" *Any* toy—there wasn't one to be seen in the suite at all—no teddy bear neatly resting on the pillow, no blocks stacked carefully in the sitting room, not even a sailboat in dry dock in the bathroom.

"A toy?" Henderson frowned.

"An item of clothing? A favorite shirt? A sweater? Anything?"

"My son hasn't played with toys for years," declared Henderson. "As for clothing, I haven't the foggiest notion what his favorite object might be. Can't you just get him back?"

"Not one thing that belongs to your son? Not even an old teddy bear?" blurted Shelby.

Ellison shot her apprentice a quelling look, but she was grateful the question had been asked.

"Of course not," said Henderson, chilling the room. "You can bring him back, can't you, Ms. Pride?"

Ellison pursed her lips in annoyance. "Of course I

can. It will be more difficult without the personal item to help focus the search, so my fee will be higher than would otherwise be the case."

"Money is no object," said Henderson.

"Very well. You're certain he disappeared from this room."

"Absolutely," snapped Henderson.

"Tell me more about this 'wench,'" commanded Ellison.

"She's got my son under some kind of spell. I'm sure of it. He's never home, except to be on the telephone or for meals. He never talks about anything else, he never goes anywhere without her or does anything without her outside of school—"

"Mr. Henderson, I need to know more about the woman herself, not her effect on your son," interjected Ellison.

"She's not a woman," Henderson said. "She's a demon. A green-eyed, red-haired, beautiful demon who has seduced my son."

Ellison raised her eyebrows, then took another look around the suite. It was still no help; there was still no sign of the resident. The sitting room still held no toys, no books, no pictures, posters, or pennants. The bathroom still held no sailboats.

"How old is your son?" asked Ellison, returning to the bedroom once more.

"Twenty-one," said Henderson promptly. "Can we get on with it?"

"Since it's not a custody case, I think we can rule all the wench-class demons but one," said Ellison to Shelby.

"Which one?"

"The one that likes boys."

"A succubus."

"That's the one," Ellison replied. "She won't be

happy about giving up her toy. She'll fight me when I call the boy. Young man," she amended. Shelby was only a few years older than the client's son.

Ellison conjured a large piece of white chalk and handed it to her apprentice.

"We need a summoning triangle," said Shelby as she carefully marked the shape on the bedroom floor. "Don't we need the protective circle, too? Won't the demon come with him?"

Ellison shook her head. "Succubae aren't generally that strong. I should be able to separate them before bringing the son back here. Dispensing with the circle will also make it easier to get through to him."

Shelby nodded. Ellison could see her thinking it through, applying her studio lessons to a real situation.

"Can we get started?" demanded Henderson.

"*We* have already started," replied Ellison. "It would be best if *you* would wait outside."

"I will not wait outside," returned Henderson. "It's my money and my son and I will keep an eye on the proceedings from right here." He folded his arms, letting Ellison know he was locked into position.

She grimaced. He wasn't the first client who had behaved this way, and she didn't expect he'd be the last. She just didn't like them underfoot or even beside her feet. Or anywhere in the same room as her feet or any part of her while she was working.

"Without the personal item," Ellison told Shelby, "we'll have to rely on place of origin to draw him back. First, however, we have to find him. That will be—" Words she didn't want to use in front of a client crossed her mind as Ellison glanced at the present client.

"Mr. Henderson. A lock of your hair, if you please," she decided.

She'd startled the man out of his control. "Excuse me?"

"A lock of your hair will give us some connection

to your son, something like him to search for. Unless, of course, he's adopted."

Henderson's face reddened. "He is not! If it is absolutely necessary, you may have a lock of my hair. I'll have my maid call—"

Ellison conjured a small pair of scissors from the sewing kit she kept in her bag. With a single snip, she procured several strands of gently curling iron-gray hair.

Henderson's jaw snapped shut. Ellison was impressed when he didn't splutter or bluster.

She conjured a clip to secure the strands and handed Shelby the scissors to return to their place in the bag. The young woman, professional cover attained, showed no sign that she'd never opened the bag before, much less handled the contents. The scissors were out of sight and in their proper place when Ellison asked her to take the first of three fat white candles.

"Place them at the vertices of the triangle, please," Ellison instructed her.

Henderson, indignant, took a step toward Ellison and the triangle. "Why is she doing this? I'm paying for you, not some underling! I want the best!"

"You have it," returned Ellison, her teeth not quite gritted. "Ms. Kusanagi is quite capable of setting up the spell. I will be saying the incantation myself. That, sir, is the critical part. That is why you called *me*."

Peeved, Ellison handed Shelby the clip of hair. "Place it precisely in the center of the triangle, Ms. Kusanagi, if you please."

Surprise flickered across Shelby's face. Ellison gave her a quick nod. Surely Shelby could manage this. Henderson had some nerve questioning Ellison's judgment with regard to her apprentice!

"Thank you, Ms. Kusanagi." Ellison handed Shelby the lighter. "Now the lighting of the candles."

Shelby's hand was *not* shaking as she struck flame from the lighter and her voice did *not* tremble as she began to speak.

"I thought—"

"Quiet!" snapped Ellison.

Shelby proceeded with the candle lighting.

"But you—"

"Shh!" hissed Ellison.

Shelby lit the third candle without further interruption from the client. The flames burned steadily and straight and in the proper color. Ellison did *not* let slip a silent breath of relief.

"You said that *you* would say the incantation!" Furious, Henderson took two steps toward Ellison and the triangle.

"The primary incantation!" snapped Ellison. "Which I am about to begin, so please keep quiet!"

Henderson closed his mouth.

Shelby stepped back from the triangle. "Please, sir, step back," she said, putting her hand on Henderson's elbow.

Henderson shook her off. Shelby, looking worried, took another step back on her own, then a third, as Henderson took yet another step forward.

Ellison noted the rage on Henderson's face as he shook off Shelby's hand, then closed her eyes. Somewhere, despite Henderson's fury, despite Shelby's uncertainty, despite her own irritation, there was a calm place. It was somewhere very close by, and she would be there soon.

"What are you waiting for?"

Or not.

"Mr. Henderson." Ellison opened her eyes and glared at her client. "Please keep quiet."

"You said there'd be an incan—"

"And there will be, if you will keep quiet." Again

Ellison kept from gritting her teeth. Her dentist would be proud.

Henderson's mouth closed. Ellison wished there were an ethical spell for keeping it that way.

Where was that calm place? Ah. There. And there was Ellison, finally in it. She stayed there for a moment, then sought the lock of hair in its triangle.

Yes. Shelby had done well. The triangle was precise, the candles were perfectly placed, and the hair in its clip was exactly where it was supposed to be. Ellison set aside gloating over her accomplishment as a teacher for later.

She felt her power begin to build, a force that always thrilled her at least a little bit, even in the most routine spells.

Raising her hands from her sides—mostly because it looked better than shoving them into her pockets—Ellison began the incantation to draw life to like life. With the hair in the triangle, Henderson's son should be drawn back to his own room. The house was new enough that there was little risk of drawing previous residents of the room.

She finished the first part, commanding the seeker to reach out. She felt the energy of the hair, harsh tendrils from it speeding away like Medusa's snakes set free.

On to part two, without shuddering: Call to the like life to meet the seeker.

Some sources claimed this part of the incantation was unnecessary. In some cases, Ellison agreed. But with a demon, and a succubus at that, involved, every word counted.

The anchoring energy seemed to fill the triangle, almost to overflowing, stifling—

Ellison's power continued to build. She let it rise. How much would she need to separate the boy from the demon? The attachment might be quite strong. Henderson hadn't said how long his son had been under the influence of the succubus. If this had been going on for weeks, or maybe months—

There. There was the like. A newer, brighter life. Gentle. Joyful?

A seeking tendril snapped around it and Ellison began the third part of the incantation: Draw the like life back to the summoning triangle. Soon the young man would be safely home, his father would be signing a large check, and Ellison and Shelby would be on their way back to the Westmoreland Avenue studio.

The bright life resisted. It rolled into a slick ball and the seeker slipped off.

Several seeking tendrils snaked around the bright ball, forming a net, and pulled toward the triangle. The ball kept resisting, pulling away from the triangle. Of course it resisted. Why would a twenty-one-year-old man want to leave a succubus?

Ellison slipped past the bright ball and twisting tendrils, her power continuing to build. If she could get between the bright ball and the energy of the succubus, the seeker would gain the upper tendril and would be able to draw the bright ball—and the young man—back to the triangle and home.

She couldn't get around the ball. Something was keeping her back. An unusually strong succubus? Something was not right here. Ellison felt beneath her chant. There was her own power. There were the harsh tendrils pulling toward the triangle and the bright ball pulling away. She could feel nothing pulling on the bright ball from the other end. But the bright ball—

"What's taking so long?"

Ellison was jerked out of the spell and back to the room. "Mr. Henderson, would you please get lost?"

she snapped. The full charge of her power was released into the spell.

And Henderson vanished from the triangle into which he'd just stepped. A young man clasping the hand of a green-eyed, red-haired young woman appeared in the center of the triangle. The clip with the lock of Henderson's hair was flattened beneath the young man's heel. Shelby, hand still outstretched to stop Henderson, drew in one short breath. Ellison was proud of her for not fainting.

"Backlash," said Ellison to Shelby. "We'll have to have a lesson on backlash. And clues."

"Clues?" said Shelby. Her voice was admirably steady.

"Succubae don't use telephones," said Ellison. She turned to the young couple. "Love," she said. "You two are in love, aren't you?"

Marcus Henderson was furious when his son's bright life gently but irresistibly tugged his sulking tendrils back to the triangle.

"I won't pay you," he said.

"I brought your son back," said Ellison calmly, handing him a neatly written bill.

"And you sent *me* to some godforsaken place in the middle of—"

"You will pay her, Dad," said Marc. "And apologize for your rudeness. And you will be on your best behavior when you speak to my fiancée or you will not see me again." He smiled gently. "I don't know if Ms. Pride would be willing to try to bring me back again."

Ellison shook her head. "There's none better in this city than the Witch of Westmoreland Avenue, but even I won't fight love. I'm not strong enough. And there's no reason."

The elder Henderson snarled, then wrote and signed the check.

Ellison accepted it, nodded to him, and turned to Marc and his thoroughly human fiancée.

"A pleasure to meet you," she said.

In the car, she conjured two chocolate bars and handed one to Shelby.

Narrator: *Marcus Henderson forgot one thing when dealing with the Witch of Westmoreland Avenue. When you hire an expert, you let that expert do the job. Still, though he caused a misspell, Marcus did come out ahead. By a daughter-in-law.*

MORGAN S. BRILLIANT was born in Kansas. But that wasn't quite like home for her parents, so they moved to New Jersey two years later. Morgan has been writing science fiction and fantasy since she was twelve, occasionally submitting her stories to magazines. At Millennium Philcon she went fangirl over George Scithers and told him she'd loved his rejection slips when she was a kid. He responded, "What have you been doing since then?" A few years later, Morgan was startled to discover that, among other things, she had spent nearly twenty years working at almost every job on the other side of publishing, from editorial assistant to typesetting. "The Witch of Westmoreland Avenue" is her first sale.

A Spell of Quality

Kate Paulk

Narrator: *The daily grind at quality control. You do your job well and no one notices. You fix the mistakes everyone else makes and no one notices. But do your job a little too well one day? Everyone will.*

There are times when being a Quality Assurance Mage sucks. The silvery gray spell-ball on my desk told me today was one of them. The ball sat on the cheap pine, its manifestation spells warping the wood.

Someone owed me a new desk.

Not that I was likely to get one—I'd probably end up restoring the desk again. It was one of the little pleasures of being employed by the stingiest son of a troll this side of the Impassable Mountains.

I sighed. I should never have created a security spell so tight even the best cracker-mages wouldn't touch it. I certainly shouldn't have released it. Imperial Mages know best, after all. They don't read instructions, not even ones that display ten foot glowing specters warning of doom if the user fails to keep an open backup in a nonmagically secured location.

The fine I'd earned from the Imperial Court put me

on the block for a five-year indenture. Of course Bottie had jumped. All of his mages were indentured.

Which left me staring at a misbegotten excuse for a spell-ball. It was going to bite me, and bite hard. Mass-producing spell components is a tricky business at the best of times, and nothing in Bottie's components shop qualified as the best of anything.

Bottie's message spell triggered as soon as I got within three paces of the desk. Unfortunately, the image in the spell was an accurate depiction of my unloved employer. He had the pasty grayish complexion typical of a troll, beady eyes perched on the bridge of a lumpy nose, and stringy hair the color of river mud. Seeing him did a whole lot of no good to my stomach.

"There's a client waiting on this, Weed, so make sure it works. You've got till sundown." The image flicked out and the spell faded out of existence.

Just wonderful. I didn't need anyone to tell me I'd be taking the fall if anything went wrong.

I took a closer look at the spell-ball. Nothing about it indicated—or even hinted at—its purpose. To the nonmagical eye, it was a featureless gray ball.

Magically . . . I groaned when saw the signature embedded in the manifestation layer. Sehkin. The most incompetent spellmaker I'd ever met. It was nothing short of a miracle that he hadn't turned himself into a lizard yet.

I probed a little further, delicately seeking the next layer. And clenched my teeth so I didn't curse. The idiot spawn of a brain-dead whore had used my security spell.

For once, he'd managed to cast it correctly—the shifting strands of power flickered in the complex algorithms I'd built, moving about ten times faster than I could build an unlocking spell. That was the point, to protect the inner workings of my spells from any prying eyes. It was supposed to be my edge, so the spells I built stayed mine.

If the Imperial Mages had actually bothered to pay attention to the warnings I built into the spell, they might have been a little less upset when the ones who tried to crack it got turned into mice. The palace cats must have had terrible indigestion.

The cracker-mages I knew took one look at the spell and congratulated me.

None of which was any help. Sehkin hadn't bothered to supply me with anything to say what his alleged masterpiece was supposed to do, so I had to go find out.

Sehkin's corner of Bottie's workshop smelled of the recent use of cleaning spells and ultramasculine pheromones. Every shelf was spotless, with not a single ingredient to be seen.

My heart would have sunk, but it was already trying to burrow into the soles of my boots. In the three years I'd been here, I'd never once seen Sehkin's work area look organized, much less pristine.

The pheromones . . . Sehkin liked to think himself the gods' gift to females of every species.

He posed artistically beside the workbench, trying for casual nonchalance and failing. His dark curls gleamed with fresh lacquer, not a strand out of place. Fabric enhancement spells rippled over his robes, making them look like the rich blue velvets of an archmage instead of the threadbare leavings they were.

I put balled fists on my hips and broke all his spells with a word. It wasn't a very nice word.

I waited while he scrambled to catch the loose ends of his spells and get them all unraveled before they could backlash. He needn't have bothered—he hadn't used anything powerful enough to damage him. The worst he could have suffered was indigestion and maybe some queasy thoughts about small animals.

When he was done, he turned to glare at me. "What did you do that for, Weed?"

"It's Sharae to you," I snarled. "You looked ridiculous."

His mouth flapped open for a while before he found something to do with it. "Aren't you supposed to be testing?"

"Sure." I spat the word out as though it tasted bad. "As soon as you give me a component that *isn't* secured."

His olive skin turned sallow. "There's no time. It needs to go to the client today."

I promised myself I'd find a way to punish Sehkin for his incompetence. "Then why send me a secured version?"

He cringed, trying to plaster himself into the corner. "Bottie said you could handle it."

I growled. I was good, but playing with magical components to see what they did was an excellent way to end up dead. If you were lucky. "I'll deal with him later." Raw magic crackled around me, giving my words an odd echo. I breathed in deeply, and forced myself to calm down.

Sehkin winced.

"So what does it do?" My voice was so controlled it shook with strain.

"It's a summoner."

I left a trail of scorched wood and overheated air as I stormed back to my office. Summoning a kindly deity to guide one's hand during spell casting was marginally less common than drawing protective circles, but only a madman would try to make a summoning component. Getting the wrong deity was the least of the potential problems.

If you weren't in the proper state of mind, getting the *right* one could be lethal.

Once I was safely inside the shielding I'd layered on my office, I took a deep breath. If Sehkin had built his summoning component correctly, it would be a miracle of the first order. The best I could hope for was that the thing didn't do anything.

I reached under my desk and pulled the locked casket out to where I could open it. Its locking spells were keyed to my magic patterns, allowing me to open the casket. Anyone else would come away with scorched fingers.

Light spilled out from my warded robes as I felt for the encapsulated recording spell. The slickness of manifestation spells rolled over my fingers until my hands finally closed around the spell-ball.

With a flick of my wrists and a murmured incantation, I glued the recording spell to the corner of the ceiling, where it could "see" everything I did. "Record: begin."

A tingle of magic flickered over my senses, telling me the spell was active.

First, I needed to cover myself against any disasters Sehkin's spell caused. "On this date, the fourth day of High Creen, I have been tasked with testing a spell component created by the indentured mage Sehkin Ahnessin. The terms of my indenture do not permit me to refuse this task."

I could imagine Bottie cursing. "My employer, Bottie Grune of Grune's Magic Shoppe, has ordered me to test this component today. The component has already been wrapped in unbreakable protection spells, so I am unable to determine if any flaws exist in the internal spell structure.

"The poor quality of the manifestation layer indicates that internal flaws are likely." I pointed to my desk. "Note the warping of the woodwork around the component, typical of faulty manifestation spells."

Now to describe how the thing should work. "Discussion with Sehkin"—a polite fiction—"indicates that the component is designed to record the name of a deity or other supernatural being when the user places thumb, forefinger, and middle finger of their right hand in the appropriate indentations."

As ideas went, this one would win prizes for stupidity. "The thumb is placed in the deep indentation on one side of the component. The forefinger is placed in the deep indentation on the other side, above the shallow indentation for the middle finger."

"Sehkin states that to call the named being's blessing on a spell, the user places thumb and forefinger over the deep indentations, and applies pressure. A standard invocation for deific blessing will be performed, using the recorded name." The thought sent shivers crawling down my spine. I could think of four different standard invocations without trying. All of them could misfire spectacularly and unpleasantly.

The *other* function of the device was worse. "To summon the named being, the user places the right thumb in the deep thumb indentation and the right forefinger in the shallow finger indentation, then applies pressure. A standard summoning spell will be performed to call the named being." No sane mage would allow anyone but himself to perform a summoning.

"To test the first function of this device, I shall record the name of my patron deity while standing in a full protective circle." With protective spells, more was better. "I will be wearing full robes with maximum shielding.

"To test the second function, while maintaining the

same level of protection, I will cast the Pickup Cantrip, asking the blessing of my deity." Every mage knew that spell and used it on a more or less regular basis. Since my recording spell also recorded spell structures, Imperial Investigators would know I had done nothing out of the ordinary.

"To test the third function, I will summon my patron deity. Again, I will be fully protected. I will summon my deity to request advice on surviving my indenture period." Not even an Imperial Justiciar could argue with that request.

I swallowed and said, "I will now prepare the protective circle."

The circle was already partially prepared, a ring three feet in diameter burned into the wooden floor. The scorch marks already anchored my preferred protective spells, which just left activating them.

By the time I was done, the circle glowed so brightly even Bottie could have seen it. Half a dozen protective shields interlaced in a circle not even a major demon could break. I still had the scars from that encounter.

The only break in the circle was an archway in the spells keyed to me—and only me. It would fry anything else that tried to use it, which was how I knew my spells would hold a major demon. It had taken weeks to get the stench out of the office.

"I will now don my full robes." That was for the benefit of whoever might watch the recording. The spell showed magic structure as an overlay to the fabric, making my robes look peculiar.

I dug the magic-slick fabric out of the casket and pulled it on over my shirt and pants. There were so many protections layered on what had begun as threadbare fabric that the robes glowed the same intense white as the circle. Archmages would kill for protection like this—it was the equivalent of knightly plate armor that repelled most weapons *and* shot back.

When it comes to keeping my soul, mind, and skin intact, I like overkill.

I adjusted my vision so the magical glare didn't blind me and picked up Sehkin's spell-ball. It felt slimy rather than slick, another indication that his manifestation layer was a mess.

"I will now enter the circle." The tingle of magical protection did nothing to ease the tension knotted between my shoulders. Whatever happened now would be trapped in the circle with me.

I held up the spell-ball, rotating it so the recording spell would see the indentations. "I will now perform the first test." It was—probably—not dangerous to speak the name of a deity without any kind of summoning or invocation spell in place.

Of course, that assumed Sehkin had cast everything correctly.

My hands trembled as I placed my fingers over the indentations, taking care to ensure that the recording spell caught every movement.

The spell-ball began to vibrate as soon as I held it correctly. I swallowed and said as clearly as I could, "Lord Order." Order was not precisely a deity, but he was close enough. Quality assurance of all kinds fell under his aegis.

I relaxed a little when several long minutes passed without disaster. "I will now perform the second test."

Ordinarily, the Pickup Cantrip was something I did without even thinking, but this time I focused intently on the magic structure. I made sure every magical line was perfectly laid before I pushed my right thumb and forefinger into the deep indentations.

What emerged was not my voice. It was no voice I recognized, and it spoke not Order's name but that of his opposite. Chaos.

The spell structure twisted, forming a summoning even as I jerked my fingers open. The spell-ball shattered at my feet, and dark smoke rose from it, twisting as it formed a portal to a realm that made the hells look cozy.

In the time it took my heart to beat once, the portal vanished. The Lord of Chaos stood where it had been.

He smiled. It was the only thing about him that stayed constant; his body and face blurred as they changed continually. All the shapes and faces were more or less human, but the movement made me nauseated.

I was too terrified to run. Like his opposite, Chaos was a force of nature. He could make me cease to exist with a flicker of what I hoped were his fingers.

"A devotee of my dear nemesis." His voice buzzed, the words arriving directly in my mind without me having to actually hear them. "What delightful irony."

He gestured casually at the circle, as though to brush it aside.

Darkness flared inside the circle, and the air filled with the smell of scorched meat.

I dived through my gateway, scrambling to my feet in time to see the protective spells bulge outward as they strained to hold the power of an enraged elemental force.

Every sound and color imaginable—and several that weren't—blasted through my office when the circle shattered. Chaos no longer looked remotely human: He was an angry blur of things that should never have been allowed to exist. With a sweep of something that might have been a tentacle, he threw me aside and surged through the wall, tearing it into shreds of . . . Well, I hoped whatever he'd turned it into wasn't alive. With Chaos, you never knew.

Behind him, several armies of darkness took shape. Death, in robes so black they seemed to suck the light into them; War astride a massive horse that still strained to carry his muscular bulk; Famine a carica-

ture of skin stretched over bone; and Pestilence . . .
oozing. Behind them ranged demons of every rank
from the highest demon lord to the lowest imp.

I swallowed in a dry throat. I was beyond dead.
There was only one being with any chance of sending
Chaos and his forces back where they belonged. Perhaps I could escape with my soul intact if I killed
myself after summoning him. Order might be counted
among the "good" deities, but that didn't mean he
was *nice*.

Not that I had a choice. Three years indentured to
Bottie might have bruised my conscience, but I still
had one. I couldn't let Chaos loose on the world.

A scream that started low and slid up into glass-
shattering heights made me wince as I scrambled to
my feet. I almost—*almost*—hoped it was Sehkin or
Bottie.

I stared at the splintered, twisted ruin of my protective circle and sighed. At least the wards on my robes
were still more or less intact. I didn't have anything
else.

A full summoning spell would have taken far too
long. Instead, I used the short version: a few drops of
my blood on the floor and an incantation that translated to "I'm in deep trouble here, please help me."

The remnants of my circle spells shifted to form a
delicate spiral, then opened out to reveal a small man
in the pinstriped robes of an accounting mage.

I bowed low enough that my head spun. "Lord
Order. I apologize for the interruption."

"A needful interruption, it would appear." His voice
sounded flat, as though he was trying not to show
anger. "Look at me, child."

I straightened and met his implacable gray eyes. For
a moment, I couldn't move, couldn't breathe. As he
held me with his eyes, he knew everything I was,
every failing.

When he released me, I stumbled back and dropped my gaze to the ruined floor, waiting for judgment.

"Impressive," he said in a dry voice. "I would suggest your allegiance go elsewhere—a mage of your talent will come into conflict with established law."

I blinked. No deity ever suggested a worshipper go elsewhere.

"I am not precisely a deity."

I felt rather than saw Order's gesture. "Come. We have business to attend to."

Disobeying him never occurred to me, although seeing what Chaos' rampage had done was not pleasant. Power built around me as I walked in his wake, and I caught glimpses of his armies manifesting.

The walls shuddered with a cry of triumph that made my bones vibrate. I didn't need to be told what it meant; the shout was the very essence of someone claiming his due.

Order quickened his step. For a moment, everything seemed to blur around me, then we stood in the mages' workroom. Or rather, the remains of the mages' workroom. I shuddered and looked away from the blood-drenched meat that lay amid shredded robes. My stomach tightened, and I clenched my teeth to keep myself from throwing up. I didn't want to know who that had been, although some small, unworthy part of my soul hoped . . .

Chaos rose from where he squatted over a . . . I gulped. Sehkin was still recognizable. Barely. Nothing that looked like that should still be alive.

Chaos glared at Order. The air between them crackled with power and mutual loathing, although Order's expression never once lost its air of mild disinterest.

Bottie himself chose that moment to charge into the ruined workroom. "Weed! What in the hells are you doing?" His bulk strained the seams of his business robes, and he seemed completely oblivious to the plight of his two indentured mages—one hopefully merely dead and the other almost dead. Typical troll. He'd probably complain about blood getting on his robes.

Chaos snared him with an arm—or tentacle—that seemed to extend to reach him. The touch was enough to make Bottie's skin sear and ooze greenish liquid. I quietly thanked all the gods I could think of that I'd been in my full robes when Chaos had thrown me against the wall.

I winced when Bottie started to scream. He sounded like a little girl.

"Stop it!" The sound of my own voice surprised me. "Whatever he's done, he doesn't deserve you." What *was* I doing defending Bottie?

"Nobody gets what they deserve, little mage." Chaos' voice buzzed and oozed. The words seemed to echo inside my head.

I fought the urge to wipe my hands.

"That," Order said in his quiet, calm voice, "is because most of our brethren offer mercy." Despite the softness of his voice, I could hear him clearly. "Is this . . . creature . . . one of yours?"

Bottie whimpered.

"No." Again, my voice was stronger than I would have believed. "He worships at the Temple of Acquisitus."

Order nodded slowly. "Then let his deity deal with him." There was steel under the soft tones. I suspected Order was going to have a word with Bottie's patron deity. That word wasn't going to be nice.

Although Chaos' blurred form hurt to look at, I could see enough. His posture said clearly that he had no intention of leaving.

I realized then that while Order and Chaos faced each other, a battle raged around them in a realm that didn't quite match the one in which I stood. Ghostly screams echoed across the realms, and on occasion a demon or demideity would drop from nowhere to land on the floor, where the body faded back into the air from which it had come. In the case of the demons, this was definitely a good thing.

My legs trembled under me. I should have taken better precautions, tried asking the blessings of a minor being like Domesticana.

Order's hand rested on my shoulder, squeezed gently. The gesture seemed to reassure as well as strengthen. Or perhaps it simply destroyed what remained of my sanity. I stepped forward, between Order and Chaos.

"You do not belong here. This world is not yours." The opening of the banishment ritual was simple enough. It was maintaining focus while I completed it that would be difficult.

Power swirled around me, eddies of darkness twisting at the graceful spirals of Order's power. I held Order's power close, focusing it into a one-way portal to the Chaos Realms. His hands rested on my shoulders, steadying me and providing a flow of power for me to channel. Strangely enough, I wasn't frightened.

The portal opened with a twist that wrenched at my gut. Insubstantial wind tore at my robes, my hair.

Weird shrieks in ranges I should not have been able to hear tore the air. I could see Chaos' creatures being sucked through the portal while Order's allies scrambled to escape its pull.

Bits of splintered wood and shattered glass lifted from the floor to shoot through the portal. I whimpered as spears of wood and glass came from behind to skim around me before disappearing into the formless darkness.

Chaos snarled as he wrapped tentacle-arms around Bottie and what remained of Sehkin.

"I think not." Order's calm voice cut through the substantial and insubstantial screams, the swirl of creatures drawn into the portal. His hands remained on my shoulders, reassuringly solid.

With a cracking sound, the tentacle-arms snapped, dropping their burdens to the floor. At least Bottie stopped screaming.

Sweat prickled under my robes, drizzled into my eyes to sting them, but I dared not release the portal. The spell had used all the power I had given it, and now it pulled directly from my soul.

Chaos slid toward the portal, tentacle-arms lashing out at Bottie, at Sehkin. The portal snared one of the arms, and power flared through me. An ululating scream sent shudders through my body and flashed red against my eyes, and then Chaos and his minions were gone.

Only Order and his allies remained.

I trembled as I closed the portal. My legs refused to hold me, and I slumped to the wreckage-strewn floor. Quality control was not supposed to include facing down elemental forces. Creatures from dimensions that shouldn't even exist weren't supposed to come and tear my fellow indenturees to pieces.

"Well done, young one." There was actually warmth in Order's voice. "You will be an asset to whomever you choose to serve. Might I suggest one of the Muses?"

I blinked. Surely I was hallucinating.

Bottie groaned and hauled himself to his feet. With green fluid staining his ruined robes and his bloodshot eyes, he looked less appealing than usual. "Weed, you lousy piece of troll dung. I'll take this out of your—"

A single gesture from Order brought welcome silence.

Bottie's eyes bulged as he stared. He opened his mouth several times, but no sound came out.

I didn't care. I was still alive. I still had my soul. At this point, I was happy to deal with anything else.

A thin, harried-looking angel in pinstriped robes

scuttled into the wreckage, picking its way to Order
with fastidious care. "The audit, Lord."

Pale wasn't an option for Bottie's grayish complexion. Instead, he went a kind of pasty color and tried
even harder to force words past whatever spell Order
had cast on him.

"The Imperium has one copy, the Academy of
Mages a second, and the Council of Priests a third,
Lord."

Order nodded. "We will wait for the Imperial Mages
to arrive. "I fear we were too late for the other culprit,
but this one will receive his due."

I shivered. Unlikely as it might seem, Sehkin might
have been fortunate.

Imperial Mages were not known for their mercy.

Bottie appeared to have reached the same conclusion: He tried to run, only to find himself caught and
held motionless by Order's spells.

"We will wait."

I stepped from bright sunlight into the shadowed hall-
ways of the Imperium's Institute of Justice. A shiver
ran through me, and my stomach knotted. Until this
moment, I'd been able to avoid thinking about my
fate.

I'd spent the last week rebuilding my strength and
my personal wards. Sending Chaos and his forces back
to the nether realms had stripped me bare of even the
simplest spells.

Fortunately, I had nothing else to do; faced with
Order's audit and depositions, the Imperial Mages had
ordered me to present myself today for judgment on
my indentures.

The arched hallway seemed to go on forever as I
walked, an endless stretch of white marble. My footsteps echoed faintly.

Sehkin had been buried as best his family could

afford. There wasn't much else that could be done for him.

It took the Imperial Investigators almost the whole week to determine that the other victim had been Bottie's other indentured mage and not one of the female visitors Sehkin "entertained." That burial was rather quieter, and the casket . . . They hadn't found all of him. What they did find was barely enough to fill a bucket.

Bottie had been sentenced to spend the rest of his life as a laborer in the Iceholt Mines. The Imperial Justiciars had decreed that his reckless endangerment of lives had built a debt no indenture period could repay.

That left me. I'd avoided the hearings, not wanting to be accused of gloating. In truth, I doubted I'd gloat over anyone, ever. It just . . . didn't seem right. Not after seeing what Chaos had done.

The doors to the Well of Justice swung open as I approached. Magic tingled over my skin, telling me that Imperial Mages had "assisted" with the effect.

I took a deep breath and entered.

My heart nearly stopped as I took in the massive hall and the hundreds—thousands—of mages crammed in. They were standing against the walls because there weren't enough seats.

I clenched my teeth and lifted my head. I might be walking to my doom, but at least I'd go with a bit of pride. I had done my best, and Order himself had complimented me.

My best robes—worn, patched, but imbued with all the protective spells I knew—glowed even to normal sight. Let the glow remind them why Chaos was not rampaging through the world.

I stopped when I came to the stairs leading to the dais and bowed. "Lord Justiciars." I saw no need to say more than that. They knew why I was here, and so did everyone else. My heart hammered in my chest as I straightened.

The Lord Justiciars in their robes of deepest purple all seemed to have been cut from the same unsympathetic stamp: twelve dried up old men whose sole pleasure came from arguing obscure branches of law. I tried not to think about how many laws had been shattered by Chaos' manifestation and rampage. "Gross endangerment of the public" was the least of the charges they could bring against me.

The Lord Justiciar at the left of the group cleared his throat. "Mage Sharae Weeden. In recognition of the public service you have performed, your indentures are hereby annulled."

My head swam. Annulled . . . that meant that I was due three years' wages—not that there was enough left of Bottie's shop to pay them. More important, it meant that the indentures would be struck from Imperial records, as though they had never occurred. I was free.

"Furthermore, in deference to the . . . unique . . . situation in which you find yourself, the Emperor himself has decreed that the College of Mages and Imperial Justiciars jointly reimburse you for three years' employment as a full Master Mage." The twist of his mouth made it clear he disagreed with the decision.

I blinked and looked stupid. The Emperor had intervened . . . for *me?*

While I wondered what I was supposed to say in reply, the Justiciar added, "This case is closed," in a sour tone, and the whole gaggle of them filed off the dais in a flock of purple robes and unhappy faces.

Well. Now what?

"Mage Sharae?"

I turned to the unfamiliar voice and saw a tired-looking man in robes whose protective spells were almost as strong as mine. "I am Archmage Justin of the

Imperial Institute of Magical Quality. I was wondering if you would be willing to join us?"

I didn't hesitate. "I'd be honored, Archmage."

Some of the other mages looked disappointed, and the crowd began to flow from the hall. My shoulders unknotted, and I smiled. "Thank you."

The Archmage studied me for a moment, and winked. "No, thank *you*. Being a Quality Assurance Mage sucks."

Narrator: *Mage Sharae Weeden returns to the daily grind, albeit in new surroundings. It's reassuring to have someone vigilant and brave on the watch for misspells by her fellow mages. Let's hope she need not work overtime.*

KATE PAULK takes interesting medication. This explains her compulsion to write science fiction and fantasy and also means you'll be seeing a lot more of her in the future. Her friends would fear for her sanity, but she claims not to have any. Her short fiction has been published in *Crossroads*, *Fate Fantastic*, and *Something Magic This Way Comes* and she is hard at work on a novel. She lives in semiurban Pennsylvania with her husband and two bossy lady cats. Whether this has any effect on her sanity is not known.

Demon in the Cupboard

Nathan Azinger

Narrator: *Men. Women. Throughout recorded time, they've tried to outguess and outsmart one another, since talking to one another hasn't worked quite yet. Behold the new battlefield. The kitchen.*

Men never really grow up—we're all boys at heart. It's one of those incontrovertible laws of nature.

Another is that women, however much they may protest otherwise, never really understand this. Oh, they *know* it all right, but knowing and understanding are two different things.

Even women who ought to know better are prone to underestimate the boy inside the man. For instance, my wife is a witch. No, really, she's got a coven, a cauldron—everything. She even keeps weird ingredients in the spice rack. Eye of newt and toe of frog—that sort of thing.

Now, if she really understood the boyish nature of men, do you think she would've left me all alone in the house mere hours before her sister and brother-in-law came over for dinner, with her pot of spaghetti and specific instructions to stir it occasionally and not to add anything? Yeah, me either.

You see, the male mind subconsciously edits out negative commands. Words like "don't" and "for the love of all that's holy, under no circumstance ever" simply fail to register.

If she'd wanted me to leave the food alone, she ought to have left detailed instructions about adding certain spices at certain times, and I would've promptly forgotten to do all of it. As it was, I heard the words "add anything" and started wondering what would taste good in spaghetti.

Answer: chili powder. The Italians never made it spicy enough anyway. So I sauntered over to the spice rack, skipped past the wool of bat and tongue of dog, and grabbed the little plastic bottle with the hot, red powder.

The spaghetti sauce was already bubbling along merrily in my wife's largest pot when I reached the stove. I unscrewed the cap and dumped a liberal amount of the powder into the pot, then stirred it in with a long-handled wooden spoon.

Afterward I lifted the spoon to my mouth and gave it a tentative lick. My nose immediately began to run, but it tasted awesome. Congratulations, I felt, were definitely in order for a job well done.

That's when I noticed the smoke. It rose into the air like steam from the surface of the spaghetti sauce, its deep purple color and sulfurous smell like no smoke I'd ever seen before. I'd started enough fires in my day—by accident mind you, well, mostly by accident—to know that this was deeply unnatural.

It hung above the pot like a lurid, purple storm cloud, roiling with an inner life all its own. For a moment I stood there frozen, ransacking my brain for the "In Case of Magical Emergency" instructions my wife had given me years ago, but before I could act or even remember, the cloud disappeared with a muted pop.

In its place hovered a scaly creature about the size

of a small dog. It had a spiky little face, replete with vicious-looking horns and fangs, and it wore what appeared to be an ill-fitting business suit.

"Tu evocaveras; ego venieram," it said, staring at me with eyes the color of burning embers.

"Er, what?" I replied.

The little creature considered this for a moment and then said, "You called, boss?"

I could not for the life of me remember doing anything of the sort, so I resorted to the old standby: "Who are you, and why are you calling me boss?"

"Oh, sorry, I forgot to introduce myself," the little creature said, taking a matte black business card case from his coat pocket and popping it open. "The name's Steve. Here's my card."

I took the proffered card from an outstretched claw and examined it:

STEVE
Demon (minor) of Wanton Destruction
Havoc & Associates, Ltd.

"So, uh, Steve," I said, turning the card over. There was nothing on the back. "You're a demon of wanton destruction, are you?"

"Minor demon," Steve corrected. "I'm new to the firm."

Pocketing the business card, I asked, "How did a minor demon of wanton destruction end up in my kitchen?"

The little demon blinked, as if confused by the question. He glanced down at the pot of spaghetti sauce simmering beneath him and said, "You summoned me here. It sure looks like a summoning to me. You've got flesh of ox . . ."

"Ground beef," I murmured, shaking my head.

". . . in a broth of blood . . ."

"Blood?" I asked, wondering what my wife had been adding to the spaghetti sauce when I wasn't looking.

". . . or acceptable blood substitute . . ."

"You've got to be kidding me."

". . . and last but not least, stuff of flame."

"If by 'stuff of flame' you mean 'chili powder,' I'm going to beat you senseless," I said, glowering at Steve.

"Don't be silly," he said, lashing a tail I hadn't noticed at first. It snapped back and forth above the surface of the spaghetti, reminding me of the single most important consideration in this whole affair: not making my wife angry.

Despite the whole demon thing, the sauce was still edible, and I needed to make sure it remained that way, so I herded Steve off the stove and down the counter a way while I said, "There must be some mistake, I didn't put any 'stuff of flame' in the spaghetti."

"Are you sure?" Steve asked.

Suddenly I wasn't. I snatched up the plastic bottle to double-check. Sure enough, written on the label in my wife's neat hand were the words, "Essence of Flame."

"Drat," I muttered.

"Hey, don't worry about it," said Steve, rummaging about on the countertop and trying to look inconspicuous about it. "It happens all the time. Why, a cousin of mine once told me about a guy who tried to make a stir-fry and ended up summoning a demon of wonton destruction. Get it? Wonton."

"I bet you're a riot at company parties."

Steve looked up from his reconnoiter long enough

to fix me with a suspicious stare and then went back
to sniffing around on the counter. That's when he
found the cookie jar, the one my wife's great aunt
Hildegaard had given us as a wedding present.

"Can I break this, boss?" he asked.

"No, you can't," I said, snatching the jar away from
the little demon and setting it down again out of his
reach. "Look, I don't need anything destroyed today.
Why don't you go back to whatever hell you came
from and take the day off."

"Can't do that boss," Steve said. "A summoning is
a legally binding contract. You've called me into this
plane of existence to do your bidding, and in exchange
I get to destroy things before I go back."

"What sort of things?"

"The world," the little demon suggested hopefully.

I shook my head.

Steve sighed, gave the laminate countertop a half-
hearted kick and said, "Oh, well, I suppose that was
too much to hope for. Truth be told, it doesn't really
matter so long as I get my quota in."

Glancing around the kitchen, I contemplated the
potential for destruction and came to the conclusion
that there was a great deal of such potential. The
counters were strewn with all the pots, pans, bowls,
and utensils my wife had used to prepare the food.

I couldn't let Steve loose in the kitchen, though; he
might ruin dinner, and at the very least I'd be tasked
with cleaning up after the little demon. That was a
prospect I did not relish at all. Clearly he had to be
let loose somewhere else. Somewhere his destructive
tendencies wouldn't cause a stir. Somewhere like . . .

The sound of the electric garage door opener humming to life interrupted my train of thought. My wife
had arrived home from her trip to the grocery store;
I'd run out of the time I needed to deal with Steve.

My new priority became hiding the evidence. Putting the essence of flame back where I'd found it was simple and quickly accomplished. Steve was another matter. I needed a cupboard and I needed it fast.

Not just any cupboard, though. It had to be one my wife wasn't likely to open any time soon, and one where there wasn't anything particularly important for him to destroy. My eyes fell on the cereal cupboard. Exactly what I was looking for.

"Steve. In. Now," I said, yanking the cupboard open and sweeping aside the boxes of cereal.

"Whatever you say, boss," the little demon said, hopping up into the cupboard. He gnawed on the corner of one of the boxes experimentally and then asked, "Can I destroy this stuff?"

"Sure. Whatever. But do it quietly, okay?"

Steve flashed a thumbs up and I slammed the cupboard shut. Just in time, it turned out. The door from the garage to the utility room off the kitchen opened, and in came my wife, carrying a couple of bags full of groceries.

"Honey," she said, "there's more out in the car. Can you help me bring it in?"

"No problem," I said, squeezing past her on my way to the garage, "but I thought you were only going to pick up some parmesan cheese?"

Her shrug was apologetic. "You know how it is. When I got to the store, I remembered that we needed salad dressing and we were running a little low on toilet paper and, well, there you have it."

I didn't really mind, but I felt certain "there you have it" included at least one item that would have to go in the cereal cupboard. In that regard I wasn't disappointed. In the trunk of the car I found three more bags of groceries, one of which contained a brand new box of cranberry almond cereal. My wife's favorite.

"Drat," I muttered, grateful that my wife was in the

kitchen and couldn't hear me. Then I remembered Steve was also in the kitchen. That thought made me snatch the grocery bags, slam the trunk closed, and hurry back posthaste.

My heart skipped a beat when I saw her standing over the spaghetti sauce, wooden spoon in hand, with a thoughtful expression on her face.

"Is something wrong?" I asked, setting the bags down on a clear patch of countertop.

"What?" she said, glancing toward me. "No, nothing's wrong. Thank you for stirring my spaghetti sauce."

Relieved, I smiled and said, "You're welcome."

A muffled thump from the cereal cupboard reminded me that I wasn't out of the woods yet.

"What was that?"

"What was what?" I asked.

My wife furrowed her brow—she looked cute when she did that—and said, "I thought I heard something in the cupboard go *thump*."

"It's probably nothing," I said, taking the box of cereal from the shopping bag. "Why don't you go set the table, and I'll put the groceries away."

"Thanks," she said, setting the wooden spoon down next to the stove.

She opened one of the drawers and took out the silverware, then gave me a quick kiss on her way out to the dining room. When I was sure she'd gone, I opened the door to the cereal cupboard to find Steve crouched among the wreckage, savaging bags of oatmeal with gusto.

"Shhh!" I hissed, whacking the little demon over the head with the cranberry almond cereal box.

"Sorry, boss," he whispered back. "Wanton destruction is physical work. There's bound to be a thump or two from time to time."

"Fine. Try to keep it down, will you?" I said, shoving the cereal box into the cupboard and closing the door. Then I thought better of it, opened the door, and snatched the box from Steve's eager claws. It wouldn't do to jump out of the frying pan and into the fire. The rest of the groceries I stored with minimal fuss.

As I finished, the doorbell rang. By the time I reached the living room, my wife had already let her sister Carol and brother-in-law Alex in. I ushered them to the dining room, then helped my wife get the food from the kitchen. As an afterthought, I brought a pitcher of water as well.

This turned out to be a clever bit of foresight.

"I made the most amusing potion today," Carol said as we dished up the food. "Its taste and color are almost indistinguishable from coffee, and it turns the subject into a five-lined skink with an unhealthy addiction to free cell."

Alex leaned over to me and whispered, "Beats being a newt, but I don't think that free cell had anything to do with the potion."

I grinned. "Ah, the joys of life with a witch. What was it like being a skink?"

"About the same as every other small, highly caffeinated vertebrate," Alex replied. "As far as coffee goes, it was almost worth being a skink."

At about this point in the conversation, I noticed two things: First, no one had so much as blinked an eyelash at the taste of the spaghetti; second, we had emptied the entire pitcher of water.

"This is great spaghetti," said Carol. "Is this Mother's recipe?"

My wife nodded. "Yes, it is. Thanks."

"I thought so," Carol said, smiling. "It seems a bit spicier, though. Did you add something to it?"

"No," my wife said, but she gave me a questioning look.

I projected innocence for all I was worth.

She looked about to say something else when a loud crash came from the kitchen. For once I was almost grateful to Steve.

"Honey," my wife said. "Can you go find out what that was?"

"Sure," I said, getting up from my chair. I already had a good idea what I'd find.

The kitchen was pretty much as I left it, so I made a beeline to the cereal cupboard and opened it to find Steve ripping apart the thin, wooden shelving.

"Sorry, boss," he said, not even bothering to look up from the debris. "It's physical work."

"That was not a thump. That was a crash."

"Relax, I'm a professional," he said. "I know what I'm doing."

I glared at him. "I've company over. Are you going to be much longer?"

The little demon shook his head. "I'm almost done in here."

"Good." I shut the cupboard door.

When I returned from the kitchen, my wife and her sister had finished their meal and wandered to the living room to discuss matters arcane, leaving me and Alex alone.

"So what was it?" Alex asked.

"A couple pots fell off the counter," I said, glancing past Alex to where my wife sat, pointing out something from the latest issue of *Witch's World* to Carol.

Alex lowered his voice. "No, really, what was it? You accidentally summon a demon?"

I glanced over at my wife again to make sure she hadn't overheard and then nodded.

"No kidding," Alex said with a chuckle, "I did that once. I will never stir-fry again."

"You're that guy? How did you get rid of it?"

Alex shrugged, "The little bastard vandalized three Chinese restaurants before he tuckered out and went home. You just have to let them wreak havoc until their quota is full."

"Great," I muttered, wondering what Steve's destruction quota was and whether I could confine it to the cupboard.

As the evening wore on and I didn't hear anything more from the kitchen, I began to hope maybe the cupboard had sufficed. Steve had mentioned he was almost done, after all. Alex and I chatted at length about cars, sports, and power tools, and before long I began to relax and enjoy myself.

When Alex and Carol decided it was time to go, we saw them out to the car and then retired to the house. When the door shut, I gave my wife a big hug.

"Great dinner, hon," I said

"You think so?" she asked.

I nodded and said, "Carol and Alex seemed to enjoy themselves."

"You didn't think the spaghetti was too spicy?"

"Not at all," I said, managing to keep a straight face with a great deal of effort. "It tasted great."

"Thanks," she said, then kissed me.

It was a long, languorous kiss, the sort of kiss that hints at things to come. Later. When it was over, I could only say, "Wow."

"I'm going to take a shower," she said, "and afterward . . ."

Her words trailed off seductively as she ran one hand down my chest. I stared, but as a husband that's my prerogative. She was gorgeous, with that long black hair and shapely hips, and the . . . and her . . . and those eyes! Gah!

"I'm just gonna do . . . check on . . . that thing . . . over there," I muttered, waving in the general direction of the kitchen.

"You do that," she said with a mysterious smile.

She headed off to her shower and I dashed into the

kitchen, grinning like the little boy I am deep down. I'd deal with Steve while my wife was in the shower, and then life would be grand.

I tossed open the door to the cupboard and peered inside. The interior was decimated. All that remained of the cereal boxes was a fine powder laced with bits of plastic and colored cardboard. The shelves were reduced to splinters. I had to hand it to Steve, he was certainly thorough.

Of the demon himself there was no sign. I could only assume he'd filled his quota of destruction and gone back to wherever it was he came from. In any case, it was over. I'd managed to survive, and things were going to go very, very well tonight.

"Honey, what's a minor demon of wanton destruction doing in the bathroom?"

Then again, maybe not.

Narrator: *As this husband discovered when he misspelled . . . three is most definitely a crowd.*

NATHAN AZINGER lives, works, and writes—no particular order—in Washington state along with his constant companion, a stuffed beaver named Winston. He likes to say that he's just an average guy, and some people actually believe this. Others note that he is, in fact, rather weird. Perhaps the beaver tipped them off. Nathan currently attends Saint Martin's University, where he majors in religious studies. In his spare time he reads and writes fiction, dabbles in local politics, and watches birds. He believes that the best education is one that never ends, and his long term goal is to be better at what he does tomorrow than he was today.

Untrained Melody

Jim C. Hines

Narrator: *It's said music can touch the soul. Most of us ignore music's true power, content to sing along or dance as we wish. But, as Laura Polaski discovers, a musician can have particular responsibilities.*

There was a dwarf on Laura Polaski's coffee table. Even as Laura searched the small apartment for something heavy to throw at him, she could hear the too-perky voice from the Kiki's Coffee House orientation video reminding her of the importance of sensitivity.

Fine. Not a dwarf. A little person. A Little African American Person, to be precise. Wearing a brown pinstripe suit and a black fedora. Sitting cross-legged on the end of her coffee table, working on the crossword puzzle in the back of the *TV Guide*. Laura stepped back into the bathroom, retrieved the still-hot curling iron, and waved it like a sword. "I don't know how you got in here, but—"

The dwarf whistled a jazzy melody that climbed two and a half octaves and ended on a chord.

The curling iron twisted out of Laura's hand and

landed on the coffee table. The cord twitched along the floor as the curling iron balanced on the handle, like a puppy begging for treats.

"How did you do that?" Laura asked.

He doffed his hat, revealing a scalp of white stubble. "You learn a few tricks over two hundred years. The secret is to hear the melody at the core of a thing, so you can—"

"No, the whistling. You whistled a D-minor chord. That's impossible. Unless you've got three throats?"

"Not that I'm aware of." He pulled a silver pocket watch from his suit and glanced at it. "My name is Aleksander Yusupov. Al, if you prefer. You're a hard woman to track down. The wedding company said they weren't using you anymore, and the fast food place told me you quit a few weeks back. Fortunately, they had your address—"

"If so, why am I still waiting for my final pay-check?" She reached toward the papers scattered over the end of the coffee table: overdue bills, junk mail, a few pay stubs. The whole apartment was a disaster. She matched Al's stare . . . then gripped the end of the table with both hands and lifted.

Al tumbled onto the floor. Laura leaped across the living room to grab the floor lamp in both hands. She raised it overhead, ready to slam the weighted end into Al's head if he so much as—

He whistled again. The electric cord whipped around Laura's arm. She switched her grip and swung the other end. Al rolled out of the way, barely dodging a spray of shattered glass.

"Easy, girl." Al raised his hands and backed into the wall. "I'm trying to *help* you."

Laura pointed the lamp at him. A broken halogen bulb fell to the floor.

"I know why you've been having nightmares," Al said. "And why you cringe from the shadows."

Slowly, Laura lowered the lamp. A sudden pounding from below made them both jump. She rolled her eyes and shouted, "Sorry about the noise, Mrs. Salvati." To Al, she said, "You've got one minute."

Al stood and removed a long, slender satchel which had been slung across his shoulder. "Landed on it when I fell," he muttered. "My chiropractor's going to be pissed."

"Fifty seconds."

Al brushed himself off. "You're a bard, Laura. When you play, you call upon powers deep within this world. Sometimes, darker things answer. You've called something to our world, and now you have to help me send it back."

He sounded so grave and serious. And he *had* managed to make both the curling iron and the lamp dance to his tune, as it were. "Fifty bucks."

"What's that?"

She crossed her arms. "I don't know anything about dark powers or magic music, but if you want me to play, that's my rate."

"You've got an obligation. It's part of being a bard."

"I've got an obligation to pay my rent on Monday." Laura tapped the plastic nametag on her shirt. "I'm no bard. I'm a Kiki's cashier, and I have to be at work in an hour."

Al sighed and pulled out his wallet. He set a crisp fifty dollar bill on the arm of the chair. "Fetch your instrument."

Laura stared. She hadn't expected him to agree. She set the lamp on the floor and went to the hall closet, where she retrieved a red box. Simply unfastening the latches helped to calm her, as did the old, leathery smell of the box. She brought it back to the loveseat and opened the lid.

"You've got to be kidding me," whispered Al.

"Shut up," Laura snapped. She lifted the accordion with both hands. The straps fit comfortably over her shoulders, smooth and supple as a baby's skin. The fingers of her right hand brushed over the piano keys. With her left hand, she slowly expanded the accordion, filling the bellows. "What would you like me to play?"

Al untied a leather cord on the end of his satchel and pulled out a long, speckled flute that appeared to be made of polished granite. "Just follow my lead. You'll provide the power, I'll shape the spell. And try to keep up."

She ran through a few quick scales, stretching her fingers. Try to keep up? She planned to leave her diminutive intruder in the dust.

Al began to play. His instrument produced a deeper sound than any flute she had heard before. At least two octaves deeper. He trilled a low B, like the call of a bird, and then his fingers began to fly over the holes. He played a fast, cheerful melody that made her want to leap out of her seat. There was a jazzy, improvisational feel to it, but it also reminded her of Russian folk music, with a slight trace of that new age, faux Native American stuff.

She grinned and squeezed her accordion. The instant she touched the keys, her body grew warm, as though she were standing on the beach in August. She kept to simple chords and harmonies as she learned Al's melody. Soon she was improvising, adding a jaunty triplet here, playing a low countermelody there. And somewhere along the line, their roles switched. Laura began to lead, with Al following along.

His eyebrows shot up when it happened, and he actually missed a note. His face turned even darker, and he scrunched his forehead as he caught up with her.

Laura laughed and played faster. She forgot about

her stupid job. She forgot about being alone and broke in the big city, stuck in a crappy apartment. Blood pounded through her shoulders and arms, and her fingers raced across the keys.

Al nodded at the window. Laura gasped. The glass at the center was cracked. As she watched, tiny shards began to fall away. The landlord would kill her! "What's—"

Al stomped his feet and played louder. He jabbed his flute at her accordion.

Laura gritted her teeth and kept playing. The stupid dwarf had broken her window. That was going to cost him extra.

The window continued to break, leaving a jagged hole the size of her two fists. Frost covered the edges, though it was the middle of July. Outside, a shadowy form twitched toward the window.

Al's playing changed, becoming slower, more seductive. Laura could feel him calling, like the most brazen prostitute trying to lure her next customer.

The floor shook. The creaky voice of Mrs. Salvati cried out, "Any more racket and I'm calling the police! And the *landlord!*"

Laura froze.

"Don't stop!" Al shouted.

The window shattered. Broken glass swirled into a miniature tornado and rushed toward her . . . fragments large and sharp enough to slice her skin to ribbons.

Al leaped in front of her and blew a single shrill note that brought tears to Laura's eyes. He turned his face away as the glass burst into powder.

And then all was quiet. The shadow was gone. The sun shone through the empty window frame. Laura was once again alone with Al, who was tucking his flute back into its case.

"What happened?" she asked.

"You interrupted a bardic spell, that's what happened." Al sat down beside her and hummed. Bits of glass dropped from his sleeves.

"Look, I'm sorry, but I can't afford to lose this apartment. I can't even afford a new window!"

"You don't understand, girl." Al doffed his hat and tapped glass from the brim. "Your music summoned that creature back here, and your music opened a portal to send it home. Then you stopped playing. You surrendered control of the spell, and he grabbed it."

"And that's bad?"

"Before, we had one nasty running loose. You just handed it the means to summon an army."

Mrs. Salvati glared from her window as Laura and Al left the building.

"A bard taking threats from some cranky old bat," Al muttered. "She's lucky you don't charm every rat within a block to come nest in her unmentionables."

"I can do that?"

Al snorted. "Better not try it. Mess up that spell like you did the gateway, and you'll be swimming in rats yourself."

Laura shivered at that image. "What was that thing at my window?"

"I think of them as puppeteers. They have no bodies of their own, so they use ours. That one was stronger than I expected. Must have been feeding from you for months."

Laura shook her head. "I think I'd have noticed a freaky shadow lurking in my apartment."

Al closed his eyes and hummed, oblivious to the passing cars and the stares of people on the sidewalk. He turned in a slow circle, then opened his eyes. "Looks like it went east. Come on."

Laura followed. It wasn't easy to hurry while carrying an accordion. "What are we doing?"

"You're a bard, Laura. That's a special kind of gift, and it carries special responsibilities. In this case, it means fixing your screw-ups." He glanced up at her. "How is it you never learned all this? A teacher should have found you the instant you started playing."

Laura flushed. "I had lessons for a while when I was younger, but I quit. I didn't want to spend all my time practicing. Mister Hartwick tried to change my mind, but I wanted to play soccer."

"Good old Bobby Hartwick." Al shook his head. "He could play a violin like it was the voice of God himself, and you quit to play soccer."

She flushed. "I started playing accordion again in high school. I didn't like the lessons, or people telling me when to practice."

Al stopped walking. "That's too bad. If you'd stayed with Bobby, he might have taught you not to stop in midspell and feed your magic to the nasties. That's one of the earliest lessons, right after *Hot Cross Buns*. Now, you see that lady, the one with the nasty leopard-fur purse?"

Laura fought the urge to turn around and head home. To let Al deal with this on his own. He was the bard, after all.

Guilt made her stay. Guilt and the fact that, no matter how annoying he might be, Al played a flute like nobody she had ever heard before. She quickly spotted the woman with the purse. "The one with the toy poodle?"

"That's no poodle. Not really a lady, either. Those are puppets, and they're coming after us." Al pulled her into an alley between a used bookstore and an Italian restaurant. The smell was a foul mix of fresh-cooked lasagna and rotting garbage.

Al raised his flute to his mouth as the silhouettes of the woman and her poodle appeared at the end of the alley. "This time, just follow along."

He began to play a variation of the melody from Laura's apartment. This time, the music had a greater sense of urgency. The beat was faster, the notes sharper. Laura added her accordion to his flute, playing softly so she wouldn't drown him out.

The poodle yipped and tore down the alley, his pink leash bouncing along the pavement with every step. Laura winced at the sound. Yippy dogs were bad enough, but this one was worse. His mere presence grated on her like a badly tuned piano. The woman was just as bad.

Al played faster. The poodle slowed to a walk, then sat in a puddle and began to lick himself. The old woman walked toward them as if she were in a trance.

The music grew louder. Each note was a hammer blow, striking the creatures within the woman and her dog. Again and again Al pounded, driving them from their puppets. He walked closer, and a faint shadow pulled away from the poodle.

The woman pointed a manicured nail. Al glanced at Laura, his expression worried. A pile of old pizza boxes flew from beside the Dumpster, lids flapping as they swarmed over him. He tried to keep playing, but soon the boxes were knocking his flute away from his mouth.

The woman smiled. A broken pizza cutter flew from the open Dumpster, disappearing in the flock of greasy cardboard. The poodle didn't move. Apparently Laura's playing was enough to hold him. What was different about his owner?

And then Laura saw it. She stopped playing and filled the bellows of her accordion.

"Don't interrupt the spell!" Al bellowed a string of harsh, foreign-sounding words. Profanity, from the sound of it. "I bet you never mastered *Hot Cross Buns*, either!"

Laura kept retreating until her back hit the Dumpster. She heard more garbage stirring within and wondered what would leap out to smother her if she failed. It would be her luck to end up garroted by moldy spaghetti.

Praying this worked, Laura blasted two simple notes as loud as she could. The woman froze, and Laura leaped forward, yanking the white earbuds from her ears, then scampered out of reach.

Laura repeated the two notes. She waited a beat, then played them a third time. Again and again, faster and faster, building the tension and fear. She added a dramatic flourish, never breaking the rhythm of those two bass notes. The woman fumbled with the earbuds, but terror made her clumsy. Her purse dropped to the ground.

The woman fled, her poodle yipping at her heels. The pizza boxes fell away from Al, and the cutter clattered to the pavement. Al's suit was torn, and blood dripped from dozens of cuts on his hands. He shivered as he bent to retrieve his flute.

"That was some powerful frightening music," he said as he inspected his instrument for damage. "Sent those puppeteers running for Mama, you did."

"It did the same to me the first time I heard it." To tell the truth, she was a bit shaken herself. Even after all these years, she couldn't watch that movie. She half expected a great white shark to burst from the Dumpster. She retrieved the fallen purse and fished around until she found the woman's iPod. She glanced at the playlist. "Looks like your flute was no match for *The Best of Tom Jones.*"

Al hummed as they walked, trying to heal his wounds. He had managed to stop the bleeding, but his hands were still swollen and bruised. "That blasted pizza cutter was bad enough, but cardboard cuts sting like the devil's piss, I tell you."

Laura rolled her eyes, willing that image from her mind as they approached an old hotel building. Polished brass gleamed in the sun. Sparrows chirped from their nests among the gargoyles.

"You feel it, don't you?" Al asked.

Laura nodded. The same wrongness she had felt back in the alley, only stronger. It was all she could do to not squeeze her hands over her ears as she walked through the revolving door.

A man in a navy suit with a hotel badge on his chest hurried around the desk to intercept her. Laura realized she was humming to block out the atonal wrongness of the man.

Al held up his battered hands. "You're on your own, Laura," he said. "Best I can do is whistle back-up."

Laura nodded and opened the purse the woman in the alley had dropped.

"I'm sorry," the man said, flashing a smile. "You'll have to leave your instruments with me. I'll be happy to store them in the hotel safe until you—"

A quick blast of pepper spray left him on the floor, rubbing his face and weeping. Everyone in the lobby stopped and stared. Another hotel employee started toward them.

Al began to whistle, and slowly everyone went back to what they were doing. Al grabbed Laura's arm and tugged her toward the elevator. Only when the doors were closed did he stop whistling.

"You know, traditionally a bard uses her instrument to fight the bad guys."

Laura handed him the pepper spray. Her hands were shaking. "I told you, I'm no bard. I don't even know what I'm doing here. I was supposed to be at work ten minutes ago."

"You have a duty, Laura. An obligation to protect this world."

"Can't you call someone else? You came here to take care of these puppeteers. Let's hit a payphone, and you can call up some friends. Tell 'em you're getting the band back together or something."

"By the time anyone arrives, it will be too late. They have a gateway, Laura."

Because of her. The doors dinged open, and Al dragged her into the hallway.

"Music is in your soul," Al said as they passed a woman with an ice bucket. An older man hurried by, dragged by a little girl who kept trying to pull the fire alarms. "You'll know what to do."

They stopped at a door marked DeVine Ballroom. An A-frame sign read *Reserved for the wedding of Julie and Roger.*

Laura stopped.

"They're inside," Al said. "Feels like a lot of them."

"I know." Laura's throat was tight. "And I know who summoned them."

"What's that?"

"I was supposed to play this wedding. Michelle called to say I wouldn't be needed after all, today or in the future. She said there simply wasn't a demand for accordion players."

"Who's Michelle?"

"The wedding planner." Laura glanced at her watch. The wedding had started over an hour ago. "She hired me for one or two gigs every week when I first moved here."

"Feeding on your power until she was strong enough to survive on her own," Al said. "Then, once she was ready, she ditched you so there'd be no chance of you learning the truth."

"She said I wasn't good enough," Laura whispered.

"I've heard you play." Al rapped the side of her accordion. "Anyone who can wrangle music out of this contraption has talent."

Laura scratched her nose with her middle finger and turned to the door. "What do I do?"

"Hit them all at once. Something powerful. Something that will grab the whole room and get them out of our way. Then we break the gateway. It's your music fueling it, so you'll have to be the one to destroy it."

"How?"

Al shrugged. "It's different from every bard. Magic is like a song. You'll feel it. Trust yourself."

"The last time you told me to wing it, I handed a magic portal over to a soul-possessing shadow from another dimension."

"True enough. And believe me, I'd much rather head to the nearest coffee shop and spend the next year filling you in on all the lessons you missed when you bailed on old Bobby. But I think I'd rather save the world first."

Right. Laura's fingers touched the keys. Her mind was blank. She knew hundreds of songs by heart, and suddenly she couldn't remember a single one.

"No time for stage fright," Al said. "Keep it simple. And remember, once you start playing, don't stop until it's over, one way or another."

Something to grab the whole room. Something powerful. Laura nodded. "I'm ready."

Al yanked open the door. Inside, a handful of people stood at a buffet line. The bride and her bridesmaids were with Michelle, posing for photos in front of a wedding cake. From the atonal filth washing over the crowd, Laura figured most of the guests were already possessed. Michelle straightened, and her eyes met Laura's.

Laura gritted her teeth and squeezed out the opening notes of the chicken dance.

"Look at the cake," Al said.

It was a typical wedding cake. Three layers, frosted

in white with lavender flowers and green curlicues. The top layer balanced on clear plastic pillars. A miniature bride and groom stood in the center of a plastic heart decorated with lavender ribbon.

Al whistled, and the tiny groom tumbled backward. His head and shoulders vanished. The cake topper was the gateway.

"But it's so small," Laura said.

"A gateway needs a frame. And a soul will fit through the eye of a needle, if you yank it hard enough. Keep playing!"

Laura picked up the tempo. Already a handful of children had run onto the dance floor, flapping their arms and laughing. Others moved to join them, compelled by Laura's music. A teenager snarled and ran toward them. He made it halfway across the room before he stumbled. His hands began to clap like a beak. An older couple tried to flee, but the chicken dance drew them back.

"Make for the cake," Al said.

Laura walked through the crowd. More and more of the possessed guests tried to reach her, but her music stopped them all. She and Al were an island of safety in a sea of dancing chickens.

The only one unaffected was Michelle. "She's absorbed a good deal of your music," Al said. "It gives her a bit of immunity."

Michelle reached out and tore several chunks from the wedding cake, which she stuffed into the bride's ears. She did the same with the closest bridesmaid, who immediately grabbed a long, ribbon-bedecked cake knife and advanced.

"Don't stop playing," Al said. He drew his flute and gripped it with both hands.

"What are you doing?" Laura asked. "You can't—"

Al swung the flute like a baseball bat, smacking the bridesmaid in the knee. She howled and fell in a cloud of purple satin and chiffon. Al grinned at Laura. "Never underestimate the power of a dwarven battle flute."

A plate shattered on Al's head. He staggered and shook his head. Bits of broken china fell like snowflakes.

The bride picked up another plate. Without thinking, Laura worked the final measure of "Pop Goes the Weasel" into her song. The plate exploded in the bride's hand.

Sweat trickled down Laura's face as she increased both the tempo and the volume. Already several of the guests had collapsed from exhaustion, but the shadow-spirits still floated above them, flapping their spectral arms to the music. The bride began to tremble, fighting the urge. She reached for another plate, and again Laura destroyed it. The bride turned away and tried to stuff more cake into her ears.

"That might work against him," Laura said, gesturing toward Al. "The flute you hear with your ears. The accordion you feel in your bones."

And then Michelle smiled. "So much power," she said. "But haven't you learned anything from your mistakes?"

Laura ignored her. Michelle was trying to distract her, to get her to stop playing. Another few steps and she would be at the portal. She could hear the portal now, a chorus of accordions and flutes, woven around a single repeating melody. Over and over it played, a single track on an infinite loop.

Michelle clapped her hands. The injured bridesmaid pulled herself up long enough to throw her knife. Propelled by magic, it flew like an arrow from a bow. The blade sank into the bellows of her accordion. Laura could barely breathe. It was as if the knife had pierced her own lungs.

"All that power you've summoned, mine for the taking," Michelle said. "A wedding feast indeed."

"Keep playing," said Al. Blood dripped down his face.

Laura squeezed the accordion, which made a sound like a dying animal. Air wheezed out of the bellows. She could barely get enough air to produce a single note. The wedding guests began to shake off the effects of her magic.

Al hummed. It was an odd melody that danced through several keys, almost at random. Slowly, the music settled into a regular tune, then grew simpler, coming back to a simple C. He hummed it again and again, bringing chaos into order.

The torn material of her bellows tightened and sealed itself around the knife.

"Finish it," Al said, then went back to humming.

Laura played. The guests might have thrown off the chicken dance, but she could do better. Never taking her eyes from Michelle, Laura began to play the "Macarena."

Al kept humming as he walked beneath the table and whacked the legs with his flute. He dove away as the table collapsed.

Michelle barely managed to seize the topper before the cake toppled onto the bride. Michelle extended her other hand, fingers spread. Smoke rose from her palm. "You're not strong enough to stop me."

Flames leaped out, but Laura only smiled. She could hear the music behind the fire. *Her* music. It swirled through the room, filling her with giddiness. Even the fire danced to her song, turning and leaping to the addictive beat of the "Macarena."

Laura's hands blazed across the keys, and she saw fear in Michelle's eyes. It was time to end this, to reclaim her music and her power. One final song to send these spirits home and seal the portal behind them.

She played a bridge, transitioning to yet another tune. Michelle's eyes widened.

Music pounded through Laura's blood. She winked at Al, then stepped around the table, backing Michelle into a corner. "Let's polka."

Laura sat at one of the few undisturbed tables, watching Al mingle through the crowd. She wondered if anyone else could hear the humming. She knew nobody else could feel the way his music reached out, nudging memories and pushing them to believe his half-assed story about a chemical reaction in the insulation and hallucinatory gases seeping into the room.

Eventually, he made his way back to her. He had picked up a bit of wedding cake . . . not a slice so much as a lump. "Not bad for a first timer," he said.

Laura ran her fingers over the hole in her accordion. This would likely need more than a patch job. The entire bellows would need to be replaced. She didn't have the money. Heck, she was more than an hour late for work. She'd be lucky if she still had a job.

"Is this normal for you people?" She waved one hand, encompassing the chaos of the ballroom.

" 'You people?' " Al repeated, raising an eyebrow.

Laura flushed. "Bards, I mean."

"I know. Girl, if you don't know what you are after all this . . ." He shook his head. "Magic or no magic, anyone who can make music with that overgrown mutation of an instrument—"

"Hey." Laura winced and lowered her voice. "Look, I'm sorry I helped Michelle conjure up her puppeteers. I'm sorry you got beat up by a bunch of pizza boxes."

"And a pizza cutter!"

"I'm sorry you can't play the flute again until your hands heal. But if you keep insulting my accordion, I'm going to take that flute and put it somewhere you'll never play it again."

Al chuckled and ate a bite of cake. "You're a bard all right. And to answer your question . . . it's a lot more normal than we'd like."

"Fine." Laura stood up. "Then I need you to hum for me. And I need to borrow this." She plucked the hat from his head.

Al looked surprised, but he did as she asked. Laura smiled as the torn bellows struggled to seal itself.

"Ladies and gentlemen," Laura said. "In all the commotion, Julie and Roger never got to share their first dance as a married couple."

She made a sad face and played a quick, mournful stanza, which drew a few chuckles. "Fortunately, I have a solution." She set Al's hat on the table, then played the opening notes of "It Had to be You."

Neither Julie nor Roger looked ready to dance, but Laura put an extra *push* into her music. Slowly, Roger took Julie's hand, leading his cake-covered bride onto the dance floor. The guests began to applaud.

Laura glared at Al, then jerked her head at the hat. "You owe me for that window."

Al shook his head, but he pulled out his wallet and tossed a fifty into the hat. Laura played a quick flourish, and he added another fifty.

"Hey," he said, reaching in to retrieve the second bill.

"Don't stop humming! Don't you know what happens when a bard interrupts his magic?" She grinned. "I won't make anyone else tip me if they don't want to. But if this stuff is going to keep happening, I need to save a little something for accordion repairs."

Al rolled his eyes, but he made no further move to retrieve the money. He wandered on to the dance floor, still humming as he held out one hand and invited a limping bridesmaid to dance.

Lauren smiled and kept on playing.

Narrator: *Ah, the power of music. The next time you start humming to an old tune, or find yourself unable to resist moving to dance? Be careful it's not a misspell taking charge.*

JIM C. HINES began writing more than a decade ago, but he tries not to think about that. He is the author of three humorous fantasy novels, *Goblin Quest*, *Goblin Hero*, and *Goblin War*, all from DAW Books. He has also published thirty-plus short stories in various magazines and anthologies. Jim lives in Michigan with his wife and children, all of whom have been amazingly supportive and tolerant of his writing career. He has never been all that fond of writing author bios, so he asked his children to help finish this one. From his six-year-old daughter: "Daddy likes Snoopy, and I just lost a tooth." From his one-year-old son: ",po ;l[;=]pl,8yu8 thh bbbbbbbbb V$# v Ecv."

Yours for Only $19.99

Shannan Palma

Narrator: *Meet Brandie Myers. She'll tell you everything that's wrong with her life. It's tough
being a teenager—the endless decisions and responsibilities, without any power. It's so not fair.
All Brandie wants is a little control over her own
destiny. Bad idea, you think? She's not listening.*

The package arrived late Thursday afternoon, the
return address blurred where the ink had gotten
wet somewhere along the way. I ran down the stairs
when I heard the doorbell ring, beating my little
brother by only a second.

"Hi," I said, a little breathless as I answered the
door. I only had the door open about halfway, and
Elliot tried to get past me by ducking under my outstretched arm. I let go of the door to shove his head
back and then grabbed it again before it swung wide.
The UPS guy snickered. I rolled my eyes. I'd bet good
money he was somebody's little brother.

"I have a package for Brandie Myers," he said,
holding out his electronic signature pad.

"That's me," I said, and gave up the struggle to
keep boy and door under control in favor of signing
the pad.

"Thanks," I said, as I handed the pad back and reached for the package. Elliott grabbed it first and ran back into the house.

The deliveryman shrugged, lips twitching. Boys, I thought, shutting the door in his face to go after the brat.

Fifteen minutes and two dollars in ice-cream truck money later, I shut myself in my bedroom with my prize. The room didn't look like it belonged to a seventeen-year-old girl, at least not like it belonged to the other seventeen-year-olds I knew. I thought of the differences as my own good taste. There were no posters or knickknacks, just books upon books covering every available surface. The only clear spot in the room was the four-poster double bed, and half of that was piled high with clean laundry I had yet to put away.

I locked the bedroom door and climbed over piles to sit on the bed, ripping at the package as I went.

The box was about a square foot across and three inches deep. Inside there was an envelope, a booklet, and a candle. I couldn't help grinning as I flipped open the booklet.

Congratulations on your purchase of a **New** and **Improved** Fairy Tale Life! Yours for only $19.99, this deluxe package includes this complete instructional booklet, the spell of your dreams, and our patented spell-delivery system capable of making your wildest fantasies come true!

I put down the booklet and picked up the envelope. Inside was a computer-generated bubble form, like the ones we always had to fill out at school. I scanned the questions for a second, then put it down and navigated my way to the window to grab a number two pencil from my book-buried desk. I grabbed a book at random to write against and returned to my seat on the bed.

The first couple of questions were pretty obvious: name and address, shoe and ball-gown sizes; then it was a series of yes or no questions. Is your mother alive? Do you have any stepparents?

> WARNING: If you have a living mother or stepparent, please call our Customer Service Department at 1-800-HRAFTER before casting spell.

My mother died when I was ten, Elliott's current age, come to think of it, and Dad had yet to remarry, so I skipped past the rest of the warnings and went down to the next section.

> SELECT the fairy tale you would most like to experience.

I chewed on my pencil, scanning the choices, then filled in the circles next to "Cinderella" and "Snow White and the Seven Dwarfs." I had seen the Disney cartoons of both when I was little and had a vague memory of singing and handsome princes. Plus, both the villains had been stepmothers and I didn't have any steps, so there was no downside.

I flipped through the booklet to the section on the "patented spell-delivery system." I read the instructions doubtfully, wondering for the first time if maybe I was being scammed.

Too late now if I was. I'd already paid for it, anyway, so I might as well finish. I was pretty sure there were no refunds on mail-order spells.

I opened the bedroom door carefully, looking from side to side in case Elliott was waiting to ambush me—he liked to hide behind doors and jump out screaming bloody murder—but the coast was clear. He wasn't back from the ice-cream truck yet. I took the form and the candle with me across the hall into my bathroom, then lit the candle over the sink and held the form over the flame. The paper combusted, but it didn't smoke. It was gone in a flash.

I waited for a couple of minutes, but that was it.

"That was anticlimactic," I said. I didn't even feel any different. I put the lid down on the toilet and sat down, hugging my knees to my chest. It had been a stupid idea anyway.

There was a knock on the bathroom door. I leaned over and unlocked it to let Elliott in, then returned to my seat.

"So what was in the package?" he asked, smears of chocolate darkening the sides of his mouth.

"Come here," I said, and dampened a wash cloth in the sink to wipe off his face. "It was a stupid mail-order thing I saw on TV. Just a scam, though. It didn't work."

"You were sure excited about it."

"Yeah, well, I'm not anymore."

"What was it supposed to do?" he asked.

"Don't laugh," I said.

He sat down on the side of the tub and looked at me with solemn brown eyes. "I won't," he said.

He was pretty cool when he wasn't being a brat, so I told him.

"It was supposed to give me a fairy tale life."

"Why'd you want one of those? Do you want dresses or something?"

"Not really," I said. "I thought it'd be nice to have the decisions all premade, and happily ever after guaranteed."

Elliott nodded, not understanding, but supportive nonetheless. "Brandie?" he said.

"Yes?"

"Why do you think it didn't work?"

"Because I'm still not sure which college I want to go to or if I want to say yes and go with Peter to the prom."

"Oh," he said.

"Yeah," I said.

"Brandie?"

"Yes?"

"Peter's a doofus."

"I know."

We sat in silence.

"Brandie?"

"Yes?"

"What's for dinner?"

So much for fairy tales. I held out my hand, and Elliott pulled me up.

"Let's go see."

I pulled my car in the driveway the next afternoon a full hour before Elliott's bus was due to arrive. There was a moving van parked in the street in front of our house.

"Aunt Mags?" I called, as my dad's sister strode past carrying a box into the house. She turned her platinum blonde head and glowered at the car.

"About time you got home," Mags said. "Don't just sit there, get out of the car and help me."

"What are you doing here?" I asked, scrambling out of the car and hurrying over to give her a hand.

"What does it look like? We're moving in."

"We?"

"Us, too." Daphne and Dru, Mags' daughters, met us in the foyer.

"Mom," said Dru, "now that Brandie's here, can we go to the movies?"

"Sure, dears. Brandie, don't just stand there, go get a box out of the van and bring it in."

"What do you mean you're moving in?" I asked, still stuck on what seemed to be a very important point.

"Your father needs help taking care of Elliott, and with you going off to college soon, he asked the girls and me to move in and lend a hand."

"He didn't say anything to me."

"Well, he called me last night," Mags said. "I'm sure he was planning to tell you eventually."

"Last night?" I asked, bewildered. Dad hadn't even gotten home until after Elliott was in bed.

"Boxes, Brandie. Work while you whine, please."

An engine started as I walked back out to the moving van. It took me a moment to realize that Daphne and Dru were pulling out in my car.

"Hey!" I shouted, but the girls waved and kept moving. I patted my pockets in alarm and realized I'd left the keys in the ignition.

"Aunt Mags," I said, running back into the house. Mags was in the kitchen mixing herself a rum and Coke. "Daphne and Dru just took off in my car!"

Mags took a seat at the kitchen table and settled in with her drink and a magazine. "Well, it's not like you could use it right now anyway," she said reasonably. "You have to finish unloading the truck."

I stared at her.

"Get a move on," Mags said. "We wouldn't want your father to come home and find out you've been shirking your responsibilities, now, would we?"

Somehow I found myself nodding and doing as she said.

It took the full hour, but I had the remaining boxes unloaded and stacked in the living room and guest room before Elliott got home. When I heard the bus pull up, I ran outside and met the crowd of kids at the corner.

"Elliott, can I talk to you?" I said, as the school of

children parted and flowed past me like fish around a rock in a stream.

My brother stopped in front of me. His brown hair was sticking up in every direction, and his T-shirt read, "You make me throw up a little." Maybe he could use a better chaperone, but Aunt Mags wasn't it.

"What's up?" he said.

I looked over my shoulder at the house, then started walking in the other direction, motioning Elliott to follow. "We have a problem," I said.

"Yeah?" He stopped and turned to look back. "What's that moving van doing there?"

"Keep moving," I hissed. "It's Aunt Mags. She's moving in."

"Why?" he said, investing the single syllable with all the horror a ten-year-old could muster. That was a lot.

"Dad called her and said he needed help with you after I go away to college." We cut through the Henderson's yard to get to the public park and headed for the swing set. I used to take Elliott here after school back when Dad first said I could be the babysitter.

"Are you going away?" Elliott asked. "I thought you hadn't decided."

"I haven't," I said, "but apparently Dad isn't waiting."

"Did you call him?"

"Not yet. I haven't had time."

"Do you have your cell?"

"Yeah."

"Well, call him then." We sat on swings next to each other, and I took out my cell phone and dialed. Elliott twisted around in his seat until the chains were wound tight and then let go, circling in the air as the chains unwound.

"Hey Lanie, it's Brandie. Is my dad in? Could I talk to him, please? It's kind of important." I waited while my dad's secretary tracked him down. "Elliott, you're going to make yourself dizzy."

Elliott grinned and started twisting again.

I shrugged.

"Dad?" I said. "Hey, um, did you call Aunt Mags last night? Yeah? Okay, well did you know she's moving in?

"When were you going to tell me?"

Elliott stopped spinning and listened to my side of the conversation with interest.

"But Elliott doesn't even like her. She made him eat brussels sprouts last Christmas."

He made a face. I made one back until something Dad said made me start.

"Lisa?" I said. "Who's Lisa?"

I hung up a few moments later and stared at the phone.

"Well?" Elliott prompted.

My shocked gaze went from the phone to my brother. "Lisa's moving in, too," I said.

"Who's Lisa?"

"Dad's new fiancée."

"Are you serious?"

I nodded, numb. "There's more."

"What?" Elliott said.

"She's moving in tonight."

"Holy—"

"Elliott!"

"I wasn't gonna say nothing bad." We swayed on the swings for a moment in perfect unison.

"Brandie?"

"Yes?"

"Is Lisa going to be our stepmother?"

I stopped swinging; Elliott put his feet down and skidded to a stop next to me.

"Elliott?" I said.

"What?"

"I think I know what's going on." I stood up. "C'mon, we've got to go home."

Elliott got up and went to stand next to me. I started forward and stopped again when I felt his hand on my arm. I turned.

"I am not eating brussels sprouts," Elliott warned.

I nodded. "Neither am I," I said, meeting his seriousness with my own. I didn't know anybody who liked brussels sprouts, no matter how old they were. "Let's hope it doesn't come to that."

We went back together.

"Here it is," I said, digging out the spell booklet from under the remaining pile of laundry. "Okay, there's a number here that you can call if you have any questions—" I scanned the table of contents and flipped through the pages until I found it. "Hand me my cell phone."

Elliott tossed me my cell and went back to listening at the door. We had snuck in past Aunt Mags during the confusion caused by the arrival of a brunette woman with a piercing voice and her own set of boxes—a woman who could only be Lisa. The two women were currently downstairs arguing loudly enough to be overheard even with the door shut about the arrival of a giant mirror Lisa claimed had been her mother's.

I had a bad feeling about all of this.

I dialed the number and got an automated system. I pressed one for customer service, two for fairy tale life, two again for mail-order center, and three to report a product malfunction. The hold music was kind of nice, a sort of eighties pop blend. I recognized George Michael.

Downstairs, the yelling stopped. Elliott and I held our breath for a second. Then it started again, louder than ever.

I gave Elliott a thumbs-up, and went back to tapping my foot to the hold music.

"This is your friendly Fairy Tale Life Customer Service Representative! My name is ANNIE! How may I assist you today?!"

My god, she spoke in permanent cheerleader.

"Hi, Annie," I said, keeping my voice as quiet as I could without whispering. "I think my spell malfunctioned. I've got some weird stuff happening."

"Don't you worry, because I WILL help you! What's the problem?!"

"My aunt just moved in with her two daughters, and they're acting really strange—"

"No problem!"

"Wait," I said, "there's more."

The silence had an exclamation point.

"My dad just got engaged to a woman we've never even heard of, and she's moving in, too."

Annie waited!

"That's it," I said. "Did you guys send me a broken spell or something?"

"Our merchandise is one hundred percent effective! We guarantee a FAIRY TALE LIFE!"

"What kind of fairy tale is this?"

"Why don't you tell me first exactly what you did when you got the spell?!"

"I filled in the little bubbles on the form and I burned it over the candle. Nothing happened at first, then all the adults went twilight zone."

"And which fairy tale did you select for your life?!"

"Cinderella," I said.

"Cinderella!"

"And then Snow White for second choice."

"SECOND choice?!"

"Yeah," I said. "Second CHOICE!"

Elliott made frantic hush motions and I waved at him to show I understood.

"So what's gone wrong?" I said. "How do I make everything normal again?"

"You didn't read the instruction booklet, did you?!" She was scolding me in cheerleader.

"I skimmed," I said, annoyed.

"If you had read the instruction booklet, you would have realized that you are required to choose ONE fairy tale, and one alone for the spell to work properly! I'm afraid you've got a PROBLEM!"

"I KNOW I have a problem," I said, ignoring Elliot's wildly waving arms. "How do I FIX the problem?"

"I'm afraid this is one we can't fix over the phone, we're going to have to send a Mobile Customer Service Representative!"

I gritted my teeth. "When can they get here?" I asked.

"I should be able to send someone out tomorrow afternoon!" Annie said.

"Nothing sooner?" I asked.

"That's the earliest I can do, but don't worry! We'll be sending DAVE!"

I gave her the address and hung up. Elliott turned.

"You suck at being sneaky," he said.

"Shut up," I said halfheartedly.

"So?" he asked.

"They'll be sending DAVE!" I said. "But not until tomorrow afternoon."

We both became aware of silence downstairs.

"That did it," Elliott said, pressing his ear back to the door. The stairs creaked as someone climbed them. The brat looked to me for rescue.

It *was* my fault.

"Get in the closet," I said. "I'll tell them you're spending the night with Jay and sneak you something to eat as soon as I can."

He nodded and scrambled into the closet. "Good luck," he said, and then hid.

The bedroom door opened just as the closet door closed. The overhead light sputtered and died, and Mags loomed, backlit by the hallway. Her eyes glittered menacingly.

"It's time for dinner," she said, and stood to the side so that I had to squeeze past her to get out the door.

Sure enough, dinner was brussels sprouts.

I did the dishes after dinner, then helped Lisa unpack her boxes in my dad's room. He wasn't home, yet, as usual, so Mags and Lisa had divided me out between them.

I managed to sneak Elliott some saltine crackers and a jar of peanut butter and tell him where my cola stash was, but that was the last moment I had to myself until well after dark.

Lisa seemed okay at first—weird, but okay. She had dark brown hair the color of chocolate and big blue eyes, and I could totally see why my dad was into her, looks-wise at least. She did sit-ups next to the bed and watched me work for a while, but she didn't try and make conversation beyond directing where things went.

Then she got chatty.

"You have a great figure, Sandy. Do you work out?"

"Brandie," I said.

"What?"

"My name is Brandie."

"That's nice. So do you?"

"Do I what?"

"Do you work out?"

Lisa was maybe a size two. Half the clothes I'd unpacked so far had been spandex.

"I take gym at school," I said, halfheartedly trying to bond. I was pretty sure she'd go away when the spell did, but my dad wouldn't have been the first guy to have a midlife crisis, and Lisa sure looked like one.

"I always work out at least two hours a day," Lisa said disapprovingly. "You should, too, you know. Don't worry, it's never too late to start."

Scratch bonding. I longed for the arrival of Dave.

Sure enough, Lisa woke me up at 5 a.m. to do aerobics with her in front of the ridiculously huge mirror she'd inherited from her mother. She'd set it up in the basement in what had been the TV room, along with a full set of weights and an exercise mat. The couch had been moved against the wall so we had more room to move.

Elliott came down at seven and found me with my head in my sweat-soaked hands at the kitchen table. He had slept in his own bed, having snuck back into his own room the night before while I'd been at dinner.

"Is the coast clear?" he whispered.

I nodded without looking up. Mags had left strict instructions not to be awakened before noon, and Lisa had gone to yoga.

"Are you okay?"

"No," I said. "That Lisa is crazy."

"What do you mean?"

I tried to raise my head. Too much effort. I settled on turning my head to the side and letting it loll. "She's a loon, a wacko, a certifiable nut job who's had some sort of mutation reaction from too many Slim-Fast bars and too much spandex."

Elliott poured himself a bowl of cereal and some milk. I swung my arm around and fished a spoon out of the silverware drawer to hand to him.

"What'd she do to you?" he said, munching.

"What didn't she do?" I said. "Jumping jacks and running in place and push-ups and sit-ups and these weird dance moves that supposedly worked muscles I didn't know we had. And the longer we were at it, the more competitive she got. I started hyperventilating at one point and she *laughed*. I swear to god. And what's weird is I think the mirror was laughing too."

Elliott nodded sagely. "She's a bad guy, all right."

"Gee, you think?"

There was silence but for the clink of Elliott's spoon against the bowl.

"Hey Brandie," Elliott said after a while.

I opened a single eye. "Yeah?" He was looking over my head at something.

"Have you looked out the window this morning?"

"No."

"Maybe you should."

I dragged myself over to the window.

Mrs. Amueller, my ninth grade English teacher, was on the front lawn facing off against seven of the younger neighborhood kids. It looked like there was going to be a rumble.

I'd Googled fairy tales last night before bed and had a better handle on my plots now.

"I'm guessing what we have here is a standoff between my fairy godmother and the seven dwarves," I said. I went back to the table and put my head down again.

"Just tell them to keep Lisa away from me," I said, and fell asleep.

It was Saturday, so we didn't have school. Elliott set up a lemonade stand in the front yard and called some of his school friends to come over and watch the show.

I spent the morning and early afternoon locked in my room trying to read, but I couldn't concentrate. Around two, I unlocked the door and tried to open it, but it was barred from the other side. Unbelievable. I pushed the screen out of the window and climbed down the drainpipe instead.

"Brandie," Elliott called, and motioned me over to the little seating area he'd set up in the bushes. His buddies grunted admiring hellos, and I figured he must have told them I was responsible for the mayhem they'd come to see.

I figured DAVE should be getting here soon, and I could do worse than hang with the rugrats until he showed. Elliott offered me some lemonade free of charge.

I sipped and studied the playing field. Three of the kids lay in a stunned puppy pile over by the sidewalk, early victims. The remaining four had put up a patio furniture barricade and were defending their position with water pistols, spitballs, and slingshots.

Mrs. Amueller had always hated spitballs.

"So these guys are all supposed to sweep in and make your life better?" Elliott asked a little skeptically.

"Theoretically," I said, as Mrs. Amueller took out yet another rugrat with a well-aimed shoe. She had a sort of boomerang-throw thing going that I attributed to magic run amuck. Shoes had a habit of taking on undue significance in fairy tales.

The remaining three kids didn't stand a chance. I hoped that didn't mean I was going to the prom next week in a pumpkin coach, although I was more in favor of that than of taking on seven more kids as full-time babysitting charges. Somehow I didn't see cooking and cleaning for seven short males as the pleasure cruise it was made out to be; one was hard enough.

A green Volkswagen Beetle pulled up and parked on the street. Now *that's* a car, I thought.

A tall, thin guy in Dockers and a button-down shirt

got out of the car and walked our way. I hoped this was our repair guy, excuse, me, I meant Mobile Customer Service Representative.

"Hi," I said when he got close enough. "Look out!"

He picked a spitball out of his hair with aplomb. "Hi!" he said, and I winced. Then, "I'm Dave," completely exclamation free.

"Thank God," I said. "Can you fix this?"

He surveyed the carnage in my front yard. "This isn't what you had in mind?" he asked, deadpan.

"Not so much," I said.

A spandex-clad Lisa came to the front door with a basket of apples, and waved one in my general direction. "Natural fruit sugars!" she called. "They'll help cleanse you!"

I looked at Dave. "Help me," I said.

It was simple enough after that. There was another bubble form to fill out, another patented spell-delivery system to light, and then a couple of forms to sign.

"They'll all wander home pretty soon," Dave said, indicating the thoroughly confused teacher and children now looking around themselves in confusion. One of the kids kept shooting spitballs even without the spell driving him. I squinted. That was Billy Pendergast. He always had been a pain in the butt.

"I'm sorry to say I can't offer you a refund," Dave continued as I handed him back his pen. He capped it and returned it to his shirt pocket. "But I can offer you an exchange. Any spell in our catalog."

I considered it. Lisa had disappeared from the doorway. I figured she was looking around at our horrible carb-filled house and packing her bags. Dave walked with me back toward the house. "Just to be sure," he said.

Mags appeared in the doorway, and called me over. I left Dave with Elliott. "I feel terrible about this, hon, but I don't know what I was thinking bringing the girls over here and promising we'd stay. I can't possibly move them into this neighborhood. It's a war zone. Do you think your dad will be horribly upset?"

I grinned. "You know this is probably for the best," I said. "I think I'm going to stay local for school, anyway." And there the decision was, made without my even having realized it. I'd miss Elliott if I left anyway. I couldn't abandon him to brussels sprouts.

She hemmed and hawed a little bit, but she was as eager to be gone as I was to have her leave. She turned to go back into the house and get their things. Lisa almost ran her down.

"I'll send movers for the rest!" Lisa called in passing, and threw her bag in the front seat of a taxi I hadn't noticed pull up. It pulled away with tires squealing.

Mags and I shared a wry look. She wasn't so bad when she wasn't bewitched. Dru and Daphne were, but Mags wasn't.

"Your young man is waiting," she said, and nodded back to where Dave stood with Elliott and his sticky-fingered pals.

"Oh, he's not—" I said, turning back to face her, but the door was already closing.

I shrugged and walked over to Dave. He was young enough, I supposed, maybe twenty? If one ignored the unfortunate bowl haircut, he was even borderline cute.

"So, thanks," I said. "I think everything's going to be o—"

"Brandie, guess what?" Elliot interrupted.

"What?" I said absently.

"Dave plays the banjo."

"Yeah?"

Dave blushed. Scratch borderline. He was cute.

"Yeah. And he does this puppet show, and he's doing it tonight at the library."

"Really?" I said, fascinated. I'd never met a banjo-playing puppeteer before. Dave was turning out to be way more interesting than high-school boys.

"So can we go?"

"Do you mind?" I asked Dave.

He shrugged. "No, of course not. I mean, it'd be nice. If you want to—"

"I do want to," I said.

"I'll get the keys," Elliott said happily, and ran into the house.

"Cool kid," Dave said. He shoved his hands into the pockets of his pants.

I smiled. Who would have thought?

Even a misspelled fairy tale ends with Prince Charming.

Narrator: *And they all lived happily ever after. (I've always wanted to say that.)*

SHANNAN PALMA is a writer, filmmaker, and academic. She was involved creatively in the production of over forty short films before deciding to move toward a more eclectic career integrating all three of her passions. Since eclectic careers take time to establish, over the years she has racked up a number of odd jobs in her ongoing quest to Pay the Rent—including flower seller, secretary, kitty litter cleaner, shoe seller, make-up artist, and court-reporting instructor. She currently lives in Atlanta, Georgia, and is working on her Ph.D. in women's studies. She has previously published nonfiction and poetry.

After years of fielding anxious phone calls from family concerning what could safely be substituted in recipes, including the now-infamous query, "Are green pork chops still okay?" JULIE E. CZERNEDA decided to toss matters into the hands of other authors for a change. *Misspelled* is the wonderful result. When not engaged in long-distance cooking salvation, Julie is a full-time science fiction and fantasy author and editor. Her eleventh novel, *Reap the Wild Wind* was published by DAW Books in July 2007, along with her most recent anthology, *Under Cover of Darkness*, coedited with Jana Paniccia (February 2007). *Polaris—A Celebration of Polar Science* was released in January as part of the International Polar Year by Star Ink Books. She'd put more about herself in this biography, but her latest kitchen experiment appears to have grown legs and be running out the door . . .

Julie E. Czerneda

Reap the Wild Wind

Stratification #1

In this earlier time of Czerneda's Trade Pact universe, the Clan has not yet learned how to manipulate the M'hir to travel between worlds. Instead, they are a people divided into small tribes, scattered over a fraction of their world, prevented from advancing by two other powerful races. But aliens have begun to explore the Clan's home planet, upsetting the delicate balance between the three intelligent races. Also in this time is one young woman on the verge of mastering the forbidden power of the M'hir—a power that could prove to be the salvation or ruin of her entire species...

978-0-7564-0456-7

"A creative voice and a distinctive vision.
A writer to watch." —C.J. Cherryh

To Order Call: 1-800-788-6262
www.dawbooks.com

DAW 80

Julie E. Czerneda

THE TRADE PACT UNIVERSE

"Space adventure mixes with romance...a heck of a
lot of fun." —*Locus*

Sira holds the answer to the survival of her
species, the Clan, within the multi-species
Trade Pact. But it will take a Human's
courage to show her the way.

A THOUSAND WORDS FOR
STRANGER
0- 88677-769-0
TIES OF POWER
0-88677-850-6
TO TRADE THE STARS
0-7564-0075-9

CJ Cherryh

Classic Novels in Omnibus Editions

THE DREAMING TREE
Contains the complete duology *The Dreamstone* and *The Tree of Swords and Jewels*.   0-88677-782-8

THE FADED SUN TRILOGY
Contains the complete novels *Kesrith*, *Shon'jir*, and *Kutath*.   0-88677-836-0

THE MORGAINE SAGA
Contains the complete novels *Gate of Ivrel*, *Well of Shiuan*, and *Fires of Azeroth*.   0-88677-877-8

THE CHANUR SAGA
Contains the complete novels *The Pride of Chanur*, *Chanur's Venture* and *The Kif Strike Back*.
0-88677-930-8

ALTERNATE REALITIES
Contains the complete novels *Port Eterntiy*, *Voyager in Night*, and *Wave Without a Shore*   0-88677-946-4

AT THE EDGE OF SPACE
Contains the complete novels *Brothers of Earth* and *Hunter of Worlds*.   0-7564-0160-7

To Order Call: 1-800-788-6262
www.dawbooks.com

DAW 9

The Novels of

Tad Williams

To Order Call: 1-800-788-6262
www.dawbooks.com

DAW 102